MURJANA

MURJANA

A NOVEL OF MEDIEVAL BAGHDAD

Ghada Karmi

Interlink Books

An imprint of Interlink Publishing Group, Inc.
Northampton, Massachusetts

First published in 2025 by

Interlink Books
An imprint of Interlink Publishing Group, Inc.
46 Crosby Street, Northampton, MA 01060
www.interlinkbooks.com

Library of Congress Cataloging-in-Publication data:
ISBN-13: 978-1-62371-664-6

Printed and bound in the United States of America

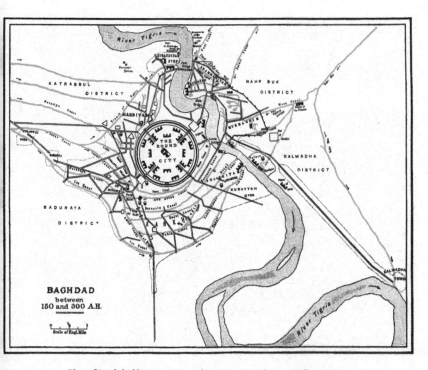

Plan of Baghdad between 767 and 912 CE, according to William Muir.

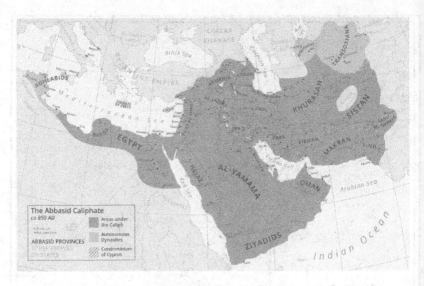

The Abbasid Caliphate circa 850 CE.
Map by Cattette, Wikimedia

PROLOGUE

Baghdad, April 830

It was early spring. The weather was mild, with no hint of the scorching summer days to follow, when the city shimmered in the heat and no one stirred in the burning afternoons.

Baghdad had become the capital of the Islamic world. Built by the second Abbasid caliph, its unique circular design was an engineering marvel. Constructed in three concentric circles, it comprised an outer double brick wall surrounded by a deep moat, a second wall inside that, and a third innermost enclosure ninety feet high with the caliph's palace and the grand mosque at its center. Unrivaled anywhere were its spacious streets and harmonious architecture, its beautiful landscaped gardens rich with flowers, trees, and fountains; its wide bridges traversing the Tigris in parallel rows; and its fine public buildings and bathhouses gracing every district.

The Round City was not even a century old. Yet, spread out majestically on the west bank of the river, it seemed eternal.

Not that the three men, hurrying forward through the crowds, had a thought for any of that as they pushed and jostled their way toward the palace. The main thoroughfare was full of people and animals: horses with and without riders, camels, and donkeys bearing huge burdens on their backs. The men picked their way as best they could over the mounds of camel dung that littered the cobblestones. The stench of so many human bodies mixed with that of animal excrement was overpowering

They walked rapidly through Baghdad's most famous Street of Booksellers, usually the doctor's favorite haunt where he was used to browsing through the bookshops at leisure. Skirting the city's poor quarters, with their squalor and filthy hovels, they passed the beautiful avenues and fine houses of the rich sitting alongside.

The road eventually branched out into a network of side streets, and the crowds thinned out. The doctor kept wondering what could have happened to cause him to be summoned in this way. What crisis was so urgent it had forced him to abandon his clinic and half-run with two guards like this to the palace?

The muezzin of the great mosque was beginning to chant verses of the Quran that preceded the call to prayer as they approached. Seeing their haste, a line of sentries quickly stood aside from the Golden Gate entrance. Inside the vestibule it was dark and cool. The attendant palace eunuchs took his outer robe and ushered him through to the central courtyard, a marvelous place of pillared cloisters and shimmering blue-green Damascene tiles. Even though his mind was on other things, it was impossible to be oblivious to the sound of water cascading from the marble fountain and the song of exotic birds that filled the air.

He was led to the Caliph's private rooms whose carved wooden doors opened directly onto the courtyard, but were now firmly shut. As he approached, one of the doors sprang open, as if the guards had been waiting for his arrival. He stepped into the small anteroom that led to the majlis, the sitting room, which as always was dimly lit by the light that filtered through ornamental grills over the windows. At normal times, this gracious room was used by the Caliph's private visitors and family members. People would recline on silk cushions for hours, or sit cross-legged with their backs resting against the walls.

This time no one was lolling on the seats and no family members were to be seen. Instead, the Caliph's chief wazir, Abu Hisham, the head eunuch, Idris, the head palace doctor, Suleiman, and several senior officials stood around in the center of the room as if not knowing what to do. In the midst of them, Durayd, the Caliph's chamberlain, was pacing up and down distractedly. As soon as he saw the doctor, he leaped forward.

"Thank God you're here, Abu Mansour!"

"I came as soon as our lord's emissaries arrived, and we walked here as fast as we could. What has happened?"

No one responded.

"Why are these ministers present?"

Normally, state officials, even ones as senior as these, were not permitted into the Caliph's private quarters. State business was conducted in the palace's audience chamber, yet here they were alongside the head eunuch and the head doctor.

Fear seized Abu Mansour. There could be only one reason for this unusual assembly of people. Some deadly harm must have befallen the ruling family. God forbid, it was not the Caliph himself. Anything but that.

He tried to quell his anxiety and looked at Durayd. The man's thin face was strained, his expression inscrutable. The chief wazir said nothing. He did not care for Abu Mansour. Neither did the palace doctor.

Where was the Caliph? The doctor had visited these apartments many times and the Caliph had never failed to receive him in person. What terrible event could have befallen his benefactor?

As if reading his mind, Durayd said, "Come with me and you will see what has happened."

"I have witnessed many terrible things in my life, Master Durayd. You can tell me what is wrong. I will not flinch or run away."

"I cannot. You must see for yourself."

With that Durayd took him to the Caliph's bedchamber, and left him there. Abu Mansour stood uncertainly on the threshold to the room. After a moment he stepped slowly inside. All was silent. He tried to accustom his eyes to the shuttered gloom. Ahead lay the velvet covered divan on which the Caliph normally slept. The doctor took another step forward.

What he saw rooted him to the spot, shaken and full of apprehension.

PART I

Baghdad, 829, nine months earlier

I

The man who stood before the Caliph was tall and dignified. He made an impressive figure in his green robe and white turban, looking at the Caliph steadily with a watchful, yet respectful, gaze. He appeared to be in his late fifties, and introduced himself as Abdulhamid ibn al-Hussein ibn Shaaban.

"I am most grateful, sir, for your graciousness in receiving me. It is a great honor and privilege to be in your presence."

It was the day of the Caliph's weekly *diwan*, when the palace was opened to anyone who wanted to have an audience with him. His cautious ministers did not approve of this practice. They thought it was dangerous for him to mix with the common people, even though the sentries outside the chamber searched every visitor and made sure no one who aroused the faintest suspicion was admitted. But no matter what the potential danger might be, the Caliph had no intention of giving up the diwans.

He had instituted these public audiences early in his reign, and no other ruler had ever done such a thing. It was at a time when he was in constant fear of his subjects' rejection for the way in which he had overthrown his self-indulgent, pleasure-seeking brother, the rightful caliph, and struck down all those who blocked his path to the caliphate.

He knew he needed to gain the people's confidence and acceptance, and he went to great lengths to do so. He even hoped that one day they might grow to love him. At the beginning, he perceived betrayal and treachery at every turn. The slightest rumor of dissent sent him into a panic. It impelled him to show his subjects a benevolence they had never seen before, in order to prove to them that he was a ruler who truly cared about them. And what better way than to bring himself physically closer to them, to show them his concern for their well-being in person and treat them all equally?

The diwans he started were held weekly, and were instantly popular. He received all who wanted to meet him in an informal, modest-sized palace chamber, humbly furnished with a few simple hangings on the walls and plain rugs on the floor. Its narrow, slit-like windows, with lamps in every corner, gave it an air of intimacy. Wooden benches were placed against the walls. More comfortable, cushioned seats, reserved for special visitors, were positioned nearer to where he sat.

People brought their complaints and problems to him, and he made sure he listened attentively and offered solutions. He hoped these friendly encounters between caliph and subject would make him seem less remote, more involved with their lives, and ever ready to offer his help with the smallest problem. And it worked.

On that particular morning, so many people had congregated to meet him that some had to be turned away and asked to return another day. He took his seat, his guards behind him and Uthman at his side, looking through the list of those waiting. Among them was this man, accompanied by two young people, who now stood before him.

Judging by their fine clothing and manner, they were clearly of respectable background, and the guards had ushered them in ahead of the rest. It was unusual for people of their class to come to these occasions, and he observed them with curiosity. Uthman was familiar with all the high-born families in Baghdad, but he did not recognize these people. The Caliph, on the other hand, had a strong feeling he had seen the man somewhere before. His tall stature and handsome demeanor were striking and not easily forgotten.

Then the Caliph remembered why the man seemed familiar. His family was among the most prominent of the Shia families of Baghdad. The Shia were known for their piety and dislike of ostentation. They lived modestly, modeling themselves on the Prophet's teachings, and did not aspire to mix with the people of the court, nor the wealthy elite of Baghdad. However, they were known to nurse a grievance against the Abbasid caliphs.

Long ago, in the early years of Abbasid rule, their trust had been shockingly betrayed. The Caliph was familiar with these Shia grievances against his ancestors, and had no patience with them, although perhaps, given his own dislike of any form of betrayal, he should have been more sympathetic. As it was, he thought their complaints were an obsessive hangover from another age, which they should have come to terms with by now. In the end, they were after all part of the Muslim community, and whether Sunna or Shia, for him there was no distinction in Islam.

Looking at Abdulhamid now, the Caliph realized that it had probably been at the mosque, when he usually led the Friday prayer, that he had seen this tall man among the worshippers.

"Thank you for coming to see me." He motioned Abdulhamid and his companions to take one of the cushioned seats. As they sat down, the Caliph noticed how the girl who accompanied Abdulhamid wrapped her blue silk cloak about her to cover her body more closely, only her feet in their soft leather shoes showing beneath its hem. In a city where all women except the poorest displayed their gold bracelets, a sort of portable wealth given them by their families, she wore no jewelry. The Caliph found he liked that.

"In what way can I help you?" he asked.

The man cleared his throat and bowed.

"I hesitate to trouble you, sir, with what might seem an unimportant matter, but it is of the utmost seriousness for my family. We own some tracts of land in Khorasan, which the family has held for more than a hundred years. We never thought the day would come when we would lose them. But that is exactly what has happened. I can only call it theft. They've been stolen from us."

The Caliph looked up at the mention of Khorasan, the Persian province he had ruled when his father was alive. The memory of his time in Merv, Khorasan's capital, where he had had his residence for years, still evoked in him a deep nostalgia and, despite the constant unrest, it pained him to hear ill news of Khorasan's people.

"I know that Khorasan has always been a source of trouble," the man continued. "But we thought the new governor you appointed would make things better."

And so had the Caliph when he gave the governorate to Abdullah ibn Rida, a local man and head of a powerful family he thought would be able to quell Khorasan's perennial rebellions against Baghdad. Up until then, he had been proved right. The people were pacified under Abdullah's rule, earning him the Caliph's trust and gratitude.

"I have approached the governor," Abdulhamid continued, "but he told me the land had been taken over by a powerful local clan and he had no control over it. Forgive me if I should offend, my lord, but I didn't believe him. I doubted that he really was as powerless over the family as he made out. That land is precious to us. It represents our inheritance, mine and that of my brother's children."

"I take it your brother is dead?"

"Yes, and I have brought up his children as if they were my own."

Including this niece, the Caliph thought, looking at the girl again. Her veil was so thin it barely disguised the features of her beautiful face. He wondered briefly how she was allowed to be seen in public like that.

"That is why Murjana and her brother Hamza, here, came with me, to beseech you, as I do, to take up our case. You are the sovereign and have the power to command Abdullah ibn Rida to see that our land is returned to us."

The girl suddenly spoke. "May I also add my voice to my uncle's, if you will permit it, my lord?"

She looked at him shyly from behind her veil.

He was taken aback at the sound of her voice. Respectable women were not encouraged to speak in public.

"Indeed, I do permit it," he replied. "Please speak freely."

She raised her eyes to his, holding his gaze, and parted her lips slowly. She had an expression of affecting entreaty, as though willing him to draw closer to her. It confused him, but there was no doubting her intention. For an intense moment it seemed to him as if the two of them were the only people in that room.

She leaned forward and spoke, hesitantly at first, but soon gaining in confidence.

"When I was a child, sir, I used to go with my father and brothers to visit our house in Khorasan."

She had large, luminous eyes, now turned fully on him.

"I have so many wonderful memories of that time."

She paused.

"Please continue," said the Caliph gently.

She sighed. "My mother would say we should move from Baghdad and live there forever. Ah...such happy days."

Her eyes filled with tears, and it touched him deeply.

"I don't know your land," he said quietly, "but I too love Khorasan, and I would also mourn the loss of any part of it."

She gave him a half-smile and seemed eager to answer him, but her uncle put a firm hand on her arm.

"You are most gracious, sir, in giving us audience," he said. "We ask permission to take our leave. I think we have told you all that was necessary..."

The Caliph raised a hand, his eyes still on the girl.

"Let your niece continue, Abdulhamid. Her words please me."

The girl had sat back again, but she retained that look of passionate entreaty. *It could not all be about her family's stolen land, surely*, he thought.

He addressed her directly.

"Is Baghdad not to your liking at all? Is your love only for Khorasan?"

"Oh no, my lord!" She looked at her uncle and brother, and seemed greatly embarrassed.

"I didn't mean that...You mustn't think I'm unhappy here, or ungrateful for my life in this glorious city...Oh no, no. I only meant...just that Khorasan has a special place in our hearts."

He found her distress enchanting, and could not take his eyes off her. Her beauty stirred and unsettled him in a way he could not explain. He let his eyes pass over her, her lips, her perfect features, the tendrils of black hair that curled over her forehead beneath the veil. A sudden urge gripped him to tear off her robes, push back her veil, and feast his eyes on her body. He wanted to possess her.

The feeling was so strong he had to try and compose himself. It was as if, in that moment, he had been returned to the breathless adolescence of long ago, an innocent boy smitten by the first beautiful woman he saw. He could scarcely remember the last time he had felt so excited, so instantly captivated, so hungry for more. Had he simply fallen prey to an old man's vulgar lust after young flesh, something to which he thought himself immune? Or was it more? He reminded himself that he was not his frivolous brother, did not succumb each time he saw a pretty face. It was the life of the mind that excited him, the attainment of knowledge that fulfilled him. He was a scholar, a lover not of women but of books, and his reaction to this young woman astonished him.

With a tremendous effort, he dragged himself back from these reflections and thanked Abdulhamid for his visit.

"Please give my secretary, Uthman, the full details of your complaint. You have a valid grievance against the people who robbed you and your family of what was yours, and I promise to do my best to put it right."

Murmuring their thanks, they rose to leave, bowing low before him.

Murjana was the last to rise. She bent her head respectfully and gave him a diffident smile that lifted the corners of her mouth and filled her eyes with light.

He looked back at her, spellbound.

2

In the weeks following the diwan, the Caliph found it difficult to forget Abdulhamid's niece, Murjana. The image of her beguiling face, her smile, and the touching entreaty in her eyes kept springing to mind, coming between him and his duties. During idle moments, he would find himself wondering what she was doing, imagining her without her veil, her black hair flowing over her shoulders.

He knew he could summon her back to the palace any time he pleased; that he could dally with her, indulge his fancy. But that was not his way, and it mortified him that he had surrendered so foolishly to a woman's charms. It did not fit with his image of himself as a serious man of intellect and reason. He vowed to put the thought of her behind him and return his attention to matters at hand.

"Your governor of Khorasan, Abdullah ibn Rida, is causing much concern, my lord," his chief commander, Abu Ubaydah, was saying. "He has been stirring up a lot of trouble among the towns and districts around Merv."

The Caliph held regular morning sessions with his government officials, during which his secretary Uthman presented him with documents to read and letters to sign. On these occasions, his army generals and tax administrators also brought him news of the various parts of the realm.

None of it was ever cheerful. They would tell him about strife, unrest, and troubles of all kinds, the same problems that had plagued his father's reign. And how else could it have been, with a vast realm that stretched from Spain to Samarkand, through North Africa, from Persia to India, and up to the borders of China?

He would find himself wishing the Arab armies that surged out of Arabia so enthusiastically after the Prophet's death, overtaking all the lands in their path, had stayed home instead. That way, he and his forebears might have been spared the burden of building the Arab empire and, what was far more onerous, holding it all together.

Unlike his father, he had no illusions that the caliphate could dominate all the reaches of its dominions forever. Neither the Romans, nor the Byzantines, nor the Persians had managed it, not even great Alexander and his heirs. And the Arabs, too, would succumb one day. In the event of this decline, however, he liked to think that Baghdad's brilliant legacy in philosophy, science, and learning, which his father and he had done so much to foster, would live on to illuminate the minds of generations until the end of time.

For now, there was little to fear. His armies and navy were strong, the world's trade, centered on Baghdad, was thriving; the port of Basra was prospering. Abbasid rule was secure. But controlling the rebellions that kept erupting in so many of his cities and provinces was still a headache, and he had no choice but to put them down before they grew to disrupt that hard-won stability.

Just the mention of Abdullah ibn Rida's name instantly brought back the memory of that magical visit to his diwan. He tried harder to concentrate on what his commander was saying. Abu Ubaydah was one of his ablest generals and the military commander in charge of the Persian territory. A Khorasani by ancestry, he was widely admired for his prowess and bravery in warfare, and the Caliph always relied on his loyalty to the Abbasid family.

"Stirring up trouble...what is so alarming about that?" he asked him irritably.

Dissidence was a constant theme of his commanders' reports, and he often found it more tedious than threatening. Keeping the far-flung parts of an empire loyal to a distant ruler was a monumental task.

"You know as well as I do that there have always been insurrections in Persia, especially in Khorasan. It's too big ever to control completely—a wonder the Umayyads ever conquered any part of Persia, let alone vast Khorasan. If the discord you describe is in the northern principalities and villages, we long ago accepted their independence from our rule."

When residing in Merv, the Caliph had made a point of receiving with appropriate pomp all the Persian aristocrats who ruled the province's important cities. The envoys from Nishapur, Bukhara, and Samarkand—the great cities of Khorasan—were treated almost as the Caliph's equals so as to flatter them and discourage sedition in their lands. But the truth was, he didn't begrudge these petty rulers their independence. Relations were often amicable, and they were left to maintain their courts and customs, while paying only lip service to the caliphate.

Although they would address the Caliph in Arabic, he knew that in their daily lives they spoke and wrote their songs and poetry in their own language. He also knew they had a barely disguised disdain for the Arabs, who, they thought, had given Persia nothing beyond their script and their religion. And not even that in the villages that lay beyond Samarkand and up to the borders of China. Baghdad had long ago abandoned any ambition to subdue the people of those lands.

The tedium that beset him at the mention of the problems of which his commander spoke was all too obvious. If only someone would relieve him of the burden of dealing with them. Abu Ubaydah straightened and looked the Caliph in the eye. He suspected the general thought him negligent, leaving it to his commanders, rather than bearing responsibility himself, for all that went on in the provinces.

He also suspected that Abu Ubaydah had never cared for him as much as he had cared for his brother. But the Caliph never had cause to doubt his loyalty. They had known each other ever since Abu Ubaydah was appointed to protect him as viceroy in Merv. He had maintained order in Khorasan on the young Caliph's behalf until he grew up, and when the time came, had fought for him against his brother.

What an evil time it had been. The Caliph shuddered to remember it, a hideous two-year struggle between brothers, one that their father strove hard to prevent. He had feared his sons would fight over the caliphate. For that reason, he made a will, affirmed by all the notables in the land, to set their inheritance so firmly that none could question it. Muhammad, the son born of his father's Arab wife, would be caliph after him. And he, Abdullah, the son born of his father's Persian concubine, would be viceroy of Khorasan and next in line.

But the arrangement broke down soon after their father's death. In the bitter battle for inheritance, Baghdad was put under siege, and much of it destroyed in street fighting. In the end, Abdullah won and his victorious forces swept into the ruined city and imposed his rule. So it was that the son of the concubine threw off his secondary status and held his own.

But at what cost? It took many years for all the damage from the war to be put right and for his great-grandfather al-Mansour's glorious city to be rebuilt. The people blamed the Caliph for the war of the brothers. But it had been his brother Muhammad's attempt to disinherit him and cut him out of the succession that had sparked the war. And Muhammad paid the price of his folly. His end was ignominious and pathetic, deserted by his troops and fleeing for his life aboard a boat on the Tigris. He did not get far, and was captured and imprisoned in the cellar of a government building.

When the Caliph heard the news of his brother's end, shivering in ragged clothes and begging for his life as the soldiers came to slit his throat, he wept. "I swear before God," he had cried out, "I never wanted any of it to happen, or wished my brother dead!" But nor could he forget Muhammad's betrayal of their father's trust and his scorn for him.

Few, other than Abu Ubaydah, knew this history. But despite everything, the general still preferred Muhammad, weak and feckless though he was. The rumor was that, to Abu Ubaydah and many others, Muhammad had been simpler and more straightforward. You knew where you stood with him, people said, even when he was plotting to keep his brother out of the succession. But this caliph, Abdullah, was cold, secretive, and elusive, difficult to like.

"We need to decide what should be done about what you've told me, Abu Ubaydah," said the Caliph, trying to summon up a sense of urgency, as he thought was expected of him.

"Indeed things have gone too far to be ignored any longer," Abu Ubaydah replied. "To prevent the situation from getting worse, the main target must be the instigator of this treachery, the governor." Although the Caliph had been satisfied with him when he was first appointed, in Abu Ubaydah's view the man had been nothing but trouble from the start. It was even rumored he had stopped invoking the Caliph's name at the Friday prayer to indicate his renunciation of Baghdad's authority.

"Sir, I hope you will permit me to propose that we should deploy the army with full strength as soon as possible to reinstate your authority over Abdullah ibn Rida and these rogue provinces. This was what we had to do when the ruler of Bukhara once defied your father."

The Caliph nodded reluctantly. How much he wished he had some of his father's drive and effectiveness in confronting these rebellions. With what relish his father used to plan his revenge on every rebel who dared to defy his rule. And when the uprisings were defeated, with what ruthlessness he punished those who had risen against Baghdad's dominion. The Caliph had none of these attributes, and every move he made to quell provincial resistance to the caliphate felt like an enormous effort and a huge burden. But he knew he had to deal with this latest insurrection decisively, or risk the rebellion spreading.

Khorasan had been the source of his family's rise to power, the strength of the army that had kept them sovereign, and the place whose culture, poetry, and art had brought beauty and refinement to his ancestors' rough desert ways. They learned to admire and emulate the customs and style of life of the Persians, intermarried with them, and the two peoples together had gone on to produce a new, inimitable Arab-Persian culture that enriched them both. It had reached its apogee in his and his father's court, with its poets, philosophers, musicians, and storytellers. It was unthinkable that those precious links should now be threatened with rupture.

"I wish for Abdullah ibn Rida to be immediately served with a notice of dismissal unless he ends these conspiracies and reaffirms his loyalty to us. Send word to our army commander in Merv and have him deliver my message. He should take an escort of our best soldiers with him when he does this. Ask them to bring Abdullah ibn Rida to Baghdad to present himself here before me. Do nothing more until I have seen him."

Abu Ubaydah bowed, but the Caliph could see he was wondering how his wishes would be carried out. The Abbasid garrison in Merv was loyal but not large and many of its soldiers had settled in the suburbs of the city, some of them married to local women. Abu Ubaydah judged them not up to the task, and the Caliph could not disagree. Khorasan's governor was a wily man who had seen to it that his own guards would defend him against any attack, including any from Baghdad.

"Uthman, draw up a formal letter of dismissal and let me see it," he commanded his secretary.

The truth was he felt compelled to face up to the matter he had been avoiding ever since his promise to Abdulhamid. He would have to confront the governor of Khorasan over his treachery, of course, but he would also have to demand a return of the lands stolen from Abdulhamid's family. He had pushed this other task to the back of his mind, fearing it would remind him of Murjana. But such cowardice was unworthy of him, he decided, and he resolved to recapture his earlier indignation at the idea that a mere girl should have been so capable of disrupting his affairs.

Bringing Abdullah ibn Rida to heel was the only way to resolve the issue of the stolen land—and end the problem of Murjana.

3

Baghdad was decked out in all its finery to welcome the ambassadors from Byzantium. Its unique circular shape, great palaces, and monumental buildings were shown off to advantage. It made the Caliph proud to see his capital city so resplendent. Through the streets, in the parks, and on the river, the banners of Byzantium flew from every boat and every building. Music played and great displays of acrobatics, juggling, and dancing filled the main streets.

Even from a distance inside the palace, he could hear great shouts, loud drum beats, and clapping as the ambassadors' cavalcade of ministers and men of high office passed by. They had come from the chief wazir's palace on the eastern bank of the Tigris, their residence during their visit, and Abu Hisham was at the head of their cavalcade. As the Caliph had instructed, their route to the Golden Gate palace, where he would hold a banquet in their honor, was lined with crowds who waved and cheered. But it was not all orchestrated by his stewards. Many among the crowd were genuine in their good wishes, tired of war and killing.

"The enmity between our two lands has continued too long," read the Byzantine emperor's missive to him. "It is time to start afresh and conjoin to make peace between our peoples. We recognize and acknowledge your great dominion as you do ours. Two such powers must be together as brothers, not as enemies."

If only it could be true. War with Byzantium had been waged for as long as the Caliph could remember. From the time of the Umayyads, who were determined to subjugate the Byzantine Empire unless it embraced Islam or paid tribute, Byzantium was the great enemy, and to do battle with it was a noble *jihad*. The history of his family from his great-grandfather's time to his was punctuated by the battles and annual military expeditions against Constantinople, and its retaliations against the Arabs.

Byzantium was the only power the Arabs feared, its navy their only rival on the Mediterranean Sea. Though the Umayyads had managed to push the frontiers of Byzantium's empire back to Asia Minor, it was not overcome. Nor did its capital, Constantinople, succumb to their armies, as had the empire of the Persians. And unlike the Persians, the Byzantine Greeks did not relinquish their faith in favor of Islam, and they learned no Arabic. They just sat in their strongholds, a perennial taunt and a provocation that infuriated the Arab armies.

The Umayyads could never resist the challenge. Each time, they failed—until the final push to bring down the Byzantine capital in 716. That time, they proclaimed, they would succeed. Their huge army and massive fleet of ships surrounded the Greek city from all sides. The siege lasted one full year and was on the verge of succeeding when the Byzantines retaliated with the terrifying weapon they called the Greek Fire. This deadly liquid, which only they possessed, was fired from their ships and set the Umayyad navy alight. Most of its ships were destroyed, and the onset of Anatolia's harsh winter carried off huge numbers of soldiers through starvation and disease. It was a great defeat from which the Umayyads never recovered.

"You know," the Caliph's father would tell him and his brother, "they used to say of my grandfather, al-Mansour, that he had two passionate desires in life: first, to build Baghdad, and, second, to conquer Constantinople and restore Arab honor after that terrible defeat. With God's help, he accomplished the first. But no matter what great armies he assembled, what brave generals, what fine fleets, he never attained the second."

To the two brothers, the very name, Constantinople, conjured up a magical city, atop a mountain so high its buildings were half-hidden in cloud, and its base washed by the sea. But they learned to accept, though uncomprehendingly, that no matter how enchanting they imagined it to be, Constantinople was their enemy.

It was finally his father who, in 806, inflicted on the Byzantines a defeat so resounding that no one thought they could rise against Baghdad for a hundred years. The Caliph grew up on tales of this victory, inflated by legend and imagination, and how it was said that his father had assembled a great army of 130,000 men, spent 200,000 gold dinars and 21 million silver dirhams, and had himself led the Arab forces into Asia Minor. Towns were captured, forts demolished, islands overrun, and people taken prisoner. Cyprus was ravaged and thousands of its people enslaved.

The Byzantine emperor had no alternative but to surrender. He was made to pay huge tribute, to relinquish the towns along the frontier of his empire, and, most humiliating of all, he and his son became personal subjects of the caliph and forced to pay the poll tax obligatory on all non-Muslims in the Islamic state. No more abject a defeat could be imagined, and it went down in the annals of Abbasid history as a most famous victory, long celebrated.

⌗

Re-reading the emperor's letter all these years later, the Caliph was glad the lesson his father had taught Constantinople was still effective. And yet, the sentiments were not all conciliatory.

"*I offer you the hand of peace,*" the letter said. "*But it will not remain outstretched for long. I pray that in your wisdom, mighty*

Commander of the Faithful, you seize our hand of friendship and do not strain our goodwill."

"Well, well," he said out loud, trying to be amused but feeling only irritated as he read the letter that Uthman had placed before him. "Not so friendly, after all."

"They say, my lord, the young emperor in Constantinople is rash and inexperienced in matters of state." Uthman echoed eagerly, pleased to be taken into the Caliph's confidence over something so important. "And hence he does not weigh up his words carefully or listen to advice."

The Caliph sighed. It was his misfortune that his forefathers' Byzantine obsession afflicted him too, and when the caliphate passed to him, the burden of the war with Byzantium passed with it. It was a duty he could not shirk or leave to his generals. He would have to resolve the issue before him.

But however he thought about it, he could summon up no appetite for renewed war with the Byzantines. No matter how arrogant the letter from the emperor might be, he preferred to pursue its peaceful message and ignore the conceited threat it held.

So he decided to make a big spectacle of the Byzantine envoys' delivery of the letter from their master and his acceptance of it. It was to be a grand ceremonial occasion to tell the people that the envoys were harbingers of a good time to come, free from war and conflict. His father's victories had ushered in a period of peace with the Byzantines that had given the country rest and prosperity for twenty years, and he refused to let the old battles against the emperor break that peace and return to the back-and-forth attacks of the past.

It was as the Caliph wished. The ambassadors were welcomed with great pomp and pageant. Inside the palace, he had his head of wardrobe dress him in ceremonial vestments, as would befit receiving the Byzantine emperor's representatives. Although Byzantium was an old enemy and their two empires were rivals, the Abbasid caliphs had come to respect the Byzantine throne and by and large regarded the emperors as their equals. But he wanted to impress on his visitors the might and grandeur of the Abbasids too.

So he had his servants select one of his most splendid silk tunics, its top sumptuously encrusted with pearls and rubies. The velvet cloak he would put around his shoulders was of deep black, the official color of the Abbasids, intricately embroidered with gold thread. On each of his fingers he wore gold rings, set with rich gems that burned and glowed in the light, and the fine silk turban that encircled the base of his black *qalansuwa*, the traditional Abbasid tall hat, was the color of pale ivory.

When the menservants had finished tending to him, smoothing his clothes and brushing his cloak, he stood tall and majestic, as befitted the commander of a great empire. He could see admiration on the faces of his chamberlain and attendants, who seldom saw him so richly fitted out, as they walked behind him toward the banqueting hall. Suddenly, he had a strange thought. *All this was not for the Greek envoys. I'm dressed like a bridegroom going to the wedding feast of his life.*

The idea was so bizarre it shook him. What betrothal, and to whom? What was he thinking of? He tried to clear his head and told himself it was no more than a trick of a tired mind. He would not dwell on it; a good night's rest was all he needed.

As he entered the great pillared banqueting hall of the palace, he was nearly blinded by the brilliant light of a myriad of lamps and candles. The dining tables had been set with silver dishes and golden goblets as befitted such a ceremonial occasion. Table stewards stood by with large ewers of scented water, awaiting the Caliph's signal for the hand washing ritual before the meal began. Courtiers and guests were already seated on cushions around the tables, chatting while they awaited his arrival. The night air that wafted into the open hall was cool, and despite the great assembly of diners, some people drew their cloaks about them.

At his entrance, the hubbub in the hall subsided as the courtiers stood up and bowed. He walked toward the dais where he would sit with his guests and principal dignitaries, and as he reached it, he turned to indicate to the assembly with a raised hand that they should sit down again and resume their conversation.

At that moment the Byzantine entourage entered from the opposite end of the hall and proceeded down between the rows of tables toward the dais. At the front were the two Greek ambassadors, richly clothed in brightly colored, embroidered tunics and short cloaks clasped at the shoulder with large gem-studded brooches. Unlike the Arabs, they were clean-shaven and wore no head covering over their short, curled hair. It gave them a less formal air than the assembled guests in their opulent multi-layered robes all around them. His chief wazir and other high-ranking men walked alongside the ambassadors, flanked by their guards and followed by a retinue of assistants and servants.

There was a hush as the party passed the tables and approached the dais on which the Caliph stood to receive them. He focused his gaze on the two envoys in their distinctive dress as they drew near, and in that moment noticed a young woman he had not seen before walking between them.

In a flash he knew it was Murjana, more beautiful than he remembered, her gown of pure white, cut low over her breast and shimmering beneath a robe of wine-red silk. Jewels sparkled in her loose black hair and flashed at her throat and hung from her ear-lobes. Her eyes were rimmed with kohl and her lips were moist and red. She was looking straight at him. He drew in his breath sharply and almost stepped forward with outstretched hands to greet her.

But no sooner had he thought to do so, than she vanished. It was a phantom. No woman would have been seen at that banquet of men, and none unveiled. No one was walking between the ambassadors. Murjana was not there or anywhere in the entire room.

The men reached the dais where he was standing and bowed low, as did their whole entourage.

"Most illustrious Commander of the Faithful," announced the first ambassador. "I bring you greetings from my master in Constantinople, his most honorable imperial majesty, and good wishes for your health and that of your subjects."

The second ambassador said much the same, and they both made speeches and heard speeches in return. The Caliph was at pains to ensure that he discharged his duties amply toward them and the other guests, notables, and courtiers. He invited the Greeks to taste the variety of dishes at the table, the most delectable his kitchens had to offer, and affected to eat heartily with them, though he had no appetite. He made appropriate conversation, looking pleased by the flattery of the emperor's envoys and sending his own compliments back. He made a show of receiving the official letters of friendship from Constantinople, which he had already read, and had his secretaries deliver Baghdad's reply to the envoys just as ceremonially. He went through every nicety that such diplomatic gatherings required and was relieved when the evening was finally over and he could leave the guests to their wine-drinking, which they would no doubt indulge in once he had gone.

It was all mechanical. He had lost every shred of interest he'd once had in the banquet and the ambassadors and their mission. The image of Murjana, as he had imagined her, took over his mind. He could think of nothing else. The old obsession was back, and his self-delusion that he had put the thought of her behind him was shattered. He had no more forgotten her than forgotten himself.

He didn't understand it and didn't want to try. Whatever it was, the compulsion to see her again could not be repressed any longer, and he would give in to it. If there was a lingering rational justification he could use for his seeing her again, it was that he would discover in that way if he had exaggerated her appeal and could put the whole madness behind him.

4

Having made the decision to see Murjana again, the Caliph could not wait for the meeting and impatiently set about arranging it. He instructed one of the secretaries, not Uthman who might put two and two togther, to inform Abdulhamid that he had news related to his land and would relay it to him if he came to see the Caliph. He also invited Abdulhamid's niece and nephew to the meeting, since he knew they had a clear interest in what was happening.

The three of them duly came to the palace and met the Caliph in an inner chamber behind the animal menagerie rarely visited by anyone. The Caliph made sure he was unobserved as he made his way there, accompanied by the secretary who had sent the letter of invitation. He asked the secretary to keep the matter confidential, as it related to an as yet unresolved state matter. Flattered, the young man promised he would do so.

The moment Abdulhamid set eyes on the Caliph, he was filled with gratitude, before even knowing what the Caliph would say. He and his nephew bowed and smiled, but the Caliph hardly noticed. His eyes were fixed on the girl with them. He watched her as she sat down next to her uncle and rolled back the edge of her robe to reveal the soft pink tunic gown she wore underneath. As before, her head was loosely covered by a thin veil, and when she looked up and her eyes met his, he felt again that charge between them. She smiled slightly, and—was he imagining it?—it was a knowing smile, as if she sensed she had some power over him, which she enjoyed. He could hardly tear his gaze away from her.

"You have some news for us, my lord?" Abdulhamid inquired.

"In a way, yes. It is not much, and I would not want to raise your hopes too high. But I wanted to keep you informed of our progress with regard to the loss of your land."

Every word the Caliph uttered made him uncomfortable, all too aware of the deception he had created by bringing the man in to see him under such false pretenses.

"I have summoned Abdullah ibn Rida to meet me here in Baghdad and answer for his crimes. It will be some time before he reaches us from Merv, of course, but it will happen. I wanted to reassure you that I had not forgotten your request, and you and your brother's children may feel secure in the knowledge that the matter is still in hand."

The Caliph's memory of the rest of that meeting was dominated by the girl and the emotions she aroused in him. It was the same as the first time.

At the very sight of her again, whole vistas of promise and renewal seemed to open before him. Her beauty was more intoxicating than when he first saw her, immeasurably enhanced by that knowingness he had noticed before. It told him she was not as innocent as she seemed, and that excited him more. Surely the girl was a virgin? But if she was not, he thought recklessly, so what? He looked at her as if he would devour her with his passion.

"My lord," she spoke unexpectedly, her eyes cast down toward her lap. "May I thank you for your concern and kindness in keeping us informed? You are busy with matters of far greater importance than what must seem to you our small problem. It is a wonder you have remembered us at all."

Her uncle and brother were looking at her in astonishment.

"Forgive my niece, sir, she is hasty and may speak out of turn. But I assure you she is truly honored to be invited here."

"Not at all, not at all. I am charmed and grateful for your niece's kindness in thanking me. There is no need. I am merely doing my duty toward you."

But the girl, undeterred by her uncle's disapproval, spoke again.

"Will you permit me to give you a little keepsake to remind you of our case, my lord?"

The Caliph watched her, enthralled, as she took a small object from the sleeve of her gown and rose. He stood up as she approached him and put a tiny velvet bag into his hand. As she did so, she appeared to trip over the hem of her long robe and had to seize his arm to stop herself from falling. Regaining her balance, she withdrew her hand, but not before slowly passing it down his arm to his fingers which she held momentarily. It had not been an accident, he was sure, and his whole body tingled at her touch.

It was as if, on seeing her, a window had opened for him onto another world. There was a mysterious aura about the young woman that went to his very core, one that evoked feelings and emotions so long suppressed and denied he didn't recognize them. His past life flashed before him: the four good women he had married, all from the finest Arab families. None had ever strayed or offended him in any way. He esteemed them all and valued their loyalty to him. As for his concubines, beautiful girls from foreign lands who vied with each other to please him, he had nothing but gratitude and praise for them.

Yet, he now realized that in all the years he knew these women not one had ever stirred him as this girl had done in a fraction of that time. But, for all that, he was unsure about these sudden, new feelings and wondered if they might stem from nothing more than boredom with his harem and the general tedium of his life.

Rousing himself from these ruminations, he heard Abdulhamid

talking of their appreciation for the time and trouble he was taking over their case, and how happy it had made them. The young man murmured something of the same. Their gratitude was dignified, not groveling, and the Caliph noted it. He thanked them and rose to end the audience.

As they took their leave, he grasped Murjana's keepsake tightly. Only one thought was in his mind: he knew he wanted her, and what she had aroused in him was no illusion and no trivial infatuation. He had been wrong to imagine he could cast her memory aside. The feeling that had come over him when he first met her, that something out of the ordinary had occurred, returned to him, and he was suddenly filled with a wild exhilaration.

▣

But it was short-lived, soon replaced by unease, even fear, about the course his infatuation might take if he let his feelings run away with him. It had been at the back of his mind ever since he was first smitten by her, and was the cause for his previous efforts to forget her.

He had to face reality. Where could such an infatuation lead? It was not appropriate or possible for him to take her, a Muslim and the daughter of a respectable Arab family, to be his concubine, and neither could he marry her. To do so would automatically mean the divorce of one of his wives to make way for a new one. Perhaps he should not have married the full quota of four wives the sharia allowed him. His father had only married two after all, more manageable, and the custom nowadays. Had he followed his father's example, he would not have boxed himself into this corner now.

But there it was. He had four wives, all of whom he had married for reasons that he judged politically wise at the time of disunity and unrest that followed his brother's unseating and murder in the war between them. And he had not been wrong. Peace had spread through the caliphate's domains, at least in part because of those unions. For him now to repudiate any of the good women who had made that happy outcome possible seemed to him callous ingratitude.

No, divorcing any of them was unthinkable, and if he did, his conscience would leave him no rest that he should have inflicted such punishment on them and their illustrious families for no crime.

In this respect, people would say he was not a man of his time. His father, who at the same age had a progeny of children with twenty-four of his concubines, would not have hesitated in this situation. Indeed, no man of position, let alone a caliph, would have been expected to show such delicacy of feeling. Everyone knew that women were expendable and largely replaceable, unless they had the exceptional talent or strength of character of a woman like his stepmother, Khadija.

That was the prevailing view, although many women of independent means ran their own affairs and could hold their own with any man. Even so, the Caliph's hesitation over the divorce of his wives would be incomprehensible to his court and the wider society. But, such was his conviction, and the best way to distance himself from his desire for Murjana, he decided, was to spend time with his favorite fourth wife, Hind. With her wit and cleverness, not to mention her beauty, she would know the way to distract him and ease the torment of his mind.

He should go to her the very next night and share her bed again after what had been a long absence. And lying with her, he would seek and might find the solace he needed to shake off this mad infatuation.

5

No one had told Idris, the head eunuch, that the Caliph would be coming to the Dar al-Huram, the women's quarters of the palace, though if he had been told, he might not have believed it. The Caliph's visits were so infrequent, it must have been a month or more since the last one. So when the young eunuch on guard at the outer door rushed to tell Idris of the Caliph's imminent arrival, Idris was taken completely by surprise. Flustered, he sent the young man to round up the other eunuchs, stewardesses, and female servants, and tell them to make preparation to receive the Caliph.

As word of his arrival spread through the Dar al-Huram, everyone started rushing about, nearly falling over each other in their haste to open windows and sprinkle rose water in the corridors and rooms, and run to alert the ladies of the Caliph's arrival. It was not that anyone feared the Caliph's wrath at finding them so unprepared; he was a courteous and considerate master. But he had so rarely visited in recent weeks that their housekeeping had become lax.

Each of the Caliph's wives had her own separate rooms where she lived with her children, slaves, and attendants. The concubines had their own shared quarters and had less privacy but more gaiety. The women of the Caliph's family should have been housed at the Dar al-Huram too, but his stepmother, sisters, and aunts had chosen to retain the independence they had in his father's time, and lived in their own palaces on the east bank of the Tigris. There they had their own social circles, parties, and musical evenings. It was a freedom they were beginning to lose, and the royal ladies who came after would live in the Dar al-Huram along with the other protected women of the household.

"My lord, forgive me," Idris stammered, bowing deeply before the Caliph. He disliked being wrong-footed when he was used to being in command. It irked him that the junior eunuchs and stewardesses, some of whom resented his power, should see him so embarrassed and unsettled.

"No one said you were coming. I had no advanced word—"

The Caliph cut him short.

"Don't upset yourself, my dear Idris. I did not warn you or anyone of my intention to come because there was no need. Is this not my home? Am I not free to go within it where I please?"

Idris noticed that he had with him just two guards, who must have walked him all the long way from his apartments through the main courtyard to the farthest reaches of the palace where the Dar al-Huram stood in seclusion.

Idris, still flustered, bowed again. But the Caliph patted his shoulder and made him straighten up. He liked the eunuch, a red-haired, blue-eyed Slav with fair skin who had been brought to his father's palace as a young boy. Captured in one of the army's raids in distant lands, he was supposedly castrated before puberty to prepare him for his role as a eunuch. But it was rumored that he already had a soft down on his cheeks when the surgeon cut out his testicles, and so too old to be a proper eunuch. No one but Idris knew if it was true, but he grew to be handsome and well-built without the effeminate looks many eunuchs had.

He was taught Arabic and brought up a Muslim. The Caliph

remembered him as a boy being tutored by the older eunuchs at the palace, and noted then how bright and inquisitive he seemed. He had gone on to excel in the service of the Caliph, who, after the death of the head eunuch, rewarded his intelligence and discretion by elevating him to the post.

The Caliph's trust was not misplaced. Idris managed the Dar al-Huram with efficiency and firmness, and most were charmed by his open face and ready smile. But for all that, people feared him. They knew his loyalty to the Caliph, like that of all eunuchs, was absolute; that he was their ruler's eyes and ears in the palace, and probably beyond. And how could it be otherwise? Idris and his like lost their families in childhood and ended up without parents, siblings, wives, or children. The palace was their family and the Caliph their father. The only affection and gratitude they knew, they owed to this family and would not betray it lightly. Knowing that, no courtier was foolish enough to criticize the Caliph, his ministers, his staff, or his womenfolk before Idris. Occasionally, an ambitious eunuch would allow himself to become embroiled in a palace intrigue that harmed the Caliph or someone close to him. But that did not detract from this general attitude.

It was the Caliph's custom on his visits to the harem to pass by all his wives' apartments, as well as the great room that housed the concubines, before settling on the one he was aiming for. It was his way of lessening the rivalry and feelings of rejection among the women vying for his attention when he chose one rather than another of them for company. This time, he did not do that but headed straight for the lady Hind's apartment. It was no surprise to Idris, who knew she was the Caliph's favorite, and he escorted him down a hallway to her rooms.

Her maidservants were waiting for him, and as the Caliph entered, he was welcomed warmly into the apartment.

"My lord," Hind cried reaching her arms out toward the Caliph.

The maids melted away, bowing, and the two were alone. There was a glint of triumph in her eyes. After more than a month of absence, when the Caliph had seen none of his women, it was she he had come first to see, and perhaps would see no other afterward. He looked into her face and saw her thoughts. But her proud self-confidence did not disturb him. It was part of her appeal and the reason why he now sought solace in her strength. Taking his hand, she drew him down to the silk cushions where she had been sitting, and slid his cloak away from his shoulders, pulling gently on the sleeves to slip them off.

Hind was a handsome woman, tall, nearly as tall as the Caliph, with warm brown eyes set wide apart, and fair-colored hair. The Caliph admired the elegance and suppleness of her figure, still redolent of youth, and so unlike the small and delicate frame of that other young woman he did not want to think about.

"It has been too long a time since you were here," Hind said. "I, *we*, have all missed you. The children of your wives ask for you every day. What matters of state have kept you away?"

They drank sherbet and went on conversing. She asked him about the news of his dominions, commenting and making suggestions for dealing with the problems he mentioned. She was as sharp and witty as ever, and he found her company delightful.

But try as he might, he could not become engaged. It was as if he were watching himself and her from afar, two people in a tableau painted on one of the walls of his palace.

They dined, she having arranged for his favorite dishes to be served—chicken zirbaj with cinnamon and almonds, smoked haddock with raisins and coriander, all hurriedly but deliciously assembled by the harem cooks. Had there been time, she would have added new savories from her own recipes. At the end of the meal, she would also have asked for the best pale honey wine to sweeten the palate following the spicy food.

He ate less heartily than normal, she noticed. She thought

he looked strained, and, despite her efforts to distract him, he remained as preoccupied as when he first arrived. Wine would have rested him, she was sure, brought color to his cheeks and a smile to his lips. But he avoided sharab* of all kinds, although in his typical open way with what he regarded as unimportant matters, he tolerated the drinking of it by others.

The night wore on, and when it was time, Hind rose, kissed the Caliph lightly on the lips, and went into the bedroom. Her maids were waiting to wash and disrobe her. He lingered on the cushions after she left, aware that he must soon follow her and reminding himself of why he had come, of the consolation that awaited him in her bed.

And yet, he was reluctant to go to her. He should not have come to see her, thinking to use her as an aid to oblivion. Hind deserved better, and he would do his husbandly duty by her.

⌗

But, lying in her bed, with the candles burning low and the distant high-pitched sound of the palace peacocks roaming the great courtyard, he could not. He passed his hands over her soft flesh, caressed her, kissed her lips, drew her naked body tightly against his. But all to no avail. The image his inner eye held was that of another body, young, urgent, untried; another face, sweet, large-eyed, not yet awakened.

"What's wrong, Abdullah?" Hind asked softly, propping herself up on her elbow and facing him.

The use of his first name was an intimacy permitted to very few. He stroked her cheek gently, and traced the line of her jaw to her lips with his finger. He sighed.

"It is not you, my dearest Hind. You are as beautiful as ever and always my favorite. But I have for some time been weighed

---

* The Arabic word for wine, not to be confused with "sherbet," meaning sweetened fruit water.

down by the problems in the country I told you about. I know I should have left them behind me at your door. But they oppress me and lose me sleep and enjoyment in life." He put out his arms to her and kissed her forehead. "That is all."

She looked back, anxiety in her eyes.

"When I have seen my way through these burdens, I swear I will be back to you, your Abdullah of old."

He almost meant it. His admiration and respect for her knew no bounds. She was the one who knew the intimate secrets of his life as no one else did, his lonely upbringing at the hands of an embittered mother, who had never recovered from his father's heartlessness in casting her aside for a younger concubine.

That unhappy mother had poured all her frustration into making him as different from his father as possible. His father had been flamboyant and pleasure-seeking, while Abdullah was quiet and studious, with no interest in the lifestyle of a man like his father: hunting, wine drinking, and the pleasures of the harem with its most beautiful young women dancing and music making for his enjoyment.

But his mother had also fed him with her bitterness and rage against his father's betrayal of her and her son, Abdullah. It gave him a lifelong horror of treachery and, if it ever happened, evoked in him a ruthless desire for revenge, which were echoes of his mother's own unrequited anger. It drove him to distrust others, while at the same time longing for affection and compassion.

Hind instinctively understood all that, and he loved her for her care of him, her empathy with the things he had suffered, when everyone thought him hard and unfeeling. But he also knew she was shrewd, and as he gave her his assurances about his temporary preoccupation with nothing more than the duties of state, he wondered if she believed him.

He certainly did not believe himself. Whatever comfort his time with her had given him, it had done nothing to sway his thoughts from Murjana or relieve his obsession with the girl. The truth was staring him in the face and could not be escaped any longer. There would be no ending to this anguish without his seeing Murjana again, whatever it might bring. If God so willed, it might even show that he had nothing to fear. All this soul-searching was over just two short meetings. If he were honest, he would recognize that his infatuation was only kept alive by the fancy of an aging man who had never known love. Seeing Murjana again, he might well discover that he had idealized her, blown up her beauty and power to seduce him out of all proportion.

And if that happened, as it was likely to, it would be the best outcome of all.

PART II

6

A bu Mansour longed for a rest from the heat that enveloped Baghdad like a thick blanket. The summer that year was very hot, and his household had already started to bottle their meat in salt and spices before it rotted. With its airy central courtyard and fountain spraying water mist into the air and over the ground, the house should have been cooler, but it was not enough. They had to drape the windows with wet cloths and hang soaking canvas sheets from the ceilings to drip water onto the floors before they could sleep.

If anyone at the time had asked Abu Mansour if he might like to be the Caliph's physician, he would have refused without hesitation. Court life, with its pomp and intrigue, did not interest him, even though several of the Caliph's ministers and state officials were his patients. They could just as well have consulted the palace's own physicians. But people were drawn by Abu Mansour's medical fame, his sharp, analytical mind, and the successful treatments he prescribed for many a disease that had seemed incurable.

By that summer, the doctor had so grown in fame and success that Baghdad's rich and powerful families fell over each other to consult him about ailments that had proved beyond the skills of other doctors. He was effusively welcomed into their homes, given every assistance, and his remarkable ability to help the patients he was asked to see astonished them and earned him their everlasting gratitude.

"How can we thank you enough, Abu Mansour?" they would ask fervently. "What gifts can we offer you?"

He was so universally admired that, had he wished it, he could have made a fortune from treating these grateful patients, and, through their connections, have gained access to the Caliph's court and his ministers. But he never accepted anything more than was his due and took up none of the connections they offered him.

"God's favor is my richest reward," he would tell them, and take his leave. If that made him sound unctuous, it did not concern him. When all physicians were known for their avarice, no one understood a man who turned his back on fame and fortune, a man so devoted to his art that he found his fulfillment and reward solely in its practice. He wished for no better life and was constantly in demand, busy from morning till night attending to his many patients.

Like the Caliph, he was in his forties. But in all other ways, their backgrounds could not have been more dissimilar.

The Caliph was born into luxury in his father's palace, indulged from childhood by all those around him, and with every material advantage in life. He was surrounded by splendor, as far removed from the lives of everyday people as it was possible to be. His capital city was largely unknown to him. He never walked its streets, saw its shops, or entered its houses.

Abu Mansour, by contrast, was a man of the people. His grandfather, Ali, had been a lowly tradesman from Tabriz in north-eastern Persia who came to Baghdad to seek his fortune, where he had heard the Arab caliphs were partial to Persians and made them welcome. He had little education and barely knew any Arabic. But he managed to pass himself off to the city authorities as a carpenter, and set up shop in the great souk at Karkh, in the west of Baghdad.

As a child Abu Mansour's biggest treat was to go with his grandfather, Ali, on a tour of the great city. They would start off at the Khorasan gate where Ali had first entered Baghdad. From there they would climb into the chamber above the gatehouse where it was said the caliph who built Baghdad had liked to sit. The panoramic view of wide fields and palm groves bordering the great river used to make the young Abu Mansour gasp with wonderment.

Then would come the greatest part of all—the grand souk. They would walk down the main thoroughfare where the major tradesmen had their brightly-lit shops, carpet sellers, paper merchants, jewelers, and perfumiers. From there, Ali would turn into the network of smaller souks of butchers, coppersmiths, tanners, and dyers.

Some of these were no more than narrow alleyways, crowded with stalls on both sides and, unlike the roofed main souk, open to the sky. The sunlight that filtered down from the narrow strips of sky above was enough to light them up in summer, but in winter they put up hanging lamps. Abu Mansour used to feel at home in his grandfather's carpentry shop, huddled close to the others in the alley, and loved going there.

The grandfather's carpentry trade passed to the doctor's father, named Mansour after the caliph who had built Baghdad and given Ali his big chance in life. And it was expected that in due course, the same trade would be handed down to Mansour's son, Hasan.

This was the modest setting of Abu Mansour's birth and upbringing. His given name was Hasan, but in accordance with Arab custom, the family's firstborn son was usually expected to name his eldest son after his father, even before any children of his own were born. So, Hasan became known as Abu Mansour, father of Mansour, from his teenage years.

At the age of twelve, he was apprenticed to his father and trained to be a carpenter according to the custom. What had been his grandfather's shop had become his father's, and in time would be his. He knew what was expected of him and meekly accepted he would continue the family tradition.

That is, until the day his grandfather fell ill. At sixty-five, Ali had attained a good age, and no one was surprised when the moment of his death arrived. But young Hasan, devoted to his grandfather as he was, would not accept it without a fight.

His parents sought out a good physician to attend Ali. Hasan watched anxiously while the doctor felt Ali's pulse, examined his urine, even tasting it for sweetness, and drew back his eyelids to see his lashes and the color around the irises of his eyes.

When he had finished, he told Hasan's parents that Ali had a hectic fever which he doubted would attain coction, when the humors mixed and cooked together, and the point that often heralded the beginning of recovery. No medical skill, he said, could now restore Ali to normal health.

As the doctor took his leave, murmuring his regrets, Hasan stared after him with something like hatred. He knelt by his grandfather's bedside, convinced with all his child's passion that, had the right doctor been found, Ali could have been cured.

It was at that moment he realized with certainty he wanted to be that doctor, wanted to cure what seemed incurable and give patients and their loved ones a hope of recovery, the greatest gift life has to offer.

That night he confided his feelings to his mother, his best friend, and told her of his sudden decision. He was determined to make medicine his chosen craft and he would have no other.

◫

And so it was that when Abu Mansour was old enough, he set out with youthful eagerness on the long, arduous journey to becoming a physician. His teachers took him through all the phases of his medical education and conferred on him an *ijaza*, an official stamp on the medical books he had studied to their satisfaction. To that was added a second ijaza on the books of philosophy he also read.

His teachers saw no conflict between the two. Philosophy was the natural complement to the medical art in its search for truth and meaning. Such learning made for the ideal Arab physician, a preeminence to which all doctors aspired: one versed in many fields, equally a philosopher, astronomer, mathematician, poet, as well as physician. This was the true *hakim*, a man of wisdom. Only few could attain such exalted status, but it seemed to his teachers that Abu Mansour might well become one of them. They saw in him a man who would one day make his mark in the world.

7

"Hasan...It's time to wake up."

His mother's hand on his shoulder woke Abu Mansour out of a deep and dreamless sleep. Her figure was dark against the sunlight that came in through the wooden shutters of his bedroom.

"Not like you to sleep so long. We've had no breakfast yet, and we're all hungry."

He struggled to sit up, yawning.

"I know," he stretched. "But I was so tired I fell back to sleep after the dawn prayer. Please don't wait for me."

"We might not, but you need to get up."

He yawned again and would have snuggled back in bed, but he threw off the bedclothes obediently instead. Somehow his mother still had the power to turn him back into a little boy again whose only desire, as throughout his childhood, was to earn her love and approval.

She had been residing with him ever since his father's death, a fate many women dreaded. In her son's household, such a woman could find herself at the mercy of his moods, or the grudging tolerance of his wife. But Um Hasan was spared all these indignities. Her son loved her, always told her she was his best friend and companion, and thought it an honor to have her share his home. It had been the same when he was a child and had never changed. And he was still unmarried, though much to her disapproval.

Satisfied that he was on his feet, Um Hasan left him. Whatever she said, he knew they would wait for him because they all cherished, as he did, the morning ritual of breakfast together. It was traditional for lunch to be the communal meal of the day, but he was often too busy to join them and usually ate later on his own. So, breakfast had become the time when they all sat cross-legged around the low table by the fountain in the courtyard and ate the freshly baked bread and the breakfast dishes the cook made so deliciously. The warm aroma of new bread had always meant home to Abu Mansour. He had grown up on the round, flat loaves baked freshly in the kitchen *tannour*, which his mother used to dip in honey for him.

The bread his household now baked was different, made according to the medical specifications he insisted on. These meant taking fine wheat flour and mixing it with carefully balanced portions of salt, borax, and yeast, the loaves made neither too thin nor too thick. In this, as in the rest of his medical practice, he aimed for balance, the Greek ideal of the golden mean between opposing elements, even in bread-making.

His mother thought it all very silly, but she humored him. "It doesn't make any difference. Bread is bread," she would say. But he insisted that the body had need of balance, in diet as in all other matters, and since bread was customarily eaten with every meal, he put the family's good health down to his bread-making recipes. "Perhaps it's God's grace that keeps us healthy and not your bread," his sisters would tease him.

The sky was partly cloudy, and it was cool in the courtyard as he walked out. The commotion of people arguing and shouting in the street outside was unusually loud that morning. It was a Wednesday, the day when small farmers from the villages outside the city came to sell their produce in the souk and passed by the houses on their way. It spared many households a journey to the market, and the farmers' visits were welcomed. Abu Mansour, who normally disliked loud noise, had a soft spot for the farmers and found the Wednesday ritual comforting.

He joined the others seated around the breakfast table. There was a dampness in the air, the first whiff of autumn, he thought. The smell of fresh vegetation watered earlier by the servants mingled with the aroma of his favorite breakfast dishes: eggs fried in clarified butter and spiced with sumac; eggplant cooked in oil and coriander; curd cheese and washed black olives; and to finish with, honeyed dates, dried figs, and a large jug of beet leaf and pomegranate sherbet. Surveying this scene as he had done so many times before, Abu Mansour thanked God for his good fortune, living with the people he loved in the comfortable house he had built for them, and absorbed by a profession he adored.

He sat down and intoned the opening of the Quran's first sura, for which they had been waiting to start the meal. "*In the name of God, the merciful, the compassionate.*"

Everyone ate heartily, chatted, and told each other their news. When they had eaten their fill, they left the table one by one. Soon after, he stood up, meaning to go and prepare for the morning's clinic. But his mother held up her hand and asked him to stay.

"Wait, Hasan. Here, sit down," she said, patting the cushions next to her.

But he remained standing. The servants had cleared the last of the breakfast table and only the two of them and his elder sister, Fatima, were left.

He knew what his mother was going to say and did not want to encourage her.

"It's time to talk again about the matter of your marriage, my son."

He detested the whole subject and had repeatedly asked her not to mention it.

"You're no longer a young man, and it is time for you to settle and have a family of your own."

"Mother, please forget this subject. If I'd wanted to marry, I would have asked for your help long ago, or Fatima's here. You would have found the best brides for me, I know. But do please understand, and you too, Fatima, that I don't want to marry anyone. I really appreciate your concern, but it's a waste of time and effort trying to persuade me to change my mind."

His mother looked unimpressed.

"Don't be stubborn, Hasan," she said, continuing as if he hadn't said a word. "You know I'm right, but you fight against it for some reason. Now, listen. I think I have found the right wife for you. There is a very good family not far from here whose eldest daughter I think might be very suitable."

For years, she had made her dislike of his bachelor status clear and insisted that marriage would complete his life, even if he did not know it himself. No protest on his part to the contrary ever convinced her, and she never stopped trying to find him a suitable wife.

"You haven't seen this girl as I have," she continued. "Fatima came with me." His sister nodded.

"Mother, I must go," he insisted. "I am late for my patients."

He turned and started to walk away.

"Stop!" Um Hasan commanded. "You must hear this before you dismiss it. The girl's family is respectable and prosperous, at least in land if not money. The girl is educated and thoughtful, both pleasing to you, I think. Her name is Ayesha, and she is handsome in a refined sort of way, though not as beautiful as her cousin, who was with her that day."

"The other girl—they called her Murjana—was younger I think," his sister added, "and indeed very beautiful, too beautiful for her own good. I would not have chosen such a one for you, Hasan. She seemed strong-willed and too sure of herself. Ayesha was gentle and sweet-tempered. I really warmed to her."

"And so did I," echoed his mother. "They knew who you were, of course, and I'm sure would jump at such a marriage, though we hadn't got to the point of speaking about it in so many words."

Abu Mansour remained silent, fighting the urge to walk off while his mother was in full flow.

"There is nothing to alarm you in this, my son," she continued. "The girl was the best for you I've seen so far. And I've invited her mother and aunt to visit us...See her. If you don't like her, I promise I won't pester you about it or bring it up again—at least, not for a while!" she smiled.

"I hope she doesn't bring her cousin when she comes here," said Fatima to her mother. "They seemed very close."

"Even if she does, it won't matter. Your brother is too wise to fall for a pretty face."

It was a tiring clinic, not least because of the irritation his mother had caused him at breakfast. It interfered with his long-held habit of making sure he was rested and composed when he saw his patients. In his experience, agitation excited the humors, and so led to disequilibrium and poor judgment.

"How many more, Younis?" he asked when the young man returned after ushering out the last patient.

"Only two, sir. First, that lady you've seen several times before, the one who always comes with her brother. And after them, a man new to us who says he is not sick himself but has a question about a sick member of his family."

Abu Mansour's mood did not improve on hearing this. He had indeed seen the woman and her brother before, and far too often for his liking. Each time, she had a different complaint: a fluttering of the stomach, a sudden palpitation of the heart, an ache in one half of her head, or a twitch in her limbs. None of these was ever serious, but they were always dramatic. Each time, he would examine her, feel her pulse, palpate the affected limb, and look at her urine. And each time, he would reassure her that, according to humoral theory, the innate heat—the vital heat that was the life force and that waned in illness—was strong. So he would prescribe a concoction of simple herbs, more for her comfort than for any medicinal effect they had.

But she was never reassured, he did not know why, and her recurrent visits irritated him. He advised that, in the future she would benefit more from seeing Nafisa, the woman healer in the souk, who was a midwife and herbalist and had helped many women with similar symptoms. But the patient stubbornly insisted he was the only healer she needed, and lately he had even thought of refusing her future access to his clinic.

"My master hasn't got the faintest idea what that woman is after," Younis would tell his sisters, chuckling, when he got home. "He doesn't realize it's him she wants. You can see it on her face plain as day, and all the 'illnesses' she comes up with are just excuses to see him. He sometimes says to me, 'What do you think of her, Younis? Is she a bit mad?' 'Mad with love of you,' I want to tell him. But he probably wouldn't believe it."

⊞

The last patient of the day gave his name as Ibrahim al-Ajami. He appeared to be in his mid-twenties and was well dressed and politely-spoken. His complexion was unhealthy and bore the scars of a past encounter with smallpox. But for that he might have been passably good-looking.

"Abu Mansour, I have been sent to ask for your help with our sick cousin."

"Do you wish to bring him to me here so I can best advise you?"

The young man looked slightly alarmed.

"No, no, that won't be possible. He lives very far away and would not be well enough to ride."

Abu Mansour waited.

The man hesitated.

"We, our family, fear he might have been poisoned."

The story was that the cousin, a man in his forties, had fallen ill mysteriously after eating something that seemed to disagree with him. The doctors could not diagnose the cause, offered no treatment, and he was being nursed by his wife and children. His condition had deteriorated rapidly and they feared for his life.

"What is your question?" asked Abu Mansour.

"You are famous for your great knowledge of medicine, Abu Mansour, and your unique experience of poisons and their antidotes. We wanted to know what sort of a poison it could be that had this effect and what antidote we might need. I can say for certain that the poison must have been tasteless and odorless for our cousin not to notice. He is known in the family for his sharp sense of taste and smell."

The man spoke hurriedly, as if anxious to tell the doctor everything he could think of.

"What sort of poison could it be that those who eat it have no suspicion there's anything wrong?"

"I am sorry to disappoint you and to have caused you a needless journey to see me. Without examining your cousin myself, it would be unwise for me to hazard guesses, on the basis of which the wrong remedies might be prescribed."

The man's face fell.

"Surely, you could suggest what sort of poisons might be disguised by the taste of ordinary food, and what sort could be so powerful that they could endanger life with such speed."

He seemed almost desperate for the information.

"You haven't told me what his symptoms are. But whatever

they might be, aren't you assuming your cousin has been poisoned? That might not be the problem."

"You're right. But poison can't be excluded, and that's why I thought you could help."

Abu Mansour shook his head.

The man realized that he would get no answer from him beyond that. Clearly dissatisfied, he reluctantly got up and left.

The doctor was puzzled.

"Do we know anything about this Ibrahim al-Ajami?" he asked Younis.

Younis shook his head.

"I've never seen him in our neighborhood before. He came alone and didn't talk to anyone while he was waiting to see you. But he was frowning and looking around all the time."

Abu Mansour didn't believe a word of the poisoning story. But he found himself wondering who the man was, and couldn't help being intrigued by what might be the real purpose of his visit.

The riddle was still on his mind when he went to the bimaristan that afternoon to give a lecture to his students. These were occasions to which many people, not just students, came: the apothecary and his apprentices, the hospital nurses and other workers who could get the time, and young doctors. Often, there were itinerant students, as well, scholars from the far reaches of the empire who set out seeking knowledge at the great centers of learning in Damascus and Baghdad. These students were assured of hospitality wherever they went, an obligation on all Muslims who believed in the tradition taught by the Prophet, to "seek learning, though it be in China."

Such was Abu Mansour's fame that people said they learned at his lectures what no book could give them, and they treasured his words. He had not yet decided on which topic he would speak that day. But with the mysterious visitor of the morning in his mind, it occurred to him that it might be useful for his lecture to be on the types of poisons and their treatments. This was a popular subject with students for its overtones of sinister plots and dark deeds that fired the imagination. Abu Mansour always had to remind them that most poisonings happened accidentally, usually through ingesting larger quantities than normal of herbs or compound medicines, which otherwise would have been harmless. Opium was a case in point. When used in small amounts for the relief of troublesome coughs, looseness of stools, or pain and headache, it was harmless. But if too much was ingested, the patient would fall into a sleep so deep as to resemble lethargy; and still more would end in death.

As he spoke, detailing the properties of dangerous plants and animal venoms, and the antidotes for each, the encounter with the strange patient he had seen that morning kept coming to mind.

The lecture ended, and the audience began to disperse. One person in particular among them drew his attention. Abu Mansour caught only a glimpse of his back as he was walking out. But for some reason, he imagined it to be the same man who had been at his clinic earlier. He realized this was unlikely and dismissed the idea. But even so, it lingered in his mind, as did the thought of murder, and unnatural death.

8

Baghdad was rife with rumors that the Caliph was sick. Throughout all the arduous times of his reign—the war with his brother, the battles against the Byzantines, the unceasing rebellions in the provinces that had to be put down, and the pestilences that overtook the city each summer to which the strongest men fell victim—the Caliph's health had never been known to falter. If illness had ever befallen him, no one knew of it except those closest to him. Any hint of such a matter would have been quickly suppressed and hidden from the public to ward off fear and unrest. This time, however, the rumors were persistent and said to be authentic, since they came from servants in the palace itself.

"The souk's full of gossip," said Saad, the chief steward of Abu Mansour's household. The doctor normally took no notice of his servants' gossip. But he had a soft spot for Saad ever since he rescued him from the bimaristan.

The hospital's chief administrator had warned him when Abu Mansour expressed his intention to adopt the youth.

"You might regret taking him into your home. Saad's head-strong and proud. We've found him disobedient when asked to do something he doesn't like."

So much so, that after only one year of working there, he was expelled from his post.

It was Abu Mansour who had carried out the medical examination on Saad at the slave market, as the doctor who normally did the slave testing was unavailable. Abu Mansour had rarely seen a man so fit. He had certified him as free of contagion, his teeth in good order, his skin clear of rashes and pustules, and his body without deformity or disease. He attested that whoever bought him could feel at ease about adding him to his household. And so the hospital had immediately bought him.

But frequent clashes with the hospital cleaners, the kitchen staff, and even the doctors, came to the notice of the hospital administrators, who tried to calm the young man and coax him into adjusting to the life of the bimaristan. He did not improve, and they were finally forced to threaten him with punishment.

None of it made any difference to his sense of grievance that he was looked down on for his color and disrespected for being a slave from the souk. Men like him were captured without regard to their family origins or social position in their native countries and could have been of noble birth or elevated status, for all the caliphate's conquering armies cared. Abu Mansour had seen such men before, brought low but with the memory of what they had been still burning in their hearts.

As luck would have it, Um Hasan took to Saad, and he to her. She treated him kindly and with a care for his feelings, took his advice on most household matters, and put him in charge of the other slave boys. Not long after, Abu Mansour emancipated him, telling him he need no longer serve them and was free to seek his fortune in the world. Saad would not hear of it. Abu Mansour and his family had become dear to him and had earned his loyalty and devotion.

"The butcher, the fruit seller, and the attar* all told me the

---

* Druggist, also spice and perfume seller.

same thing. All morning, the bakery's been full of people talking about it. They say the Caliph is very sick and cannot attend to his duties. The chief wazir has taken change."

"Is this any more than market gossip?" Abu Mansour wondered aloud.

He was in the small room off the corridor which he used as his dispensary, mixing a new batch of remedies. He always prepared his own medications, simples, and even compounds with many ingredients. Only in that way could he be sure of their purity and efficacy. Assisting him was his pupil, who was weighing each ingredient to the measure Abu Mansour specified, before passing it on to him.

"You see how we do it, Ahmad? Put the myrrh, tamarind seeds, yellow gentian, and birthwort together as I am doing, and then knead them all with three times their weight of honey until you have the right consistency."

He showed Ahmad the mixture he was stirring with a wooden spatula as it was forming at the bottom of the basin until the sticky cohesiveness of the blend was to his satisfaction.

"And there you have it!" he announced triumphantly. "The Theriac of Four, the best cure there is for diseases of the stomach, liver, and spleen."

His young pupil looked impressed, as did Younis, standing in the doorway, although he had seen Abu Mansour dispense his drugs a hundred times before.

"So, Younis, is there anything in these rumors?"

"No one knows, sir. But they say the Caliph hasn't been seen outside the palace for weeks, and the kitchen servants who go to the shops every day do their business quickly and hurry back. Some of them talk about the Caliph's sickness, but the rest are afraid to with the palace spies everywhere."

Abu Mansour said no more.

But as the days wore on, and there was still no sighting of the Caliph in public, alarm and speculation about his alleged ill health grew. Abu Mansour even heard of it at the house of the Banu Aziz, wealthy patrons of learning and prominent public figures, the head of whose household, Abu Aziz, was his patient. He had been called earlier to attend to the old man for another bout of dysentery.

This illness attacked him with regularity and Abu Mansour had warned him repeatedly to avoid drinking undiluted wine and eating sour, salty, or spicy foods. Abu Aziz, who had great respect for the doctor, always acquiesced and adopted this regimen for a while, but he always went back to the wine and the savory foods. Seeing him this time, Abu Mansour diagnosed the cause of the attack as an excess of phlegm in the stomach, which had pushed food down through his intestines too quickly. He prescribed a constipating *hiera*[*] compound and a diet of barley water and quince juice. His only nourishment was to be a daily meal of rice in sour milk or boiled egg yolk with sumac.

"God bless you as always, Abu Mansour," said the patient with fervent gratitude, sitting up on his cushions as if invigorated just by seeing Abu Mansour. "All will be well now you are here." He smiled up at the doctor. "At least my state is not as grave as that of our Caliph, eh? You've heard the news of course?"

"I thought it was just a rumor, not news."

Abu Aziz, a stout but handsome man in his early sixties, paused and lowered his voice.

"It is definite. I heard it from Sadiq, the minister, who heard it from the Caliph's chamberlain, no less. Our master is sick and so weak he has taken to his bed and cannot rise."

---

[*] *Hieras*, drugs of Greek origin and rendered as *iyarijat* in Arabic, were bitter compound medicines widely used in the treatment of many ailments.

"What do his doctors say?"

"That's just it." Abu Aziz replied slowly, obviously relishing the story. "They don't know. It seems they've tried every remedy—daily blood-letting, emetics, purges, ointments, and many other things. But nothing's worked."

Abu Mansour wondered where Abu Aziz had obtained these medical details, and concluded that wherever it was, the man was taking far too close an interest in the Caliph's condition. It was well known that he had been a supporter of the Caliph's brother and that, like many others, he had never truly accepted the legitimacy of the victor.

"So, what do the Caliph's doctors propose to do?"

"It seems they're close to seeking an opinion from a physician of great and exceptional learning, who might be more successful than they've been. It hasn't been easy for them to admit defeat. But they can't afford to endanger the Caliph's life by further delay."

He looked pointedly at Abu Mansour and winked.

The doctor ignored the hint and rose to leave, telling the patient's attendants to ensure the patient took the drugs and diet as prescribed. He said his goodbyes to Abu Aziz and his anxious sons, and made his way out.

As he walked toward the bimaristan with Younis and Ahmad, who had accompanied him on the visit, Abu Mansour had to admit that, disdainful as he normally was of gossip about the Caliph and his court, this time his curiosity had been stirred. He wondered what disease it was that afflicted the Caliph, what were its signs and symptoms, what humor was involved, and what superfluities had accumulated in the Caliph's body. Aside from his wealthy patients, Abu Mansour knew no one connected with palace circles to ask. And he did not trust the testimony of Abu Aziz, who was almost certainly exaggerating the severity of the Caliph's illness.

But to his surprise, the talk at the bimaristan was of the same topic.

"The palace doctors' envoys have just been here," Ismail, the young doctor in the fevers section, told Abu Mansour.

"They wanted to know of any physicians we had with special expertise in the treatment of loss of appetite and debility. They wanted to see you first."

"What did you tell them?"

"We asked who the patient was, because you would need that information, and it seemed to annoy them. They demanded to know what that had to do with their inquiry. Isaac, the Jewish doctor who's come to us from Fez, explained that the patient's age, and whether man or woman, were important in finding the right expert for the condition. But they would say nothing more and seemed very disappointed."

"They left?"

"Yes, sir. But of course we all knew it was the Caliph."

Not long after, news circulated about a celebrated Persian physician, the Prince of Bukhara's personal doctor. A man of great knowledge and skill who had cured many a difficult ailment, he had been in nearby Rayy on some business and was hurriedly invited to the palace.

Then the rumors died down, and it was assumed that the Caliph was recovering. Abu Mansour ceased reflecting on the Caliph's illness and resumed his routine activities: seeing his patients and warding off his mother's attempts to marry him off to some girl or other.

But the gossip started up again.

The Persian doctor had not been successful in alleviating the Caliph's condition and had been dismissed in favor of a doctor from India, who was a famous sage in his own country, deeply versed in Ayurvedic medicine. The Caliph was a lover of Indian mythology and admired India's ancient learning. He had traditionally welcomed such doctors to his court. It was only right they should now come to the Caliph's aid and put their wisdom to good use.

At the same time, the astrologers, officially frowned on by the men of religion in Baghdad, cast their horoscopes, attempting to divine the cause of the Caliph's illness and the time of his recovery. As the mystery of his ailment grew, they were in as much demand as the doctors. They pored over their zodiacal charts, studied the conjunctions of the stars, and pronounced on the most favorable time for the Caliph's treatment and recovery. Powerful talismans, containing especially engraved gemstones, were fashioned to be placed on the Caliph's forehead and around his neck. But he, a skeptic who regarded astrologers and their works as no better than magic and necromancy, refused them all.

Hearing this, Abu Mansour regretted the Caliph's attitude. He was no less a believer than the Caliph in the importance of reason over superstition. But he took it as natural that the motion of the planets, the sun, and the moon should affect the human body in health and disease. After all, reduced to its rudiments, the body was composed of the same four elements—earth, water, fire, and air—as those of which the world was made. It seemed to him self-evident, therefore, that the body was in microcosm a reflection of the universe. And had not Hippocrates, the great teacher and founder of the medical art, once said that the science of the stars was no small part of the science of medicine?

Ahmad, coming from Harran in northern Iraq, whose Sabian star worshippers were barely converted to Islam, could not have agreed more. Astrology was paramount in their lives, and the horoscope guided each step of their everyday activities. The idea that anyone in the Caliph's parlous state would reject the astrologers' help was to him almost incomprehensible. He was emboldened enough by the general bafflement about the Caliph's condition to say so and offer his own advice.

"If only our prince would believe it," he mused timidly, "his cure would surely come about if he submitted to the counsel of his astrologers and acted precisely according to their predictions."

Much as Abu Mansour was inclined to the same view, he was not so certain that such practices would be effective in what sounded like a very complex illness. He was by now increasingly intrigued by the Caliph's story and curious about its outcome. Rather like his mother and sisters and the rest of the household, he found himself waiting eagerly for the latest news from the palace.

Two weeks went by in this fashion, and it was said that the doctors had finally despaired. The Indian sage had been no more successful than those before him, and the Caliph was sinking fast.

It was at this point that they came to Abu Mansour.

◻

One morning, as he was finishing his clinic and contemplating a few quiet hours writing his manual for *mutatattibs*,[*] Younis came to tell him that three visitors from the palace were waiting to see him. He had been half-expecting this and motioned for them to be brought in.

They turned out to be the head palace physician, Suleiman, and two younger doctors with him. Abu Mansour had met Suleiman previously, a stout, shortish man with close-set eyes and a small mouth. But he did not know the other two, also from the palace and apparently subordinate to Suleiman.

"Gentlemen, please come in," he said.

Abu Mansour invited them into his inner office which no one normally entered without permission and where privacy was assured. It was a small room closed off from the main house by wooden double doors.

---

[*] Everyday medical practitioners who concentrated on the practical side of medicine and lacked the erudition and theoretical knowledge of physicians like Abu Mansour.

As the visitors came in, Abu Mansour could sense an awkwardness in the air. But they made themselves comfortable enough on the cushions and smiled at Younis when he came back shortly afterward with fresh mulberry sherbet. The head of the delegation then spoke.

"Forgive this intrusion, Abu Mansour. We would have sought your help before, but your..." He hesitated. "Your dislike of the court is well known."

He made it clear that he disapproved of this attitude, but Abu Mansour doubted that it was the real reason for his not having made contact before. Far more likely, it was the humiliation of being forced into consulting him on a case, and thus having to admit failure and acknowledge Abu Mansor's superior medical skills.

Abu Mansour had come across professional jealousy often enough in the past to make him shun many would-be colleagues, like Suleiman, and confirm him in his decision to work alone.

"I won't hide the truth from you," Suleiman went on. "Our lord, the Caliph, is mortally sick. He fell ill some two months ago and has grown worse over time. The details are not a matter of public knowledge, and we would be grateful for your discretion. Rumors and gossip have given a false picture of the situation, but unfortunately, servants' talk can't be avoided."

He paused, searching for the right words.

"Many physicians have been consulted about our master's state. I am myself...er...not unconnected in the world of medical learning, and have personally sought out the best, most well-known doctors. But all the medicaments we or they prescribed have been useless."

His colleagues nodded in silent agreement, observing Abu Mansour intently.

"I am sorry to hear this bad news," Abu Mansour responded. "Were you sent here by the Caliph himself, or by some other person?"

The doctors looked at one another.

"Why should that matter to you?" countered Suleiman. "We are the Caliph's official physicians and empowered to do whatever is necessary to ensure his recovery. The important thing is that you should agree to offer your services gladly for our prince—indeed should be anxious to."

"Don't misunderstand me," Abu Mansour responded quietly. "I am just as concerned as you about the health of our sovereign."

Abu Mansour was aware these men didn't like him and had power to do him harm. It seemed to him that Suleiman, in particular, had come against his will, only out of desperation to save the Caliph and his own professional reputation. Suleiman's failure to treat his master successfully must have been noted.

"Am I right that the Caliph knows nothing of your request for my assistance?"

"No, he does not. It is the chief wazir, Abu Hisham's request, and ours. I repeat, you should be more than ready to accept."

Abu Mansour considered this for a moment.

"My esteemed friends, please don't think I hesitate because I'm any less zealous than you to cure our Caliph, far from it. But it is not my way to attend to a patient who has not asked to see me. In my experience, the benefit of my help is far greater if the patient has specifically requested it from me."

There was a silence.

"So, if you would still like me to treat our master, please inquire of him first. If he approves, I am of course ready to serve him faithfully and to the best of my capacity."

"Abu Mansour," said Suleiman wearily, his high-handed manner suddenly gone. "I don't think you realize how sick our Caliph is. He lies on his bed all day, listless and hardly speaking to anyone. He's neither asleep nor fully awake. If we approach him with a question, he just turns toward the wall and doesn't respond. I honestly wouldn't know how to get an answer from him to what you ask."

For the first time, Abu Mansour saw that the other doctor

was in genuine distress, as well he might be if matters with the Caliph had reached this point.

"Perhaps you should tell me the whole story, from the beginning," he said. "Then I would understand better and we could start again."

◫

The tale that emerged was one of a slow, insidious decline, barely noticeable as illness at first and ascribed to a passing distemper, or a change in the weather, or a pollution of bad air, until the symptoms worsened to a point where they could no longer be explained away so simply. It did not help that the patient himself, being normally accustomed to robust health, attributed his symptoms to overwork and worry about the unrest in various parts of the caliphate, in fact to anything but disease.

It had all begun with the Caliph's insomnia. He would pace his bedchamber sleeplessly each night until the dawn prayer, when his eyes would finally close, only to open a short time later. This happened night after night, and the Caliph found that only a draft of hemp, drunk at bedtime, would induce a few hours' rest.

"You must have realized that hemp was dangerous when used so often."

"Of course we did, and we suggested that the Caliph find another way. But before we could find an alternative, the next stage of his illness began. He lost all appetite for food and became increasingly listless, to the point of abandoning many of his duties and regular activities. It was happening more and more that the gatherings with his secretaries and army commanders, which he had never missed before, were taking place without him. And the same with other important palace meetings.

"He grew pale and thin from lack of nourishment and fresh air. He stopped his daily strolls in the great courtyard, one of the special pleasures of his life, and began to sit alone, his eyes half-closed, as if in deep meditation. The chief wazir, one of the few allowed to be in the Caliph's presence, did his best to cover official duties. But there were many he could not do, and they had to be suspended until the Caliph recovered."

"What treatments did you prescribe?"

Suleiman turned to the other doctors. One of them now spoke.

"Once everyone accepted that the Caliph's condition was no simple case of fatigue and tension, we gave him the remedies known to be effective in cases like his."

"And what are those cases, in your opinion?"

The doctors looked at one another in consternation. Finally, Suleiman replied.

"I must admit that defining the cause of the Caliph's illness has been the main stumbling block in all this. We were unsure, and I couldn't remember having seen a case like it before.

"At first, when it seemed to me the Caliph had developed a yellow tinge to his complexion and the whites of his eyes, I put it down to a choleric disturbance of the liver, perhaps a hot inflammation or nature pushing the yellow bile to the surface of the body. It was for that reason that I prescribed emetic herbs and purgative medicines for evacuating the yellow bile, and gave him a cooling diet for the liver. But none of it worked, and I began to wonder if I'd just mistaken his pallor and tired eyes for an excess of yellow bile."

He paused, looking suddenly at a loss.

"What did you do then?"

"As the days wore on and our master declined further, no longer talking to anyone, but often sighing deeply as if remembering some great sorrow and showing no interest in the life around him, it occurred to me that I could have been right about his liver malady all along, and that the combustion of the yellow bile filling his liver had turned it into black bile."[*]

---

[*] Black bile was one of the four humors. It is obscure in origin, but was believed to have been formed by pathological processes in the body. Its vapor arising to the brain caused various neurological diseases, most notably, madness and melancholia.

"So, you assumed the black bile's vapor had then ascended to the brain?"

"Yes," responded Suleiman, pleased that Abu Mansour was following his line of thought. "And the vapor had given rise to melancholia, which was the Caliph's true diagnosis."

He paused, and looked at the others.

"The more my colleagues and I thought about it, the more feasible it seemed."

Suleiman had dropped his superior attitude by now and showed himself to be an ordinary and not unpleasant man underneath, to whom Abu Mansour found himself sympathetic. The process of deductive clinical reasoning that was unfolding was something close to Abu Mansour's heart, and so engrossing that he wondered how to include his pupil in the discussion, which was turning out to be of prime educational value. But Suleiman would not hear of it. The information he was giving Abu Mansour, he insisted, was for his ears alone. No one outside the room should know how deplorable the Caliph's condition was.

"His symptoms were not entirely typical. He showed no signs of morbid fear or a longing for death, as many melancholics do, nor, like them, did he wish to sit in graveyards, or imagine he was a beast or someone other than himself. Even so, there were enough signs to convince us that our diagnosis was correct. So, we applied the black bile regimen with every expectation of success."*

"That is a strenuous regimen. Did the Caliph not object to the treatments?"

Suleiman and the others shook their heads.

"He was too apathetic, too unconcerned about the world around him to care about what we were doing. He accepted it all silently."

---

* Blood-letting and medicines designed to evacuate the black bile from the body.

The rest of the story was soon told. Disappointingly, the Caliph did not respond to the new regimen, and when visiting physicians came to assess his state, their suggestions about the origin of his malady and prescriptions were no more helpful than those of the palace doctors.

Suleiman looked Abu Mansour in the eye. "We are at our wits' end, Abu Mansour. There is no more that we can do. If you cannot help, then God only knows what could happen."

There was a silence.

Abu Mansour said nothing, but he was quite disturbed. This account was of the utmost seriousness. If the Caliph's condition was in fact as Suleiman had described, it suggested that a completely different approach to the diagnosis and treatment of the illness was urgently needed. Even then, it could be too late to save the Caliph.

"Gentlemen, I'm deeply alarmed by the story you tell. It's an urgent situation, and I'm entirely at the disposal of our Caliph."

A look of relief spread over the doctors' faces and they leaned forward to shake his hand. But he laid his hand against his breast and continued with some severity. "It's astonishing you didn't call me in sooner. A different sort of man might take offense at the disrespect implied in leaving a consultation with me to the end, when no one else could be found to come to the Caliph's aid, and such a man might have shown his anger at this insult by dragging his heels, or not cooperating with your request at all."

Suleiman looked uncomfortable, sensing that Abu Mansour's comments were directed at him.

"But my first concern is my duty to a sick man, whoever he might be and whoever has wanted to undermine my professional standing."

Suleiman's younger companions stared at the floor.

"Whether or not I can succeed, where others more noted than myself have failed, I cannot promise. But if our lord's condition is as you describe, there's no time to lose. And if you're certain that the Caliph, who has not asked me for my services, will not object to my visit"—Suleiman nodded vigorously—"then I will come with you to the palace at once."

9

The four doctors soon covered the short distance to the palace, where they found Durayd, the chamberlain, waiting in the antechamber. With him was Idris, the head eunuch. Both men looked anxious. Durayd came forward to greet Abu Mansour.

"Peace be upon you, Abu Mansour. We're most relieved to see you, and I hope to God you're in time. Your fame has reached all the corners of these lands. If you can't cure our master, no one can."

Suleiman went ahead, and the rest followed. Flanked by Durayd and Idris, Abu Mansour walked toward the doors of the Caliph's private quarters. So often a bustling meeting place for his family members, close associates, and special visitors, it was now desolately empty. From there, an unlit back corridor led to the Caliph's bedchamber and an assembly of servants standing outside the closed door. An atmosphere of gloom hung over the gathering, made worse by the semidarkness.

As they made their way to the chamber door, it opened, and an elderly woman wearing black with a long veil over her head came out, two maids holding her arms on either side to steady her. Suleiman and Durayd bowed low. Abu Mansour recognized the old woman as the Caliph's stepmother. Khadija was no beauty, and age had not improved what looks she might once have had. But there was character in her face, and she exuded an air of natural command that immediately impressed itself on Abu Mansour. She paused, seeming to recognize him in her turn, and looked directly into his face.

"So you are the famous doctor, and you're going to cure my stepson of his malady?"

It was an order, not a question.

"Will you succeed where everyone else has failed, I wonder?"

"I cannot say, madam. I must examine the Prince of the Faithful first and make my tests. Only then can I judge."

She did not like his answer.

"There's no time for niceties, doctor. We've had enough of them from the so-called experts our head physician here called in."

Suleiman flushed, but she continued, her voice softening a little. "Abu Mansour, I'm grieved to see the Caliph brought so low. It's that which makes me testy. His father would have moved heaven and earth to ensure his recovery. You must help him. You are our best hope, and I will pray for you and him that you find the right course."

▣

A young eunuch ushered them, tiptoeing, into the bedchamber.

The room was airless, and the light that filtered in through the window shutters was insufficient to illuminate it. The lone candle burning in the corner made little difference. Servants hovered about in the shadows.

Against the far wall stood a low bed, and when his eyes had grown accustomed to the semidarkness, Abu Mansour could make out an elongated shape outlined by the blankets on top. Next to the bed was a silver tray bearing a water pitcher and goblets, a crystal glass decanter of rose water sherbet, and a large bowl of fruit. Nothing looked as if it had been touched, the grapes and fresh figs still glistening with the water they were washed in. Vases of artfully arranged flowers adorned the room and gave off scents that would have been refreshing had they not been confined in an airless room.

Suleiman walked ahead of the others and, drawing near to the bed, bowed and beckoned to Abu Mansour to follow him.

"My lord," he said in hushed tones. "Forgive me for disturbing you again. I have taken the liberty of inviting a new doctor to see you."

There was no movement from the bed.

"It is someone in whom we have much confidence, and we pray that he will find favor with you, too."

There was still no reaction. Suleiman turned to Abu Mansour with what looked like exasperation.

Abu Mansour could hardly contain his discomfiture and regret at having ever consented to this doomed enterprise. He felt no better than a hired hand, brought in for no other purpose than to save Suleiman's skin. Even the lowliest of his students would have rejected such a role.

"Perhaps the Caliph does not want to see someone he never asked for, has never met, and may not wish to."

But Suleiman would not be deflected from what he saw as the only course open to him to redeem his reputation and score some success with a case that had seen nothing but failure at his hands. He addressed the Caliph again with desperate eagerness.

"The man who spoke is too modest, my lord. He is the best physician in all Iraq, the most learned and celebrated Abu Mansour Hasan ibn Mansour al-Tabrizi."

The room was utterly silent. All eyes were fixed intently on the bed. Suddenly, the shape beneath the bedclothes shifted, and the Caliph opened his eyes.

The servants hurried forward to help him up onto the pillows which they pumped up behind his head. He groaned slightly with the effort, but kept his eyes open. Durayd came forward and Suleiman bowed again.

When the Caliph spoke, it was in a hoarse whisper.

"Who does not know Abu Mansour al-Tabrizi? Let him draw near."

Abu Mansour leaned over the edge of the bed and looked into the Caliph's face. What he saw shocked him. It was not that the Caliph looked exctly ill, but his face was almost lifeless, without any expression. His bare head, shorn of its customary turban, looked small and vulnerable.

Seeing Abu Mansour's intent expression, the Caliph averted his eyes, and slowly his eyelids began to droop, the spurt of energy he had briefly displayed fading away. He closed his eyes and, sighing, lay back on his cushions.

A collective sigh of dismay escaped from those standing nearby, and they looked at him and at each other with uncertainty.

At this, Abu Mansour made a sudden decision. With firm resolve, he straightened up and asked the servants to draw the shutters aside, open the windows, and light the room with more candles. Durayd and Suleiman both frowned.

"The Caliph needs rest and quietude," said Suleiman. "There must be no bright lights or loud noises. I've had the care of him from the beginning, and I must insist on that."

Durayd agreed.

"And I must insist that if you wish me to take on this case, I will make my examination in my own way and do what tests I need to do without interference. I'd also like the room cleared, so I can be alone with the Caliph."

Suleiman frowned more deeply, but acquiesced.

The servants opened the shutters and the windows as requested, and brought in enough candles to transform the Caliph's bedchamber from the stuffy morgue it had been into an airy, bright, and sunny space. As everyone filed out, Suleiman lingered behind. But Abu Mansour was adamant, and, looking resentful, the head physician left too.

The room was finally empty. Abu Mansour waited for a moment or two after they had gone. He then turned to the Caliph, who appeared to have noticed no change in his surroundings.

"My lord, it's me, Abu Mansour, who is with you. There's no one else here, and we're alone. Will you allow me to examine you and try to understand your condition?"

The Caliph did not respond, but his eyes were open again and trained on the wall.

"Will you talk to me, tell me the story of how you came to be so ill? There's no one to hear us, and it is my sacred duty never to speak to anyone of anything you might tell me."

The Caliph still said nothing, but rolled onto his back and looked up to the ceiling. Abu Mansour waited.

"How did the problem begin?" he prodded. "Will you trust me with your story, sir? It will make it easier for me to help. Was there some happening, some unexpended event, or some sudden illness with which it all started?"

He waited, but the Caliph continued to stare at the ceiling without a flicker of response.

Abu Mansour waited again, but saw it was no use. He realized that, contrary to his normal practice and the teachings of his art, he would have to reverse the clinical order in which the doctor normally diagnosed his patients, starting first with the story of how the symptoms developed, next examining the body for signs of the illness, and finally testing the body fluids, the blood and urine, for what they might reveal of the state of the humors. In the Caliph's case, this method would not succeed.

Sitting down by the bed, he took the Caliph's wrist in both his hands, and placed his finger on the pulse. It was weak and irregular. He observed the rise and fall of the Caliph's chest, the breathing shallow and interrupted by frequent deep sighs. He then passed his hand over the arms and the face. The skin was cold and dry. He looked carefully into the Caliph's expressionless eyes. There was no trace of tearing or moisture, and the lashes were slightly flaky with dryness. Apologizing to the Caliph, who took no notice, Abu Mansour brushed his lashes and touched the inside of his eyes lightly with the edge of the towel folded across the side table. The caliph blinked, but, despite the irritation the towel must have caused, his eyes remained dry. The whites were clouded and pink, but there was no hint of yellow in them.

Apologizing again, he felt for the Caliph's liver and spleen, watching for any signs of pain as he pressed down. There were none, but he thought he felt a swelling high up in the stomach, just beneath the diaphragm. The rest of the Caliph's abdomen and his legs and feet showed no swellings, no gout, distended veins, or other abnormality. He avoided examining the intimate parts of the Caliph's body; he already knew he would not need to. Rising from the bedside, he went to the door and asked the head page of the bedchamber to call Ahmad, the student who had come with him. Returning to the Caliph, he asked if he could disturb him again.

"My lord, I will need to examine your urine and your blood. It is necessary for the completion of my assessment. Will you help me?"

The Caliph gave a slight nod, but showed no curiosity. He cooperated when a flask was brought and was able to provide a specimen.

Inspecting it against the light, Abu Mansour was not surprised to see that the urine was turbid and dark. For the next test, he took out from the pocket of his outer robe the medical pouch he had brought from his house in case it was needed. Inside was an elegant small scalpel with a mother-of-pearl handle, the bloodletting tool of his craft. He normally discouraged phlebotomy, except in cases of absolute necessity, and did not have the enthusiasm for it of his colleagues who used it for the most minor ailment. He believed it weakened the patient at the onset of illness when he most needed his strength. In the case of the Caliph, however, Abu Mansour considered it essential, not as therapy, but as a tool for diagnosis.

"Forgive me, my lord, but I will have to bleed you. It is the last test. I promise."

Once again, the Caliph made no objection, as if he was long past caring. Abu Mansour asked the page to fetch a basin and instructed Ahmad, desperately anxious to assist in tending to their illustrious patient, to remove the belt at the top of his sirwal. Together they rolled up the Caliph's sleeve, and the doctor wound the belt tightly around the arm above the elbow.

Leaning over the Caliph, Abu Mansour unsheathed his knife, positioned it carefully on top of the swollen vein in the crook of the Caliph's elbow, and made several rapid small slits in the skin. There was a sharp intake of breath at the touch of the scalpel, but otherwise no complaint. The blood trickled out into the basin Ahmad was holding against the Caliph's arm. As the blood collected at the bottom of the bowl, Abu Mansour released the pressure of the ligature and bent the Caliph's arm upwards to staunch the bleeding.

"There. It is over, my lord."

Taking the basin to the light, he examined it keenly. The blood was dark, almost black, and slightly viscous. Without a doubt, Abu Mansour was looking at an excess of black bile both in the blood and the urine. So much was clear to him: the major cause of the Caliph's symptoms was an accumulation of black bile in the brain, almost certainly arising from the swelling of black bile he had felt in the Caliph's stomach. The coldness and dryness of the Caliph's skin were further evidence, if any were needed, of the presence of this coldest and driest of the four humors. So much also had been suspected by Suleiman and perhaps some of the doctors who had seen the Caliph before. On the basis of this supposition, they had applied the regimen for evacuating the black bile. But it had produced no cure, and the mystery remained.

◫

The question that had eluded them, in Abu Mansour's opinion, and without an answer to which the Caliph would not recover, was why? Why had the black bile so increased in the Caliph's body as to bring him close to death? What had provoked the deadly increase of this malign humor? Everyone knew its presence in the body usually followed on a corruption in some organ or tissue. But the Caliph had not been ill when the disease struck. He was fit and healthy. Something had brought him to this pass, some event had occurred in his life to cause it, and a suspicion was beginning to form in Abu Mansour's mind. A memory of something that had crossed his path some years before came back to him, a previous diagnosis he had made in similar circumstances.

He thanked Ahmad and the page for their assistance and asked that the chamberlain should come to see him without delay.

Checking on the Caliph, he saw he had closed his eyes again. In a few moments the door opened and Durayd appeared, a look of worry mixed with curiosity on his thin face.

"Come here, Master Durayd."

Abu Mansour was sitting by the Caliph's bed. In normal circumstances, neither man would have known the other, and Durayd would never have allowed himself to be spoken to like that. He was a powerful person at court, influential with the Caliph, and people were anxious for his favor. Abu Mansour, reputed as he was, would not normally have been in a position to send a servant to summon him, or question him, as he was clearly about to do. But the Caliph's long illness had upset everything and turned Durayd's world upside down. He was determined that whatever Abu Mansour required to end the nightmare he and the palace had been living through, he should have it without hesitation.

"Am I right that you are the person in the palace who is best placed to know the Caliph's movements, the people he meets and keeps company with?" asked the doctor.

Durayd nodded, unsure where this line of questioning was leading.

"I keep our master's appointments and remind him every day of where he must be. But there are others, like Uthman, his head secretary, who do the same."

Abu Mansour doubted that. Durayd was the man known to keep the Caliph's innermost secrets. He continued.

"I want you to cast your mind back to the time immediately before the Caliph fell ill. Did he change his routine in any way that you remember, meet people he did not normally spend time with, go somewhere that was unusual for him?"

The other man thought hard.

"I remember that about that time, our master was worried about the unrest in the provinces, especially in Khorasan. It concerned him that the governor was behaving treacherously."

At this Abu Mansour saw that the Caliph had suddenly opened his eyes, although the rest of him remained inert.

"Was the governor of Khorasan's issue unusual? Had he given any trouble before?"

Durayd was not sure, but he could not recall the Caliph previously commenting on such a thing. Then he spoke suddenly.

"In fact, I do remember that the business of the governor came up again. It wasn't about his treachery, but something to do with stolen land under his charge." The chamberlain was frowning with the effort of recall.

Abu Mansour was beginning to think this was a blind alley and wanted to move on.

"Who did the Caliph meet with at the time of the news from Khorasan?"

Since opening his eyes, the Caliph had continued to stare straight ahead, without making any other motion.

"How could I know? Our master meets with many officials, and also ordinary citizens every week at the diwan. I remember that he went through a period when he was quite preoccupied. Not worried, I'd say, but as if he was far away. That wasn't unusual for him. He would often be thinking about something or other to do with his intellectual friends."

"Please try and remember if the preoccupation you describe came after meeting a visitor, or after a particular diwan."

Neither man had noticed that while this exchange was taking place the Caliph had blinked several times. At Abu Mansour's last mention of the diwan, a low moan escaped the Caliph's lips that made them both jump.

Durayd darted forward toward the Caliph, but Abu Mansour shook his head vigorously to stop him. Taking the Caliph's wrist in his hands again, he placed his finger on the pulse. It was as weak as before, but beating faster. Durayd drew back and forced himself to concentrate on the doctor's request.

"I can't be sure, but I seem to think the Caliph's preoccupation was around the time of one of the diwans. I remember him talking about a request he'd received from a man with a problem. The man was above the usual cut of people who came to the diwan, and I know that intrigued him."

At this, the Caliph's pulse quickened.

"What was the problem? Who was the man? Any detail you can remember will help us."

"Our master doesn't usually tell me everything that happens at his meetings, unless it's something exceptional. Uthman was the one who told me about the man with the problem at the diwan that day. The man's family had land in Khorasan, I think, which a local Khorasani landlord had taken over without the governor intervening."

The Caliph's pulse rate was still raised, although his eyes had closed again. "But you can't date the Caliph's preoccupation from that event?" persisted Abu Mansour.

"I don't remember anything that might have caused it. But in any case, his mood went back to normal after a short while, and I forgot about it."

"When Uthman told you about the man, did he mention if he was alone?"

Abu Mansour kept his finger on the Caliph's pulse. Yet again, it increased in rate and his breathing became audible.

Durayd thought for a moment.

"No, he wasn't. Uthman noticed that because it was unusual. The man had a youth with him and a girl, his niece. Uthman remarked that she was strikingly beautiful."

Abu Mansour could not contain his excitement.

"Is the girl unmarried? Did Uthman know her name or that of her uncle?"

The distress and agitation that swept over the Caliph's body could not be ignored. His pulse was racing; he sighed and frowned by turns. Abu Mansour took the towel by the bed and wetted it with water from the pitcher. He applied it to the Caliph's forehead for a moment or two and then passed it over the rest of his face and neck. Gesturing to Durayd to remain silent, he sat by the Caliph and held his hand. After a few moments, the Caliph's distress receded and he grew calm again, appearing to have fallen asleep.

Abu Mansour sighed and stood up.

"We are at a critical moment in this sad story. I now know what has made our master sick, and it's a difficult condition."

Durayd stared at the doctor in disbelief. Could it really be true that the riddle of his master's illness had been finally solved?

That a cure was possible? An urgent knock at the door interrupted his thoughts.

Suleiman, who had waited outside impatiently, refused to wait any longer. He pushed his way in, the other palace doctors behind him, and, not looking at the Caliph, confronted Abu Mansour.

"Well, Abu Mansour, you've had ample time with our master and must have reached your own conclusions. Are you as puzzled as we've been?"

His tone was frosty. Word had reached him of the urine test and phlebotomy Abu Mansour had performed on the Caliph, as if his and the other doctors' previous tests had been worthless and needed repeating.

"Come in, my friends. Let's talk, but not here. Our lord should be left to resume his rest."

<hr/>

They filed out silently and walked to the sitting room, with Durayd at the head. Ahmad hung back, but Abu Mansour urged him to come with them. Everyone sat down, their eyes on Abu Mansour expectantly.

"Let me first thank you for your efforts to cure our master of his illness. I have no doubt you worked with dedication and commitment. It's not anyone's fault that the Caliph's ailment was so difficult to recognize. Unfortunately, it is one of those conditions which you diagnose only after you've already thought of it."

They waited.

"The cause of his ailment is abundantly clear, and the mystery is solved." All stared at him.

"Our Caliph has the disease of *'ishq*—love. It is severe, but we must not despair, as the cure may be at hand. We have little time, but if I'm right we might still be able to save him."

There was a long silence.

Suleiman bit his lip. Thoughts swirled round in his head.

Shouldn't he himself have thought of it without having to resort to this conceited man? He was familiar with the disease of '*ishq*, which had once afflicted a cousin of his, but he had to confess it never crossed his mind in the Caliph's case. He felt humiliated and embarrassed.

"I believe the object of his passion is a young woman, whose name and address we don't know as yet. Locating her will lead us to the cure for this terrible malady."

There was a look of stupefaction on the faces of his listeners, as if they could hardly absorb what they were hearing.

"It's a great pity our master was not diagnosed before he sank so low. The excess of black bile in his body did indeed cause most of the symptoms, and love is a black bile disease as you know. It was making the link between the two that was needed. But there it is."

Abu Mansour's authority could not be denied. The doctors knew they were in the presence of a master. All except Suleiman, who was not to be won over so easily.

"Good thinking, Abu Mansour. And it is good of you to come and see the Caliph. Love is something one must consider in such an illness of course, but just thinking of the possibility does not make the diagnosis certain. What's the evidence this is the disease of love? I gather you just repeated our tests for the black bile and found what we already knew."

"I will go through the pulse test with you Master Suleiman, if you want. You know it is the definitive test for this disease and it was strongly positive. The change in pulse rate and character led us to identify the precipitating cause, which is not always easy and in many cases, might never be known."

Suleiman was about to speak, when Durayd stood up.

"Enough, gentlemen. Surely to God we must be grateful that Abu Mansour has solved the problem. I am no physician, but even I can see that, thanks to the treatment Abu Mansour will administer, all will be well with our lord."

"Thank you, Master Durayd," Abu Mansour followed. "But we are only at the beginning of our journey to cure the Caliph, and we still have to find the lady he loves. Even then, who knows how she will respond when we find her? These are all unknowns. But they are crucial to the Caliph's recovery."

He carefully avoided looking at Suleiman.

"For now we must thank God that we can at last begin the therapy our Caliph should have had from the start. And with God's help, he will recover."*

---

* The disease of love, '*ishq* in Arabic and denoting passionate love, was considered to be a type of insanity and included among "organic," not psychological, diseases of the brain in medieval Arabic medicine. Its signs and symptoms were as displayed by the Caliph, and the gold standard for diagnosing it was by the method of the pulse rate, as used by Abu Mansour. The ideal cure was a union between the patient and his beloved.

10

From that time on Abu Mansour became the undisputed head physician in charge of the Caliph's health. Suleiman and the other doctors withdrew, assuring him they would be on hand if he needed assistance. Durayd informed the chief wazir of the situation and asked him to continue covering duties for the Caliph's absence as he had been doing. Abu Mansour reorganized his work to make himself totally available for his new role.

The palace accorded him a special status and assigned servants to take his orders at all times. Ahmad unhappily agreed to train with another doctor while Abu Mansour was away. Abu Mansour's family, fascinated by the Caliph's illness and expecting to be kept up to date with his progress, reluctantly accepted they would be without their head of household for some time to come.

⊡

The Caliph's condition was said to have worsened overnight. As soon as Abu Mansour reached the palace the next day and was taken to the Caliph's quarters, he immediately started the full therapeutic regimen for the disease of love. This was a many-pronged approach to the illness, in order to deal with its several effects on the body and mind. A complete change of diet, environment, and daily routine were required, to be followed by more specific measures when the Caliph's health allowed.

Abu Mansour's first task was to have the Caliph moved from the Golden Gate to the Small Palace on the west bank of the Tigris. This had been an occasional residence for the Caliph and his brother as young men when their father stayed at Raqqa, a town in northern Syria he had always preferred to Baghdad.

It was a pretty house, homely and bright, without a hint of the grandeur of the Golden Gate. Its chief merits, from Abu Mansour's point of view, were the large gardens that surrounded it on all sides and reached to the river's edge. The trees and bushes that grew thickly all over the grounds enveloped the house in a shady, green mantle, not yet affected by the arrival of autumn. It ensured that each time the Caliph looked out from his window, he would see an expanse of green, the color of tranquillity recommended by all Greek physicians to soothe an anguished mind. In this restful place, the Caliph could repose, away from the prying eyes and ears of the Golden Gate's myriad officials, secretaries, and eunuchs. The servants who accompanied him answered strictly to the discipline imposed by Abu Mansour: to go about their work quietly and report any changes in the Caliph's condition immediately.

The doctor's next task was to engage the services of a band of musicians to play for the Caliph. The musical soirees at court were well known, and the Caliph was patron to the best players in the land. His illness had suspended all such enjoyment, but Abu Mansour had something different in mind.

The musicians he invited to the Small Palace were not court minstrels, but the very same ones who entertained the patients at the bimaristan and were skilled at playing for the sick and injured. The effect of their music-making on the most agitated of patients—those in pain, or racked by fever, women in childbirth, consumptives, and melancholics determined to take their own lives—was marvelous. They had power to calm even the raging maniacs, wretched creatures no one else could control, who grew quiet, tamed by their music. Abu Mansour had no doubt that the same music would ease the Caliph's distress.

He asked the musicians to take up position in the garden where everyone could hear them, and as their sweet tunes flowed through the windows into the palace, the servants paused in their duties to listen and feel their tiredness lift. The Caliph, sitting up on his cushions by the open window of his room, responded too, smiling with pleasure, his eyes gently closed and his face softening.

But Abu Mansour knew the battle with the Caliph's disease could not stop there. Among the many errors his previous doctors had committed, the most serious had been to solate him, believing wrongly that rest and quiet were all he needed. In his case, it was precisely the opposite, for the mental obsession he had developed fed on fantasy and dreams from loneliness.

Rather than depriving him of contact with reality, he should constantly have been in the company of others and distractions found to draw him away from fixating on the object of his infatuation. Visitors were encouraged to come and see him. But members of the family, and those from his life at the palace, were excluded to avoid reaggravating the stresses he had so recently suffered. There would be time enough for that when he grew stronger, and anyone who objected was told those were the orders of Abu Mansour, whose status was such that no one argued.

Continuing with his line of treatment, Abu Mansour went on to engage the most artful professional storytellers in Baghdad to entertain the Caliph nightly. They had also performed at the bimaristan to help the sleepless pass the hours away and help patients forget about their symptoms. Their stories cast a spell on the listener who could not wait to hear more. Abu Mansour encouraged them to surpass themselves for the Caliph. And so, each night they told him a different tale, some exciting, some adventurous, and some comical. But none told of love or romance, just as Abu Mansour had insisted. Any mention of *ghazal* love poetry was omitted, nor were the stories interspersed with poetic verses, as was the custom. Instead, they were told with as much amusement as they could muster, without any romantic embellishments.

It succeeded—beyond Abu Mansour's expectations.

The Caliph had never been interested in storytellers and had even barred them from the palace because of what he regarded as their frivolity. He was unaccustomed to such diversions, but listening to them now he began to find them pleasing and absorbing enough to look forward each night to the next installment.

The storytellers were so well accepted that Abu Mansour began to allow occasional visits from a passing scholar who would discourse on the subject of his studies. These visits were of special interest to the Caliph who began to regain some of his previous animation as he conversed, leaving him afterward to mull over the issues the scholar had brought up. After such visits, it even seemed that the Caliph briefly became his old self again, and he would discuss with Abu Mansour the questions the scholar's conversation had raised in his mind.

The next step, thought Abu Mansour, was to gather a number of scholars and revive the tradition the Caliph cherished and had lived by for years with his circle of philosophers and intellectuals.

Throughout this time, the Caliph also had been made to follow a regimen of daily baths, fresh air, and gentle exercise, as Abu Mansour prescribed. He was given a moistening diet of clear water, lettuce, and cucumber to offset the dryness of the black bile inside him. He was prescribed to wear raw silk during the day and warm wool at night, even though the weather did not warrant such clothes, in order to counter the humor's coldness.

To these measures, Abu Mansour added a daily dose of gentle *hieras* to evacuate the bile from the Caliph's body. He also advised him to take a generous helping of wine at night, which the Caliph declined, but which the doctor insisted on. He was too weak to argue and drank the nightly draught obediently. The effect was such that not long after swallowing the wine, the Caliph's eyes would close, his head would droop down on his chest, and he would drift off into a deep slumber for many hours.

After a few weeks of this routine, the Caliph was showing signs of improvement. He had regained some of his appetite, was alert for most of the day, and showed fewer signs of distress. He spoke of wanting to ride his horse again and asked for news of the outside world. His attendants were happy at these signs of returning health and asked Abu Mansour if they might soon return to Golden Gate Palace. Suleiman, Durayd, and Abu Hisham, the chief wazir, all sent daily messages inquiring about the Caliph's progress. His stepmother was particularly insistent, and also his sisters. The Caliph's siblings were not usually close, having been born of different mothers and not reared in a tradition of family life. At court, it was normally everyone out for themselves. But these times were exceptional, and the Caliph's illness was at the forefront of everyone's attention.

Abu Mansour responded to all inquiries in the same neutral way. He knew that, as encouraging as the Caliph's improvement was, it was mainly due to the reduction in the level of black bile in his body, and would be only temporary. Unless the cause of his disease was addressed, the black bile would increase again, and he would soon relapse to a worse state than before. The doctor was merely waiting to build up his patient's strength sufficiently to move on to the next, and hopefully final, stage of treatment. Professional pride stopped him from wanting to share these plans with anyone, wary that a dissenting opinion might interfere with the delicate therapeutic web he was weaving so carefully around the Caliph. Modest in so many ways, Abu Mansour privately believed himself superior to his colleagues on most medical questions, and jealously guarded his reputation and standing.

In the weeks he had spent caring for the Caliph, a closeness had grown between the two men. To a certain extent, it was inevitable that the Caliph, grateful to Abu Mansour for saving him from an inexorable decline, would form an attachment to the doctor. But there was more to it than that.

Though he and Abu Mansour had barely conversed, he had an intuitive sense that if they had, they would discover a certain commonality of outlook, a shared way of thinking, even perhaps a similar view of what in life had value and meaning. For reasons he could not have defined, the Caliph trusted Abu Mansour and had no reservations about confiding in him, if asked.

So it was that when the doctor broached the subject that would lead them to the next phase of the Caliph's treatment, he was not instantly rebuffed as he had feared.

"My lord, now that you're feeling a little better, we need to talk about what it was that brought you so low."

The Caliph said nothing.

"It's not that I want to pry into your affairs, sir. But it's necessary for me to understand the events that might have provoked your illness."

The Caliph nodded, but remained silent.

"When I first met you in your bedchamber at the Golden Gate and you were very ill, I asked about your activities in the time just before you fell ill. They mentioned your meeting a young woman who'd come with her uncle to visit your diwan. They said she was very beautiful. Do you remember that?"

The Caliph, who was sitting by the window overlooking the garden, turned his head away from the doctor and stared at the far horizon in reverie.

Did he remember? How could he ever forget, was the better question. Every moment of that first encounter with Murjana was etched on his memory, no less than his second meeting with her, that meeting which cemented his adoration and longing for her. It came back to him now, distant, almost part of another life.

"My lord?"

Abu Mansour's voice broke into his reverie.

"Have you remembered now?"

The Caliph turned from the window toward him and nodded. Sighing deeply, he asked the doctor to sit by him, and when he had done so the Caliph began his tale.

Hesitant at first to say things he had confided to no one, it became suddenly easier to talk. A deluge of confession poured from his lips. How he had first met Murjana, the emotions she had excited in him, his attempts to escape her spell, his battle with himself to forget her. And then, their second meeting when he could no longer deny the strength of his passion for her and the powerful urge that drove him to succumb to it.

"But you didn't."

The Caliph shook his head. His expression was colorless, but Abu Mansour could see sorrow in his eyes.

"I couldn't."

Without waiting for the doctor's inevitable next question, he related the rest of his story: the tussle between his appetites and his conscience, his agonizing dilemma over hurting his wives; and in the end, after the thrill of his second meeting with Murjana had temporarily receded, the victory of principle over self-indulgence—his decision to give her up for good.

And the effect of your decision, thought Abu Mansour, *brought you to death's door. Was it really worth it?*

There was something pathetic about the Caliph, he reflected, a man with the world at his feet and the might of an empire at his back, destroying himself for the sake of an abstract notion of justice. Who in his position would have hesitated or been held back by such scruples? The wives of a ruler expected to be supplanted by others, younger and fresher; it was the way of men with power, and also men without. But it was not the only reason, Abu Mansour felt sure.

The Caliph was a man of lofty ideals and high moral standards. It took courage and strength to hold to those ideals, and the Caliph had always admired the uncompromising resolve with which the philosophers of the past upheld their beliefs, even in the face of death. Casting those noble principles aside and surrendering to carnal desires was something the Caliph despised in others. He would never accept such weakness in himself, and he regarded his obsession with Murjana as nothing short of that.

Abu Mansour saw he would have to wean the Caliph off these self-sacrificing ideals and persuade him to give in to his natural instincts and the desire to find happiness all humankind shares. It was not that the doctor disregarded the Caliph's moral stance, but that he had come to feel compassion for a man who had lost all understanding of human feeling and who strove to destroy the chance of happiness that life was offering him.

But above all, Abu Mansour was driven by the conviction that the cure for the Caliph's illness lay in his union with the girl. No other treatment would serve. If the Caliph did not seize the opportunity, he would soon be buried along with his ideals.

Abu Mansour could not allow that to happen.

Twilight was approaching, the time when the storytellers would arrive. Abu Mansour rose from the Caliph's side and let the pages waiting outside into the chamber. He took his leave, saying they would talk in the morning. The Caliph looked at him, a little of the old haunted expression clouding his features.

"Talk?" he muttered wearily, as if to himself. "What more is there to talk about?"

Abu Mansour walked out without replying.

The Caliph's tale of unfulfilled love had made him pensive. In his imagination he had lived every scene and every emotion the Caliph described. And Abu Mansour wondered why he himself had never felt such things. In all his encounters with women, patients, relatives, family, friends, not one had excited such passion or such desire. No wonder he could summon up no enthusiasm for marriage, to the despair of his mother and the rest of his family. It was not dislike of women or blindness to their charms, but that his profession—his books and his family—enriched his life every waking moment of the day. He never missed the company of people or felt the need for a woman to share his bed or his life.

And yet there was a magic in the Caliph's story that enticed him. He sensed the power of the girl's spell over him and found himself thinking that if ever something as remarkable as that happened to him, he would break the habit of a lifetime and marry without hesitation. This realization convinced him that the Caliph's story should not end there, but had to progress to the next phase.

And he, Abu Mansour, would make sure that it did.

11

The next morning, Abu Mansour rose early and sent word to his house for Younis to come to him as soon as possible. Without preliminaries or excuses, he told the Caliph, "I propose to make inquiries about the lady Murjana, my lord, to establish if she is married or betrothed."

The Caliph did not look rested after his night's sleep. He stared vacantly at Abu Mansour. If he was surprised that the doctor had gone expressly against his decision to give up Murjana, he made no mention of it and remained morosely silent.

Abu Mansour continued briskly.

"I think it's important before we go any further to find out her situation. I hope you agree."

The Caliph still said nothing. It was obvious he had suffered a setback after the confidences of the day before. But it did not overly disturb Abu Mansour to see the deterioration in his state. It was to be expected as the root of his problem was laid bare.

When Younis arrived, happy to see his master again and telling him that Ahmad was miserable in his new post and waiting to return, his errand was explained to him and he was sent off. Abu Mansour had chosen Younis to carry out this delicate task for good reason. He could rely on the boy's loyalty and discretion that any inquiries he made would not find their way to the palace.

The next day, he returned to report on the information he had collected.

"I found the house all right and watched it for a while. I then put word out with the neighbors that I was making inquiries on behalf of a family looking for a bride for their son. I said they'd been told about the daughter of that house and wanted to know if she was available, and did they know anything bad about the family. While I was standing in the street chatting, something funny happened. I saw a man walk into the house, and I could swear it was the same one who came to your clinic about his relative, the man who said his name was Ibrahim al-Ajami.

"I wanted to ask the neighbors who he was, but they started to tell me about the lady Murjana. I gathered she was not married or betrothed to anyone. She's quite young, with two brothers. They had been three, but one had died recently. They live with their uncle and aunt, and generally keep to themselves, maybe because they're Shiites. But everyone said they were decent, God-fearing people and nothing was known against them."

Abu Mansour thanked Younis for having been so efficient. The next task was now before him, to bring the girl to the Caliph and let matters take their course.

It was going to be difficult, but there was no choice, and he had little time. Just that morning a message had come from the chief wazir that he had urgent matters to discuss with the Caliph that could no longer be put off, and he was intending to pay a visit. The day before, the Caliph's stepmother had announced she would not wait any longer to see him, and she was asking if Abu Mansour had become his jailer. He managed to hold them off, but it would not be for long, and he had to move fast.

He waited until the Caliph had awoken from his afternoon sleep and went to his chamber.

He found him drinking a sherbet of rosewater, which seemed to revive him.

"I have news of the lady Murjana, my lord."

Abu Mansour smiled at the Caliph, as if all was well with the world and he was simply responding to an inquiry that the Caliph himself had made about the girl.

The Caliph, who had been about to smile back, frowned, and his body visibly tensed. Blithely, the doctor continued in the same cheerful voice.

"The news is good. She is not married or betrothed and is free to marry whoever she pleases."

"What use is that to me?" complained the Caliph, "Why are you telling me this? I made a decision I will not go back on, and there is nothing more to be said."

Ignoring these words, Abu Mansour plunged in. He knew that, to the Caliph, he was in the end just an ordinary citizen, as subject to the rule of the palace as anyone else, that if the Caliph wished it, he could destroy him, even have him put to death. Doctor or not, he had no power over the Caliph, and, in acting as he was intending to do, he might have already overstepped the mark. But he was compelled to complete what he had started and would not give up.

"On the contrary, there is much more to say, as for example that the lady is yours for the taking and you must marry her."

The Caliph, looking angry now, got up and towered over Abu Mansour threateningly. But undeterred, the latter went on.

"You might not like what you hear, my lord, but it is time you faced the truth."

Despite his inner nervousness, Abu Mansour's voice was firm and his expression serious.

"If you don't take my advice, I can't answer for your life, it is as simple as that. The disease of love, your malady, is not a joke. It is no foolishness or a fancy of the imagination. You saw for yourself what a state you were in. If you'd continued with the useless treatment your doctors were giving you, I don't exaggerate when I say you would not be standing here today. I saved you from that in the nick of time, but I have not cured you yet. Your cure lies in one thing only: to bring you together with your beloved in the eyes of God and according to law."

The Caliph glared angrily at Abu Mansour. Then gradually it passed, and he shook his head from side to side piteously.

"I cannot do it. I *cannot* do it. How can I bring an end to the contentment of my wives and my children, who are innocent of any wrongdoing toward me?"

"But who will not die, as you assuredly will if you ignore my advice." Abu Mansour wanted to comfort the poor man and leave him to his misery. But the kinder course was the harsher one.

"I hope you will allow me to be frank with you, my lord. Far from decrying your fate, you should be prostrate with gratitude before God, who in his munificence has put the cure of your malady within your reach. If the lady is as willing as she is available, you will be returned to health and vigor as before." He now had the Caliph's full attention.

"If I were to tell you of the wretches I have attended with a disease as severe as yours, but for whom there was no cure, I would break your heart: men, whose beloveds were married already or did not return their affection, and who struggled with their obsessions unrequited. I saw them pine away and die of melancholy, or live stunted, ailing lives without hope. How every one of them would have longed to be in your position, to risk the temporary unhappiness of a wife or a child, yes, but in return for their own precious lives!"

The doctor had dramatized the details of his old patients' stories, used every piece of eloquence at his command, and now felt he could say no more. He waited for the Caliph's response.

The latter remained silent. He had sat down as Abu Mansour was speaking, listening intently to every word. Finally, he spoke heavily, and with effort.

"I thank you for your care of me, Abu Mansour. I cannot doubt your devotion or your skills. If I could only trust those around me as I trust you. But there are those in my life who trust me also not to betray them, not to hurt or set them aside."

The Caliph paused, searching for the right words.

"It is not in my power to put my own fleshly desires ahead of their welfare. In spite of what you say, Abu Mansour, I know I will be master of myself once again without having to resort to the cure you have prescribed. Till that happens, I will do nothing to harm the innocents in my charge."

He turned his face away.

Abu Mansour was alarmed. He had not seen the Caliph do that since the time he was so desperately ill at the Golden Gate. He hung about in the bedchamber uncertainly, but the Caliph made no further motion.

⊞

That evening, the Caliph grew worse, rejected all food and drink, and spoke to no one. It was clear to Abu Mansour that the level of black bile in his body was rising, provoked by the emotional upheaval he had undergone, and its vapors would soon cloud his brain. He was fast relapsing, the weeks of improvement the physician had worked so hard to achieve evaporating before his very eyes.

Abu Mansour's noted ability to remain calm in a crisis deserted him. He paced the garden restlessly as evening set in, dismissing any servant who approached, and berating himself repeatedly for the crass haste with which he had tried to goad the Caliph into abandoning his long-held scruples and rush headlong into an action alien to his nature. How could he have been so stupid?

On the other hand, he told himself, how could he have avoided it, given the short time he had to put his plan into effect before the people from the palace appeared and disrupted everything? Had it not been for that, he felt sure he would have taken a slower, more cautious approach to bringing the Caliph round to the idea.

But it was no use. He could not justify his folly by such excuses. It was at such times that he wished he had someone to confide in, a companion who had his welfare at heart and whom he could trust. His professional pride and belief in his own medical prowess had prevented him from making friendships with other medical colleagues that could have provided this; and his thoughts turned back once more to the question of marriage.

Perhaps he was wrong to have dismissed that possibility for so many years. Perhaps an intelligent, loving wife, such as his mother had been to his father, was the companion he needed to share his concerns and dilemmas. He could suddenly imagine a kind and sympathetic woman who saw his perplexity and offered her help, who listened quietly to his worries and gave him her support.

He pulled himself up sharply. This was no time to contemplate what had not happened and was unlikely to. No, he was alone, and would have to find the way to halt the Caliph's deterioration and redirect him toward the cure.

He sat on the ground under the tall palm tree and made a plan. It was bold and risky, and if it failed, his contact with the Caliph would be terminated forever, or worse. But he could see no alternative to following the method that had guided his therapeutic regimen for the Caliph from the start and yielded such good results, until this setback.

⊞

The next morning, word was sent to Abdulhamid that the Caliph had asked to see him and his niece. The matter was urgent, he was told, and they must come to the palace without delay. There was no further explanation.

Like everyone in Baghdad, the Banu Shaaban knew that the Caliph was very ill and had been moved to another palace from where hardly any news of him leaked out. They assumed he must have recovered, although the request had come out of the blue. But it was a summons from the Caliph, and neither Abdulhamid nor the rest of the family could refuse. A heated argument arose about the reason for the Caliph's invitation and where it might lead. Murjana's brothers, Hamza, and the younger, Yazan, were eager for them to go, but their uncle was not.

"The Caliph might want to see me, but why should he ask to see Murjana, as well? It's true she came with us both times we met him, but it was on a matter of business, nothing else. I can't understand what he could possibly want by inviting her now."

Murjana looked at her uncle beneath her lashes, thinking, *Much you know about it.* But she remained silent.

"After what these Abbasids have done to us, we ought to have nothing to do with them," her uncle continued. "I went to see the Caliph much against my will because there was no other way to reclaim our land, although I have to admit I did find him courteous and gentlemanly. He always had more sympathy with our community than any of his ancestors, and I showed him my respect for that when I saw him. But I find it hard to understand why such a man persecutes our young men and keeps our imam confined."

"Because in the end he's a true member of his family, that's why, Uncle," said Hamza. "But you can't refuse to go. It could be something to do with our lands."

Abdulhamid looked doubtful.

"Maybe. But I don't like it. I'm afraid he has something in mind for Murjana, and we don't need to ask our imam to work out what that might be. And if I'm right, then what?"

At the palace Abu Mansour awaited their arrival with impatience. He was conscious of every hour that passed and every suspicious glance the palace eunuchs threw in his direction. He had known from the start that his actions were being monitored by several of them and duly reported to the Golden Gate. It had not mattered up until then; all that happened had been quite innocuous. But from the moment he had summoned the Banu Shaaban on the pretense it came from the Caliph, he knew he would have something to fear from their spying, and it increased his sense of urgency. Then, seemingly from nowhere, they appeared.

"Peace be upon you! I am Abu Mansour al-Tabrizi, physician to the Caliph."

As requested, Abdulhamid had brought Murjana, but also Murjana's cousin, Ayesha.

Abu Mansour looked at Murjana with considerable interest. She was covered in a dark cloak, her head and face hidden behind a long white veil. Even with that, he saw the other girl could not hold a candle to her.

"Is my lord ready to receive us?"

"Indeed, but only the lady Murjana may come into our lord's presence. Those were his express orders. The rest of you are welcome to take a glass of sherbet here while you wait."

Abdulhamid was scandalized.

"But it is not proper. My niece cannot be left to enter into the Caliph's presence on her own. I assume her cousin will go with her at least?"

Abu Mansour shook his head regretfully.

"Our lord has made his orders clear. It is not for us to question but to obey." *The man must be very sure of himself to question the Caliph's commands*, Abu Mansour thought. No subject, not even the wealthy, had such daring. He must have someone powerful behind him to speak in that way; either that or he was innocent in the ways of the world.

"That's all right, Uncle." Murjana stepped forward. "I will obey. I will not be alone with the Caliph, and nothing that shouldn't will happen, I'm sure."

Abu Mansour was arrested by her beauty as the sunlight penetrated through the veil to her face. No wonder the Caliph was besotted to the point of madness, he thought.

He made a small bow and indicated she should follow him. Behind him Abdulhamid looked at Ayesha and shook his head. They watched from afar Murjana's receding figure.

12

Silently, Murjana and the doctor walked to the Caliph's quarters. Then they stopped outside a closed door. He told her to wait and went in, knowing the high stakes he was playing for.

The room was in semi-darkness, as before at the Golden Gate, and the Caliph lay on his bed, his eyes wide open but unseeing.

Abu Mansour bent over him.

"My lord, there is a visitor to see you."

This was met without response; the Caliph's eyes did not blink.

"It is the Lady Murjana, the niece of the man who came to see you about his lands in Khoasan, you remember. Will you permit her to enter?"

The Caliph suddenly turned round in his bed and stared at Abu Mansour. His expression was one of alarm, and he began to sit up.

Abu Mansour quickly moved away before anything more could happen and opened the bedroom door, ushering in Murjana.

He beckoned for her to go to the Caliph's bedside.

"The Lady Murjana is here," he announced, and with that left them alone.

Murjana walked uncertainly into the half-dark room. The small windows were shaded, and there was a scent of ambergris in the air. The gloom did not frighten her. Rather, it gave the bedchamber an atmosphere of intimacy she found oddly familiar, as if she had been in her own bedroom at home. But it also made her keenly aware of being alone with the Caliph. Not a single page or attendant was in the room. She had not expected this and it mystified her.

When her uncle received the Caliph's summons to his presence, everyone assumed he had recovered from his illness. Why else would he see anyone, let alone a family of little importance like theirs? Yet, here she was in what looked like a sick room, and the Caliph appeared far from recovered.

There must be some mistake. Perhaps her uncle had got it all wrong. For a moment she considered turning back to the door and leaving. Yet it was the Caliph's own doctor who had received them and ushered her in, and he of all people knew the Caliph's situation. She couldn't make sense of it, but felt she had no choice other than to force herself to go further into the room.

Ahead of her, she could see the dark outline of a bed against the opposite wall where the Caliph had sat up on his cushions when she came in. She could see he was watching her, and hesitated in confusion. He raised his arm and seemed to be beckoning to her.

As she drew closer, he suddenly straightened his back against the wall. She had never seen a man in his position without his turban and formal robes before. In his simple linen tunic now, he looked younger and like a different man to the Caliph she had met formally before. Though he said nothing, the tension in his taut body communicated itself to her. Her steps faltered and she stopped, not knowing what to do. They looked at each other.

Even at that distance, she sensed his brooding absorption in her every movement, and it excited and frightened her. That she should have such an effect on the most powerful man in the world was thrilling. It suspended her in the moment, not knowing what he would do next.

Wordlessly, he put out his hand to her and, instantly obeying, she went forward and took it in hers. She wondered if she was expected to kiss it in the manner of all those who came into the Caliph's presence.

He stood up slowly, steadying himself against the wall. She watched him, holding her breath. There was a moment of stillness. And then he suddenly lunged forward, took her in his arms and crushed her body against his, breathing harshly. It happened so quickly she could do nothing but submit. He pulled her head into the crook of his neck, pushed back her veil and ran his hand feverishly over her hair, her neck, her shoulders, and then her face, caressing her features roughly, until he found her mouth in a frenzy of passion. She could feel his heart pounding through the material of his tunic and the rapid, rasping breaths he took.

Holding her body tight against his as if he feared she would slip from his grasp, he pulled her down to the bed. Still nothing was said. When he eased his hold of her, she turned toward him. He lifted her hand to his face, his hot breath passing though her fingers, and kissed the palm lingeringly. She was stiff with fright; her only resort to ward off his terrifying passion by trying to appease him with flattery. She broke the silence.

"I am so glad to see you, my lord. When you sent for me to come and visit you, I could hardly wait to be here," she lied. "If you only knew how terrible it's been to hear that you were ill all those long weeks and be so powerless to help you. It upsets me to see what a toll it has taken of your health."

She tried to look into his eyes with genuine concern. It seemed to confuse him, as if he had not expected her to speak in that way. She wondered if anyone ever dared to show any feeling toward him.

As if in a rush of gratitude, he took her face in his hands and put his lips on hers, softly at first, but then with increasing passion as if his very soul would pass from him to hers through their lips. He gathered her to him, his eyes closed in ecstasy, and in that state, he kissed her face, her hair, her ears, and the hollows at the base of her neck. He opened the top of her gown to reach her breasts, beside himself with desire. He passed his lips over the soft, smooth flesh slowly to prolong the moment. And then, with unstoppable urgency, he started to move down her body.

But with a small cry, Murjana put her hands against his chest and pushed him away with difficulty. When he first kissed her, she had found his ardor compelling and could not help responding, opening her lips to him and kissing him back, which made him wilder. The more he reacted the more she was tempted to entice him to greater passion.

Murjana was not altogether naive. From early on in her life, she had seen the effect her extraordinary beauty had on men, young and old, and the way it influenced how they acted. She quickly learned how to use that beauty and natural allure to achieve her ends. But the encounter with the Caliph was no simple game of the sort she had known with her brothers' and uncle's male friends, and it had moved with an inexorable speed she had not anticipated. She was alarmed by his passion and the forces she seemed to have unleashed in him.

"No more, my lord, I beg you! No more!" she said, extricating herself from his arms and standing up. "I do not wish to displease you, but I am not versed in these matters. Yet, as I am alone here with you, you might have thought that I...that I wanted...I mean, you are the Caliph and can command me, while I...I am far beneath you and cannot refuse."

He stood up also, trying to regain control of himself as his rapid breathing began to subside. When he was calmer he took her tenderly in his arms, soothing her with his hands, his fervor momentarily stilled.

"Forgive me for being so insensitive," he said, kissing her hand. "I've forced myself on you and shocked you. You're not beneath me. It's me who has been a fool, trying to pretend you meant nothing to me and that I could forget you just like that. I will show you it's exactly the opposite. I swear!"

"Please, don't say such things, my lord. You really mustn't."

Murjana was now well out of her depth. She had put on a credible pretense of caring for the Caliph and reciprocating his interest in her as instructed. "Make him want you," Hamza had instructed. "Flatter and seduce him." But in all his tutoring, her brother had not warned her of such a serious development, and she did not know how to behave.

"Shhh…" The Caliph put his finger gently to her lips.

"I will say more, and what I say will please you."

He paused, his face calm and determined. Even through her fright and the ravages of his illness, she saw what a handsome man the Caliph was. His strong, manly features, his deep, arresting eyes, the wide, generous mouth, and his lean, upright body. There was a pride and majesty in his demeanor that made him unforgettable. How could she not be spellbound by the attentions of such a man?

"Murjana." He released her from his embrace and looked solemnly into her eyes. "I'm not used to making declarations of love, and I don't know how to make flowery speeches or lovers' odes like my court poets can dream up in a second. But I do know, sincerely, that I love you, and that I want you to be my wife. I swear I never planned to meet you, or in this way. But it's happened and I am grateful for it. It has shown me what I must do, and should have done years ago."

Murjana was shocked to the core of her being. Inexperienced though she was, she could not fail to recognize the heartfelt honesty in the Caliph's artless speech, and, much against her will, it touched her. But at the same time, she wished he had said nothing at all, at least, not now, not yet. Her rapid success in what she had set out to do stunned her into silence. She had expected a longer courtship: more ingenious excuses she and her brother would need to think up to get her together with the Caliph, and a host of seductive tricks she would have to play on him when they met. In fact, she had been rather looking forward to the challenge. This rapid collapse in his defenses was unexpected and unplanned for. It made her wonder if it was the illness, from which he had evidently not recovered, that was the cause; a fever of the brain that played havoc with his judgment and made him say things he would later take back.

She gazed down at the floor as if thinking about what he had said. In reality, she had no idea what to do. Was it the marriage proposal of a man of sound mind, or the fantasy desire of a feverish delusion?

The Caliph, seeing her perplexity and misinterpreting it, put his arm around her shoulders gently.

"I've startled you, beloved Murjana. I don't expect you to answer me at this moment. I realize you weren't expecting to hear what I said, and you'll need to reflect on it. And, of course, you must have time to think and talk it over with your family."

He smiled at her.

"And for that to happen you should be with them and not with me. You're free to leave whenever you wish."

She turned away from him at once, relieved to be released, and made quickly for the door. He followed her and, as she turned the handle, he stayed her hand with his and took her in his arms one last time. Tenderly, he held her to him, kissed her hair, and then let her go.

"Don't keep me waiting long."

◻

In Abdulhamid's household there was much outrage and consternation. Abdulhamid was still shocked at his treatment by the Caliph, even more so when Murjana told him about her audience with him. She omitted all mention that the meeting had taken place in the Caliph's bedchamber and that he was in his sickbed. And, of course, she said nothing of the physical intimacy that had occurred and the fear she had felt, but merely talked about the Caliph's confession that he had developed feelings of affection for her, which led him to ask for her hand in marriage. That was why he had called them to the palace.

But her uncle sensed she was not telling him the full story.

"How is it possible that I, your uncle, was excluded from these important discussions? It is to me the Caliph should have addressed himself, not you. Who else was there to hear this proposal?"

She replied vaguely that she did not know any of the men with the Caliph, but they played no role in the proceedings.

Abdulhamid shook his head disapprovingly.

"You should not have allowed it, my daughter. You should have insisted that I was present."

Hamza quickly came to Murjana's rescue.

"What are you saying, Uncle? He is the Caliph and can do what he likes. We have no say in the matter, and nor does Murjana."

Abdulhamid shook his head again unhappily.

Enthralled by the whole story, Yazan wasn't at all worried by the Caliph's conduct.

"When is he going to approach us formally for your hand?" he asked.

"I don't know, but I suppose it will be after I have thought about his proposal."

Murjana looked inquiringly at Hamza and her uncle. "What do you think?"

Abdulhamid did not answer immediately, but Hamza did.

"I think that no matter what he said, we don't have any choice but to accept the proposal."

His tone was one of feigned resignation to hide his inner satisfaction at this surprisingly favorable outcome.

"But we do!" thundered his uncle. "If Murjana says the Caliph asked her to think about it, then we have time. He could have taken her at once, willing or not, like all his kind." Abdulhamid could not hide his disgust. "But at least he didn't."

"I must say he was very courteous," said Murjana. "He did not command, he begged. It was very strange."

"That's good. It gives us time to work out how to delay the decision and send you as far away from the court as possible."

The memory of the Caliph's ardent caresses still fresh in her mind, Murjana shook her head.

"That will be impossible, Uncle. He won't allow it, I assure you. It's true he was gentle, but he was most insistent I give him my answer very soon."

She stole a glance at Hamza.

Yazan, usually careful not to displease his uncle, summoned up the courage to agree with his siblings.

"They're right, Uncle. We must obey. Spiriting Murjana away against the Caliph's wishes would be very dangerous."

Abdulhamid stared at the three of them in disbelief.

"Have you all lost your minds?" The anger in his voice was palpable. "Do I have to remind you who your sister's 'suitor' is, God help me. He's not an ordinary man. He's an *Abbasid*, for God's sake, a son of that evil, treacherous family that's done us no end of harm. They used our help when they needed it, and then threw us to the dogs when they got what they wanted. How many of our imams have they murdered, or sent to prison, or hounded all their lives?"

This was a history that went back a hundred years or more. No one who had witnessed those bloody events was alive to tell the tale, but for Shiites like them, it had become a folk memory of murder and betrayal, passed down the generations, and had lost none of its vividness over time. The three siblings bowed their heads in silence.

But Hamza saw with alarm that if his uncle was allowed to continue in this vein, all the careful plans he had laid would unravel. Things were going well. His careful training had led Murjana to ensnare the Caliph, who would soon be at their mercy for the sweet revenge Hamza dreamed of night and day. Nothing must be allowed to interfere with it.

"We all know it, Uncle. No one is saying the Caliph is innocent. But hasn't our imam always told us to be peaceable in the face of our persecutors? Doesn't that mean going along with the Caliph's proposal rather than fighting it?"

Not everyone agreed with the imam's conciliatory approach, as Hamza well knew. There were many who broke away from the consensus and rebelled against the authorities. If caught, they usually paid for their insurrection with their freedom or their lives. But Hamza said nothing of this.

"After all, he's not intending to hurt Murjana, just to marry her. Doesn't that make any difference?"

"I am surprised at you, nephew. Do you want to stand by and see your sister dishonored? You should have been the first to defend her, not cave in to that tyrant. I can't get over the shame of her going in to see him on her own like some concubine."

That stung Hamza, whose pride in his family and its standing was known to all its members. He flushed deeply and tried to bite back the angry words on the tip of his tongue.

"That's unfair, Uncle. Murjana's honor is our honor. Why do you want to insult me?"

Murjana, who had been quiet until then, spoke. "Will you allow me to give my opinion, dear Uncle?"

She knew Abdulhamid had a soft spot for her and found it hard to deny her anything.

"I'm the one who's most affected by this marriage if it happens. And if it does, wouldn't that be the best protection for our community and even maybe the end of our persecution? Do you imagine the Caliph would want to hurt me by hurting my family and friends? And, in any case, what is so shocking about a marriage between one of us and one of them? We are all part of the Dar al-Islam, the family of Islam, aren't we, Uncle? Don't all of us belong together?"

Abdulhamid looked at her affectionately.

"You argue the case well, Murjana, and as you say, it will be you who marries this man. You talk of wishing to make what is an enormous sacrifice for the sake of our community. That is an honorable intention, my dearest niece, but it's not easy. How do you truthfully in your heart feel about marrying him? Do you think you'll be able to carry such a burden?"

Oh Uncle, thought Murjana silently, *if you only knew how much bigger a burden I'm asked to carry if Hamza carries out his plan.*

Abdulhamid puckered his brow and continued,

"I ask myself how your father, God have mercy on him, would feel if he saw me, his brother and the guardian of his children, aiding you in such a terrible venture. Would he himself have offered you, his only daughter, in sacrifice to the Abbasids?" He shook his head vigorously. "I don't think he would."

Her brothers looked at Murjana. Hamza's face was expressionless. As her uncle was speaking, she had been asking herself the same question. How *did* she feel about marrying the Caliph?

When Hamza first put his plan to her, she had been nervous, but believed wholeheartedly in what motivated him. He was her elder brother and had always loved her and taken her side. She trusted him implicitly. But now she realized that when she agreed, it was to an idea, a worthy aim, without an understanding of its tangible reality. The object of the plan, the Caliph, had been to her a remote figure in a distant palace. He could have been a stuffed puppet that children played with. And what she was asked to do to him was just as unreal.

But then, through a fortuitous event that Hamza had not anticipated, their uncle decided to seek the Caliph's help over the family's stolen land. That visit to the palace, when Hamza saw the Caliph's interest in Murjana, gave him an idea. The second meeting, miraculously sought by the Caliph himself, made the idea more concrete. And from there, events had moved with a momentum that brought them amazingly within reach of the final goal. Hamza was jubilant.

But Murjana was not so certain. Seeing the Caliph in the flesh had given her a sense of unease. It was not that it made her go back on her mission, but it gave a concrete reality to what until then had been only a plan. "*If* we can get you together with the Caliph," her brother had said, "And *if* he likes you... And *if* he decides he likes you enough to want to see you again, or in the best case to fall in love with you, *if* all that happens without him or his spies suspecting..." There were so many "ifs" that she had almost put the whole idea out of her head.

But now there was no uncertainty. The Caliph not only liked her, he liked her enough to want her for his wife, better than what her brother had thought the best possible scenario, and in his heart of hearts probably unattainable. But it had happened, and Murjana found herself confronting a real man in a real world. And given that, would she be able to go through with it?

She closed her eyes and prayed for guidance.

13

It was ten days since Abu Mansour's return to his own house. He had not intended to leave the Caliph's side so soon, but events had forced his hand.

A delegation including the chief wazir, the Caliph's chamberlain, the head doctor, and the grand eunuch had suddenly arrived from the Golden Gate Palace. Frustrated by waiting for permission from Abu Mansour, whom they regarded as having acted beyond his authority, they had decided to override the doctor's instructions and come to see the Caliph for themselves. Suleiman doubted that the Caliph's health had improved. In fact, he secretly hoped it had not, thus showing Abu Mansour's treatment to have been ineffective.

It was clear Abu Mansour had offended protocol, and his erratic advice to remove the Caliph beyond the palace's reach had only been tolerated out of desperation over his plight. Even then, only Durayd believed the doctor could really save him. That skepticism had seeped into the atmosphere of the court in spite of the ban on all discussion of the Caliph's health. Talk of a successor had already started, and various courtiers were lining themselves up to take sides once the Caliph died.

When the entourage of dignitaries from the Golden Gate

arrived, Abu Mansour did not come out to greet them, and no one from their side asked to see him. He had gathered up his papers and few personal belongings, and, leaving the visitors hovering around the Caliph's bedchamber, he had left the palace quietly and ridden toward his house. Once there, and in the midst of his household's warm welcome, he had tried to put aside his anxieties about the Caliph. He told himself he had done his duty as best he could and the rest was in God's hands. But was that really true?

When he watched the Caliph's bedroom door close behind the young woman, Abu Mansour had experienced a moment of doubt. Had he done the right thing, he wondered? What if the shock of seeing the woman who haunted his dreams had been too much for the Caliph, ill once more and depleted of strength? Abu Mansour had gone out into the garden and paced among the trees, trying to calm himself. It was not just his attachment to the Caliph, but also his professional *amour propre* that had made him fearful of failure. He dreaded seeing the Caliph again and possibly finding him angry, or even sicker than before.

Perhaps that was why no news had come from the palace for a whole ten days. Normally sanguine and self-assured, Abu Mansour could not repress a growing nervousness about this silence and what it might mean about the Caliph's progress. Had he recovered or was he worse? If the latter, Abu Mansour did not give much for his own chances of a future, and the enormity of his gamble with the Caliph's health was borne in on him once again.

Of the household, only Younis knew of his master's concerns. Without being asked, he would tell Abu Mansour each day, "No news from the palace this morning, sir. And Saad has heard nothing from the souk either."

Finally, and as Abu Mansour was debating whether he should go to the palace himself without an invitation, a messenger from the Caliph arrived at the house with a summons for him to attend. There had been no warning, and he was given no time to prepare himself for the visit. He was to accompany the man at once and be taken into the Caliph's presence on arrival.

"It must mean that our master has recovered, sir!" Younis ventured hopefully.

But Abu Mansour shook his head, "I don't know what it means."

Uneasily, he walked out with the emissary.

◻

The atmosphere in the palace was unremarkable. There were no signs of agitation or groups of worried courtiers standing about, and no high official to greet him as had happened the first time.

He was shown into a small audience chamber and asked to wait. Guards stood outside, exchanging a few words with the attendants who passed them, but no one entered the room.

After a short while, he saw the sentries stand to attention at the sound of approaching footsteps, and the arched doorway suddenly darkened with the figures of people coming in. Expecting these to be court officials who would take him to the Caliph, Abu Mansour was surprised to see the Caliph himself in their midst.

He entered the chamber, and seeing the doctor standing to receive him, he asked the attendants to wait outside. As the last of them left, Abu Mansour bowed deeply, but did not prostrate himself on the ground and kiss it as was the custom. He knew the Caliph disliked this display of subservience so beloved of his forebears.

"Peace be upon you, Abu Mansour. You probably expected to come to me instead of the other way round. But since my recovery, I have felt the need for exercise, and I walk inside the palace whenever I can."

His recovery was indeed impressive. He was still thin and had walked in with a slight stoop. His face had not yet filled out, but it had regained its color, and his eyes shone with something like their former brightness. The restoration from the poor, semi-co-matose creature he had been when Abu Mansour first saw him to what was now more or less his normal self struck the doctor as nothing short of miraculous. He stared at the Caliph.

"You may well look surprised," said the Caliph, seeing his expression. "But you shouldn't be. It is all your doing. How can I ever thank you for snatching me from the jaws of death and returning me to the world once more?"

To Abu Mansour's discomfiture, the Caliph came forward and grasped him warmly by the shoulders, smiling.

"Surely, there is no greater gift one man can give to another than this."

"My lord, I am overcome with happiness at seeing you so well. I only did what was my duty toward you." Abu Mansour was riveted by curiosity to know what had happened after his departure from the place where he had last seen the sickly Caliph.

The Caliph shook his head.

"No. Not only your duty. Suleiman and his doctors also did their duty, and you know the result. No, it was your bravery, your wisdom, and your skill, for which you are so rightly famous, that saved me. Come, let us sit."

He indicated the cushioned divan, and as Abu Mansour sat down next to the Caliph, he was aware of a pleasurable but unfamiliar feeling of self-approbation.

Whenever Abu Mansour's wealthy patients praised him too extravagantly for his treatments, it made him uncomfortable. He always felt that if he should ever fail them, they would turn on him for disappointing them. That was why he preferred to work among the ordinary people and the poor who came to the bimaristan. Yet, the gratitude of the Caliph, whose rank was far above that of the wealthiest of his patients and should have caused him even greater fears, did not. There was an honesty in the Caliph that Abu Mansour recognized as much like his own.

"Let me first apologize for having left you in the dark these last many days. It was because of returning here and the mountain of tasks waiting for me. Though I was much improved, I was still weak and had to rest frequently. I called for you as soon as I could."

He turned his eyes on Abu Mansour. "I wanted you to come so you should know how you saved me and what joy you have brought into my life."

Abu Mansour cleared his throat, unsure how to respond.

"You may think that a Caliph has a hundred companions, brothers, wives, and all kinds of men and women eager to share his company where he can find a true friend. But you'd be wrong. There are things so intimate, so secret to the heart, for the telling of which no confidant, no *nadim*, soulmate, exists. I've longed for such a person. But I've had to keep my thoughts and secret desires to myself. Only you, Abu Mansour, will understand what they are, since it was you who led me to them."

The Caliph paused.

"You knew before I did that my illness was love and that my cure was to be found in the one I loved. You ignored my objections and brought her to me. I know you must have braved your fear of my anger in order to help me, and I will bless you for that all my life. You are the one true friend I have, and I will trust you with everything that is dear to me. From now on you will be my physician, and no one else will take your place."

Abu Mansour was ineffably moved. Speechless with emotion, he could only look at the floor, humbled by the great honor the Caliph had done him.

"When I was a child, my mother used to be my one true friend," the Caliph continued. "My father and his wife, and all his concubines had nothing to do with us, and my brother was my father's favorite. As I grew up, my interests were different from my brother's and those of the court and I was often lonely. The greatest loss of my life was the death of my mother when I was twelve."

Abu Mansour thought of his own mother, likewise his true friend, and thanked God for her long life.

"I managed, of course, but I was never happy, and my life has turned out to be about duty and control...Until now."

His face lit up.

"Murjana has changed all that. I want her for my wife, and I'm waiting for her reply to my proposal made the very day when you brought her to me. Since that moment, my vigor has come back. I want to live every moment of the time I have left and make up for all the years I lost."

Abu Mansour understood him. Who could not? But at the same time, he wondered if Murjana's youth and inexperience were equal to the needs of this passionate, difficult man. He marveled at the Caliph's indulgence of her and her family's boldness in keeping him waiting for her decision when he could have commanded her acquiescence at a stroke. For people of such modest background and means to behave so high-handedly seemed defiant, or simply foolhardy.

Was it because they were among the followers of Ali? Although there were many like them in Baghdad, hardly anyone noticed them. But not all were so unobtrusive. It was said that there were angry men among them who rebelled against the Caliph. Each rebellion they mounted was put down with great force, and shown no mercy. It caused much bitterness among the Shia, and Abu Mansour wondered if the Banu Shaaban were influenced enough by these events to feel an antipathy toward the Caliph.

On balance, he thought it was unlikely, since the majority of Shiites were peaceable citizens. The only reason he was thinking about them at all was the Caliph's proposal of marriage to the daughter of a Shiite house.

"Will you wait for the lady's response much longer, my lord? You know that you don't have to."

The Caliph looked earnestly into his face.

"If you mean I could command her to obey me, you're right, I could. But I'd never do it. She must come to me of her own free choice and out of love for me. If she agrees because of fear or the persuasion of her family, I will not accept her, though it would tear me apart."

He looked into the far distance.

"She's young and doesn't know me yet. But what I saw of her showed me that, even if she doesn't love me fully now, she's started to. And that's already more than I could ever have hoped for."

14

The imam had visitors. He always did. Renowned for his knowledge and wisdom, many scholars and learned persons from far and wide sought his company. They came to study, to dispute various points of theology with him, or simply to seek his advice and listen to him reflect on faith, philosophy, and the meaning of piety. His interests were not confined to religious matters, however. He had among his pupils alchemists and astronomers, eager young men whom he loved to teach and whom he helped to develop into experts, each in their field.

With such a following, it was rare to find him alone, and Abdulhamid, who knew and revered the imam, was familiar with his way of life. On previous occasions when he had found him busy, he would leave and return on another day. But this time he felt his business was so urgent he would have waited all night if need be.

He was shown into a side room with an open door from where he could see people's comings and goings. It was a modest house, its rooms and reception hall, where the imam saw his visitors, often not large enough to accommodate them.

The walls were largely unadorned, except for the occasional plain hanging. The furniture was simple and basic. There was no silk or brocade here, nor any hint of luxury, and Abdulhamid sat waiting on sparse, woollen cushions, his back propped up against the bare wall.

The imam's house was in keeping with the poor neighborhood in which it stood, not far from that of the Banu Shaaban. All around were small and crowded mud or wooden houses, not strong enough to withstand extremes of weather. But for the street cleaners who came by from time to time, the narrow alleys would soon have been choked with refuse. The artisans and stall holders who lived there were not destitute, as in some parts of Baghdad. But most of them struggled to keep body and soul together.

It was sunset by the time the last visitor was shown out. Abdulhamid rose and went into the hall. As soon as he appeared, the imam held out his hand in greeting and beckoned him to draw near. They had been friends ever since the imam was forcibly moved on the Caliph's orders from Medina to Baghdad. When at first Abdulhamid had commiserated with him on what amounted to an expulsion from his native city, he had smiled and shaken his head gently.

"No need to feel sorry for me, my friend. It is better by far than being thrown into prison!"

He had been in and out of Abbasid jails enough times when the Caliph's father was alive to have no desire ever to return there. But the price for his relative freedom was that he should be confined to his home, unable to come and go as he pleased, and kept under constant surveillance. "Why?" his many followers would ask angrily. "What is there in this gentle, peaceable man to be afraid of?"

Meeting each other that day, both the imam and Abdulhamid knew they were observed. However, the Caliph's men rarely intruded into the imam's home, instructed by their master to show him respect and consideration at all times. Not that it reassured the imam's visitors, who always avoided speaking to each other within earshot of his house. This Caliph, they said, might have a better record toward the followers of Ali than his ancestors, but he was still an Abbasid and not to be trusted.

The pity of it, though, people said, was the loss to the Caliph of a friendship with a man whose interests so harmonized with his own. While the imam's mystical beliefs were not those of the Caliph's, his concern with jurisprudence, philosophy, and the sciences was close to the Caliph's. A more suitable candidate for the intellectual circle of the palace could hardly have been imagined.

Abdulhamid sat down, spreading his robe around himself, and looked at the imam. They were of an age, but the imam, with his open, serene expression and clear eyes, looked younger. He was short in stature with a fair complexion. Like Abdulhamid, he wore green, and his turban was rounder and flatter than the more usual pointed style. Although his demeanor was friendly, there was a spirituality, an otherworldliness, about him that inspired wonder and awe.

"What is troubling you?"

The imam's voice was soothing, and Abdulhamid sighed deeply.

"It's a personal matter on which I need guidance. I don't know what to do and have come to you, our dearest Imam, for help."

The imam waited while Abdulhamid collected himself.

"It's about my niece, Murjana, and the Caliph's marriage proposal to her."

If anything was capable of attracting the imam's instant attention, this could hardly be bettered. He had been speaking all day about matters of faith and worship, interrupted only by prayer times, and he was tired. But hearing this unusual request made him sit up. He asked Abdulhamid to continue, and the whole story was soon told.

"As you see, whatever I do will be wrong. If I turn down the proposal that's surely coming, as the Caliph won't wait much longer, I will bring his wrath down on my head. And if I accept, I will put your followers and all good people to shame."

The misery Abdulhamid had been feeling for days lifted with the relief of unburdening himself to the one person he trusted implicitly.

"This is a predicament, I must say," the imam replied. He was pensive. For a while he said nothing, and when his servant approached, he waved him away.

Abdulhamid went on.

"I've been hoping the Caliph would change his mind. To begin with, he has four wives and can't take a fifth."

Even as he said this, Abdulhamid knew it was no bar to the Caliph's wishes. Divorce for a man, and especially one in the Caliph's position, was easy. An inconvenient wife could be cast off and replaced by another at a moment's notice. So, he tried another tack.

"Such men are capricious, and the Caliph has been ill. It could be that he sees Murjana as an amusement while he convalesces. So, I reckon that if I make an excuse for a further delay while I take her off somewhere far away for some reason, he may forget and find another to take his fancy. What do you think?"

The imam looked at him sympathetically.

"No, Abdulhamid, the Caliph will not forget. Only your desperation makes you even consider an idea like that. You and I know the Caliph is a serious man, not given to whims of the kind you were hoping for."

Abdulhamid bowed his head.

"Well, then, what's to be done? I can't surrender my niece to an Abbasid and I won't. There must some way, Imam, isn't there?"

"What does your niece say? Has she agreed to the Caliph's proposal?"

"Not formally, yet. But, like her brothers, she thinks we have no choice but to accept. She even thinks she could help our people by this marriage. But she doesn't know what she's saying, Imam. She's young and inexperienced."

The imam looked impressed.

"On the contrary, your niece's high ideals are to be commended. She must be a young woman of worth. Before you do anything more, bring her here, so I can talk to her."

□

The next evening, and much against his will, Abdulhamid took Murjana to see the imam. He had not planned on taking her to what he saw as a strictly private meeting, and had been taken aback by the imam's invitation to her. As a young girl and incapable of fending for herself, she must defer to his and the imam's greater wisdom, of course, and he could see no useful purpose in allowing her to express her opinion. It still worried him that he had come away the day before without the imam's unequivocal support for his plan to evade the Caliph's proposal. He was at a loss to understand the imam's exact position. However, he comforted himself with the thought that the imam might simply want to see Murjana in order to dissuade her from taking a step she would regret.

Murjana had never seen the imam before, and she found herself much in awe of him at first. But before long, she started to feel at ease. He had a fatherly air she warmed to, never having had a father she could remember. She had been a young child when she and her brothers were orphaned and had longed for years to have known their father. Abdulhamid was a good and dutiful uncle. But, although he tried to be kind, there was no affection in him.

The imam looked at her with warmth and kindness, and she had an instinctive sense that she could trust him, even with all her life's secrets if need be. "Your uncle has told me of your proposal of marriage. I know his view of the matter, but I want to know yours, and in your own words."

122

She found no difficulty in giving him an account of what had happened with the Caliph similar to the one she had given her uncle, and stressing the Caliph's determination to marry her.

"And by this marriage, you feel you can help the poor and the disadvantaged?"

She nodded vigorously, encouraged by his interest, and explained again what she had told her uncle earlier. The imam smiled at her with admiration in his eyes.

"There, Abdulhamid, you have your answer. Your niece wants this marriage, and I agree with her. You will accept the Caliph's proposal, and that will be the end of your quandary."

Abdulhamid was shocked.

"It's one thing for this foolish girl to imagine she will have power over the Abbasid once she marries him. But it's another for you to encourage her. How can you ask me to offer her up so tamely? Do I strike you as something less than a man who can't fight to shield my family and our community from dishonor?" Abdulhamid was so agitated that Murjana put her hand on his arm to quieten him.

"Please calm yourself and listen to me, Abdulhamid," the imam answered. "The caliphs have done us Shia great harm. I know that they are in the wrong, but we have to be steadfast in the face of adversity. Defiance and trickery are not our ways. Submission to the will of God is the only way."

Seeing Abdulhamid's distress, the imam softened his tone. "Our ruler has set his heart on your niece, and you must give her up. You have no choice."

Abdulhamid shook his head unhappily.

"I venerate you, Imam, and have always been strengthened by your wisdom. But how can you speak like this, after what he and his father have done to you and yours? How can you ask us to submit to injustice and tyranny?"

"No, my friend. Our submission is not to tyranny, but to our true faith, to waiting quietly, and with patience, for the time when justice will prevail. As it must."

This was the advice the imam always gave to those who complained to him about ill-treatment at the hands of the state.

"These caliphs have gone astray," he would tell them. "They have turned their backs on justice and the equality of all before God, which our Prophet and our first imam, Ali, taught, in favor of wealth and luxury. But our duty is to pray that they find guidance, and to walk the true path of justice ourselves, so that, by our example, those who are misguided will learn."

These views were duly reported to the Caliph by the spies who watched the imam. But the imam remained undeterred and continued preaching the same doctrine.

"I am serene in the knowledge that the rule of the unjust will not last, and you must be, too," he assured Abdulhamid.

Yet, Abdulhamid wondered how the imam could be so certain. Surely, he must know about the young Shia rebels who did not accept his creed of passivity and who ran off to join the opposition to the Caliph. They had no faith in the virtue of endurance and dreamed of overthrowing the caliphate, replacing it with what they believed the Prophet had always intended: that the heirs of his bloodline, from his cousin Ali to his sons and their sons, in an unbroken line of imams, should lead the Muslims righteously, and with justice. Some revolutionaries had broken off entirely from their Shia brethren and set up new groupings with new names. Abdulhamid could not refrain from bringing up these young rebels.

"I know about them, of course," the imam replied. "But they're wrong, and I don't agree with what they do. It is not for us to fight the Caliph. God, in his own good time, will do it. Let us remain peaceful, patient, and *undivided* while we await God's justice." He nodded toward Murjana.

"It is with conciliation and friendship that we will succeed. And in that Abdulhamid, your niece will be the standard bearer."

⊞

Not long after, Uthman, the Caliph's secretary, came to the Banu Shaaban's house delivering a sealed letter from the Caliph. Receiving him, Abdulhamid felt he was facing his executioner.

The letter, which was addressed to him, was short and to the point. It asked for Murjana's hand in marriage and his permission for the Caliph to approach her for that purpose. With a heavy heart, Abdulhamid had Murjana join them and read her the Caliph's letter. But afterward, when Uthman had left them with her reply to the Caliph, Abdulhamid hardly said a word. He went to his room and sat alone.

15

I n the Dar al-Huram, the women's quarters at the Golden Gate palace, there was much agitation. It was usually an amicable place, a secluded world of its own, where bickering and disagreements were quickly contained, and to which the Caliph went from time to time for repose and leisure.

His visits, which had become less frequent than in the past, were typically occasions of enjoyment in the company of his wives and children. Sometimes he might ask for one or two of his more gifted concubines to sing and recite poetry, a custom that had been a regular pastime for his father and brother and their companions when they used to spend many evenings drinking and consorting with the girls.

The Caliph's sober ways were different, but they had their advantages. The women of his harem, whom he treated with fairness and respect, were peaceable and less inclined to rivalry. And the eunuchs who guarded them were likewise less quarrelsome. As a result, the Caliph's harem was quite unlike the seething hotbeds of ambition and competition that plagued so many others.

Rumors that the caliph was intending to take a new wife had run through the Dar al-Huram ever since his return to the Golden Gate and the start of his recovery. The fact that he had made no official announcement led some of the women to hope it was mere gossip.

"But we must be prepared for the rumors to be true," insisted Um Jaafar. She was the eldest of the Caliph's four wives and was held in great respect by the others for her calmness and common sense. But Um Jaafar was also realistic and had long expected the Caliph to acquire a new wife. It was only his tardiness in doing so that had made them all so complacent and accustomed to the status and security of being equal in his eyes. If the rumors were true, then he must divorce at least one of them, and Um Jaafar had long accepted that, as the eldest and the least physically appealing of the four, she would be the first to go.

"I don't agree," said Zeinab, who, being his cousin, thought she understood the Caliph best. "I'd be very surprised if there was truth in any of it. There's never been a time when our master showed any interest in a new woman, not even in the ones people give him as presents."

Hind, more concerned by the rumors than any of them, shook her head. "That's nothing to go by. He's never liked those dancing girls because he knows they're bribes other men offer him to get something in return."

As was her custom, Sulafa remained quiet, listening to the others. But she was anxious, nonetheless.

"Maybe you're right," said Zeinab, shrugging. "But I still say it isn't in his nature to run after women. Let's face it now, he's not much interested in any of us, is he? Or in the concubines. I can't remember the last time he came to me, for example."

She laughed.

But Hind certainly remembered that last night he had been with her, his disheartening tepidness toward her, his excuse about being preoccupied with affairs of state which she had sensed was insincere. Had he been thinking of the other woman even then? She disagreed with Zeinab's assessment of the Caliph's character, perhaps because of all the wives, she was still in love with him and knew what passions smoldered in him beneath that outward tranquillity and self-control. And because she knew this, she was worried. If it turned out that he really was after someone else, she felt it would devastate her.

In her heart of hearts, Hind had always been convinced he would be hers for as long as they both lived, never to be supplanted by another. She couldn't believe she was wrong and was determined to find out the truth. Idris was close to Durayd, who knew all the Caliph's secrets. He was the person to talk to.

⊞

"Idris, what do you think of all the talk that the Caliph might be wanting to marry again?"

Anticipating questions from the Caliph's wives and dreading them, the head eunuch professed ignorance. Hind was unimpressed by his denials. The Caliph had requested that the matter of his impending marriage be kept secret until he himself had spoken to his wives, and Durayd had passed this on to Idris. Idris had laughed at the idea of keeping something like that a secret, since everyone had been talking about nothing else for weeks.

Hind pressed him further, wheedling and threatening by turn. In the end, Idris gave way and told her. But he asked for her discretion. Had he only known it, she was the one wife among all the others the Caliph had most wanted kept in the dark about his marriage plans. While he had feared to hurt his other wives' feelings, he judged them able in the end to take his disloyalty in their stride. But Hind's reaction would be different, he knew, and he was anxious that she should hear the news directly from him.

Idris saw the crash of disappointment on Hind's face, the sudden pallor of her complexion, and it pierced his heart. They were alone in her rooms.

"Is there no doubt, Idris? Has our master truly made up his mind to take this step?"

Idris sighed regretfully and nodded his head. She looked at him desperately. "Tell me about the girl the Caliph wants to marry. Who is she? What does she look like? Is she as beautiful as they say?"

"I have not seen her, my lady. Few of us have. They say she is young and her family is God-fearing and respectable. That is all I know."

"When will the wedding be? How soon?"

"I haven't been told," Idris said, wanting to spare her the knowledge that the Caliph was in a fever of haste for the nuptials to take place as soon as they could be arranged.

"It can't be soon, surely?" There was a note of entreaty in her voice. "The Caliph will have to...to...divorce one of us first."

Idris was silent and as she turned away from him, he saw her shoulders shake with silent sobs. Unable to bear her grief, he reached out impulsively and put his arms around her. He turned her toward him and held her. She wept uncontrollably, clinging to him, oblivious to the situation they were in.

He let his mouth rest lightly against her forehead, wiped her tears, and she let him soothe her. Idris was not a complete man after all, she told herself. His ministrations were almost those of another woman, expressions of kindness, and no one should blame her for taking comfort from it. But she also knew better than that. Idris was in fact a eunuch, or so they said, and yet ever since her marriage to the Caliph and her residence at the Dar al-Huram, she'd sensed he had a special interest in her well above the call of duty.

"Idris, I'm so wretched. First, the Caliph's illness when we weren't allowed to go to him, and now this. I don't think I can bear it."

She moved away from him, and Idris, seeing her sorrow, was full of anguish for her. *If only she did not love the Caliph so much*, he thought. He couldn't fault his master for his kindness and consideration, and was devoted to him. But in matters of the heart, he judged him cold and unfeeling. A woman so fine, so spirited and beautiful as the lady Hind, deserved a different sort of man, one who would not just love her, but adore her.

⊞

When the Caliph came at last to visit the harem, he began with his first three wives. He had not relished the task of talking to any of them about his forthcoming marriage and still felt guilty. But he had lost the remorse that nearly cost him his life, and finding that they were at least partially prepared for his news made his task easier.

Um Jaafar was the easiest to talk to. Over the years she had become more like a sister to him than a spouse, and he always found her company restful and undemanding.

"It is high time you took another wife, Abu Jaafar," she told him generously. "I'm surprised it took you so long. I hope your new bride is worthy of you and may God bless you both."

Sulafa was as generous, always wanting to please and afraid to offend him. He could not help noting how faded she looked and how mouse-like in her meekness she was. Had that been his doing, he wondered? Had his uninterest in these women as anything other than old friends dried up their flesh?

Zeinab, always livelier than the rest, was outspoken when he told her. "And what happens to us, then? Thrown off like old shoes? Do we stop being your wives or what?" In another harem, she would not have dared berate her husband for marrying a new wife, much as she might have resented it inside herself. Wives in that position were expected to put a good face on their misfortunes so as not to offend their husbands, but often ended up taking out their frustrations on the other wives or their children. But Zeinab was accustomed to the Caliph's respectful and considerate ways, and was his cousin to boot, and felt free to speak her mind.

"Of course not. You know that your place in my heart remains the same and that I will treat you as I have always done. Your status is assured."

She did not doubt the sincerity of his intentions. But with a new young wife to pamper and dally with, he would have little appetite for any of them. However, she did take solace from the fact that he'd made no mention of divorcing her, or Sulafa, or Um Jaafar for that matter.

When the Caliph finally came to Hind's apartments, he found her resplendent in a gown of dark green brocade, a color he had always liked on her. Her honey-colored hair was coiled around her head, showing off her long elegant neck, and she wore emerald earrings to match her dress. She was pale and looked as if she'd been crying. But she smiled gaily enough and welcomed him with her usual warmth. Her wide, intelligent eyes and the cast of her features appealed to him as strongly as they ever had, and for a moment he almost wished she could again arouse the old passion he had once felt for her. How much simpler matters would be if that could return.

She offered him sweet sherbet and fruit, as if to delay the conversation she knew would have to take place. He sipped his drink slowly, looking down at the floor. And then he took her hand in his.

"My dear Hind, I'm sure you already know what I'm going to say. I didn't intend for you to hear it from others, but I was too late, and by now you've heard about my impending marriage to a new wife."

Before coming, he had debated long and hard with himself about how best to tell her, and had decided to be truthful and direct without going into detail. It would hurt her less that way.

"This marriage is something I want, but not because I've lost my regard for you or that I find you displeasing in any way. Please don't think that."

Hind looked at him expectantly. But he said nothing more and there was an awkward silence. She could not stop herself from wanting him to go on.

"If I do not displease you, my lord, why do you want to marry this...woman?"

He hesitated, afraid to upset her. "I desire it, that's all."

But Hind would not be put off.

"Surely there is more to it than that. Please tell me. You've always been able to talk to me. We have no secrets from each other. Don't I deserve your confidence over something as important as this?"

She was right, and he had known she was too clever to be satisfied with his tactful but curt explanations. Looking at her eager expression, he wondered if, after all, he could risk speaking more honestly. Of all the women he had known, she was the most imaginative, the most open to new ideas, the most capable of appreciating his feelings. And he longed to tell her about his new-found happiness, to accord her the respect her intelligence and self-esteem deserved by explaining that she had not been cast aside for some trifling infatuation or flight of fancy, but rather for genuine and deeply held feelings about his own life and future. But he could not permit himself such indulgence, and so instead he reiterated his admiration for her and the special place she occupied in his life which, he insisted, nothing could change.

Hind was dismayed. It was not an answer to her question, and not even true. Though she recognized the concern behind his words, she did not think it likely his attachment to her would long survive this new marriage. His evasiveness alarmed her more than any admission he could have made. If he had talked of a physical infatuation, or a need to regain his youth with a fresh young woman, or a desire for distraction from the burdens of state, she could have understood and perhaps forgiven him. But his reluctance to describe the reasons for this momentous step in a life never previously devoted to the pleasures of the flesh could mean only one thing—he was in love.

That was the real reason for his marrying. Despite the secrecy surrounding his recent illness, rumor had still seeped through about its exact nature. She had not believed it, but now saw all too clearly the sequence of events.

"You are not candid with me, my lord. You have reasons for wanting to contract this marriage, but will not say what they are. I ask, I plead, that you tell me; it is only my due."

He raised his eyebrows at that but still said nothing. Hind's urgings and pleadings grew louder and more insistent. She couldn't help herself. She went on interrogating the Caliph about the woman he intended to marry. Where and when had he met her? Was it at the time of his last visit to the Dar al-Huram? Had he known the woman then and betrayed Hind, even as he dined with her and lay in her bed that night?

The torrent of words that poured out of her was choked by sobs, but she would not stop, even though she was dimly aware of an ominous change in the Caliph's mood. She went back over their past relationship, how they had met and married, and the many years of love and companionship they had known. Had he forgotten their closeness of thinking, the intellectual bonds that united them, the books they shared, and the philosophical arguments that had engaged them?

Her face was flushed with passion as she brought up every aspect of their past compatibility and plucked every sentimental chord in the Caliph's memory. Her implication, cleverly and movingly argued, was clear. How could he throw all that away for the sake of some new liaison, however desirable it might seem to him for the moment?

"It always grieved me that I could not give you children, strong sons to be proud of. But you were magnanimous, told me that you loved me just the same, and I believed you. I wonder now, is that what is behind this? Do you want more sons, and are you punishing me for my failure?"

At that she burst into tears, reached out toward him piteously, and tried to touch his arm.

But he drew back, and, wrapping his robe around him, stood up.

His face was closed. He had come to her full of remorse and desperate to make amends. That she would be upset was only natural and he had expected it. But as she ranted against him with ever more hysterical accusations, his sense of guilt gave way to annoyance, made all the sharper by that guilt, and then her pleadings and complaints left him cold. Perhaps his chamberlain had been right to suggest that he was too indulgent of his wives and gave them too much license. Why else would Hind feel herself at liberty to harangue him like a tradesman's wife in the souk? Favored though she was, she had presumed too much, and it angered him.

"You are right that the matter of your childlessness is important to me," he said coldly. "But it is not as you think, and not the reason for my marriage, though it will be the reason for my divorce. As you know, I can't marry again without repudiating one of my wives. And because, unlike them, you have no children, it's only right that you should be the one I have decided to divorce."

She had stopped crying and seemed numb with shock.

"You needn't fear for your future. There is no question of you having to move from the palace after the divorce. This is your home and you can remain here for as long as you like."

With that, he turned on his heel abruptly and left.

Idris was waiting at the door. After the Caliph walked quickly past, frowning and waving him away, Idris returned to Hind's apartment.

Not waiting for him to make the first move this time, she threw herself in his arms and broke down in a storm of anguished tears.

"What will I do now, Idris? What will I do?"

16

Abdullah ibn Rida, the governor of Khorasan, was not enjoying his captivity in Baghdad. He was furious that he had fallen for the trick played on him by Abu Ubaydah and hated being outmaneuvered by the Caliph's shrewd commander. Although news that the Caliph was inquiring about the land of the Banu Shaaban had reached him long before Abu Ubaydah came to the governorate at Merv, he had not taken it seriously.

He had seen no reason why such a trivial matter as a transfer of land from one owner to another—even by way of alleged theft—should be important enough to claim the Caliph's attention. These "transactions," as he preferred to call them, were regrettable but not uncommon, and one had to make allowances for cases of necessity, as happened from time to time when his friends and family needed land. But Baghdad rarely got involved with local issues, and Abdullah ibn Rida had paid no attention to the rumors, until one morning when one of his sentries came to see him urgently.

"I'm sorry to disturb you, sir," the captain had said urgently. "But we have word that a convoy of soldiers was sighted on the road to Nishapur. They say it's not a large force, but it looks as if it's come from Baghdad."

Abdullah ibn Rida, who was looking forward to a day of leisure with his favorite concubine, was irritated.

"What about it?"

"They say that the Caliph's chief commander is at its head."

Abdullah was now fully alert.

Abu Ubaydah would not have been dispatched from Baghdad for a minor reason, and the governor's immediate thought was that the Caliph had got wind of the plots he and the heads of the neighboring districts had been hatching to escape Abbasid jurisdiction. If so, he was more than ready to hold his ground against the Caliph's delegation. He had no fear of the Caliph's armies; by all accounts they were engaged on the various fronts of the empire, and he doubted that the reportedly small number of soldiers in Abu Ubaydah's convoy would give him much trouble. Nevertheless, he was taking no chances and summoned the head of his soldiery.

"Our scouts say it is only a small force, sir. Do you really think they have come to fight us?" asked the captain, "that they'll head here from Nishapur?"

"Why not? Nishapur is not far, and I don't trust the people of Baghdad. I want us to be ready for whatever might happen. How are our outer defenses? How many soldiers can we call on?"

The captain hesitated, looking unconvinced, but did his best to comply. Abdullah ignored his obvious skepticism. The years he had been governor of Khorasan had given him a freedom of maneuver and independence he valued. He had become accustomed to conducting the affairs of his province without reference to the caliphate, which he increasingly regarded as irrelevant and a foreign imposition. He would resist any threat to the position he had created for himself, and to that end had assembled a small but well-trained local army to guard him. He had also built a network of powerful supporters among the local gentry who had frequently benefited from his favors.

To the governor's surprise, however, the delegation from Baghdad came no nearer to Merv. After a day or two, word reached Abdullah that Abu Ubaydah had reached Nishapur and was being hosted by Abdullah ibn Rida's sub-governor. Shortly after that, a message from Abu Ubaydah arrived telling Abdullah that he had come with letters of greeting from the Caliph and an assurance that Khorasan's tax debts to the central treasury had been suspended until such time as the provinces could pay.

For the past two years, the harvest had failed and the tax revenue from farmers had become erratic. Provinces were required to pay a proportion of their tax revenue to Baghdad. But little had been forthcoming from Khorasan, and Abdullah had lived in fear of retribution. This was partly his reason for spearheading the movement to escape from Baghdad's control.

That the Caliph himself should now be making this unsolicited offer of financial relief to the governor's treasury was almost unbelievable, and Abdullah did not know whether to be pleased or wary. But then, on balance, he decided it was due to his deft maneuvering around the Caliph and his officials, always covering his tracks and being one step ahead. In that frame of mind, he decided to take Abu Ubaydah at his word and sent five of his men to Nishapur, ostensibly to receive the Caliph's letters, but in reality to spy out the situation and report back.

In the days that followed, he waited anxiously for them to return with the letters, or to at least send word. Even making allowances for the distance to Nishapur, a three-day journey to the south of Merv, he still expected some response in the time they had been away.

When nothing happened, he began to get worried and started thinking about going to Nishapur himself with a deployment of his best soldiers. But before he could take further steps, his scouts reported that Abu Ubaydah himself was riding toward Merv and was not far away. Mystified and apprehensive, Abdullah rode out to meet him.

As Abu Ubaydah approached the city gate, he waved to the governor and smiled, with all evidence of friendship. As he slowed his horse to a halt alongside that of Abdullah, he stood up in the saddle and leaned over to embrace him. Abdullah, taken aback, did likewise.

"*Al-salam-u-aleikum!*" declared Abu Ubaydah.

"And peace upon you too, commander! You are most welcome in Merv," rejoined Abdullah with strained enthusiasm.

The contingent of men he could see behind Abu Ubaydah did not look small to him, but he couldn't be sure. He turned his horse around and indicated for Abu Ubaydah to go in front. The other man insisted it was Abdullah who should precede him, only for Abdullah to refuse and ask that the commander should go first.

This elaborate back-and-forth made for a great spectacle and the people cheered. It had been a long time since so high a commander from Baghdad had visited them, and it was cause for much excitement. Despite the bonhomie, however, Abdullah remained wary, though he had to admit there was nothing to indicate that Abu Ubaydah meant him any harm. He even started to wonder if he had been too suspicious, as his captain had implied. They rode together toward his palace, where the visitors were invited to rest and offered delicious Persian food and pomegranate sherbet.

After they had eaten and drunk their fill—Abu Ubaydah, the sherbet, and Abdullah, the wine, which he imbibed in large quantities, being still nervous and unsure—Abu Ubaydah addressed his host.

"Now, Master Abdullah, I have brought our Caliph's greeting and letters from him to give to you. But first I would ask that your men leave us, for these matters are private and intended for you only."

Abdullah was surprised at this. But he nodded at his attendants and sentries, who left the room. Meanwhile, those of Abu Ubaydah's men who had come into the dining chamber with their commander remained. Abdullah wanted to point this out, but seeing Abu Ubaydah unroll the Caliph's letter and prepare to read it, he said nothing.

"To the thief and traitor, Abdullah ibn Rida," intoned Abu Ubaydah sonorously, as if he were the Caliph himself suddenly incarnated before them. "You are charged with offenses against the office of the caliphate and against me personally, working to subvert my authority by encouraging sedition and treachery among my people. You are not only a traitor, but also a thief who has connived in transferring lands rightfully belonging to the Banu Shaaban over to your thieving friends."

Abu Ubaydah paused to draw breath, while Abdullah stood pale and disbelieving, trying desperately to clear his head of its alcoholic fog.

Abu Ubaydah continued.

"You are hereby instantly dismissed from your position, honors, and offices, which you will relinquish to your successor, and all the wealth you have accumulated will be confiscated forthwith. I have appointed my commander, Abu Ubaydah, to arrest your secretaries, agents, guards, and anyone who stands in the way of our decree and to bring you in chains to me in Baghdad."

Before Abdullah could do anything, Abu Ubaydah's soldiers had jumped forward, seized him, and shackled his arms and legs. They put a robe around him and with a soldier on each side, made him walk, dragging his chained feet forward as best he could along the ground.

Once outside, he could see that his guards had been overpowered by the Caliph's men, while terrified slaves looked on helplessly from the shadows. Abu Ubaydah's men marched Abdullah out of the palace and toward the horses. His soldiery had not sprung to his aid, as he had expected, and all his plans and strategies had come to nothing.

⊞

Only gradually had he come to understand the extent of his folly in thinking he could outwit the Caliph. He learned that Abu Ubaydah had carefully laid the ground for his arrest well before coming to see him at Merv, feigning friendship. Abdullah's emissaries to Nishapur had been taken captive, and Abu Ubaydah had placed his men at strategic points on the route to Merv and appointed new district heads in place of those who supported Abdullah.

The commander's last act as they left for Baghdad, and Abdullah's final humiliation, was the appointment of a new governor to replace him, one of the hated *Abna'*, descendants of members of the original Abbasid armies that had lifted the Abbasid caliphate to power—and ever loyal to the Caliph.[*]

---

[*]   The *Abna'*, meaning the Sons, were descendants of members of the original Abbasid armies that had secured the rise of the Abbasid caliphate to power, and mostly lived in Baghdad. The landowners and aristocratic families of Khorasan disliked and distrusted them.

PART III

PART III

17

When he returned to Baghdad, Abu Ubaydah won many accolades for his prowess in having trapped the notoriously devious and slippery governor of Khorasan, and the Caliph bestowed great honors on him. Abdullah was brought to the Caliph in chains, disgraced, and sent to prison, an object lesson in punishment widely publicized to deter any others from contemplating a similar treachery. The offender had been spared from execution to make him a living reminder of the dire consequences of rebellion. It was a vain hope, the Caliph and his ministers knew; autonomous rebellions were constantly erupting in far-off parts of the empire. But it might serve to stem the tide for a while.

The Caliph resumed his daily meetings with his secretaries and military commanders, and everyone noticed how remarkably revived he was after his illness. He even managed to appear interested in the field reports of his generals.

"Now that the governor of Khorasan has been arrested, where have we got to in the matter of land restoration to the Banu Shaaban, Abu Ubaydah?"

"I'm pleased to say, my lord, that we were able to arrange for a return of the land, and I can report that the transfer will take place shortly."

The Caliph smiled with satisfaction, imagining Abdulhamid's delight when he heard the news. Seeing his master so energized, Abu Ubaydah wondered if it was the Caliph's approaching nuptials that had brought about this remarkable change. If that was so, he was glad of it, but of nothing else about the marriage.

As soon as he heard about it, Abu Ubaydah had maintained a reserved silence and not joined in the congratulations of the other officials. A memory connected with the bride gnawed at him. He knew it was something important, but also unpleasant, and had a feeling that a marriage to a daughter of the Banu Shaaban was not one the Caliph should contemplate. Abu Ubaydah knew he would worry at it until he remembered. In the meantime, his spies should make enquiries about the family, and, if it turned out as he feared, he would have to inform his master and warn him off a course of action he might come to regret.

Abu Ubaydah's reluctance to mention the marriage and his obvious lack of enthusiasm for it, so unlike that of his colleagues, had not escaped the Caliph's attention. It added to his growing realization that his matrimonial plans were a cause for concern not just to his wives. He thought back over his last encounter with Hind. It had left him with a lingering regret, and however much she deserved it in his estimation, he disliked having had to be cruel to her. Some show of enthusiasm on the part of others around him would have ameliorated these feelings. But everywhere he looked he found muted responses and little comment. His stepmother, however, had not been slow to voice her criticisms to his face.

"My son, you should not honor this girl by marrying her," Khadija had said to him. "She is from a low family and too far beneath you. Remember your wives, each one of high birth and good standing. This girl is a passing dalliance no one would blame you for desiring. Marry another woman if you wish, but you should set her aside," she sighed. "I can't deny that your father took many concubines, including your mother. But he never married any of them."

Khadija had been good to him as a child, although he knew she held it against him that he was born to her rival, one of lesser rank whose appeal for her husband she had resented. Not only that, but this concubine's son had taken the place of her own, and she had never really forgiven him for that either. He understood her feelings, and although her objections hurt him, he could expect nothing else from her.

But it was the reactions of the others close to him he could not explain. While Idris might be worried about the effect of the Caliph's new liaison on the women of the harem, whom he had long served and was probably attached to, what had Durayd, his chamberlain, or Abu Hisham, his chief wazir, against this marriage? They had congratulated him politely enough and wished him well in the usual manner, but otherwise maintained a near silence over the whole subject. It puzzled and concerned him. Finally, he turned to Uthman, his secretary and the person who had been entrusted with the task of asking for Murjana's hand in his name. In addition, Uthman was one of those who had shown enthusiasm for the Caliph's betrothal.

"Don't be afraid to tell me the truth, Uthman. I value your common sense in this matter and rely on you to be my eyes and ears. What do my officials have against the marriage I have chosen… Or is it the lady Murjana who is the cause of these objections?" he added, mindful of his stepmother's words.

Uthman was uncomfortable at the Caliph's request. He did not want to be put in a position that was more properly someone else's. After all, it was the chamberlain's duty to deal with such delicate matters, not a secretary's, and he told the Caliph so.

"Perhaps it's Durayd you should ask, my lord. He will know what the problem is and be candid with you, I'm sure."

The Caliph brushed this aside impatiently. "If I thought he'd help, I wouldn't have asked you. Now I think you should tell me what you know."

Uthman sighed.

"Well, my lord, I can speak about the discomfort of your chamberlain and ministers, but not of Idris. I don't know why he objects. But as for the others, there has been talk about the lady Murjana's family."

"Do they say that it's low class? Is that it?"

"Not exactly. It's to do with her uncle's closeness to the imam, and the likely influence he has on her and her brothers."

"They might be close for all I know," the Caliph frowned. "But what do they say is wrong with that?"

Uthman could not believe that the Caliph did not know. It was more likely a ruse to draw him out further, as was the Caliph's way, to listen rather than talk. He decided to confide all that he had heard.

"The lady's uncle, who is a strong-willed man, as it seemed to me when I met him, is devoted to the imam and consults him on many matters. It is said, my lord, he bears a grudge against you and your family for what he claims is unfair treatment of the imam, and all the imams who went before him, and it's feared he doesn't mean you well. He's spoken out many times against the imam's confinement, for which he blames you entirely, and it's rumored he was not agreeable to your offer of marriage to his niece."

"Continue."

"Well, with all that, my lord," Uthman was anxious not to exaggerate his account to the Caliph, "your ministers are concerned that your bride may have been influenced to...to..." The secretary hesitated, afraid to say too much.

"To do me harm?" the Caliph finished the sentence for him, bursting out laughing. "Yes, I see what troubles them. My chamberlain and chief minister have vivid imaginations and are given to much fancy," he laughed again. "Inform them, Uthman, that I have no such fears. What my ancestors were forced to do in the name of ensuring the safety of the state and protecting its authority against dissent and division is now long past. The imam knows, even if Abdulhamid doesn't, that I have no personal animosity toward him or his followers. He is free to receive whoever he likes and to say whatever he likes on all matters, other than to question the authority of the state. In fact, I respect and value the imam's knowledge and wisdom on many matters. Indeed, he and I could be friends."

And then the Caliph concluded, "None of them has anything to fear from me. As for Abdulhamid, he came to me with a request for restitution of land owing to him."

Uthman well remembered that morning of the Caliph's diwan and the arrival of the tall, green-robed elderly man and his beautiful niece.

"That land will now be restored to his family in accordance with his request. So you see, Uthman, it's not as my chamberlain and ministers think. Please tell them so, and let me hear no more of worries and fears and disquiets. My marriage is a cause for joy and happiness, and I want you all to celebrate it and spread the good news everywhere."

But despite the self-confidence he had shown his secretary, the Caliph was uneasy. It did not please him that a course of action he had decided on should be so overhung with doubts and criticisms. A man as much in love as he wanted the whole world to rejoice with him, to wish him well, to applaud his good fortune in finding a happiness given to very few. He wanted everything to run smoothly from the first moment, without hitch or mishap. In this he cared little for the fears of his officials and felt that in some magical way his life would be untroubled from the moment of his wedding and long after into the future.

Nevertheless, there remained a kernel of doubt inside him, as if there was indeed something to worry about, though he did not know what it was. It was inconceivable that Murjana could wish him ill, but what of the people around her? Her brothers had come to the palace and paid their respects, and they had seemed sincere enough. As for Abdulhamid, he was certainly reserved and difficult to like, but harmless, even if he did hold a grievance against the Caliph's ancestors. Such maunderings were the hobby of old men who lived in the past, and meant little more.

However, the niggling doubt remained, and he decided to consult the one man who understood him and whose advice he totally trusted.

▣

Abu Mansour had not visited the palace for some weeks, receiving almost daily reports about the Caliph's health from the palace doctors. As these were always satisfactory, and the Caliph had not summoned him, he was content to be left to attend to his patients, his drug dispensing, and his writing.

His medical compendium, based on the notes he made during his clinical practice, was progressing well. It looked as if it would run to several volumes of detailed descriptions of the diseases he came across and the treatments he used to help the mutatattibs who would use it. So, when a summons came from the palace, he was least expecting it and immediately wondered if something had happened to the Caliph.

When he arrived at the Golden Gate, the Caliph was waiting to greet him. "Salam, Abu Mansour. I'm very glad to see you."

The Caliph did not look as well as when Abu Mansour had last seen him. He was pale and his cheeks were beginning to lose a little of their roundness. One had to remember that his disease was in remission for the time being, but only in anticipation of his marriage. It would not remain so for much longer. The disease

148

of love was as insidious and pernicious a condition as any he had ever dealt with, and Abu Mansour was conscience-stricken that he had left the Caliph unattended for so long.

It was obvious the man was preoccupied, but with something other than his health. Barely waiting for the attendants to leave, he invited Abu Mansour to sit down, and, not pausing to engage in the usual polite preambles, he launched straightaway into an account of what he had heard from his secretary regarding his proposed marriage and the general unease among his officials.

"My agents have been watching Abdulhamid's house and that of the imam, and have reported nothing suspicious. So I don't believe what my officials say. But I wish they'd never raised these doubts, and it's led me to consult you, Abu Mansour."

He looked troubled.

"If you don't believe them, what do you fear?"

The Caliph looked into the doctor's eyes. But he did not answer his question directly.

"Tell me honestly, Abu Mansour, and setting aside my love for Murjana, of which you know more than anyone, do I have any option but to marry her?"

The question took Abu Mansour by surprise. He did not reply immediately.

"I can only speak as your physician, my lord. And as your physician, it is my firm view that you have no choice but to be intimate with the lady, and, given her situation, that is best ful-filled by marriage. It is essential for your health to do this, in fact for your very survival. So, no, you have no choice, and you should marry as soon as you can."

Privately, he wondered if it was the officials' anticipated loss of influence over the Caliph as a result of the marriage that they really objected to.

The Caliph looked relieved, but Abu Mansour sensed he had not fully answered the question. The Caliph had wanted reassurance that marrying Murjana was not a caprice. But it was evident he had other doubts surrounding her that Abu Mansour had not stilled. What they were, the doctor could not imagine, and neither at that time could the Caliph.

□

Meanwhile, and far away from the palace, Abdullah ibn Rida festered in his prison cell, brooding on his plight and planning his revenge. He intended to bribe his way out of prison as soon as possible. He had money, embezzled over the years from Khorasan's taxes, and he would use it to good effect. He would find accomplices, among disaffected Shia rebels if need be. The Caliph, like all absolute rulers, had enemies everywhere, and he would find them. Working with them, Abdullah would do the Caliph great damage, and through it, wipe out his humiliation for good.

□

When the summons came from the palace for Abdulhamid and his family to attend on the Caliph, they guessed it might be connected with their lands in Khorasan. But for a moment, a wild hope sprang up inside Abdulhamid that the Caliph had had a change of heart about Murjana and wanted to abandon his proposal to her. No arguments on the part of Murjana and her brothers, nor even the imam's, had succeeded in persuading him to accept the impending marriage, and he had gone on stubbornly searching for ways to escape it. He asked Murjana if she or her brothers had received any word from the Caliph he did not know about, but they had not. He confided his hopes to them that the Caliph's summons might mean the end of their ordeal.

Standing now before the Caliph in the audience chamber, Abdulhamid could only feel how puny his anger and his hatred was in the face of the majestic man who waited to greet them.

A feeling of helplessness in the presence of power came over him. This was the first time he was meeting the Caliph after the latter's illness and in the shadow of the imminent change in their relationship if the marriage proceeded. More than ever, he longed to hear that the Caliph had reversed his decision and would set Murjana and the family free. Seeing a tall, strongly built man standing beside the Caliph, as well as the secretary Abdulhamid remembered from his visit to their house with the Caliph's marriage proposal, he was not so sure.

"Greetings to you all! I have good news which should gladden your heart, Abdulhamid, and I hope the rest of your family."

The Caliph gestured for them to sit down.

"You first came to me asking for my help in reclaiming your land." Abdulhamid well recalled that original visit to the palace and how it had led them to this accursed pass. He felt a sense of acute disappointment.

"This is my commander, Abu Ubaydah," said the Caliph, indicating the tall man beside him. "He will tell you the rest of the story."

Abu Ubaydah explained how he had confronted the governor of Khorasan and forced him to acknowledge the theft of the Banu Shaaban's land, after which its fraudulent landlords were evicted. All that was left was for the Banu Shaaban to repossess it.

At this news, and despite all his reservations, Abdulhamid could not help but feel an irrepressible surge of joy, and also of gratitude. Yet, how could he be grateful to such a man as the Caliph? Had he helped them out of magnanimity, or because he had set his sights on Murjana even at that early time? Was it all a ruse to win Abdulhamid's agreement to what would happen next?

"Look on it as my first wedding gift to you and the family."

There was no response until Murjana stood up.

"My lord, my uncle and brothers are overwhelmed, or they would be thanking you before me."

Hamza nodded and Yazan blushed. They looked awkward and unpolished, and it embarrassed her.

"I cannot express my gratitude enough for your generosity in giving us back our inheritance. Your kindness overwhelms me just as much as it does my family." She looked so charming with her modest attire and gentle voice that the Caliph had to look away to control his emotions. Murjana's words had also broken through her uncle's reserve, and he now rose and bowed stiffly before the Caliph.

"My lord, I thank you with all my heart. You have been our champion and protector, and neither I nor my family will ever forget your benevolence."

"Thank you. But isn't that as it should be between relatives?" replied the Caliph.

Abdulhamid repressed a slight internal shudder.

"Now, Uthman, please take our friends and help them with the administrative work needed for the land transfer. Abu Ubaydah here will assist you."

When the chamber had emptied but for Murjana, whom the Caliph had asked to stay behind with her uncle's permission, he led her to the cushioned seats set against the wall, took her hands, and kissed them. She could see he was making an effort to be restrained.

"I've missed you so much, I'm almost in pain. I can't hold out much longer until we are together as man and wife."

Like the time before, she forgot everything her brother told her, and was filled instead with the thrill of being in the Caliph's presence. For a moment, she wondered excitedly if he would kiss and embrace her as he had done the last time, and was slightly disappointed when he didn't.

"Murjana, I want to tell you that I've divorced my wife, Hind, and can now marry again. So you mustn't have any worries on that score."

It had never even occurred to Murjana to wonder about his wives or whether he would divorce or not. She simply accepted that he was the Caliph and all powerful to do as he pleased.

"Everything is prepared for our marriage. But there is something you must know, my dearest. It pains me to tell you, so forgive me, but it must be said. My chamberlain and others around me are not happy about our marriage. They say your uncle has no love for me and perhaps does not wish me well."

Murjana blanched. She felt like a child who had been caught stealing. How would she deal with this? What should she say to the Caliph?

"I don't expect you to answer for your uncle," the Caliph said, taking her hand in his. "But I was sure you would know if there was anything to these rumors. Is there?"

She thought it best to say as little as she could get away with. "My uncle is a difficult man, my lord, and he takes against many people. But he does not wish you ill. I would swear to that."

He kissed her fingers.

"I won't upset you with more questions, my love, but there is one other thing. Your uncle's close to the imam, I'm told, and holds it against me that I may have treated him badly. Have you heard talk of such things from your uncle?"

Murjana felt trapped. She feared that the Caliph knew more than he admitted to and wondered when his questioning would lead him to her and her brother.

"No, no," she said a little too quickly and emphatically. "My uncle often speaks of the past and gets upset when he remembers bad things, that is his way. But there's no more to it than that."

The Caliph believed her. Her large eyes radiated innocence, and they melted away his doubts.

"No more questions, my dearest love. You and I will soon be together, and no rumor, no suspicion, will ever separate us."

18

The wedding was set for the twelfth of Rabi' al-Thani, two weeks away. The Caliph had instructed that the wonderful news be proclaimed far and wide. But at the Dar al-Huram, none of the women thought the news was wonderful.

It wasn't that the wedding was a surprise to them. The Caliph's wives were already resigned to his marriage. But the prospect of a new wife arriving to live among them, with him either visiting her daily and avoiding them, or she leaving them to go to him, was hard to stomach. There had been no new rival to any of them for many years, and they had grown comfortable with their situation. One or two would have wanted to attend the wedding out of curiosity, had any of them been invited. That they had not was another of the indignities now pushed upon them as discarded women.

For Hind it was different. She did not include herself among the cast-off wives any more now than she had ever done. After the Caliph announced his intention to divorce her, he had sent a message to her family in Mecca. Then, not waiting for their response or their efforts at reconciliation, as was the custom before a couple broke apart, he had divorced her in a simple one-sentence repudiation, all that was required by sharia law.

Sent to her by letter, it read:

"*I divorce you.*"

Nothing more. It was cruel and it was final. She had no close relative in Baghdad to whom she could turn when this happened, except for a distant uncle. So she consoled herself with the thought that the Caliph might change his mind before the three months of '*iddah* were ended.[*] After a while, that consolation turned into a conviction that he would think better of his infatuation with the Banu Shaaban girl, since it was nothing more in her view, and return to her.

The days passed without word from him, and she had no way of knowing what was happening in the palace except through Idris and the visitors to the Dar al-Huram, whose gossip she did not trust. Since the head eunuch made no mention of any new marriage, she began tentatively to hope once more. Idris noticed her revive and take an interest in her appearance again. She smiled and began to eat and chat in the old way. The other wives had stopped talking about the Caliph's marriage, and life slowly went back to normal. If they pitied Hind for what they saw as her vain hope for the Caliph's return, they didn't show it. Though it was only weeks since that cruel meeting with him, to Hind it felt like a lifetime ago and she wanted to forget.

So the wedding announcement, coming in the midst of this newfound optimism, was a shattering blow to her, and the loss of hope this time was unbearable. '*Iddah* or no, in her grief she made a decision. She would leave her apartments and the palace altogether rather than stay on as the Caliph's castoff; she would not accept the sad resignation as the other wives had. First, she would go to her uncle's house in Baghdad, even if she

---

[*] This period of three menstrual cycles was obligatory on Islamic divorce in case the woman was pregnant, in which case the husband was obliged to accept responsibility for the child. It was also a time in which the couple could get back together without the need for remarriage, so providing an opportunity for reconciliation.

hardly knew him, and then return to her family in Mecca soon after that.

⊞

Hind was not alone in her unhappiness at the Caliph's marriage. As she was making her plans to leave, elsewhere in the palace a conclave of the Caliph's closest advisors—his chamberlain Durayd, his chief wazir Abu Hisham, the head eunuch Idris, and the palace doctor Suleiman—gathered in earnest discussion. There also was Uthman, the Caliph's personal secretary, who normally would have been considered too junior for such a meeting. But he had been the Caliph's messenger to the Banu Shaaban, and the information he could provide about the family was likely to be important.

Turning to the palace doctor, Abu Hisham asked him, "In your medical view, Suleiman, do you think our master is sufficiently recovered to do without this marriage now?"

Suleiman had not liked taking a backseat when Abu Mansour was appointed the Caliph's personal physician in his place. Nor was he certain that the remedy prescribed for the Caliph's malady was any longer the best one. Although, if he were honest, he would have to admit this was not based on medical opinion, but on prejudice and emotion. For if the Caliph's illness returned, it was Abu Mansour who would be blamed.

"In my view our master is now recovered. He has no need of this marriage or this young woman. But he has been persuaded by others that his permanent cure will only happen in that way."

"Well then, perhaps we should ask Abu Mansour to release him from this illusion," suggested Durayd, understanding what he meant. "Would you talk to him, Suleiman?"

That was not something the doctor had in mind at all. He had imagined the Caliph's chief wazir would do it and had no confidence that, given his strained relations with Abu Mansour, he himself would be successful.

Then Idris spoke up for the first time.

"The Caliph will not change his mind. He didn't hesitate to divorce the lady Hind, his favorite wife and the one who has been his favorite among the women for years. I never thought he could do such a thing. But I believe he's determined to marry the Banu Shaaban daughter and will not be deterred."

Everyone knew of the head eunuch's closeness to the Caliph and his almost feminine intuition with regard to his master's needs and emotions. The chief wazir pursed his lips determinedly.

"Even so, he must be deflected. It is not in his or the state's interest for him to contract this marriage. Durayd knows what our agents have uncovered about the Banu Shaaban. The loyalty of a family so close to the imam, whose sons have sympathies with the rebels outside Baghdad, cannot be relied on."

"But the Caliph already knows that," said Uthman. "He told me so himself, and he ordered me to inform you that he has no concerns about the Banu Shaaban or the imam." He recounted his conversation with the Caliph.

They digested this silently. "So," Uthman said finally, "What actual harm could come to him from marrying this girl?"

"She's a source of influence over him," explained Durayd patiently, as if to a child. "She could come with secret instructions from her family or the imam to hurt him or expose him to danger from his enemies among them. She could spy on him and tell them what she hears at the palace, which might be to their advantage. The people of the imam are not our friends, Uthman, and I don't understand why our master is so complacent."

Abu Hisham agreed. "However good the Caliph's spies are, they wouldn't be able to pick up on things like that. We can't leave the Caliph unprotected, no matter what he says."

Everyone nodded, but they couldn't decide what to do. The more they discussed it, the more hopeless it all seemed. In the end, they managed to agree that an attempt must at least be made to cancel the marriage, especially now that the wedding date was so imminent. Durayd and Abu Hisham would speak to the Caliph, and Suleiman would approach Abu Mansour. Much to his relief, Idris was not included in these plans. He feared that the passion with which he would have tried to dissuade the Caliph from marrying, and seeing Hind happy once again as a result, would reveal his feelings for her. Never before had there been a rival in his devotion to the Caliph, but Hind, with her beauty and her sad helplessness and grief, had touched his heart and made him love her.

Suleiman was reluctant to face Abu Mansour. Though he would never admit it, he was intimidated by the other man's superior knowledge and greater medical skills. The collegiate relations they had briefly developed over the Caliph's illness had ended with his recovery. He wrote to Abu Mansour, asking him to dissuade the Caliph from the marriage, since his recovery had made the medical need for it redundant.

Abu Mansour had no difficulty refuting the other doctor's arguments, and made clear that the Caliph's marriage would have to go ahead for the sake of his health, and that Suleiman should have been the first to know that. Suleiman had known it was no use approaching Abu Mansour, and he smarted from the insult in his response. He could only hope the others would fare better.

They did not. The Caliph was incensed that his chamberlain and chief wazir should presume to tell him how to conduct his personal affairs. He dismissed their anxieties as unfounded rumors, and accused them of taking him for some half-witted provincial governor who knew nothing of what went on under his own nose.

They were alarmed. Their project had gone badly wrong. But it wasn't fair of the Caliph to have reacted like that, said Abu

Hisham afterward. Their suspicions about the Banu Shaaban were not gossip, he insisted, but based on their agents' reports, and these made clear the family's association with elements hostile to the Caliph. It was true that no one had been caught red-handed yet, but surely what they had learned was evidence enough to justify their concerns.

Durayd was quiet for a moment. "Whatever proof we can provide, our master won't believe it because he doesn't want to."

"So, does that mean we can do nothing?" asked Abu Hisham. "What happens if our fears turn out to be justified and the Caliph comes to harm? Won't we be the first to be held responsible? Surely we can't just stand by and let that happen."

"We won't, Abu Hisham, never fear," Durayd replied firmly. "But it will make it the more important for us to be extra vigilant, and suspicious of his new wife and her family. We have no other choice."

◫

Abu Ubaydah was usually cool-headed, one reason why he was such a successful general. His men respected his patient, calm authority and shrewd military sense. But on that particular morning when preparations for the Caliph's wedding were already moving ahead, he felt those qualities had deserted him as he waited restlessly to hear from the men he had sent to investigate the Banu Shaaban.

They were certainly taking their time, he thought, and it annoyed him, although in fairness they were working according to the usual schedule of well-tried methods. They had posed as door-to-door peddlers, beggars, and itinerant laborers, frequenting the family's neighborhood and befriending the people who lived there.

Doing so, they were able to observe and track the comings and goings of the Abu Shaaban household, follow Abdulhamid and his nephews wherever they went, and even tail the old servant's movements. Occasionally, they saw a veiled young woman emerge from the house with a servant, but they didn't bother with her, assuming it was the men of the household who were of interest to Abu Ubaydah.

More than a week had passed without word from Talha, the man Abu Ubaydah had made the head of the spy team, a ruffianly former soldier with coarse manners but sharp intelligence, on whom Abu Ubaydah depended for many of his secret missions.

Talha had been in Abu Ubaydah's service for many years. In his youth, he had proved a reliable foot soldier, and so the commander promoted him. He later accepted his retirement from active service due to a leg injury he had sustained in battle that became troublesome. Having noted his streetwise astuteness and native intelligence, Abu Ubaydah transferred him to work as an agent, which he relished and was successful at doing. It had struck Abu Ubaydah more than once that, had he set Talha onto the governor of Khorasan, instead of the dolts he had employed, Abdullah ibn Rida would have been apprehended much sooner.

"Well, Talha, where have you and your men got to with the assignment I gave you? I told you I wanted the information as soon as possible. What's holding you up, or are you spinning out the time to get more pay? If you are, let me tell you, you won't get anything at all unless you give me the information I need. You have another two days, and then it's over, whether you find anything or not."

A vague sense of urgency had dogged Abu Ubaydah ever since he had learned the name of the girl the Caliph intended to marry. He was certain the unease it stirred in him was significant. But he couldn't pin down exactly why or recall where he had come across the Banu Shaaban before. He was strictly acting on a hunch and kept the matter to himself, pending the outcome. If it turned out he was wrong and there was nothing to justify his fears, then no one would know. But time was short, and the Caliph's wedding was soon to take place. He made it his mission to solve the riddle before that happened.

The deadline passed. Finally, Talha arrived at the military barracks adjacent to the palace. From there he was taken to Abu Ubaydah's quarters. Making his soldier's salute even though he was no longer in active combat, he stood to attention before Abu Ubyadah.

"I have nothing to report," Talha growled.

He was a short man with broad shoulders and thick arms. His coarse, bushy beard was untrimmed, and his tunic and over-robe were grubby. Sometimes Abu Ubaydah wondered why he kept putting up with him.

"All right, Talha, at ease. Sit down and make your report."

The man coughed, phlegm rising in his chest. He wiped his mouth with his sleeve and cleared his throat noisily. He could see Abu Ubaydah was displeased and it upset him. Beneath his gruff exterior, he was devoted to the general and wanted his approval at all times.

"As you instructed, Abu Ubaydah, we watched the Banu Shaaban day and night."

It was his custom to address all superior officers, even Abu Ubaydah, directly by their names without using the conventional titles of "sir" or "commander." It was his crude way, and Abu Ubaydah was used to it. "Problem was, the Caliph's men were doing the same thing. We didn't know who they were at first and nearly beat them up. But when we found out, we worked out an agreement with them so we wouldn't interfere with one another, if you see what I mean."

Talha chuckled, clearly having enjoyed the arrangement. But it irritated Abu Ubaydah.

"This wasn't supposed to be a game, Talha. The Banu Shaaban could easily have found you out and the Caliph's men with you. Did they?"

"They noticed nothing, I swear."

"And did you continue your assignment for me like that, you and the Caliph's spies working together, swapping information and covering breaks for each other, maybe cosily feasting together at my expense?" Abu Ubaydah was angry and disappointed.

"I swear on my father's life there was nothing of that," Talha said. "We worked hard, we saw everything they did, the neighbors told us all they knew. We had no more to do with the Caliph's men, nor they with us. We worked with no rest for ten days, I swear it."

His voice was hoarse, and he started to cough again.

Abu Ubaydah relented a little. He'd never known Talha to lie, despite his rough speech. "All right, what have you found out?"

"Whatever they're doing that's wrong, we couldn't find it. The old man went to see the imam a few times and his older nephew went with him once, but the other younger one didn't. He came here and met what we reckoned was his friend who works at the Barid, the post headquarters. He waited for him outside the palace gates, and then they went off to the souk. The girl went on a visit somewhere with her aunt once or twice. But no one did anything out of the ordinary."

"So, you've drawn a blank. Hmm..." Abu Ubaydah frowned in thought. "Are you sure there was nothing else you could have done?"

Talha pushed a dirty finger nail under his cap and scratched his hairline. He thought for a moment and then shook his head.

"No. If they're doing anything, they're hiding it very cleverly. Beyond us to find at any rate."

"All right. Thank you, Talha, and pass my thanks on to your men. You'll get your final payment when I've thought what to do and feel sure I need nothing more from you."

Abu Ubaydah was frustrated. He couldn't believe his hunch about the family was wrong. The sense of foreboding that had assailed him on hearing of the Caliph's wedding couldn't have been an accident. He or Talha must have missed something. For a moment, he considered watching the Banu Shaaban himself, but it was out of the question. Whatever disguise he wore, a large man like himself loitering anywhere near them would never go unnoticed.

There had to be something he could do. He worried at it overnight and into the next day, going over everything Talha had told him, but still came up with nothing. Finally, and in some desperation, he wondered about the younger Shaaban nephew, and if seeing him on his next visit to the palace might yield a clue. He wasn't sure what to look for, or how to get information from the boy once he saw him, but he could think of no other course of action, and perhaps if he just played it by ear some inspiration would come to him.

He ordered Talha back to his quarters and asked for exact details of the visits the Banu Shaaban nephew paid to the palace. But it seemed these were random and could not be anticipated. So, one of Talha's men, who had become familiar with the family, was stationed at the palace entrance to watch out for the young man.

Abu Ubaydah requested a list of workers at the Barid on the pretext that he was looking for former soldiers among them. Examining the list, he had no idea what he was expecting to find, but he scrutinized it carefully. None of the names meant a thing to him or gave any suggestion of who their associates might be. He could detect nothing unusual about any of them or their duties as inscribed in the Barid register. Nor was there any reason why he would. But then, the commander's duties were military ones; he'd never had—or wanted to have—anything to do with the bureaucracy of palace officials. Completely frustrated, he now wished he had.

Abu Ubaydah waited irritably for the Shaaban nephew to visit the palace. Then, as he was beginning to give up on his quest, his sentry ushered Talha in to see him. The man was breathless and his clothes more unkempt than usual.

"Got him! My man caught the Shaaban boy just as he was coming up to the outer gate. We're holding him in the stables."

"What! Who told you to do that? I only told you to let me know when he turned up."

"What if he ran off again while we went to find you?" Talha was hurt and surly. "It's a wonder we got him at all. A worker at the Barid named Khalid was waiting for him just inside the gate. The two of them seemed to be in a hurry."

"So, now Khalid's been dragged into this blunder, too?" Abu Ubaydah was even angrier. "I didn't want any of this to happen, don't you understand? I'm not pleased."

Talha was definitely not the man he used to be. Although Abu Ubaydah had to admit his agent had a point, and he was aware he had not been explicit enough in his instructions, he had always known Talha to be quick-witted enough to pick up what was really behind the orders he was given. He had never needed to have everything spelled out, and it occurred to the commander he might have to do without him sooner than planned.

"Talha, I want you to go to where you're holding the boy and explain that he was mistaken for someone else. Apologize to him and let him go. I'll go to the entrance and stand outside at the spot where you caught him. Make sure he walks past me as he leaves."

Talha still looked hurt but also skeptical, as if he thought the whole idea was stupid.

"That friend of his, Khalid, has gone to join him. What do I do with him?"

"Tell him the same thing. And apologize to him as well."

With that, Abu Ubaydah called for some of his senior soldiers to accompany him to the palace entrance. They picked their way through the antechamber to the barracks, cluttered with discarded armor, swords, riding boots, and saddles. As they walked out into the fresh air, a light drizzle was falling. Following Abu Ubaydah, they went toward the main gateway, where they stopped. He watched the palace entrance intently and waited.

Not long after, two young men came out with Talha behind them and walked past him. One was taller than the other and obviously older. Beneath his sleeveless robe he wore a short tunic over his sirwal, its collar and sides edged with black, the uniform of junior palace employees. That must be Khalid, thought Abu Ubaydah. But it was the younger companion who arrested his attention.

The boy's features, his gestures, and his facial expressions evoked a memory so unpleasant it instantly jogged Abu Ubaydah into recalling what had eluded him for weeks. It vindicated his plan to see the Shaaban nephew, far-fetched and pointless though it had seemed, even to himself. It was not the boy himself who captured his attention but his striking resemblance to another man whom Abu Ubaydah recalled as older, darker, and more thickly built. That man must have been a brother to this boy, so close was the resemblance, and Abu Ubaydah vividly remembered the pugnacious and fanatical rebel he had met.

For more than a year the man had managed to elude the Caliph's soldiers before he was finally captured by Abu Ubaydah's troops, who had been recalled from Khorasan to quash the rebellion. Abu Ubaydah did not normally register the names or faces of the dissidents who fought in the uprisings and rebellions his soldiers had to put down. To him they were anonymous outlaws who had to be eradicated like vermin. But on that occasion, and contrary to his usual habit, he had been moved to speak to a few of the ringleaders, curious to understand what had motivated them to risk what would be certain imprisonment or death.

He particularly remembered the man who resembled the Shaaban boy, his fanaticism and extreme hostility toward the Caliph. He seemed intelligent and cultured, and Abu Ubaydah had tried to talk him out of his recalcitrant ways, promising him leniency if he would explain what his grievance was against the Caliph. The man had looked at Abu Ubaydah with crazed, blood-shot eyes and shouted at him.

"He's a tyrant like all his ancestors, and cannot lead the Muslims in righteousness. Only our imams have that authority." He spat in Abu Ubaydah's face. "You will never understand. You're just his servant, stupid and ignorant like all the rest. You only know how to kill and oppress in his name."

The man's vehemence shook the commander. This was no ordinary rebel, and he continued trying to speak to him. But the man remained obdurate.

Soon after he managed to escape until, in a final ambush outside the city, he was caught, and, together with many of his fellow rebels, he was put to the sword. The uprising was merci-lessly crushed. When the news of his men's success reached Abu Ubaydah, they brought him the heads of the ringleaders. The man's grotesquely grinning face among the decapitated heads—as if still mocking Abu Ubaydah—was unmistakeable. The executed man's name was Yahya ibn Shaaban. The connections that had eluded Abu Ubaydah for weeks seemed to snap into place.

But facial resemblance, however suggestive, was not defin-itive proof. Abu Ubaydah asked his men to find out discreetly from Khalid at the Barid if his friend, Yazan ibn Shaaban, had any brothers and other family details. They could say that a new palace ruling required all friends of employees to be checked for safety reasons.

Whether Khalid believed them or not, he was too frightened to disobey. He only knew that Yazan's eldest brother, Yahya, was dead. But it was enough to confirm Abu Ubaydah's suspicions.

With this discovery, terrible thoughts crowded into Abu Ubaydah's head. The woman the Caliph was about to marry was none other than the rebel's sister. And the sinister plot that would soon engulf the Caliph became suddenly clear. His master was in danger, and there was no time to waste.

He would go at once with the information he had and alert the Caliph. Whatever happened, the wedding had to be stopped.

19

As her wedding day drew near, Murjana was both nervous and excited. Careful to show her brother only the nervousness, she hid from him the tremulous anticipation she was also feeling. She knew she should take no pleasure in her forthcoming union with the Caliph who, she kept telling herself, was their enemy, but she could not help it. To her uncle she said little. He preferred to be alone or to visit the imam, and in any case was morose and quiet, behaving like a man grieving for a recently deceased relative.

When the dressmakers and seamstresses from the Dar al-Tiraz, the palace's weaving and embroidery quarters, arrived at the house to make her wedding dress, Murjana was thrilled. She knew she was not of the Caliph's household yet and did not merit that privilege reserved for its royal members only. But the Caliph had ignored protocol and sent them to her just the same to fashion, as he instructed, the most sumptuous, most expensive, and most beautiful dress in the world. Only the finest silks from Khuzistan and the most resplendent brocades from Damascus would be used in its making; the smoothest Persian velvet would go to make her overgown, and the softest leathers would be cut by expert craftsmen to fashion her shoes.

As they spread out the rich fabrics before her, and asked which colors she favored, she could hardly speak. Their gorgeous hues lit up the drab room the dressmakers had grudgingly been assigned by Abdulhamid, and the precious stones that spilled out of the silver casket they opened to show her how her dress and shoes would be adorned imbued the atmosphere with a magical glow. When they described how the gown would look at the end, Murjana was filled with awe and delight.

"How wonderful!" enthused her cousin Ayesha, the only person she could confide in. "I can't wait to see it when it's finished." She had come to help Murjana choose her fabrics and designs. Something of a dressmaker herself, she understood the basics of sewing, but had no expertise in something as grand as the project underway. The girls spent their time mainly whispering to each other and giggling.

The color of material and choice of gem having been decided, the dressmakers measured up the bride and set about their work. The rest of the household kept out of the way, but Murjana could feel the weight of displeasure that emanated from them. Only Yazan surreptitiously shared her excitement, though he dared show none of it to his uncle or brother. She wished her mother, who had died in childbirth when she was seven, had been with her. It was certain that, along with everyone else, she would not have approved of the marriage. But Murjana felt in her heart her mother would have understood her dilemma and taken pity on her.

Such longings, however, were of no use. She was alone in the world, and no one could imagine the fears and anxieties she lived with. Her feelings for the Caliph were not allowed to be her own. They were driven by the will of others—on the one hand, the domination of the Caliph's desire for her, and on the other, the equal domination of her brother's hatred of him. Where her own needs and desires lay in all that she did not know, and she could only respond to the mood of the moment. Each visit of the palace dressmakers made her thrill with anticipation, and each time they went and she was alone, the weight of responsibility returned to dampen her mood.

□

The house of the Banu Shaban was transformed. Up until the Caliph's proposal of marriage, it had been a modest dwelling that suited the needs of Abdulhamid, his small family, and their few servants. But from the moment of that first visit the palace dressmakers made when they came to measure Murjana for her wedding dress, everything changed. The narrow alleyway where the house stood was soon choked with the workers from the Dar al-Tiraz, their horses, and baggage. The neighbors' lives were also transformed as they watched these happenings and gossiped about who came and went. They found trivial excuses to knock on the Banu Shaaban's door and make irrelevant offers of help. The truth was that none of them could understand why the family had been so favored by the Caliph. It was a mystery that provoked a lot of conjecture and not a little envy.

Abdulhamid did not like any of it. In a last pathetic attempt at resistance, he had countered the Caliph's wishes for Murjana to be fitted at the Dar al-Tiraz, which would have been easier for the staff and left the family undisturbed. The Caliph had acquiesced to his soon-to-be kinsman's request and sent the dressmakers to the Shaaban house instead. This turned out to be a mistake. Strangers began to appear in the Banu Shaaban's vicinity, and the family started to imagine they were being watched; the number of people wanting to sell them something or offering casual labor grew by the day. These suspicious occurrences made Abdulhamid so uneasy that after a while he allowed no one to go out, and they shut themselves in the house.

But his precautions did not stop the strange visits or the

constant prying, and by the time of the wedding, a positive invasion of palace dressmakers, jewelers, and shoemakers took over the house and made it virtually uninhabitable. None of the menfolk in the household felt able to enter the courtyard or the rooms, which were spread with fabrics, clothes, veils, shoes, and an array of jars, unguents, and perfumes. Abdulhamid escaped and spent most of his time at the imam's house, and Murjana's brothers, bemused by the proceedings, especially Yazan, hung about on the margins in an ineffectual show of family authority. The old servant offered drinks and cleared up after each visitation. He was stunned by the change in their surroundings, but not altogether displeased. To feel the dour atmosphere of the house enlivened by so much merry noise and so many people was a welcome change and made him wish it happened more often.

Murjana stood in the middle of what was now the sewing room, wearing her wedding gown. The dressmakers walked slowly around her, putting in last minute stitches, tucking in folds, and checking hems. The leather of her sandals was polished and its fastenings carefully aligned. The jewels adorning her head dress and gown were polished to a bright sparkle, and the kohl for her eyelids was prepared. A choice of perfumes for each part of her wedding day was assembled, and, finally satisfied, the dressmakers and their assistants disrobed the bride and packed everything away in large bags and caskets. The next time they would dress Murjana in all that finery was the wedding day itself.

When they had gone Murjana sat down, exhausted, leaned her head back against the wall and closed her eyes, her mind reliving the scenes she had just experienced. Despite her fatigue, she was exhilarated by the jumble of pleasurable thoughts and images that raced across her mind's eye. The scents of expensive perfumes that would anoint her body on the wedding day still hung in the air, and she breathed them in sensuously. The time was fast approaching when she would be the finest bride in the world, she thought extravagantly, when men and women would look upon her with wonderment and delight, and she abandoned herself to the anticipation of it.

Her eyes still closed, she heard the door handle of her room being quietly turned. She opened them to see Hamza steal into the room as if he did not want to disturb her sleep.

"Come in, brother. I am awake."

"I thought you'd be tired after all that fussing around and all those people."

He sat down on the cushions opposite her. Though his words sounded sympathetic, his face was unsmiling and his expression inscrutable. She could see he was not relaxed as he sat awkwardly with his back stiffly upright. The pleasure she had felt before he came rapidly ebbed away, and she waited for what would come next.

"I hope you're not letting yourself get carried away, Murjana. All those rich clothes and jewelry and pomp could go to your head. But you must resist."

She turned away in case he saw her dismay, but he seized her arm in a tight grip.

"You're carried away already, aren't you?"

She shook off his hand and composed herself.

"I can't lie and pretend that I don't like all those pretty things. I do, but it goes no further."

He stared into her face, searching for signs that she was deceiving him. She looked back steadily.

"I hope that's true. I don't want to have to remind you we have a mission. If it hadn't been for that, we would never have arranged for you to meet the Caliph in the first place, and none of this would be happening now. So don't flatter yourself that he would ever have wanted to marry you otherwise. Your duty is to keep him duped until you've earned his complete trust and you're well entrenched in the palace. And then we can get on with our real business."

She wanted to remind him he had arranged no meetings with the Caliph—they had been fortuitous coincidences. But she remained silent.

Hamza was short and slight. His complexion was sallow and his eyes close-set, his face bearing the ugly scars of smallpox contracted in childhood. He had always looked insignificant beside their older brother, Yahya, and Murjana used to feel that Hamza resented him for it.

Yahya was tall and well-built, his open face dark and handsome. He had loved and cherished her as if he had been her father. How she missed him and how she longed for him to be still alive. The loss of a brother so fine brought back the anger and despair she had felt at his death. It was not a day she could ever forget, and the memory of it now still made her shudder.

⊡

It was spring and the weather was mild. Yahya had been away on one of his trade journeys to Khorasan, or so he told their uncle. Her brother was employed by a family of merchants who dealt in ivory and metal and had a shop in the grand souk. They had taken on several apprentices, Yahya among them.

It was good work, and at first he made money for the family. But the competition with merchants selling similar products gradually reduced his employers' income to the point that it affected his own. His apprenticeship might have come to an end there and then but for the fortuitous establishment of the great pottery near the Golden Gate palace that saved them all.

The glazed ceramics the factory produced were much in demand, and the trade in such ceramics became ever more lucrative. In response, Yahya's merchants switched their business from ivory and metals to pottery. Noting an opportunity in the market, they changed to dealing not so much in the finished products as in cobalt and silver, the ingredients used to make the glaze.

Yahya and the other apprentices were sent on missions to buy blue cobalt from Khuzistan and silver and copper from Khorasan, which were then sold on to the royal kilns. The business was so successful that Yahya was promoted to commercial agent for the merchant family, and he was regularly traveling either overland to Persia or by river to the port of Basra, where he was commissioned to buy expensive porcelain imported from China for sale to wealthy clients. His uncle, seeing how well Yahya was doing, had observed, "It's time you thought of taking a wife, my son. You have enough means now to set up your own family." Yahya was his favorite nephew of the three, and while Abdulhamid was in no hurry to share him with a wife, he had a duty to his deceased brother to see his children settled. And so, he started to think of a suitable girl for him from among their friends. But Yahya resisted.

"I'm not doing as well as you think, Uncle. I need more time to establish myself, really, I do."

Outwardly, his behavior was unchanged, but all the time, and unknown to the family, he was becoming embroiled in a totally different project.

One of his fellow apprentices, a young man named Musa and another of the followers of Ali, introduced Yahya to a group of other young followers who had defected from the authority of the imam. They had set up makeshift, movable camps among the rich palm groves and orchards east of the Tigris where they joined the vagrants and outlaws who lived amongst the trees. There they preached a doctrine of resistance to the Caliph in Baghdad, and Yahya, reared by his uncle on a diet of resentment toward the Abbasids, was a willing disciple.

He started to frequent the dissidents' camp. Although he saw that there were men among them who were not followers of Ali at all but a collection of misfits, thugs, and beggars who had tagged on, it did not deter him. He met fiery young men who denounced the Caliph and his ancestors. They reviled what they called the godless tyranny of the caliphate, its profligacy and oppression of the poor, and they bemoaned the depths to which Islam had been brought by these "apostates." When the young men spoke of a new age of justice and piety that would ensue once the Caliph was overthrown, they aroused a fervor of idealism in Yahya he had not known existed in him, and he came to see them as more his brothers than those of his own blood.

The passions ignited within him could not remain hidden for long. He told his siblings about the new community he had found and the speeches they made, how their beliefs had become his own, and how he felt he belonged with them.

"Do you not love us anymore, dear Yahya?" Murjana had asked him, on the verge of tears.

He hugged her and ruffled her hair as he used to do when she was a little girl.

"Of course I do, I love you all. But I want you to see things through my eyes. Our father died serving the Caliph and left us orphans. Did the Caliph do anything to help us? Did he even know we existed? Had it not been for our uncle, where would we have been?"

"But it's not this Caliph who did that," said Yazan. "It was his father."

"Do you think this Caliph will be any more just or God-fearing than the rest of them?"

Hamza intervened.

"Why did your friends abandon our imam?"

"Because he only knows the way of peace and forgiveness, and that is not the Abbasid way. Where has the patience and fortitude he has preached for so long got us? Our people are in prison or afraid for themselves and their families. No. Battle is the only answer against these tyrants. When they are overthrown, a new era will begin. You'll see," he said, his eyes taking on a dreamy expression.

Murjana remembered how they had all looked at each other in the wake of Yahya's words. Where were these oppressed people Yahya talked about? Limited though her experience of life was, she did not see them around her or notice that things were so bad. It was as if he perceived a world she did not, and wondered if her other brothers thought the same.

"What will you do now?" asked Hamza.

"I will join my friends and fight with them. It's the only honorable way. Why don't you come too?"

Yahya knew that was not possible. Hamza did not have the stamina needed for battle. He had been sickly since childhood and would not be able to withstand the physical demands of fighting. It was one of the things Hamza held against his elder brother, that Yahya should have been blessed with a strong constitution, while he, Hamza, was doomed to be as feeble as a woman.

"You fight if you want to. I have another way. After all, in the end we all want the Caliph gone, don't we? My route to that result is different to yours."

"Will you tell us what it is?"

Hamza shook his head slyly, as if implying his method was superior to the crude strategy of Yahya and his friends, and likely to be more effective. In reality, he had no plan at all, and just thought up something to say on the spur of the moment to assert himself in the face of his brother's authority. All this talk frightened Murjana. Yazan, being the youngest and unable to keep up with the conversation, just looked bewildered.

"Please don't leave us, Yahya. I am afraid for you."

"Don't be, Murjana. I need to do my duty, and with God's help it will end in success. Then I will come back and be with you all as before."

"But what shall we tell uncle?" she asked.

They knew Abdulhamid's views to be close to the imam's. He abhorred violence and preferred the peaceable approach, even though the imam's patience in the face of the authorities' aggression against those they called dissidents often struck him as excessive; and he had often thought that the imam should be more assertive. But in no case would he ever have condoned the course of action his nephew had espoused.

"I'll tell uncle I've gone on another of my trade trips, this time to Bukhara. The distance to there will explain my long absence, and in any case I'm due to go to Nishapur on my merchants' business. But in reality, you will all know I'm not far away from you."

"When will we see you again?" asked Yazan, who loved Yahya and was looking forward to being taken on as a junior apprentice to the same merchant family his brother worked for.

"It depends on the outcome of our battle with the Caliph's soldiers. We have reports that they're not up to the fight because they don't take us seriously, and they've left the youngest and most inexperienced recruits to man their positions." He chuckled confidently. "So, I don't expect to be away for long."

"Please, Yahya, don't do this. Don't go."

Some premonition told Murjana he was wrong and that only harm could come to him from this adventure.

"Dearest Murjana, have you forgotten what the caliphs have done? Have you forgotten their cruelty, the injustices and crimes they've committed against us? Should we stay silent in the face of their despotism?"

She looked down at her lap. If ever she even thought about the Caliph, who at the time she had never seen nor expected to see, it was only as a shadowy, sinister figure, rather as she might imagine Satan to be. In that way, she could understand her brother's position. She embraced him and gave him her blessing.

It was the last Murjana was to see of him. The fight with the Caliph's army did not go as her brother had expected. At first, the soldiers who had been sent to put down the rebellion were unsuccessful. They consisted mainly of mercenaries and former slaves, with little understanding of who they were fighting. They just knew that they had to defeat a bunch of rebels and outlaws who had defied the Caliph. Thinking the assignment would be short, they did not expect to meet the rebels' fierce resistance and were roundly defeated. Reinforcements soon arrived to bolster their efforts, with orders to kill or arrest the ringleaders, among whom Yahya had become prominent. But the rebels escaped each time, breaking up into small groups and hiding in the encampments that surrounded Baghdad, and after resting, regrouping for the next fight.

This went on for weeks, and Yahya was triumphant, as his side began to get the better of the Caliph's troops, who were finding they had no stomach for the skirmishes with the rebels. Unlike them, the rebels were highly motivated and passionate about their cause. On their side by contrast there was only apathy, and some soldiers had begun to filter back to the city, bored by the fight with hot-headed young men who could have been their own kin.

Emboldened by the relative lull in the fighting, Yahya's friends started preaching their mission once more, and found new recruits in the nearby villages. It was in this phase of rebel self-confidence, and as Yahya was thinking to return home and reassure his siblings about their progress, that Abu Ubaydah took charge. He dismissed the mercenaries and brought a battalion of his own Khorasani soldiers to the battle. But he could not deny he was surprised by the Caliph's orders to deploy the army for this fight. Small-scale uprisings like this one were commonplace and did not normally call for the attentions of a regular army.

"What is special about this uprising, my lord?" Abu Ubaydah

had inquired when called to attend on the Caliph. "These skirmishes are common among discontented subjects, and they flare up from time to time. Or is it that they've attached themselves to the Shiite dissidents this time?"

"My information is that followers of Ali have instigated the rebellion. We must crush them with enough force to extinguish their movement, and all others like it, for good."

"Forgive me, my lord, but the so-called rebels hardly require this attention. Shiites are not a group separate from us. Even if they have a few young tearaways among them, why is it necessary to take such extreme measures against them?" The Caliph's brother, the former caliph, would not have reacted in the same way, Abu Ubaydah thought. He would probably have ignored the whole thing, and it would have fizzled out in due course. Taking it so seriously as to set his best troops against the rebels was like taking a sledge hammer to a gnat.

The Caliph shook his head at the commander. "It is from such small beginnings that mighty rebellions grow, Abu Ubaydah. My ancestors saw that the Shia were a source of trouble right from the beginning. The first imams wanted all religious authority for themselves, and that can't be allowed to happen. There can be no rivals to our authority. Al-Mansour knew that, and every one of my ancestors after him."

Abu Ubaydah had not meant for the Caliph to give him a history lesson. But the Caliph continued with animation, "These young Shiites are not seeking domination—yet. But their talk about social justice, the end of poverty and the equality of all men, is far more dangerous. That's the message of the imams, and it's found an echo among the people who mistake a promise for its fulfillment, who understand nothing about the protections they enjoy under my rule and the vigilance that guards their security."

"It is not as you think, my lord. Hardly anyone notices the rebels."

"Even so, when they speak openly of my overthrow, I'm forced to act. I can't have such feckless people challenging my authority. They must be silenced, no matter how unimportant they might seem now. And you, Abu Ubaydah, best know the way. It is a wise ruler who destroys the snake's egg before it is hatched."

Abu Ubaydah was unconvinced. He wanted to warn the Caliph that disproportionate violence could provoke even greater resistance and help to solidify a nascent opposition that, if left alone, might have faded away on its own. But he could see the Caliph was determined.

After that, it was only a matter of time. The rebels were no match for professional soldiers and they were soon overwhelmed. Most surrendered without a further fight, and Yahya and the other leaders were arrested. Yahya escaped, but was soon recaptured. News of his beheading at the hands of the Caliph's soldiers was relayed to his brothers by Musa who met them at the house when Abdulhamid was out. Murjana sat silently looking at Musa through her veil.

"We've lost so many of our best men," wept Musa, scarcely able to contain his grief. "It is God's will, I know, but they were taken from us too soon, with no time to prepare for new leaders to take their place."

He gave a harrowing account of that final battle. He had joined the fighters as they rested before the confrontation with the army. Their spirits were high after seeing off the last battalion of soldiers, and they felt invincible. But that was before Abu Ubaydah's men appeared. Musa remembered how the Caliph's soldiers had sat in their saddles watching them from the edge of the wood, making no move to attack, and silent but for the snorts of the horses and the pummelling of their hooves into the ground. It frightened him, but Yahya and the others did not lose their nerve as they checked their weapons and reserve ammunition they could use.

They were proud of the armaments they had managed to assemble over months of preparation. Many of them had been stolen or bought from the Caliph's mercenary soldiers, and some were smuggled directly from the palace arsenal by Shiite friends working inside.

Yahya and the other leaders wore suits of padded cloth armor, also smuggled out of the palace, and many fighters carried wooden shields. They had no horses, but instead relied on hand-to-hand combat, which had served them well in the previous battles. They had learned to lure enemy troops off their mounts and draw them into the palm groves where they attacked them with daggers, double-edged axes, and short swords. A few archers would perch on higher ground and shoot arrows at them and their horses.

The rebels' military skills had improved with each skirmish, and Yahya and his friends felt they had good reason to be confident, although this time the numbers on their side had dwindled. The outlaws and petty criminals who had swelled their ranks, giving them the appearance of being a much larger force, had run off. But the rebels were unwilling to give up without a fight, even though it was now against superior forces.

"Why?" Yazan cried out to Musa in distress. "Why not run away as well when you saw the soldiers?"

"If we had, they'd have attacked us for sure. But we never thought the army would do much more than the previous troops had done. And your brother urged everyone on. Anyway, we reckoned our numbers and theirs were about equal, maybe three hundred on either side. Yahya said it was more of a show to scare us off than anything else, and we all thought so too.

"When the Caliph's troops first advanced, it wasn't to attack, but to watch us After a while, they turned their horses around and rode away. It seemed like your brother was vindicated, and we all heaved a sigh of relief. But in no time the soldiers were back. Again, they didn't attack, but this time they made a ring around our fighters and then moved in to make the circle smaller. No one dared escape. The villagers who were stealing up to watch were ignored.

"I'd gone to get provisions for what we thought was going to be a long wait, but when I saw what was happening I stopped and hid."

Musa stared straight ahead, his eyes large with remembered fear. "I saw it all. When they had surrounded our boys, their leader stood up in his saddle and signaled. Then they charged as one man with their swords and maces swinging to and fro, slashing and mowing down everyone in their path. Our side put up a strong fight. They dragged the soldiers down and clubbed and knifed them where they could. But it was no use. We were up against superior arms and a deadly attack plan we couldn't break. It was horrible. I never saw so much blood.

"I wanted to reach Yahya and the others, and tried to find a way to get through. But before I could work it out, the battle was over."

Musa could say no more. He just sat staring, dry-eyed. After a time, he told them the rest, how Yahya had escaped briefly, was caught again, and how he met his gruesome end.

Murjana was numb with anguish. "Where is his body for us to wash and shroud for burial? How can we say farewell to him in the proper way and send him to his Creator?"

She let out a mournful sigh and intoned the Quranic verse of condolence.

"To Allah we belong, and to Him we shall return."

In an unusual display of affection, Hamza put his arms around his sister and hugged her closely.

"I promise you, those who have done this shall pay. They will meet their fate, no matter how high and powerful. I swear it on his blood."

They kept the truth from their uncle. After Musa had gone, they told Abdulhamid another story, the same that Musa would tell the merchants: Yahya had been ambushed by robbers on the road to Bukhara, as was known to happen on some stretches of that route. His belongings were taken and his corpse strapped on his horse's back and driven off to where Musa did not know. He himself, having accompanied Yahya up to that point, had managed to escape and hide in the bushes until the bandits departed.

Abdulhamid knew of many such tragedies, and was overcome with grief for his favorite nephew. All he could do was lament over and over, "Why him? Of all the travelers on that road, why him?"

His sense of loss was indescribable.

"Do not question, Abdulhamid. It is God's will," said his sister, weeping. She too had loved Yahya and thought of him as a potential husband for Ayesha. Their only consolation was that the poor boy's parents were not alive to suffer the grief of their child's death.

The memory of that terrible time came back to Murjana, and with it her rage at the killer who had stolen her brother from her. The afterglow of that special day she had been enjoying was entirely banished by her anger. It was as if a jet of ice-cold water had been splashed over her, and she regained her sense of purpose.

"I will not falter, Hamza. Never fear. I will do all that is required of me."

But despite the decisiveness of her words, Murjana knew that the only way she would succeed was to keep her resolve alive every minute of her marriage to the Caliph for however long it lasted, and remind herself continually of her anger and thirst for revenge. If she did not, her mission would end in a failure so shameful she would never recover.

20

The boat sailed slowly down the river, its reflection undulating with the rippling waters. Bouquets of flowers adorned its deck and spilled over its sides to trail in the water like the hem of a long and beautiful dress. A lone figure clothed all in white stood on the deck gazing ahead, her slender form silhouetted against the horizon.

The day had dawned cloudy and cool. But as the flowered boat came into view of the watching crowds massed on the near bank of the Tigris, the sun suddenly broke through the clouds and bathed the passenger in golden light. To the people gathered there the boat looked unearthly, and the straight-backed, silent girl who sailed in it no human figure but a *houri* from a magic land. A hush fell over the crowd. The fine veil that covered her face fluttered in the breeze, and those near enough to see her features through it were captivated by her beauty.

The Caliph had wanted it so, had wanted Murjana to be visible to all. He had expressly forbidden her to sail in a curtained boat or have her face covered by anything thicker than the gauze she wore. God had created her for all mankind to marvel at, and all who saw her should praise Him for her beauty.

Abu Mansour was one of those who stood amidst the crowd

on the river's edge, gazing with them at the spectacle. By his side Younis looked on with rapt attention.

"How wonderful it all is! Thank you for bringing me here, master." His eyes were shining. "I never saw such wonders in my life. And to think I can go with you to the wedding! What stories I shall have to tell the family!"

From early on that morning, they had watched the resplendent pageant of gaily colored skiffs and boats bearing the wedding guests down river to the estate of Harthama ibn Fadl, a man of fabled wealth and one of the favored Abna'. The Caliph's party had gone on ahead of the bride by a few days, and as the Caliph's boat sailed along the river the crowd had cheered him enthusiastically. The celebratory mood was infectious and they wished him well in this new marriage, so unexpected a thing for a man of his austere nature. Everyone liked a good love story, and they enjoyed the snippets of gossip that reached them of an impassioned prince and a beautiful maiden.

Murjana's Shiite origins, the cause of so much anxiety at the palace, were mostly unknown to them, and in any case of no concern. It was enough that she was young and beautiful and from all accounts had enchanted their stern and mighty ruler. They expected some largesse from the palace in the wake of this happy occasion.

As Murjana's boat passed before Abu Mansour and he looked at her youthful figure bravely standing on deck, he thought there was something vulnerable, even tragic, about her. A strange fancy to have on a festive day like that, he said to himself, a fairy tale come true for a humble girl who would soon have the world at her feet. Looking more carefully he saw she was not really alone in the boat. Behind the curtains at the rear of the deck he could make out various shapes, her female relatives, he presumed. He could also see Abdulhamid sitting on deck and two young men with him, one of whom he recognized with a shock that made both him and Younis start.

"Sir! Sir! That's the man I told you went into the Banu Shaaban house when you sent me there. He looked familiar then, and I've just realized why."

Abu Mansour nodded, "And I recognize him too. I assume he's the bride's relative, but he was definitely our visitor that day at the clinic." The man's unconvincing story and his interest in poisons came back to the doctor. He could make no more of it now than he had then. Perhaps the two events were unconnected, but he doubted that. However, now was not the time to unravel the mystery.

"Come, Younis, let us return home." The boy was reluctant to leave, enjoying the panorama, the cheers and chatter of the crowd, and the excitement in the air. "Let's stay a bit longer please, sir." But Abu Mansour was firm.

"There will be more to see on our journey, and much more at the wedding. For now, we must prepare ourselves for travel and follow on."

As they walked away from the river bank, Abu Mansour could not put Murjana out of his mind. The image of her standing immobile as a statue on that boat deck haunted him, and he was full of strange misgivings.

⊡

For all Abu Ubaydah's desperate haste to prevent the marriage ever taking place, he was too late. The Caliph he had rushed to see had already left Baghdad and was soon to arrive at Harthama ibn Fadl's estate where the wedding ceremony would take place. The formal contracts of marriage had already been exchanged, and Abu Ubaydah's intervention was now irrelevant. But the commander was only defeated for the moment; he decided to bide his time until an opportunity arose to warn the Caliph. Even the cleverest plot against him would surely need time to come to fruition, and much could happen before it did.

Harthama ibn Fadl's estate was a sprawling assemblage of houses and outbuildings set well back from the river's edge. It stood on the outskirts of Famm al-Silh, a small farming town rich with palm groves and lush orchards to the south-east of Baghdad. In the center of the estate was a spacious house where Harthama and his household lived, and it was this he opened up for the wedding party. The source of Harthama's wealth was unclear, but it was said to be the favor he had enjoyed for years from the Caliph and his father.

It had not always been so. At one time Harthama had been appointed governor over an unruly Khorasan he was unable to pacify, and had so displeased the Caliph he was removed from office. Abdullah ibn Rida had replaced him in a bid to bring the situation under control, and he was banished in disgrace. It was a humiliation he had found hard to accept. But with the news of his successor's fall from grace, Harthama's spirits revived, and he had gone to the Caliph to congratulate him on his forthcoming marriage.

"Nothing, my lord, would give me greater happiness or express my repentance better than for your glorious wedding to take place in my home. I pray you will accept this humble invitation."

The Caliph was pleased, and not unmindful of the usefulness of the offer. It would mean a journey for the wedding party along the Tigris all the way to Famm al-Silh and a great opportunity to mount a festive pageant for the people. They loved a spectacle to distract them from their hard lives, and it would ward off unrest and discontent. The Caliph's previous weddings had all been celebrated in the privacy of the palace. But this union would be displayed to the world, and he intended it to be an occasion so splendid, so luxurious, it would eclipse all others.

"You are most kind, Harthama, and I will look on your generosity as proof of your goodwill and true repentance. My wedding shall mark the end of our displeasure with you and the renewal of our ties of friendship."

田

Abu Mansour arrived in Famm al-Silh at the time of the evening prayer. He found the Caliph's party well settled, and an air of bustle and festivity hung in the air. One of the stewards took him to his chamber, while Younis went to separate quarters with the other staff. It was cool and dark outside, and the wind swished incessantly through the tall palm trees that surrounded the house.

When the prayer ended, Abu Mansour was shown into the main hall where the Caliph was seated with his courtiers. It had been carpeted with rich and colorful rugs, and the walls and pillars hung with flowers. Men sat around the Caliph on cushioned seats or on the floor, and a buzz of conversation and laughter filled the air. Durayd stood to the side, watching over the gathering. When he saw Abu Mansour, the chamberlain came forward to welcome him with a genuine show of pleasure. The doctor bowed.

"Come, my dear Abu Mansour!" the Caliph called out from across the hall. "Join us."

With him was his favorite son, Jaafar, who alone among his half-brothers had been invited to the wedding, the others excluded out of respect for their mothers' feelings. Abdulhamid was also seated by the Caliph, looking ill at ease; he nodded gloomily at the doctor. Next to him were the two young men Abu Mansour had seen on the boat.

"Peace be upon you, Abu Mansour. May I introduce my nephews, Hamza and Yazan?"

So, thought Abu Mansour, the man was Murjana's brother. Hamza flushed, visibly embarrassed at meeting the doctor again, and his complexion mottled over with dark red patches. He saw that Abu Mansour had recognized him, and tried to smile at the doctor in salutation, making as if to stand up. But no one was looking at him as all heads were turned toward the door and the entry of the court musicians. At the sight of them, Abu Mansour's heart sank. He had no love for the new maqams they would no doubt play, which he thought repetitive and tedious.

The musicians came forward and bowed deeply. They were identically dressed in white shirts and short black velvet tunics over white woollen sirwals. On their heads each man wore a tall qalansuwa cap covered in black velvet and wrapped around at the base with white ribbon. The Caliph clapped his hands in delighted anticipation; he was proud of his court musicians and had them play at all his literary soirees.

As they set up their instruments and strummed their lutes and tested their drums and flutes, a new attraction appeared. Four *qiyan* ran in, Harthama's most talented slave-girls, summoned especially for the Caliph's pleasure. Only the richest of men could afford to own these special girls, whose training from childhood in music and dancing and the literary arts cost a fortune. They could compose and recite poetry, sing like angels, hold their own in learned discourse on a diversity of topics from philosophy to science, and enslave many a man with their beauty.

Young and confident, the qiyan swept their eyes boldly over the male assembly. The coins strung around their gold anklets jingled merrily as they danced until, stopping by the Caliph, they paused, looked down demurely, and inclined their graceful bodies before him. In their wide linen trousers and colorful over-tunics, their long hair braided with gold thread and flowing over their shoulders, they had a joyful, carefree air that set them apart from "respectable" women.

The men with the Caliph were riveted by the slave girls, calling out to them to dance again, and itched to touch them. But it was wishful thinking; such women were not for hire. They might tempt and delight, but were not available for anything more—except to their owners. The air in the room grew thick and warm with the smoke of guttering candles and the heat of the lamps that burned against the walls.

Abu Mansour felt hot and uncomfortable. He could sense the growing lustfulness of the men despite their attempts at self-control, and he wondered if there was any way he could leave the gathering without anyone noticing. He had never enjoyed seeing lascivious men with dancing girls, whose fleeting power over their owners lasted only so long as they kept their sharp wits and good looks.

The Caliph looked on contentedly at the singing and the dancing. He seemed like a new man in a new world that he was learning to savor, and Abu Mansour was happy for him. He saw Harthama beckoning to his servants to bring forth the wine.

"Do I have your permission to celebrate this happy occasion with a glass of wine, my lord?"

Everyone knew the Caliph was not a drinker, but usually had no objection to others drinking. However, Harthama could not be sure that his capricious ruler would not have had a change heart.

"It seemed only fitting for us to drink to your happy future, sir."

There was an anxious pause.

"Of course you can," the Caliph declared, "We must celebrate and be happy!"

As the servants came through with flagons of Harthama's finest pale, old wines and richest reds from the famous vineyards of Falluja, the Caliph bent forward and to everyone's surprise took a cup for himself and one for Abdulhamid. He was smiling.

"Drink with me, Abdulhamid. It's a special occasion, is it not?"

Seeing the older man's consternation at this suggestion, Abu Mansour made another effort to extricate himself from what he anticipated would be a painful scene. It was a step too far for Abdulhamid, who adamantly refused. But, taking the Caliph's cue, his court poet, Abu Firas, who seemed already inebriated, raised his glass at Abdulhamid and laughed gaily. Durayd looked on with some distaste. He and many others found it hard to understand the Caliph's affection for this man who was a reprobate and drunkard.

Raising his wine goblet to the light, he declaimed with a flourish,

"Wine is a ruby, the glass is a pearl.
Served by the hand of a slim-fingered girl.
When she serves you the wine from her hand and her mouth.
You will be drunk twice over!"

The slave girls now joined in, responding to Abu Firas in verse, and the musicians struck up a languorous melody to echo the poem's sentiment. More poems extolling the virtues of wine followed. But then Abu Firas changed mood. Raising his glass again to the Caliph, he started to recite an extravagant love sonnet he had written for him and his new bride. He entranced the assembly with his eloquence and the passion of his words. The Caliph closed his eyes, listening pleasurably.

Abu Mansour, seeing the Caliph so absorbed, seized the opportunity to slip away, bowing and excusing himself without anyone noticing. He walked out into the dim courtyard, lit by torches that barely penetrated the blackness of the night. The sky was covered in cloud, through which neither moon nor stars penetrated. The air felt cold on his face, and he heard voices coming from the kitchens where the great banquet of the next day was being prepared. The sound of the guards and their horses moving about their tents reached into the night, but muted by the thick clouds. As he reached the far side of the courtyard that led to his chamber, footsteps on the stone floor sounded behind him. He turned to see Abdulhamid's nephew following him.

"God greet you, Abu Mansour." Hamza was out of breath.

The doctor stopped, peering into the young man's face.

"I wanted a word if you will kindly give me a moment." His tone was courteous, if slightly whining.

"It's a matter of little importance, and you won't remember, but I once came to see you at your house."

Abu Mansour waited.

"I had a question about a sick relative of mine, which you might have thought strange."

"I remember perfectly well. And yes, your question was strange."

"Well, you see we were worried about my relative, and I don't think I explained myself well at the time. I don't want you to have had the wrong impression."

"I'm not sure what you mean. Perhaps you could tell me what happened to your relative in the end?"

"He...um..." stammered Hamza. "He's, he's fine. It was nothing after all, and nothing to do with what I asked you about. I just wanted to apologize for having seemed odd at the time."

"Don't worry. I'm used to people asking for guidance on many different matters."

The young man looked relieved.

"The main thing is that your relative has recovered, whatever the cause of his malady."

"What...? Oh yes, yes, thank you." Hamza seemed hardly to be listening. "Peace be upon you, and God's mercy and blessings, sir," he said abruptly as if he had accomplished what he had set out to do. He turned and walked back across the courtyard.

Abu Mansour watched him go. What did he want, I wonder, and what wrong impression was he talking about? The sick relative story seemed as implausible now as it had before, but Hamza had stuck to it, and his only concern it seemed was to give a good account of himself to the doctor. Yet, there was no doubt the young man had been interested in the matter of poisons, although, for the life of him, Abu Mansour could not think why. It crossed his mind briefly that Hamza might have been planning to use a poison himself for some purpose. But if so, how foolish of him to remind the doctor of the incident.

⊞

In the women's quarters of the house, Murjana lay awake, restless and unable to sleep. She longed to let herself feel the excitement of anticipation of her wedding day, yet held back because of her sense of duty to her dead brother and the promise she had made to Hamza. The Caliph's image swam before her eyes, his eager passion and the depth of his emotion for her. She dallied a while with a daydream of how their wedding night would be. It made her breathless with excitement and a jumble of emotions she could hardly control.

Her aunt and cousins had urged her to sleep early the night before, so she would be fresh and ready for the next day. No one had told her where the Caliph was, beyond the fact that he had preceded the women's party to Harthama's estate. Had he been any other man, he would have been carousing with his courtiers, since it was what royal bridegrooms did on the eve of their weddings. But she knew it was not like him. Whatever he was doing, she felt he was thinking of her, patiently holding himself in check until they met again. And as she thought it, a rush of unexpected warmth for him ran through her.

21

The dawn could not come soon enough. Murjana was the first to be up and ready for the seamstresses from the Dar al-Tiraz, who had accompanied the party in order to ensure that the bride's apparel on the wedding day was impeccable. They had removed the clothes from their wrappings the night before and hung them up to straighten the creases. Murjana's aunt and cousins awoke soon after and sat waiting for their breakfast. But she had no appetite and only picked at the fresh bread and honey that the servants brought.

Her journey along the Tigris in the preceding days had been tiring, made worse by her aunt Zubeida's constant ranting, on top of her uncle's grumbles. "How could the Caliph ask you to do something like that?" her aunt complained. "No Muslim girl can allow herself to be on show like that, unveiled like a dancing girl."

"I wasn't unveiled, Aunt."

"As good as!"

"I don't usually veil any more than that anyway. Uncle has allowed it."

"My brother is not always wise, and in any case, a short trip here and there in Baghdad is not the same thing. This was not

194

proper and an insult to your virtue. Had it not been the Caliph, the marriage would have been called off by now, I can tell you."

She had gone on like this all through the henna night when Murjana's hands and feet were dyed orange in the traditional manner for brides before their weddings. All the womenfolk of the house took part—Murjana's cousins, the ladies of the Caliph's household who had come from the palace, Harthama's two wives and his daughters, and, unexpectedly, the Caliph's stepmother, Khadija, who had arrived in the morning with his stepsister, Hasna. Khadija made sure that Murjana's aunt said no more about the veiling.

"You mustn't worry, dear lady. No one doubts the virtue of your niece. I'm sure she won the hearts of all who saw her."

Privately, Khadija, considering Murjana to belong to the lower classes of women who went around unveiled, didn't care one way or the other. She had decided to attend her stepson's wedding with as good a grace as she could muster.

Despite her continuing dismay at his choice of bride, she had become persuaded of his genuine love for the girl, and realized he would not change his mind. Khadija was a clever woman who had managed her husband's infidelities with skill, ensuring he had no cause to repudiate her or remove her son from the succession. The war between the brothers subsequently had spoiled her plan and ended with her son's death. But it did not blind her to the need to look out for her own survival at the court of his successor. Since it seemed that the Caliph now was set on this marriage, she was determined to retain his support by taking his future wife under her wing.

When the women came to dress Murjana, she looked pale and had dark shadows under her eyes. They bathed her in attar of roses and smoothed milk and melon water lotion over her body to make her skin as soft as silk. Her hair was combed until it shone, and the auburn tinge from the henna dye they had used gave it luster and richness. Persian black kohl was painted inside her lids to enhance the beauty of her dark eyes, and her cheeks were dusted with rouge. When they came to apply the borax and white marble powder to lighten her complexion, as was fashionable, she shook her head. Her ivory skin was one of her best features and she did not want it any paler than it was already. She was perfumed with ambergris and musk, and then stood up to be dressed.

All the women of the house gathered to watch. They sat on cushions against the walls of the room staring at Murjana. It made her nervous. The seamstresses brought out her sleeveless shift, which they slipped over her head. Then they held out the wide-legged silver sirwal for her to step into. She leaned against the seamstresses as she pushed her legs into it, and when they came to fasten the waist with a satin band, she suddenly swayed forward and would have fallen had the women not supported her. They lay her down on the floor and called for water.

With a cry her cousins sprang over and knelt down beside her. There was general consternation among the women. What if the bride was too ill to attend her own wedding party? It was already past the noonday prayer, and she would soon have to go down to the hall for the start of the wedding banquet.

The servants fetched cold water and toweled Murjana's face. She opened her eyes, but did not move. She saw the Caliph's stepmother and his sister bending over her.

"There's nothing to be afraid of," said Khadija to the women crowding round. "Too much excitement, that's all. Let her rest for a bit."

Her main concern was that no word of this should reach the Caliph waiting with the other men. When she greeted him that morning, he had seemed elated but also on edge. She did not think he would tolerate the slightest hitch to the festivities he was so eagerly awaiting.

And in a short while, Murjana revived and sat up, much to the relief of her attendants. She was given a draught of camomile infusion and a spoonful of honey, and was soon up on her feet again. The sirwal was adjusted and her waistband secured once more. She waited for the seamstresses to bring out the overdress that would cover her body down to her ankles.

The gown they slipped off the hanger and carried over their arms was of a magnificence few of the women had ever seen. Even Murjana's aunt and cousins, who had sat with her as she was fitted with the dress at home, did not remember that it was so fine. It was of a style between the caftan that men were beginning to wear and the traditional women's over-tunic. The sleeves were wide and flowing, and the rounded neck and slit bodice were patterned with silver thread, in whose twisting loops and turns pearls gleamed and diamonds sparkled. It fell to her feet in a shimmer, the color of the clear sky at dawn. The turquoise silk brocade set off her black hair and dark eyes to perfection.

Around her neck the women fastened a collar of silver and pearls, and a circlet of aquamarine and diamonds was fitted to her brow. From its center, a long pearl hung down to rest between her eyes. Rings adorned her fingers, and the pale leather of her sandals was encrusted with gems.

Seeing them, Khadija smiled. It was she who had introduced the fashion of jeweled sandals to the court of her husband, and she was pleased to see it looking so well on this young woman's shapely feet.

When the seamstresses finished with Murjana, she was allowed to take a seat and rest again. Her cousins sat on each side and held her hands, careful not to disarrange her dress or jewelry. Their mother would accompany the bride and the women of the Caliph's family into a chamber specially set aside for the meeting with the Caliph. There Murjana would be brought together with him, her uncle, and her brothers. Afterward, and in accordance with custom, the men and women guests would separate, each side to enjoy the wedding festivities apart.

The women pulled their veils over their heads and covered their faces. They walked downstairs with Murjana toward the chamber where the men waited. Her gossamer veil, though it covered her whole head, did nothing to conceal her beautiful face or her lustrous hair. She knew it was what the Caliph would have wanted. As she walked a little ahead of the others, she felt disconnected from reality, like a sleepwalker heading toward the edge of a precipice.

The Caliph waited for his bride in a chamber especially prepared for the wedding party. It would be the first meeting between them since their formal nuptials, when she had been represented by her uncle. As the day of their wedding celebration approached, he had tried to put her out of his thoughts, did not allow himself to dwell on the memory of her deep, dark eyes and her half-innocent, half-knowing smile. Time enough for that when he had her to himself.

After performing the noon prayer, he and the others sat waiting for the bride's party. He was distracted by anticipation. Jaafar, his son, a spirited young man of seventeen who had no fear of his father and behaved in every way like a future caliph, chattered away. His invitation to the wedding had made his mother secretly joyful. It was a mark of the Caliph's partiality for the boy, she thought, and boded well for his chances of becoming his heir, whatever happened with the new wife.

The wives and concubines of the harem all dreamed of being the mothers of the future caliph. It was a status like no other, bestowing power and privilege that put such a woman far above the others. She would have her own house, her own servants and secretaries, and become the center of a web of influence that reached far into palace politics.

Much of this went well beyond Um Jaafar's ambitions for herself. She had no interest in palace affairs, and everyone knew her as a kindly, modest woman whose chief pleasure in life was that her children should gain their father's favor and prosper. But she could not deny that being mother to the next caliph was an honor that pleased and flattered her, and, she thought, was only fitting for the daughter of a family of ancient lineage like herself.

Abdulhamid was quiet. He had not slept well after the wine drinking and depravity of the night before, as he saw it. In his view, the slave girls, the poetry, and the music were all works of the devil, and he could only shudder with horror at what his poor niece would have to endure with such a man as the Caliph. For his part, the end of the wedding festivities couldn't come soon enough, and he was anxious to be released from what he saw as his captivity in Harthama's house. Neither of his nephews had voiced an opinion yet, but he had not liked Yazan's obvious enjoyment of the spectacle of the night before. Hamza remained inscrutably quiet, and it was impossible to know what he was thinking.

The sound of footsteps and voices interrupted his thoughts as the servants suddenly flung open the chamber doors. The Caliph rose to his feet, and the other men followed suit. There was a pause and then, with the Caliph's stepmother and his sister on either side of her, Murjana walked slowly into the room.

⊞

She looked resplendent in her wedding dress. Abu Firas should be here, thought the Caliph. Only he had the words to describe her magical beauty and the spell she cast over everyone who saw her.

As she drew up to stand before him, he bent forward and lifted the veil from her face, oblivious that there were men present not of her family, before whom by custom she should not go unveiled. It brought back vividly the time when he had first seen her at his diwan and had had a sudden impulse to push her veil away from her face.

Jaafar, not much younger than she, stood staring at her with undisguised admiration. She was like a doll, and the boy thought of his mother's plump, maternal figure and homely features.

The Caliph took Murjana's hands in his and led her to sit beside him. As they faced the room, no one, however insensitive, could doubt the Caliph's happiness or fail to be touched by it. It radiated from him like a beacon in the night. He held Murjana's hand tightly and raised it to his lips.

The wedding guests came forward to give their blessings. When it was Khadija's turn, she bowed and kissed the Caliph's hand.

"Dear son. Allow me to wish you and your bride long life and happiness."

She then turned to one of the Abbasid ladies who was holding a golden tray covered in velvet, and pulled off the cover to reveal a pyramid of the most exquisite pearls. Taking the tray carefully in her hands, Khadija went up to the bride, raised it high in the air and poured the pearls over Murjana's head. They cascaded like snow drops through her hair and over her shoulders, spilled into her lap, and clattered delicately onto the floor. The company clapped their hands at the spectacle, and Khadija smiled with satisfaction. It would stand her in good stead for the future.

The Caliph smiled too.

"Now that you have received your wedding present from the lady Khadija, it is my turn. Ask me for anything you desire, and I will grant it if it is in my power."

No one thought Murjana would know how to answer him. The Caliph's uncle was watching her intently, and her brothers, not expecting the Caliph's offer, looked uneasy. Murjana cast her eyes down and said nothing.

"Speak to your lord, Murjana," her aunt urged her. "Ask him for what you want."

Nothing would normally have induced Zubeida to speak at such a gathering. Like her brother, though he tried to pretend otherwise, she was intimidated by the Caliph's presence and the unfamiliar situation they were in. But the prospect of her niece attaining untold favors just by asking for them was too tempting to throw aside, and she was afraid Murjana's silence might offend the Caliph.

Murjana raised her eyes and looked into his.

"My lord, I ask nothing for myself, but I beg that you hear my plea for others. I know it's not my place to interfere in matters I'm ignorant of. So please forgive me if I express to you my desire that there should be no more enmity or anger in your life."

Abdulhamid knew his niece to be strong-minded and often wise beyond her years, but he could not imagine what was in her mind.

"Our imam has suffered your displeasure for many years. He is a good man and means you no harm. Is there not some way you could find it in your heart to reconcile with him and give him back his freedom? He has often spoken of you with the greatest admiration and respect."

Abdulhamid was astounded at his niece's audacity. The family members looked anxiously at each other. The Caliph thought quietly for a moment.

"In the matter of the imam, I have no doubt you mean well, Murjana, and I admire your generosity of spirit in pleading on his behalf. But these are not easy requests to grant."

Murjana looked downcast. No one had primed her to plead for the imam. She had spoken of her own volition.

"I don't want enmity or anger in my life either. But the imam is another matter."

Putting his hand under Murjana's chin, he lifted her face to be level with his. "However, I give you my word that I will earnestly consider your request."

With that, he turned to Abdulhamid and asked him what

land he desired to become his. When there was no more reply than an embarrassed stuttering, the Caliph ordered the gift of an estate not far from Famm al-Silh to be made to Abdulhamid and his family.

He then asked for Harthama to come in, and presented him with two fine Arabian horses and a gold-edged black Abbasid robe of honor.

More sherbet was called for and the tension lifted—though not for Hamza. He was furious at his sister's unwise mention of the imam and her silly request for the Caliph's clemency on his behalf. Who knew what tongues would wag at hearing such news? That the Caliph's new wife should intercede on behalf of the Shia imam, a known enemy of the Abbasids, would strike people as strange. How long before they started to suspect her of disloyalty, and from there to the total ruination of his plans? What had the stupid girl been thinking of?

His expression hardened. He saw that his sister was weak and unreliable, and he must remain vigilant she did not make another error. Not for the first time, he wished he did not have to depend on her for a mission so delicate, yet so crucial.

22

Younis watched the wedding banquet from the sidelines. He had edged his way in without permission from anyone, gauging that he would not be noticed amid the flurry of guests finding their seats and stewards rushing in and out. No one looked at him as he flattened himself against the wall.

The gathering was not as large as he had expected in view of the number of people camped on the grounds of the house. But the atmosphere was merry, and everyone looked as if they were enjoying themselves. It was a cold night, but the many candles made it feel warmer. He knew nothing about the protocol of such occasions and had never attended a banquet in his life. Mealtimes at home were simple affairs, all the family seated on the floor, dipping their bread together into the dishes his mother and sisters put in the center of the floor mat, and when each had had their fill, rising one by one to wash their hands. By contrast, here the tables were laid with Chinese porcelain, silver spoons, and silver goblets, and basins of rose water were brought round for the guests to wash their hands before the meal.

Trays piled high with delicacies of every sort to make his mouth water were set at each table, and, as had happened the night before, there was wine in abundance. The Caliph sat facing the room, the men of his family beside him, along with Harthama and his sons. His attire was magnificent. Gaping in admiration, Younis could not have known that the Caliph was in the identical clothes he had worn to the banquet with the Byzantine ambassadors all those months before. He had wanted to evoke the precious memory of the premonition he had had that night and which had now come true.

Younis saw his master sitting uncomfortably with the Caliph's party, dressed in unaccustomed finery and looking out of place. He was doing his best to appear happy, but it was obvious to Younis that he would rather not have been there at all. He knew that he was thinking of the patients left behind and how they would miss him, and he wished that his master could enjoy a respite from the daily chores of his life.

The smell of delicious food drifting toward him was too much for Younis. He began to feel hungry and wondered how much longer he should stay. The other attendants were being catered for in a tent outside the house, and he decided he had probably seen enough of the spectacle to make a good story for his family.

He strolled unobtrusively toward the entrance, and as he did so nearly collided with another man going the same way. At their touch, the man shrank away as if he'd been stung, and slunk off rapidly into the night. Younis was in time to notice the man's black beard and his plain brown cloak wrapped tightly around him. He did not remember seeing him in the dining chamber, although he might have been lurking in one of the shadowy corners. It was possible he was one of the guards outside the house who had strayed into the banqueting room by mistake. Younis would have forgotten all about him but for the fact of seeing him again outside the tent where the servants' food was laid. He had his back to him, but Younis recognized him. He seemed to be deep in conversation with another man, a soldier by his dress, who was listening attentively. The soldier was a short, stocky man with a bushy gray-specked mustache that curled around his mouth. The two men moved off, still talking, and the sight of them struck Younis as curious, though he could not have said why.

He mentioned the incident later to his master. Years of sifting through the many requests from patients wanting to see Abu Mansour had given Younis a keen nose for what was potentially significant. He was rarely wrong, and when he saw Abu Mansour emerge from the dining hall, he went over to him.

"I hope you've dined well, sir."

When his master nodded he went on.

"There's something I want to draw your attention to."

He told him about the strange man in the dining room and the earnest conversation he had subsequently seen him have with the soldier, which Younis thought looked secretive, even conspiratorial.

"Aren't you being overly imaginative, Younis? And what would the conspiracy be about?"

"I don't know, but it's the second odd thing that's happened since we came."

Abu Mansour looked at him inquiringly.

"Well, there's the business of the man who's here and who called himself Ibrahim al-Ajami when he came to see you, and now turns out to be the bride's brother. Why not give his real name?"

"What's that got to do with the strange man you saw at the banquet and his conversation with the soldier?"

Younis was at a loss to explain.

"I don't know, sir. But I feel it in my bones they're somehow connected."

Abu Mansour considered him for a moment. He was not impressed by Younis's hunches on this occasion. But he did not want to discourage him.

"All right, keep an eye out and let me know if you spot anything else that strikes you as important."

The women's dancing and singing at their separate banquet had grown louder and merrier. Murjana, getting up to dance at her cousins' urging, did not hear the announcement of the Caliph's impending visit, which was just as well, as it would have stopped her there and then. It had taken much persuasion and pleading on their part, and that of their mother and the slave-girls, to get her to join the dancers. Having taken the plunge and done so, she was so absorbed watching the *qiyan* leading the dance that she did not notice the flurry of activity as the other women reached for their veils before the Caliph appeared. Standing poised to start, with everyone eager to see her wedding dance, she drew herself up to her full height, raised her arms elegantly above her head, the wide sleeves of her caftan falling back to her elbows, and waited for the rhythm of the drums to draw her in. The *qiyan* quietly withdrew to the side, creating a space for her in the center of the room.

As she took the first steps in time with the music, Murjana's supple body seemed to take on a life of its own. It swam into the rhythm of the drum beat, moved and swayed, at first slowly and then, gaining pace, she arched her back as far as it would go and in that position swiveled her agile hips from side to side. Her step did not falter once, and as she straightened again with superb control, her arms outstretched, her face flushed and her long hair tousled, she shook her shoulders and her breasts provocatively at the watchers with a fluidity of motion that far surpassed the skill of the other women.

Everyone was silent, looking at her. *Where had she learned to dance like that?* wondered Khadija; when the other girls had danced, it was nothing like this. Their innocence and verve were fresh and youthful and delighted the older women. But when Murjana danced, it was different. Though she smiled at her aunt and at Khadija as she glided across the floor, they knew her dancing was not meant for them.

There was to her movements an allure, a hidden invitation that the women who saw it recognized was meant only for men, and would enslave any who saw her. Yet Murjana had no dance teacher, no one had trained her to dance like that. It was something innate, instinctive, as if she had been born for pleasure.

Unnoticed, the Caliph stood watching her in the shadows behind the archway. She stirred him in a thousand ways, his eyes filled with the image of her dancing body. *You're going to dance like that for me tonight and every night*, he thought with fierce tenderness.

Seeing the Caliph, the *qiyan* called a sudden halt to the music, and bowed. Turning toward him, Murjana put up her hands and covered her face with embarrassment, as if caught in a shameful act. He came into the light and walked to the center of the room.

"Ladies, please don't be ill at ease. I come here to thank you for your celebration of me and my bride and your good wishes."

Some of the women murmured a response, but the rest were mute, flustered at his appearance among them. Murjana's cousins, who had never seen the Caliph before, were overawed by his commanding presence. How would Murjana be able to live with him? His sister, Hasna, came forward and took his arm, but he made no move to sit beside Murjana, as his guests were expecting. Seeing her dance had inflamed him unbearably, and he did not want to put off the moment when they would be alone a minute longer.

"I'm pleased to see you, my lord, and I'm sorry I was dancing like that when you came. I did not mean to offend."

"How could you offend me, Murjana? What put such an idea into your head?"

She flushed. "We were women together, and it did not matter how we danced."

"And indeed it does not matter. I am pleased that you and the others have been enjoying this festive day."

The *qiyan* saw how the Caliph looked at her. What a man. Not one of them would have turned down the chance of having such attention, and if they had, what pleasure, singly or together, they could give him. If only their overweight and ageing master, who repelled them, would give them to him! But even as they thought it, they saw it was a hopeless ambition: he had no eyes except for the girl. He held out his hand to her. She hesitated until her aunt pushed her toward him. She looked so young, so overwhelmed, as she put her hand in his obediently and let him lead her away.

The bedchamber that Harthama had prepared for the Caliph's wedding night was large and chilly. Murjana stood alone where her husband had left her to disrobe. Its hangings were handsome and the rugs on the wooden floor were thick and colorful, but they imparted no warmth. The wind whistled outside and increased the atmosphere of bleak isolation. A huge candle, the largest Murjana had ever seen, burned in a heavy brass holder, guttering and smoking. It was Harthama's most expensive wedding gift to the Caliph and weighed some six or seven pounds. The ambergris which permeated its wax must have cost a fortune, and it filled the air with a powerful scent that made Murjana cough.

Her aunt, who joined her in the room, had also coughed. She told her to undress, and then lie down on the bed to await her lord.

"Remember, my daughter, you must do whatever he asks of you, however strange it might seem. You must not complain and you should try to look as if it pleases you."

Murjana's anxious face expressed the exact opposite, and she knew that if she wanted comfort and a different guidance on her wedding night with the Caliph, Zubeida was the last person to give it. All she did was preach obedience and submission, but

Murjana humored her and was glad when her aunt left.

Finally alone, she got up, unable to contain the apprehension that gripped her. All she had known of the Caliph as a lover was that one encounter in his bedroom in the palace in Baghdad. The memory of his ardor then only increased her anxiety. She did not know what to say to him when he came, or what he might want of her—supine obedience as her aunt suggested, or someone who knew how to give pleasure? In her nervousness, she started to pace the room, staring at the door through which he would enter. All thought of Hamza and her mission had fled, and whenever it came into her mind she pushed it back.

As she looked at the door, she thought she saw a shadow darken the gap at the bottom, as of someone standing there. It was him; there could be no doubt of it. She stopped and braced herself, took a step backward, and, least expecting to, slammed into him standing behind her. It was so sudden she gasped. Concentrating as she had been on the shadows beneath the door in front of her, she had not heard him enter through the back door, the one she had earlier used to come in.

Distractedly, she realized the sound of his entry must have been obscured by the noise outside. He said nothing, gripped her round the waist, and pulled her tightly against him. The heat of his body on her back was like a furnace. Keeping one arm around her waist, he pushed her hair aside with the other, and kissed her neck. She stood paralyzed, hardly able to breathe, conscious that beneath her thin shift she was naked. It made her feel vulnerable. But her will seemed suspended and her mind empty of thought.

His lips still on her neck, he passed his hand slowly over her, feeling her body through her shift, cupping each of her breasts gently. His breathing quickened. He turned her to face him and kissed her deeply and lingeringly. Parting his woolen robe, he took her into it and enveloped her inside. Despite her fear, his touch had aroused Murjana, and she was as absorbed by him as he by her. They stood close together inside his robe, unmoving, until he took her hand and led her slowly to the bed. Her heart began to thud. She knew this would be the moment when he would expect her to perform, and it excited and frightened her. Would he give her time, be patient with her? She recalled his frenzied passion that time before, the way he nearly devoured her. If anything, it would be worse this time. He was the Caliph and, though he had always shown her consideration and respect, even when he was ill and not in proper charge of himself, somewhere in his mind must have been the thought that he now possessed her utterly, to do with as he wished, even have her killed if she displeased him enough.

The realization sobered her and brought her out of her paralysis. There was nothing for it, she would have to do her best and hope he would not be too disappointed. They lay down together. He took off his robe and covered them both with the bedclothes. Then he drew her to him and rested her head on his chest. She shivered, and he held her closer.

"Don't be afraid, Murjana, I have all I want. You are with me, in my bed, your body against mine. When I saw you dance tonight, I thought I would go mad. I wanted to seize you, make you dance again and again, only for me."

He kissed her hair, and stroked her face tenderly, but there was no more. He did not touch the private areas of her body, or make any attempt to disrobe her as she had expected. He seemed content to just lie beside her and close his eyes.

A spasm of disappointment shot through her. The memory of how he was before, his hunger for her, and the feel of his hands on her breasts had made her restless. She was confused. Was that it? Was that really all he wanted of her on this night of all nights, to lie with her in a chaste embrace? Before he arrived, she had been afraid of him, his wild passion, the attack she expected him to mount on her defenseless body, and his inevitable disappointment in her response. But now, with him beside her, calm and strong, her fear had receded, and she thought of the excitement he had stirred in her before, the thrill of power she had felt over him. Though she hardly dared to admit it to herself, she was eager for that again, but did not know how to provoke it. She moved against him and put her hand hesitantly on his chest. It did nothing except increase his tenderness toward her. He lifted her hand, kissed it, and held it to his heart.

After a while and to her dismay, Murjana thought he had fallen asleep. She lay beside him, her eyes wide open. The candle sputtered again, and more smoke filled the air, putting her into a paroxysm of coughing. The Caliph was instantly alert. His whole attention taken up with her, he had not noticed the candle in the corner when he came in. But he now rose, took his robe, and went to see. Wax was dripping down the candle's sides and pooling into the holder beneath. Smoke billowed intermittently from its molten top as its flame came and went. He strode to the bedroom door and shouted out for the attendants. When they came scurrying and flustered, half asleep, the Caliph was incensed.

"Look at this candle. It's not fit to put into a room, let alone a bedchamber."

"My master had wanted to give you the pleasure of enjoying its light and scent," said the chief steward.

"It gives us no pleasure. You see how it smokes and sputters. Take it away."

Two servants carried out the candle still smoking in its holder, and the steward asked if he could help with anything else. The Caliph shook his head and watched them depart. He stood for a moment looking at the space where the candle had been and thinking he would have to explain the situation later to Harthama, who had obviously wanted to impress, as tactfully as he could.

He returned to the bed to see Murjana sitting up. He could hardly make out her features in the early dawn light, and her hair was like a black cloud around her face. When he drew closer, he saw she was looking at him in a strange way. He disrobed again and lay down beside her.

"I hate to see you disturbed, my darling. The candle's gone. Now come back again and rest."

But she remained sitting up, and as he drew the bedclothes back and eased himself onto the cushions, she turned toward him and slipped down into the bed until her face was against his. She suddenly put her arm around his neck and felt for his lips. The kiss she gave him was full of passion. Its urgency evoked those early sexual adventures of his youth, when his only guide had been a blind need that drove without thought for the consequences. He lay still, letting her kiss him, feeling her breath on his face. This was not what he had planned. He had resolved to control his desires, to give her time until she was used to the feel of his body beside hers, and then to let her guide him to do whatever she wanted. His instinct had from the first picked up something in her she was not aware of, a sensuousness, a passion that came out in her dancing. But he had not anticipated her hot kisses so soon. It provoked in him something halfway between tenderness for her youth and arousal by her womanhood. Uncertain what to do, he lay still.

"Do I displease you?" she asked.

It was impossible to resist. He could hold out no longer. He seized her in his arms and, all restraint gone, kissed and caressed her with mounting intensity, stroked her body with rough passion, and let his hands linger over its secret areas, until, like that time before, he thought he would go mad with desire. She did not flinch or try to stop him. It was not some hidden experience, only her instinct that answered to his and told her what to do. Their coming together, when at last it happened, was the sweetest thing he'd ever known.

As the weak winter sunlight filtered through the shutters, he felt his ardor finally abate. Murjana lay exhausted and asleep. He looked at her rumpled hair, her flushed face and glistening skin, the perspiration on her brow that dampened the hair above it into curls, and he bent down and kissed her gently. She did not wake, and he was careful not to disturb her. A surge of happiness such as he had never felt passed through him. The time of the dawn prayer had gone. But the noon prayer was still to come, and when it did, he would arise and pray as he had never done before, humbly prostrate himself before God and, with his whole heart, thank him for his bounty.

23

The Caliph stayed at Harthama's house for seventeen days. No one could remember a time when any wedding festivities had lasted so long. The Caliph spent the days and nights with Murjana, as he could not bear to be away from her and was oblivious to everything else. The word on the street was that the Caliph was bewitched, besotted beyond reason, with his new bride, and so entranced by her that he might not be able to resume his normal duties ever again.

Abu Hisham, still overseeing his duties in Baghdad, had begun to feel impatient with the Caliph's long absence. Too many matters needed his attention and could not wait much longer. Durayd was of the same opinion. He had seen the guests depart the day after the wedding, and then the Caliph's family left, followed by Murjana's. But there was no sign of the Caliph preparing to do the same.

Abdulhamid said goodbye to Murjana, and her aunt and cousins kissed her. "You have a husband now, my daughter, and you are under his protection," he had told her, trying to keep his voice from betraying his worry about her and his dislike of the situation she was in. "Be obedient and give no cause for offense. But always remember we are there at home if you should need anything."

Murjana was moved and kissed her uncle's hand.

Hamza gave her a meaningful look as he left, and whispered, "Remember to whom you owe your first duty." Yazan hugged her closely and said they'd miss her at home.

☐

Once they had gone, Murjana felt momentarily bereft. But the Caliph's overwhelming presence soon swept all thought from her mind. She found his company intoxicating. No one had ever cherished her, satisfied her every wish, or anticipated her every mood as he did. In those first days, as she surrendered herself to his tireless passion, he seemed to her like a father, a lover, and a teacher all in one. She luxuriated in his indulgence of her, his adoration, his ceaseless attention. It made her feel precious, special, taught her to see herself through his eyes and love herself for the first time. She reveled in it.

When, much later, she looked back on those days, it seemed to her that she had lived in a sort of sexual haze, her body not her own but part of his, entwined with him in an endless embrace. He made her discover pleasures she never knew existed. She felt the thrill of them every time he looked at her and could think of nothing else. The everyday routines of eating, bathing, dressing, and attending to the prayer times went by unnoticed; even taking strolls outside in the environs of the house hardly impinged on her consciousness. Her only reality was the Caliph, the smell of him, his touch on her, the frequent times they lay together. He dazzled her by the extravagance of his love and the wealth and glamor of the world he had brought her into.

In all those days, he hardly left her side but for the times when he tore himself away to dine with Harthama and his sons out of courtesy. Mostly, their meals were brought to their room, when it pleased him sometimes not to let her eat unless he fed her with his own hand, teasing the food tenderly into her mouth as if she were a child. When once on another whim he gave her wine to drink, and it made her cough and splutter, he took her in his arms and with his tongue licked every droplet from her lips.

As the days and nights passed in a passionate dalliance that never seemed to pause, Murjana felt herself ever more tied to the Caliph by a bond of emotion, which he fed with his insatiable love for her. In the darkness of the night, he would hold her in his embrace and whisper into her hair, "I love you Murjana. You are my life, my soul, my beloved." He spoke to her of his past life, his childhood, the mother whose memory he treasured, and the hardships he had seen. She understood little of the things he described, but sensed his great relief that he could confide his secrets, and lay quietly listening to him. He loved her for it, and one night, unable to express the emotion that filled him, sank down on his knees and put his head in her lap. At such times she feared the strength of his feelings for her.

Murjana had been virginal before her wedding, but not ignorant of what went on between men and women. She knew many girls younger than herself who were already long married. They gossiped about relations with their husbands, spoke frankly about their often disappointing experiences, and complained about men's boorishness and insensitivity. None of this bore any resemblance to her few days with the Caliph, nor did it help her to understand his extreme ardor. She did not know if his adoration was normal, or how to control it.

But she was now as caught up with him, as he with her, and did not let it worry her for long. She was still unsure that she could trust him entirely, but there was a peculiar joy in her complete abandonment to him, letting him do with her what he desired, and she forgot her qualms. Her uncle, her brothers, the imam, and every burdensome obligation she had ever taken on in the time before vanished from her mind. It was a freedom from care she had not known since childhood, and a wonderful sense of liberation filled her, as if Hamza had sprung up before her and said, "Dear sister, don't worry. I will not hold you to your promise anymore." If only it could be true, she thought, and not a fantasy where no sooner had the image of her brother appeared than it faded away.

✠

As their stay at Famm al-Silh drew to a close, Murjana felt that she had changed. In those seventeen days with the Caliph, she had matured and blossomed into womanhood. Her skin glowed, her eyes shone, and her vibrant young body pulsated with promise. She did not know it, but she was every inch a seducer of men. Never again would the Caliph permit her to be shown off in public, as he had once desired. The thought that lecherous men should feast their eyes on her radiant beauty was intolerable to him. Henceforth, she would be covered in the thickest of veils before strangers, too precious to share with even their most casual glance. And when they were back in Baghdad, he decided she would live with him at his private apartments in the palace, not at the Dar al-Huram as would have been expected. They would be as inseparable there as they had been at Harthama's house, and when the frenzy of his passion gradually calmed, they would settle into a quiet happiness that none should disturb.

✠

"What have you got to tell me?" asked Abu Ubaydah when Talha came to report. The commander's anxiety about the Caliph's marriage had not been relieved with the wedding, and he was as determined as before to protect his ruler. He had had the wedding guests and every activity at Harthama's house watched from the moment the Caliph arrived at Famm al-Silh.

Talha scratched his neck. He was looking more than usually scruffy, his mustache in bad need of a trim, and his tunic crumpled as if he'd slept in it, which he probably had.

"Well," he coughed to clear his throat. "I set one of my best men on it, and he watched the lady's brothers, especially the ugly one, and hung around the wedding banquet. He saw the brother talk to Abu Mansour, the doctor, in the courtyard. Looked as if it was something important."

Abu Ubaydah was puzzled. How was Abu Mansour involved? "Did your man hear what was said?"

"Not all of it, but something about a visit the brother made to the doctor and a sick relative. Nothing more happened until the next day when the brother said goodbye to the lady and whispered something in her ear which made her look unhappy."

"Is that all?"

"I called my man off. There didn't seem much point because our master and the lady hardly ever came out of their room after everyone had gone."

"Didn't you watch out for the Caliph as I told you to?" Abu Ubaydah was annoyed.

Talha shrugged, unruffled.

"Like I said, seemed no point to it. But we kept an eye on her brothers and her uncle all the way back to Baghdad. Nothing happened, and after they got home we left it at that."

Abu Ubaydah considered the man for a moment, but could think of nothing more to ask him. "All right," he muttered, and threw him a bag of dirhams, which Talha caught deftly in one hand.

He didn't leave, as the general had expected, but hung about hesitantly.

"I was wondering if we couldn't wait for a few weeks and then start watching the Banu Shaaban house again. I mean, if they were going to do anything, they wouldn't want to do it straightaway, would they? And from what I saw of the brother, he didn't look right. Sort of sly and underhand."

Abu Ubaydah had never told Talha the reason for his wish to have the family watched, but the man had inferred for himself that they still posed a threat. His suggestion made sense. Even so, Abu Ubaydah felt all at sea and could not decide on the best way forward. Perhaps his suspicions were exaggerated after all.

On the one hand, there was a definite case to be made that the Banu Shaaban family constituted a source of potential danger to the Caliph. As Shiites, they were hostile to him, and some of their kind had taken up arms against him. One of those rebels had been the bride's own brother, put to death by the Caliph's soldiers, which had caused the family much grief and bitterness. Doubtless there were moments when they must have wanted revenge.

But on the other hand, was it not a stretch too far from there to the idea of the family deciding to do the Caliph actual harm, and do so by way of his new bride? Had he, Abu Ubaydah, got too carried away by the startling discovery of a close link between the bride and the executed rebel and inflated it into some imminent threat against the Caliph? He could not make up his mind, and wondered again if he should share his suspicions with Abu Hisham or Durayd.

Talha was looking at him expectantly. "Thank you, Talha. I'm not sure for the time being. I'll think about it and let you know."

When the man had gone, Abu Ubaydah thought some more and then made a decision. He was a soldier, more used to drawing up military strategies and anticipating enemy moves in battle than working out the plans of devious men in peace time. That being so, he would take his suspicions to those more accustomed to that sort of intrigue and discharge his duty to the Caliph with their help.

But whatever his doubts about his own judgment, Abu Ubaydah could not dispel the fear that there was danger, be it from Murjana's family or someone else, and he would not rest until he was satisfied that it existed no more.

24

At the Dar al-Huram, the Caliph's wedding came and went, and still Hind had not left her apartments. In despair, she had reached out to her uncle soon after the Caliph repudiated her, and went to plead for his help.

"Please, Uncle, let me come and live with you. My mother and father are far away, and I can't travel there until they know what has happened."

"Well, why don't you wait till then?"

Her uncle was old and infirm, but not senile. It had never occurred to her that he was anything but soft-hearted and kind, and being her father's brother, he would surely stand in for him. She was at a loss.

"Has the Caliph thrown you out?"

She shook her head miserably. "He no longer wants me. He has divorced me and taken a new wife. He hasn't asked me to leave, but I can't stay there."

"And you can't come here," said the old man firmly.

He sat up on his cushions with surprising vigor. "My daughter, women are divorced every day in our land, there's nothing unusual in that. It's just the order of things that men marry new wives. You're no different from many other women. At least the

Caliph has let you stay in your apartments, and I can't displease him by sheltering you here."

Hind returned to the palace in a state of dejection, feeling utterly alone in the world. In fact, her position was not much different from what it had been before—her family far away in Mecca, and her uncle a man she hardly ever saw. But it didn't matter. The Caliph had made her feel a part of him and his world, and she wanted no other. Back in her rooms, she avoided the other wives and sat alone in the dark. She would have to wait for her letter to her father to reach Mecca and then leave. Yet, she did not want to go. The visit to her uncle had made her realize it. If she left the palace, she could never come back, and the thin thread that still bound her to the Caliph would be severed forever.

Idris, her sole confidant, and the only person from whom she did not hide her wretchedness, had accompanied her to her uncle's house and seen her despair on leaving it. It irked him to see how much she still yearned for the Caliph, as if she didn't realize she was actually divorced and had no rights of any kind.

"I'm sure you know what they're saying about his new marriage." He didn't want to be unkind, but her persistent denial of reality irritated him.

She winced at his words. She had heard the gossip from Zeinab and some of the concubines. Still smarting from the Caliph's abandonment of them all, Zeinab told her how the happy couple had not left their bedroom for two weeks.

"Apparently, our lord was so enamored he couldn't tear himself away. They say he does as little as possible, so he can get back to her. God knows how he's going to govern the land if he goes on like that."

Hind's sudden pallor told Zeinab she'd hit home. *Not the Caliph's favorite now, are we?* she thought spitefully. *You're no better than the rest of us here. At least he didn't divorce us.*

Um Jaafar took the gossip equably.

"It's not our business anymore. We must put it behind us. And if our lord is happy with his new wife, then all the better for him. It wasn't long ago that we feared for his life. We should wish him well."

She can talk, Zeinab thought. It was her son who was the Caliph's favorite; Jaafar even lived with him in his private apartments, along with the new wife.

Hind remained silent, as if struck dumb. Without a word, she nodded at Zeinab and the other wives, and went back to her apartment. Um Jaafar looked after her and shook her head.

"She really should make good on her resolve and leave. She won't be able to accept what's happened as long as she's here." Um Jaafar had more charity for the younger woman than Zeinab did. Once she too had loved the Caliph and nurtured hopes of his marrying no other. But she was realistic and knew it was an idle dream, as indeed it turned out to be when he married Sulafa, and then the others. However, over the years, his respect for her opinion and advice helped to compensate her for her disappointment, and she found substitute contentment in bringing up her children.

But even she was unprepared for an event that none of them anticipated.

▣

"You don't have to do that, my darling, at least not yet," the Caliph had said when Murjana told him of her plan to visit the Dar al-Huram.

He worried about her going alone among his resentful wives, especially Hind. He did not think she would be able to deal with them.

"I must meet them sooner or later," said Murjana. "I can't hide away as if I was ashamed of what I've done, and we must make peace. They will surely see I don't mean any harm. Maybe we could grow to be friends."

She had lived in the Caliph's private apartments ever since they came to the palace. He was reluctant for her to leave them, and each morning he had no sooner gone to his daily meetings with his officials than he was back to take sherbet with her in the courtyard amid the chirping of his songbirds. Tearing himself away again, he would return for lunch as the tables were laid with the best foods the palace cooks could provide. His official duties became a sort of punctuation in the flow of his life with her, tedious diversions he was forced to accommodate. They mostly dined alone, but at times he would permit others to join them for lunch and had invited Abu Mansour more often than anyone else.

In the long afternoons after lunch as the Caliph lay with Murjana, he would stroke her hair and tell her what he had done that day and all the thoughts that passed through his head. It was at such times that she felt able to put in her usually modest requests. Having gained his permission, although reluctantly, to visit his harem, she felt emboldened to ask for a second favor.

"My dearest lord, I'm not used to staying in one place all the time. In my uncle's house, I used to go to visit with my aunt, see my cousins, or go with them to their friends. Since we returned from Famm al-Silh, I've been nowhere but in these rooms."

"You've been free to roam the palace, Murjana. Your family has come to see you, and I've said they're welcome any time. Weren't you happy to see them?"

"Of course. But I'm still not used to it here, and I'd like to go home every now and then."

He took her in his arms. "But this is your home, here with me."

He hated her leaving him, even on such an innocent mission. Still, it was agreed that one of her brothers, and her cousin, Ayesha, should come to the palace and take her to her uncle's house.

In the weeks since her return to Baghdad, Hamza had not paid her a single visit and had sent no word. She feared his silence more than anything and took it to mean she was failing in the mission they had agreed, a mission she still didn't really understand, but it made her feel guilty.

more than anything and took it to mean she was failing in the mission they had agreed, a mission she still didn't really understand, but it made her feel guilty.

Idris was at Murjana's side when she set out across the palace grounds one afternoon to go to the women's quarters. She was apprehensive about meeting the Caliph's wives. But she was also determined to neutralize what she felt sure was their resentment of her, even if they never became her friends. The Dar al-Huram had been forewarned of her coming, and all the women, wives, concubines, slaves, and stewardesses were curious to see the girl who had enslaved their Caliph.

"Salam!"

Murjana made her way into Um Jaafar's apartment and took off her veil. It was a smaller room than she had expected, nothing like the spacious chambers of the Caliph's private apartments. Two other women sat on the cushions staring at her, and she wondered which of the wives they were.

"Peace upon you too," Um Jaafar welcomed her, inviting her to sit down. She clapped her hands for a stewardess to bring in refreshments. "This is the lady Sulafa, and this, the lady Zeinab."

Murjana knew them to be the Caliph's second and third wives. There was an awkward silence. However they had imagined Murjana, they had not expected to see a girl of such warm and exquisite beauty.

"I thought it was time I made myself known to you," said Murjana, flushing. They waited.

"I would have come to live here with you, but our lord did not wish it. I'm sorry."

Zeinab regarded her unsmilingly. "What makes you think we would have wanted you here?"

She was annoyed by the girl's beauty and couldn't understand why she had come. In her shoes, Zeinab would have gone nowhere near the Caliph's other wives. After all, she had won and they had lost. Was she there to gloat or what?

Sulafa coughed. She too was struck by Murjana's looks and could understand why the Caliph was in love. Sulafa had known from the beginning that her own marriage to him was one of convenience. He had never loved or desired her, but had always been kind and dutiful. Expecting nothing more, she had accepted her role as mother to his children with meek resignation. Murjana's beauty only reminded her of her own plain looks and underlined her irrelevance to the Caliph's life.

Murjana was flustered.

"I don't know if you want me here or not. But I had to let you know that it was not my choice to exclude you."

"And how could you do that?" Hind had come in time to hear the conversation. Earlier, she had declined Um Jaafar's invitation to receive Murjana with the others. But her curiosity to see the woman who had captivated her lord and lured him away from her was too strong to resist. A turmoil of emotion churned inside her as she came to Um Jaafar's room when Idris told her that Murjana had arrived. She tried to remind herself that she was no longer the Caliph's wife and that Um Jaafar had only invited her out of courtesy. But it made no difference to her sense that she was still his wife, just waiting for him to realize it, once his silly infatuation was over.

Now she stood in the doorway and saw what she had dreaded for months. The girl was entrancing in exactly the way the Caliph liked: intelligent eyes, lissom body, sensual beauty. It was worse than her worst imaginings. She walked further into the room.

"What made you think anything *you* did could exclude *us*?" Her eyes flashed. "We are the Caliph's longstanding loyal wives, not some bit of short-term amusement. However he may stray, we know it won't be for long."

She looked as if she might attack the other woman with her fists. Um Jaafar was not pleased.

"Please remember, Hind, you are in my apartment. The lady Murjana is my guest. We will all treat her with courtesy and respect."

She took Murjana's hand and sat her down. Um Jaafar was not blind to the girl's attractiveness, which confirmed the descriptions her son had given her. She was uneasy about his adolescent admiration for the Caliph's new bride. But the boy was young and easily impressed, and Um Jaafar had no fears for her own place in his affections. Even so, and with all the composure she could muster, she found it galling to have this winsome young woman set both her husband's and her son's hearts on fire.

"It was very kind of you to come and visit us, Lady Murjana. I am sure everyone appreciates your good intentions." Um Jaafar warned Hind off with a stern look, but which had no effect on her.

"It wasn't kind of her at all! She wanted to feel sorry for us, to rub our noses in it, show us what failures we were!"

"No," protested Murjana in distress. "No. It's not like that at all. I wanted to greet you and get to know you. I thought perhaps we could be friends."

She waited for a response, and when none came, she continued a little desperately. "Making anyone unhappy was the last thing I wanted."

"Well, we're all unhappy. So there." Hind's nostrils flared and her eyes were wild. She frightened Murjana.

Um Jaafar stood up and faced her. "Hind, you must stop."

"So, you want to defend this slut who's taken our place? Can't you see she's a cheap little schemer who's used her wiles on our lord and got him to marry her?" Crude though she was, her words struck a deep chord with the wives' feelings.

Before anyone could stop her, Hind suddenly lunged forward and dragged Murjana up from her seat. She pushed her in front of her and into the corridor. Then, reaching the front door, she wrenched it open and threw her out.

Murjana lost her balance and fell over onto the ground. Idris was too late to intervene. He rushed to help Murjana to her feet, and, along with the servant Um Jaafar had despatched after her, they helped brush her off and gave her back her veil.

When Idris caught up with Hind, he shook his head at her.

"What have you done? What have you done? I will have to tell the Caliph, even if the lady doesn't tell him first."

Hind shrugged her shoulders defiantly.

"Tell him all you want. I don't care. He needs a shock to see what his foolishness has led to. She must be unmasked." And she wanted to add, *Then he can return to me.*

Idris could only pity her the more. He knew what the Caliph would do, and she must have feared it too.

⊞

"Inform the lady Hind that I expect her to leave the palace as soon as she can," the Caliph said coldly when Idris recounted the story to him. Murjana had concealed the incident from him, and he was shocked and angry. Idris tried to soften the details, but it didn't fool the Caliph.

"I believe she has an uncle still living in Baghdad."

Idris nodded.

"Let her go there. Inform him that he must take her in at once. Tell the lady also that she is allowed to stay out the period of her 'iddah at her uncle's house."

Idris duly delivered the Caliph's message to Hind's uncle, and then, much against his will, to her. He found her sitting stiffly upright in her room, as if frozen.

"I'm sure you didn't want that to happen?"

She was silent, but eventually she raised her eyes to his. They were bloodshot, puffy, and full of pain. She spoke in a dull monotone that alarmed him even more than her hysterical weeping.

"I want only one thing. He is mine and always will be. I will not let her have him, no matter what it takes."

She seemed half-crazed, and he didn't know what to say. She stood up and looked into his eyes.

"If you have any love for me, Idris, you will help me. I have no one but you."

With that, she ran to him and put her arms tightly around him. Her body quivered as she wept, and despite the situation, an unaccustomed thrill went through him. Sensing his reaction, she stopped sobbing, looked into his eyes, and then, without warning, kissed him full on the lips. He found himself hesitantly responding. It was all wrong and, had anyone walked in, he would have been exposed as the worst of traitors to his master. But he didn't think about that and gave himself up to the pleasure of the moment.

What she meant by her threat to the Caliph's young wife, he didn't know, but didn't take it seriously. She was filled with the bitter rage of all spurned wives. He had seen it before among the harem of the Caliph's predecessor, though never among his master's women, until now.

He would let her storm and grieve and wallow in self-pity to her heart's content. She was trapped, a divorced and discarded woman, with no one to turn to but him. The thought of her helplessness made him tender toward her. There was no need for her to have asked. He would help her faithfully, and also love and serve her. And in time, he hoped she might learn to forget the Caliph and her former life.

25

The days were growing longer and warmer, and the sky had become cloudless most of the time. It was the season of the year Abu Mansour liked most, cool enough to carry out his work at home and in the bimaristan without the interruption of an afternoon sleep. Abu Mansour couldn't understand why everyone needed to do that. Left to himself, he would have recommended a rest in the shade at the hottest time of day, preferably upright and with eyes closed, but not actually sleeping. Whenever he gave in to the dozy afternoon silence and inactivity of everything around him, he would invariably wake up thirsty, with a bad taste in his mouth, and feeling more tired than before. It could take an hour or more to shake off the lassitude and regain his energy. His mother, who herself slept deeply when it was hot, didn't agree with him.

"Sleep refreshes you, my son, and helps you to enjoy the rest of the day. Of course, if there was a wife to lie down with, you'd soon be enjoying your afternoon naps!"

She said this teasingly, but he never rose to the bait.

※

Younis had not been around much lately, Abu Mansour noticed.

He carried out his duties as scrupulously as before, but didn't hang around when he finished. Ahmad, who used to know Younis's whereabouts, had been raised to the status of apprentice and now worked at the bimaristan.

"You're free to go whenever you want, of course, Younis. But is there some reason why you don't want to spend time here as you used to? Has something happened with your family?"

Younis shook his head. "Nothing like that, sir."

"Well, what then?" persisted Abu Mansour, more curious than ever at the boy's reluctance to speak.

They were in the dispensary where Younis was helping to prepare a jar of oxymel, a mixture of honey and vinegar, and the standby of physicians for the preservation of health. A draught, taken first thing in the morning, was cleansing and restorative. Abu Mansour himself took a spoonful daily and prescribed the same for the rest of the family.

Younis looked uncomfortable. "If I tell you, sir, you'll only be annoyed with me."

Abu Mansour paused his mixing and looked up at him.

"How do you know unless you tell me?"

Younis still hesitated. "All right, but please hear me out before passing judgment."

Abu Mansour nodded, and they both sat down on the dispensary stools.

"A week ago I was in the spice-sellers' souk to get cinnamon and cardamom for my mother. You know, the big shop in the grand souk. On my way there, I passed by the apothecary's, the one we always use, and saw a man talking to the apothecary. He had his back to me, but when I got closer, he turned round and I recognized him. It was Hamza, the son of the Banu Shaaban—no doubt about it. I'm sure he didn't know who I was, so I stopped at the edge of the shop and made as if I was looking among the medicine jars and sniffing the herb baskets. And I overheard him ask the apothecary how soon could he get him *some*? The apothecary said, they ran low this time of year, but he was expecting a delivery of freshly cut flowers any day now. Hamza could come back in a few days. Or he might find the doctors still had a stock, why not go to one of them? Hamza said he'd rather buy it from this shop. He took some money out of his pocket and gave it to him. It must have been a lot, because the apothecary looked pleased and told Hamza to leave it to him."

"Was that it?"

"No. I saw Hamza go off and join another man I hadn't noticed who was standing nearby. He looked older and rather grim, I thought. He held out his hand to Hamza, but Hamza shook his head, as if to say he hadn't got it. Then they left."

Abu Mansour looked at Younis, expecting him to continue. Younis cleared his throat with the air of a storyteller coming to his fable's climax.

"I managed to find the apothecary's boy I always deal with. He was weighing out batches of snuff, and I asked him what the man who'd been speaking to his master had wanted. I thought he might have me ask the apothecary, but he didn't hesitate. 'Opium,' he said. 'Oh, is that all?' I said, pretending I wasn't that interested anymore. I asked what he wanted it for, but the boy didn't hear that part."

Younis paused to let this clue sink in.

"I've thought a lot about it since then. I mean there was that time when Hamza came here and asked you about his relative. I know he wanted to get you to tell him about poisons."

"How did you know? I never told you."

Younis flushed red and looked flustered. Abu Mansour had long suspected that Younis routinely listened at the door and overheard what went on inside his consulting room. But he usually didn't mind it because his apprentice was loyal and discreet.

"And what if he did?"

"Well, this is what I think." Younis paused again for dramatic effect. "There must have been a reason for his wanting that information, and I reckon Hamza was up to no good. So when I saw him in the market and there he was again trying to get something that could be used as a poison, I decided to watch him. And I've been going to that apothecary's shop all week to see if he came back."

"So that's where you've been going," said Abu Mansour with growing impatience.

"Sorry, sir, it is. And yesterday I saw Hamza come back and pick up a package from the apothecary. It was quite small. He tucked it under his arm and left like he was in a hurry. He was alone this time."

Younis stood there with a look of triumph on his face.

"Why are you so interested in this story?" asked Abu Mansour in disbelief. "A young man goes to the apothecary and tries to buy some opium. He probably should have gone to a doctor instead. But so what?"

"Don't you see, sir? Hamza isn't *any* man. He's the brother of the Caliph's wife. What he does could affect the Caliph. And he's got himself a load of poison. What for?"

Abu Mansour took Younis by the shoulders. "Listen, Younis, this nonsense has to stop. I know you've done all this spying in your own time, and you're not shirking your work. But you've let yourself get carried away, like that time at the Caliph's wedding when you thought all sorts of strange things were happening."

Younis looked hurt.

"Hamza has done nothing wrong as far as I can see. His interest in poisons could have all sorts of reasons, and opium isn't normally used as a poison. People take it for everything—sleeplessness, cough, diarrhea, for every kind of pain. It's true Hamza's related to the Caliph through marriage, but what's that got to do with his buying opium?"

Younis remained silent, and Abu Mansour went on, though not unkindly.

"I suppose this comes from the time I sent you to spy on the lady Murjana. But that's over. From now on, I don't want to hear another word about strange happenings and dark plots. Just pay attention to your work here and don't worry about Hamza or his quest for opium. Or anything else about him."

In one of the small chambers of the palace, Abu Ubaydah sat with the Caliph's chief officers. They all respected the commander and knew he would not have asked to meet them without good reason.

"Greetings to you all. I thought long and hard before deciding to confide to you my suspicions and fears for our master relating to his new marriage."

They were suddenly alert. Abu Ubaydah got to the point.

"It's not my place to approve or disapprove of the Caliph's new marriage. But I have had private misgivings about the lady Murjana's family from the start. Much too late, I remembered an incident that happened a time ago."

Everyone waited for him to continue.

"It came back to me that the lady Murjana's brother, named Yahya, was a Shia rebel who'd joined a group of dissidents I later learned was headed by a man called Ismail. The Caliph ordered me to put an end to the rebellion. It turned out to be a limited operation and not difficult to do."

He reflected silently for a moment.

"In the battle, just a skirmish really, I rounded up the ring-leaders and had them put to death. Lady Murjana's brother, Yahya, was among them. By the time I remembered the incident and went to alert our master to the danger he might be in, the wedding had already happened."

The Caliph's chamberlain spoke up. "If you had alerted the Caliph since he came back to Baghdad, I would have known," he said.

Abu Ubaydah shook his head.

"Telling him something so uncertain could have caused grave offense for no good reason. The truth is, I'm unsure of what to do, and so I decided it was time to share my concerns with you gentlemen."

"You did right, Abu Ubaydah," said Durayd. "The matters you've brought up are extremely serious."

"What are you afraid of?" asked the Caliph's secretary, Uthman.

"I couldn't help thinking that Yahya's death must have aroused his family's anger and enmity toward our master. What if Yahya's brothers, or uncle, or all of them wanted revenge against the Caliph for killing him? It's not that unlikely. In our military world of killing and counter-killing, only blood for blood will wipe out dishonor and bring satisfaction."

"And you're worried the lady Murjana's family will try to avenge Yahya's death by harming our master in some way?" asked Durayd.

Abu Ubaydah nodded.

"But we have no actual evidence for any of this," said Uthman. "Have threats been made? Do we know of any actual preparations for some attack on our master?"

His overconfident tone irritated the Caliph's chief wazir. "Following that kind of logic, the crime would have been over and done with while you were still looking for clues." Abu Hisham turned to Abu Ubaydah. "All of us had similar anxieties about the bride's family before the Caliph married her. We tried to warn him. And that was before we had any idea about Yahya or his death. What you've told us about the brother makes the case for our worries even stronger."

He looked round at the others. They were as nonplussed as he was. He turned back again to Abu Ubaydah. "Have you acted on your suspicions?"

"I assigned my best spies to observe the bride's family, before and after the wedding. But nothing out of the ordinary happened. Now I'm at a loss to know what to do."

No one spoke, but in all their minds was the fear of the Caliph's wife and what she might be capable of.

"Shouldn't we set a watch on the imam?" asked Uthman. "Wouldn't the Banu Shaaban be sure to consult him on something like this?"

Abu Hisham dismissed the idea. The imam was renowned for his gentleness and humanity and would never agree to such a thing as cold-blooded revenge.

At last, Durayd spoke.

"We've got to face it. The lady Murjana is the best channel to our master. If her family really is planning revenge, then it is most likely to come through her, not some hired assassin."

He had finally uttered the two unmentionable things they had all been skirting around: that the Banu Shaaban's aim could be no less than the Caliph's murder, and that the assassin could be none other than their daughter, his wife, and the woman he adored most in the world.

At this point, Abu Ubaydah, whose lifelong focus had been on action, not sentiment, and who had been frustrated by the slow pace of events so far, took charge.

"No need for hesitation. Forewarned is forearmed. We simply cannot let this happen. And the surest way to do that is to go direct to the intended victim—the Caliph himself. He must be warned to be on his guard. And we should consider putting the Banu Shaaban brothers and their uncle under house arrest until they're proved innocent."

"I understand how you feel, Abu Ubaydah," said the chief wazir. "But we can't do any of that."

"Why not?"

"If you were to see our master these days," Durayd cut in, "you would understand. He's been transformed by this marriage.

He is inseparable from the lady Murjana and so deeply in love he can barely think of anything else. In all the years I've known him, I have never seen him so happy, or content. It would be a brave man who interferes and smashes his dreams. I will not be that man, and, if you value your life, commander, neither will you."

⊞

Abu Ubaydah left the meeting at the palace, dissatisfied. It had done nothing to solve his predicament, and the Caliph remained in danger. He was not convinced that their master was too delicate, or however they had put it, to withstand being alerted to his situation, and needed to think of a way to tell him. It did not improve his mood to learn just after the meeting that Abdullah ibn Rida, that scoundrel of a governor he had succeeded in trapping, was out of prison. Unbelievably, he had escaped from one of the Caliph's best fortified jails disguised as a woman.

Questioning the prison guards, they put it down to the visits Abdullah had received from one or two people described as friends, just before the escape.

"But you knew it was forbidden for him to receive visitors or have any special treatment."

Abu Ubaydah was furious. The guards each denied being bribed by the prisoner. They claimed that someone had smuggled a sack of women's clothing to Abdullah, which he put on while being moved from one cell to another when no one was looking. The commander didn't believe a word of it, and saw only too well that Abdullah's considerable wealth had been put to good use to contrive his escape.

Once out of prison, he disappeared into the streets of Baghdad, and weeks later, reports surfaced of a man answering to his description being overheard making threats against the Caliph. It seemed Abdullah was engaged in a secretive vendetta, seeking to gather supporters to his cause from among dissidents and troublemakers in the city. Abu Ubaydah did not think he would succeed in making good his threats, however bitter his anger. But he could still rally enemies who opposed the Caliph.

Abdullah Ibn Rida was at large now, and that was that. It was only a matter of time before he was caught again, and this time, executed.

Abu Ubaydah turned his attention once more to the far more real threat of the Caliph's wife and her family. But his resolve to warn the Caliph face to face faltered once he thought about it again. Perhaps it wasn't a wise move after all. The only thing left was to set a watch on the lady, which he probably should have done much earlier. If she were in fact the chosen weapon of her family's revenge, it was she who would lead him to their treachery.

Even as he thought of the idea, he knew it could never happen. For a servant of the Caliph like himself to spy on the Caliph's wife was outside the bounds of protocol and well beyond his military authority. The surveillance he had already carried out on her family had been risky enough, and he had often wondered if the Caliph's spies ever reported their encounters with his own. Since nothing came of it, he assumed they had not and that he had got away with it. But the risk of discovery and its consequences, if he were to repeat the exercise with the Caliph's wife, were unconscionable, and he put the matter out of his mind.

26

In a modest house, not far from the quarter where the Banu Shaaban lived, four men were holding a secret meeting. The room, which was seldom used, was sparsely furnished, with no rugs covering the floor or adorning the walls. The doors and windows were closed and the room was stuffy and airless. A lamp burned in one corner, casting a weak glow over the huddled group. The men sat cross-legged on flat cushions around a coarsely woven brown mat on which several papers were spread out.

A sudden knock at the door startled them. But it was the house boy, asking if they wanted some refreshment. No one did and he was sent away.

The eldest in the group, Ismail, who appeared to be the most authoritative of the four, spoke.

"Why didn't you bring your brother, Yazan, with you?"

Hamza looked flustered. "Should I have done? He's young and...a bit unreliable."

Ismail frowned. "What do you mean?"

Hamza became more flustered.

"I just mean he's easily impressed. He gets taken in by all that wealth and glamor at the palace. Not that he's not a good kid, far from it. He's one of us, I'm sure of it. He loved Yahya more than anyone, and I'd vouch for his loyalty any time."

Hamza knew he was saying too much, as if he had something to hide.

"Is there any chance your brother might do or say something that could give us away?"

"No! I didn't mean that at all. Ask Musa, he knows him."

"Yes, I do," said Musa. "He's a good, honest boy. But we probably shouldn't rely too much on his help with our work here, brother Ismail."

"What do you think, Usama?" asked Ismail of the fourth man.

"I say you're being overcautious, and we're wasting time. Why not take the brother's word for it and get on with what's brought us here?"

Ismail nodded. He was a stern-looking man of about forty, with jet black hair and a long, thick beard. Usama, who was a little younger, was also dark and had a thin, haunted-looking face. The two were leaders of the dissident Shia group that Yahya had embraced with enthusiasm.

"For over a year now we've been planning this, brothers," said Ismail. "Ever since Yahya's execution. The long nights, the meetings, the near misses when we thought we'd lost our chance. Remember how often we thought our aim was too ambitious, that we'd need to forget it and think of some other way."

"I don't remember any of that because I wasn't with you till Hamza asked me to join," said Musa. "I have no idea how you began, and I'm still not sure we can succeed. It's too hard to get to the Caliph, and we could easily be found out."

Usama looked at Musa with dismay.

"Why are you saying that now, brother Musa, when we're getting so close to our goal? If you're still asking questions like that after all this time, maybe you shouldn't have joined us."

"No, wait," said Hamza, "Musa didn't mean to lower our

spirits. He's always cautious and careful to follow through on what he sets out to do, which is what we need, brothers." He turned to Musa. "I did try to tell you how we started, but..."

Ismail put up a hand to silence Hamza. He then went on to tell Musa how they had sworn to avenge Yahya's death, a pledge on which his siblings were also agreed. There was no choice but to resist the Caliph. He had to be stopped, and for good. Consulting the imam was useless, as he would only advise patience and persistence until God in His wisdom delivered them from oppression.

"So we knew we had to find our own way to the Caliph. And that's where brother Hamza came in."

Hamza told them about the visit to the palace to recover their land, which by chance brought the Caliph together with Murjana, and how Ismail had spotted an opportunity to make something of it. When Ismail heard from Hamza about this unexpected meeting, he urged him to train his sister in the art of seduction.

Luckily, events developed in an amazing direction that opened a path straight to the Caliph. When Hamza reported back to Ismail and Usama, the three men conferred and came out with a daring plan that, if successful, would satisfy their wildest desires and give them the sweetest revenge.

"From that moment on," said Ismail, "we saw our plan work out better than we'd expected, truly a miracle from God. And here we are on the verge of carrying it out."

There was a silence as everyone took in the significance of the moment. Musa was the first to speak.

"So now we're here, how is it to be done?" He looked troubled. They all turned to Hamza.

"My sister needs a bit more preparation," he said guardedly. "She's known all along her job was to ensnare the Caliph, and she's done that so well she's got him eating out of her hand."

"Does your sister know what she has to do?" asked Usama.

"Well...not exactly. I haven't spelled it out, yet. I wanted to give her time to settle into living with the Caliph first. But I've been reminding her of her mission."

"Yes, but is it clear? Does she understand what we're after?"

"Have no fear, brother. Murjana is as keen as we are to avenge our brother's killing. She's sworn it."

Ismail's stern expression returned.

"You didn't answer the question, Hamza. Does your sister know that the Caliph must die?"

There it was. What no one had been willing to say clearly and unequivocally before had now been said and heard.

In all the months of planning, they had spoken of their goal only in oblique ways, avoiding any mention of the necessity of killing, as if it would tempt fate to thwart their plans by doing so. But now that it had been said, a silence fell over the men as the enormity of what they were contemplating sank in.

Ismail was still looking at Hamza, waiting for him to reply. "Well?"

"I know my sister better than any of you." Hamza's face had hardened, as if it only then struck him that he now had the upper hand. Without Murjana, all their plans would come to nothing.

"So, I will choose the best time to tell her and prepare her for what she must do."

Ismail looked at Usama, and they nodded.

Musa, who had been listening quietly, took Hamza's arm and made for both of them to rise.

"Goodnight, brothers. Hamza, it's time we went."

27

There was a flurry of excitement at the palace, as servants prepared the majlis sitting room for the gathering of jurists and theologians to take place that day. Before the Caliph's illness, these meetings of jurists, philosophers, poets, and literati had been a regular feature of the palace calendar and famous throughout the land, even as far as Byzantium. It was said the Byzantine emperor admired his old enemy in Baghdad for what he heard about the majlis gatherings, how they drew men of talent and learning from all over the Islamic lands, and what glittering occasions they could be. He had nothing at his court that could compare.

In the months of his sickness, and then his absorbing marriage to Murjana, the Caliph had missed these gatherings. Their intellectual vigor and mental stimulation had always delighted him, especially the ones on jurisprudence and theology, which were closest to his ceaseless inquiry into the nature of the divine. For that reason, they were held more regularly than the others. That day's majlis was more eagerly awaited than usual by all who had been invited.

When the Caliph presided over the previous meeting, the controversy over the Quran's createdness was at its height. The factions on each side of the debate were at daggers drawn when he fell ill, and their differences had not narrowed since. Once he recovered, the Caliph started to follow their heated arguments once more, and had invited proponents of both positions to the majlis that day.

It was the same day as Murjana's visit to her family. The Caliph had arranged it that way so as not to miss her absence too much. He was already unaccustomed to life without her. But it surprised him that he should feel so bereft at what would only be a brief parting. Murjana had not left his side for weeks, and, though his formal duties took him physically away from her every day, he carried her around in his head all the time they were apart. It would be the first time she was not there to return to when he had finished the business of the day. The thought opened up a well of nameless anxiety inside him that he could not allay.

Murjana's cousin Ayesha and her younger brother Yazan, keen to see Khalid, his friend in the Barid while at the palace, came to get her. With them would go the head eunuch, and a palace guard to escort them to Abdulhamid's house and accompany Murjana back.

On his way to the majlis, the Caliph embraced her and held her close for a few moments.

"I hate you leaving me."

"It will not be for long, my lord. You will be busy with the majlis and I will be back before you know it."

◫

When the Caliph entered the majlis, the discussion was well underway and growing more animated. These meetings were run along egalitarian lines where the Caliph insisted that the participants, no matter where they ranked in professional or social importance, had an equal share of time to present their arguments. He did not like to dominate the gatherings or give himself privileges over anyone else, but would sit listening attentively and, if he joined in, it was usually at the end. Of course, the guests were only too aware of his intelligent, watchful presence, and vied with each other to impress him.

As he came into the room, everyone stood up and bowed. It had been a long time since the last majlis, and many dramatic events had occurred in the Caliph's life. It was partly in salute to his recovery and new marriage that they stood up to greet him. He smiled and waved them back to their seats. Then he took his place in the center of the rectangular room's long wall facing the arched windows. On warm days, the majlis moved to the courtyard, but it was still too cool for that.

"Please continue your discussions. Let me listen to you before I speak."

They took him at his word. Sheikh Amr Ibn Uthal, a pale, ascetic-looking man with heavy-lidded eyes, and one of the foremost theological scholars to make the traditionist case against the Quran creationists, did not need much encouragement. He resumed his address to a man sitting opposite.

"I don't accept what you say. The purposes of God are not for us to understand. We don't ask why he created such and such, however mysterious it seems to us. And we're not entitled to take a position that questions God's wisdom."

Anas, the man to whom he was addressing this, looked at his companions sitting on the cushions next to him. And then he looked to the Caliph, who was listening intently.

"On which side of what I might call the divide between reason and faith do you place yourself and those who think like you, Sheikh Amr?" interjected the Caliph.

Several of the scholars in the room said they supported the use of reason for understanding the laws of nature and investigating its secrets. How else would one appreciate the breadth of God's power and the marvels of his creation? Ibn Uthal looked round at the theologians who had come with him and saw they disapproved of the way the discussion was going. He had never made any secret of his dislike for the group of unorthodox thinkers now sitting opposite him, members of a sect he and other traditionists dubbed pejoratively, "mu'tazilites," those who set themselves apart because they saw themselves as an elite among a herd of ignorant believers. It dismayed Ibn Uthal that the Caliph had always rejected these criticisms of them. He seemed to be impressed by their ideas, and everyone knew he was now their greatest champion. Without him, thought Ibn Uthal, they might long ago have sunk into the obscurity they deserved.

"I don't fit myself or any believer into a category, my lord," said Ibn Uthal defiantly. "We believe in the wisdom of God and the Last Day. All the knowledge we need is in our holy Quran and the Prophet's Sunna and his Hadith. We don't need question or sophistry. The Quran is uncreated and eternal, and it sets out the truth for all our needs. Why should we put any of it to question or debate? That way can only lead to schism and *kufr*, unbelief."

⊡

Durayd, who was there to see to the guests' comfort, now directed the stewards to serve the various fruit sherbets, and bring in the trays of dates and quinces. He was bored stiff. The conversation was like so many others he had heard before at the palace and usually avoided—fiddly arguments about obscure issues he cared nothing about. He was a practical man, his job was to ensure the smooth day-to-day running of the Caliph's life, not to sit around mooning over meaningless riddles. He looked at the fifteen learned and reputable men in the room, and for the life of him couldn't understand how they let themselves sit for hours wasting time over some minute point of religion or philosophy no one had ever heard of until they dredged it up.

He resented being there. It should have been Uthman, who normally assisted at such gatherings but could not be found that day for some reason, and so he had been forced to step in. Durayd wouldn't have minded attending some others of the Caliph's gatherings, like the ones on poetry, or the musical evenings when the girls came out and danced, which he enjoyed best of all. And even the gatherings of scientists and artists could be interesting, like the one to be held after this one, when the great mathematician from Khwarizm was due to present the Caliph with his famous book on algebra. The Caliph had bestowed exceptional patronage on this scientist, whom he greatly admired, and it would be a grand occasion.

But what he regretted most of all was not to be allowed to go with the lady Murjana's party instead of staying at the majlis. That surely was where the really important events to the Caliph's life were likely to be happening. The Caliph and his guests, meanwhile, were oblivious to anything other than their own disputations, and Durayd could see no hope of the meeting ending for many hours to come.

"Let me ask you to set your differences aside," the Caliph was saying. "My friends, you have rehearsed these issues many times and there's no point restating where you stand. I know that you, Sheikh Amr and the *ulama'* here, are opposed to the use of reason in religious matters. I would agree with you that some of the philosophers have gone too far in saying that religion is just dogma and old wives' tales. But our mu'tazilite friends are not the same. I know they think many stories in the holy text are just allegories and must not be taken literally."

The *ulama'* shifted uncomfortably in their seats.

"But they insist," continued the Caliph calmly, "that rational inquiry can be brought to bear on all aspects of religion. And why not? Our faith in God should be strong enough to withstand that, even to welcome it, don't you agree?"

Several of his listeners nodded in assent. But Ibn Uthal said nothing.

"Like you and me, they see God's essence as justice, and, like us, they know that God' retribution is not absolute, for if a sinner repents, he will receive God's mercy. There is no vengeance in Islam."

The *ulama'* murmured their agreement.

"So you see, despite these differing approaches to our faith, in the end they are true believers just as you are, and their path to the worship of God is as valid as yours. Shall we now agree to make peace and end this unnecessary dispute?"

Ibn Uthal shook his head. "No, my lord. I don't wish to offend, but we cannot. They must first withdraw the blasphemy of claiming the holy Quran was created."

He folded his arms across his chest and sat back. The Caliph looked toward the mu'tazilites, who made no response and seemed intimidated by Ibn Uthal and his companions. Finally, one of them spoke.

"I ask Sheikh Amr this simple question. Is the Quran the actual word of God or not?"

Sheikh Amr would not answer.

"It is," continued the mu'tazilite equably. "And since it is, it must have emanated from God. And that could not happen unless God was there before his word. Ergo, the Quran is subsequent to God, and since God created all things and nothing can exist of itself, it follows he created the Quran. Do you fault this argument?"

Ibn Uthal remained silent. He suddenly gathered his robe around him and stood up. His fellow theologians made to do the same.

"Please give me permission to leave your presence, my lord. I cannot stay to hear our faith slandered in profane arguments copied from godless Greeks. If you allow me, I will go from here and pray for God's forgiveness that I have listened to such men as these."

The Caliph considered him. Amr Ibn Uthal was a man to be reckoned with. He was widely admired for his piety and humble ways. He had an impressive following, and a school of Islamic jurisprudence was named after him. Many taught his ideas and spread them among the people. While the Caliph was ill, languishing in danger of his life, the *ulama'* had been left free to widen their circles and gain more teachers and disciples to spread their message. Some of the foremost madrasas of Baghdad were already teaching religion according to Ibn Uthal. The version of Islam they propounded allowed for no diversions from orthodox belief or practice. Even *Ahl al-Kitab*, people of the book like Christians and Jews, and respected in Islam, ranked second in Ibn Uthal's and his followers' estimation.

Such teachings were utterly alien to a man who prized intellectual freedom like the Caliph. Seeing their popular success, he castigated himself for having allowed it to happen through his negligence of the religious life of his subjects. It was not what he had dedicated his life to do. Through his own studious example, he had sought to direct the people toward a similar learning and enlightenment; had provided them with books in their own languages; libraries, and schools for their education. Above all, he had offered them a new vision of the world, one to be understood through reason and scientific investigation, not obscured by superstition and ignorance. Was he to see all that destroyed by these *ulama's* narrow creed?

The insolence veiled as piety he saw that day from Ibn Uthal and his friends, and the license they seemed to give themselves to express their ideas and prejudices, ostensibly directed at the mu'tazilites, but implicitly at him, showed him the extent of his failure to stop them long before they grew so arrogant. The sight of Ibn Uthal standing before him, expecting to walk out after a perfunctory request for his permission as if it were a foregone conclusion, was like a red rag to a bull. It brought out that hard, unforgiving side of his nature which his subjects last saw in the war with his brother; which Abdullah ibn Rida, the feckless governor of Khorasan, had got a taste of in his harsh prison; and which Murjana tried not to think about after the execution of her brother.

"Sit down, Sheikh Amr."

Silence fell, as everyone in the room started to feel uneasy.

"Close the doors, Durayd, and see to it there are no interruptions of any kind."

He turned to the assembly. "I brought you here today for one last opportunity to resolve our differences through dialogue, courteous discussion, and debate."

He stared Ibn Uthal in the eye.

"I was wrong. What I found were closed minds and arrogance on the part of some of you, the same who preach to naïve and uneducated people all over this city."

Ibn Uthal opened his mouth to speak, but thought better of it.

"The *ulama'* say they oppose the doctrine of the Quran's createdness, and for that they would persecute my mu'tazilite friends here, who try to meet them with rational argument."

"It's not rational argument, my lord, but kufr—blasphemy," Ibn Utal objected.

"We will have to disagree on that, Sheikh Amr. But if you were being honest, you would admit that the Quran's createdness is the symbol of your objections, not the substance. What you and the *ulama'* really oppose is the exercise of reason in the service of truth, something I have made my life's mission. And I will not permit you to overturn it."

His eyes took in the room.

"I have been patient and not interfered in your activities, Sheikh Amr. You and your colleagues have been free to speak, teach, and spread your message. But my tolerance has been abused. You have set yourselves up as a rival authority to the Caliph's. That cannot be allowed to happen. There can only be one authority in these lands, and that is the Commander of the Faithful."

He paused for everyone to take this in, even though it was primarily aimed at the *ulama'*. After a moment he went on.

"I have decided that from this day on, the doctrine of the created Quran will be the official doctrine of these lands. Anyone who opposes my decree will be subject to the *mihna* inquisition, the full punishment of the law until they recant, and my judges are ready to exercise the powers I will give them to enact my decrees."[*]

Ibn Uthal was shocked. He knew the Caliph was displeased, but he had not expected this. He looked at the other *ulama'*, who seemed equally stunned. After a moment, he recovered himself and said with quiet dignity, "We are your subjects, my lord, and yours to command. But there is a higher authority than even the Commander of the Faithful. And it is to that I submit myself over any other."

No one uttered a sound at this foolhardy, some thought admirable, show of defiance.

"You don't seem to have heard me, Sheikh Amr," responded the Caliph coldly. "I have made my decree clear and absolute. And everyone, including you, will obey it."

With that, he rose from his seat, and the gathering stood up and bowed. Durayd opened the doors, and the Caliph left the chamber.

◻

Murjana's party left the palace soon after Yazan and Ayesha arrived that morning. They had gathered in the anteroom to

---

[*] This was the *mihna,* the inquisition instituted by the caliph al-Ma'mun in 833, to impose the doctrine of the created Quran. Theologians, judges, and jurists had to affirm their acceptance of the doctrine. Those who refused were coerced, threatened, and sometimes tortured.

the Caliph's private apartments, avoiding the majlis where they could see men in formal dark robes and tall turbans arriving. Yazan wanted to hang around, curious to see more, but Murjana dragged him away.

It was a fine, spring morning, a little cool, and the girls were sheltered inside a litter carriage through whose discreetly parted curtains they could see the streets of Baghdad. Both found the journey exciting. Neither had ever been so far into the city, and as they took in the scenes of people and animals, the ubiquitous river glinting in the background, they chatted animatedly. Their route took them past a large new building with a tall tower and a platform all around the top. Who could possibly want to stand so high above the ground?

"What is that place?" Ayesha called out to Yazan, walking beside them, as he must have often passed it on his way to the palace.

Yazan did not know, and it was Idris who answered.

"The Caliph's new observatory, madam. It has not been there long, but it already has many scholars working in it. They study the stars and measure their distances and motions. It is a great undertaking, and our lord is very proud of it."

Murjana's heart contracted with emotion at mention of the Caliph. She too felt pride at the sight. The buildings adjacent to the observatory seemed also new.

"Those were built before," said Idris before they asked. "They belong to the translation academy the Caliph set up many years ago. But they've expanded recently because of more translators and a bigger library."

He continued to be their guide to the city landmarks they passed. Murjana stared at the public gardens on the opposite side of the road that ran alongside the river, and longed to get out of the litter and walk in the free air. The early spring flowers looked so fresh and innocent she wanted to touch their soft petals. The desire that came over her to feel the air on her face and the soil beneath her feet was overwhelming. It showed her the extent of her discomfort at living within the confines of the palace. If only she could be allowed to go out into this wonderful city, full of color and people and life, whenever she wished.

They passed the great Hammam, the public bath, its ornamental gates open to receive men and women through their separate entrances. Even at that early hour, people were gathered outside chatting, some having already bathed, and others about to go in. Once past the Hammam, they turned into that part of the city where Abdulhamid lived. Here the streets and houses were quite different, smaller and more crowded together.

As the group walked on, the alleys became narrower and soon would become impassable for the litter. To the right and left were warrens of alleyways, confusing for strangers, and at times even for people who normally lived there. The roads and alleys here were unpaved and the air was dusty. If there ever had been a building plan for this quarter of the city, it must have been long since abandoned. Houses looked as if they had sprung up wherever there was space, and were so densely packed together that if one fell down the rest in the row were likely to collapse.

After the grandeur of central Baghdad's wide streets, its parks and monuments, it was hard to believe they were still in the same city. But to Murjana it was home. She did not see the dilapidated buildings or the rundown streets. It was by no means the poorest section of Baghdad, and a far cry from the city's slums with their hovels and filthy alleyway. Her heart lifted as they neared her uncle's house.

⊞

Murjana's homecoming was made a special occasion. The house had been especially cleaned, and the best hangings and cushions brought out. Zubeida and Ayesha's sister were there with the rest of the family to welcome her. Their immediate neighbors had also turned up to see the glamorous group from the palace, and the ones further down the street came out in front of their houses to wave and stare. One or two greeted Yazan and tried to talk to the guards, but were ignored.

"How high and mighty these Banu Shaaban have got," one of them grumbled.

The welcome Abdulhamid put on for Murjana was touching. Bouquets of flowers decorated the entrance, and a broth of mixed pulses and honey reserved for special celebrations was served to the party as they entered. It was a kind gesture since she knew her uncle had still not accepted her marriage and thought she had sacrificed herself needlessly for the sake of their community.

"The Abbasid cannot change," he had said to the imam. "I pray she will be spared his worst excesses."

The imam advised Abdulhamid to set aside his anxieties and leave it to the will of God and the common sense of his niece. And one had only to look at Murjana to admit she looked exceptionally well, radiant, his sister said. He supposed it was the goodness in her heart and her patience in the face of adversity shining through.

"Sometimes, I think you're very foolish, brother," said Zubeida. "It's nothing to do with any of that. Can't you see? Murjana's young and the Caliph adores her, just what any girl longs for in a husband. Let her enjoy it while she can."

She was thinking of her own unmarried daughters, and how that hoped-for betrothal to the son of the Tabrizi family had come to nothing. She took little interest in public affairs and did not share her brother's dislike of the Caliph, who had behaved well toward them, she thought.

But her remark had made Abdulhamid uneasy. He studied Murjana's face and her behavior more closely. She certainly did not appear unhappy, rather the opposite, and he could not fit that into his understanding of her situation with the Caliph. The more he observed her, the more serene and self-confident she looked to him. He would have to discuss it with Hamza afterward, he decided.

The noon prayer behind them, the family sat down to lunch. Idris had tactfully turned down the invitation to join them, and stayed with the guard in another room. The meal was a feast unlike any the frugal Abdulhamid had ever offered. A sheep had been slaughtered for the occasion, roasted on a spit at the butcher's, and then stuffed with saffron rice and dried fruit. The carcass, decorated with herbs and covered with toasted almonds, was served on a huge platter borrowed from Zubeida's well-to-do neighbors. It looked sumptuous. They ate heartily, but it was impossible to eat much of the rich meat. When the household and the visitors had had their fill, the rest of the sheep was sent to the mosque to be distributed among the poor of the neighborhood in the time-honored custom after such celebrations.

Murjana thanked her uncle. She was happy to be among them again, to feel normal. By contrast, her life at the palace was an aberration. It felt temporary, as if she would wake up one morning to be told she could now go home and forget all about the palace. But did that apply to the Caliph too? Was he also temporary in her life? She realized that he loomed so large in that life it was impossible to imagine him no longer there. As the thought came into her mind, she saw Hamza's eyes on her. He had embraced her warmly when she arrived and behaved so pleasantly, she had wondered if it was possible she could get away without having the talk about the mission.

It was not to be. When everyone retired to rest after lunch, Hamza took her arm and led her out into the small courtyard of the house. He looked around to make sure they were not overheard and sat her down next to him. She tried to smile, but he didn't smile back.

"Well, sister, have you been thinking about what we must do?" Murjana sensed he was holding himself in check, as if he did not want to frighten her off. But she was already frightened by his expression. Gone was the warmth and pleasantness of his welcome, and in its place was a grim sense of purpose. He looked at her as if weighing up where to start.

"I don't want to go over everything again. You know what this is about. And the time has come to do what we've been planning ever since we swore to find justice for Yahya's death."

"Planning? What have we been planning?" Her heart beat faster.

He sighed. "Murjana, don't play the innocent. You were eager enough to go along with the meetings we set up for you to see the Caliph. You were happy to see him when you got him to notice you. Luckily for us, he did the rest himself. And here you are, in just the place we need you to be."

She felt confused, but also guilty that she didn't understand exactly what he meant. Who's *we*? And what was she supposed to do? She realized she had never known what Hamza intended for her, once she had married the Caliph. She had a vague idea that she was to assist in some plan to get him to make amends for her brother's death. But what that entailed, Hamza had never told her. At times, she had imagined what it might be. But it was all too frightening to contemplate, and she told herself that her brother could never think like that. But if not, what sort of justice did he have in mind?

Hamza looked around again before he spoke again. But the courtyard was as empty as when they had entered it. Then he lowered his voice to a whisper and began to explain.

⊞

Around the corner from Abdulhamid's house, the watcher moved away from the wall as soon as he spotted the young woman. The wall was in shadow, which was why he had chosen it, leaning against it as unobtrusively as he could while he waited. His cloak was a dull beige color that merged into the color of the sacks full of bricks someone had dumped against the wall. He stood among them as if he were another sack. It was successful, and no one took any notice of him.

The area in front of the main entrance to Abdulhamid's house was in full view at all times, just as he wanted. By turning his head round slightly, he could also see the back entrance, from where a servant had earlier emptied a sack of vegetable peelings into the alleyway.

As he waited, watching both entrances, a heavily veiled young woman came quietly out of the back door. She walked fast and silently along the wall of the house, not looking to right or left. The watcher was certain she had not seen him. He could not tell which of the women she was, or even if it was a woman at all and not one of the brothers in disguise. The thought was not as absurd as it seemed; such cases were not unknown in Baghdad when a man was desperate to evade pursuit.

The watcher had a quandary. What if the veiled woman were not the lady, who was his target, but her cousin? They were both about the same height and build. Could he risk leaving his primary target unattended, if that was how it turned out, while he followed her cousin, whose movements were of no interest? If he made a mistake now the unique opportunity that chance had offered those who wanted the lady watched would be squandered.

It was a heavy responsibility, and he hesitated. The lithe speed with which the figure was walking, and beginning to disappear down the street while he dithered, spurred him to action. He prayed he was right.

After a time of shadowing her as unobtrusively as he could, the woman turned off into a side street. It led into a dense network of alleys she seemed to know well. There were fewer people out, and he feared he would attract attention. But the woman seemed oblivious, intent on her journey.

He had to dodge a vegetable cart and the donkey pulling it. But he hurried ahead in time to see her round a corner into another alley that led to a cul-de-sac. At the end of it was a house, a little like Abdulhamid's, with a number of people standing outside.

The watcher stopped in his tracks and crouched down as if examining his shoe. Peering out, he saw the woman stop at the door of the house. The men outside said something to her and then knocked at the door. It was opened by someone he couldn't see, and the woman disappeared inside.

The watcher turned round and walked out of the cul-de-sac. He went a little way, looking for someone to ask, and found a boy staggering along with a bucket of water.

"Tell me, my son, whose house is that at the end of the alley behind us?"

"The imam's," said the boy scornfully. "Everyone knows that."

28

On their return to the palace, Idris reported to Abu Hisham and Durayd. He recounted how Hamza had behaved with brotherly affection toward his sister, except for a conversation they had in the courtyard of the house after lunch. Idris couldn't hear what was said, but the lady Murjana seemed distressed afterward. On the way back to the palace, Idris noticed that she was subdued and kept peering out of the litter as if she was afraid someone was following them. He could see she was worried and unhappy.

He had no more to tell them, and they didn't know what to make of it. So they decided to share this new information with Abu Ubaydah, while continuing their surveillance of Murjana and her family. It was a feeble plan, but it was the best they could come up with.

Idris walked wearily toward the Dar al-Huram. He hoped there would be no problems waiting for him in the women's quarters. His emotions were in turmoil; on the one hand, there was his loyalty and devotion to the Caliph, and on the other, his attachment to Hind. She had sent him several letters since going to her uncle's house, all sorrowful and forlorn. She said she had finally accepted her fate and resigned herself to a loveless life back in her family's home in Mecca. There was no mention of the Caliph in any of the letters, for which he was grateful.

The eunuch who opened the door of the Dar al-Huram accompanied him to his room and heated a water jug for his bath. It was only after the young man had massaged the tension from Idris's muscles as he sat on the bath stool and poured water over his soapy body that Idris felt restored enough to ask for news of the harem.

"All is well, but I have a letter for you. It came from outside the palace, I think from the same place as other letters you've received."

The lady Hind, thought Idris. I wonder what now. When the boy had gone, he broke the envelope seal and read.

"*My dear Idris. I want to confess to you that I have been living a lie ever since I left the palace. I have led you to believe that I accepted my final separation from my lord, that I am resigned to life with my family once more. But none of it is true. I can't forgive or forget. Only I know what my life with my husband has been all these years. Blissful, harmonious, the happiest that he and I have ever known. Never were two people more suited, more content. And in his heart of hearts, he knows it too. I cannot take the infatuation he has fallen into seriously. I know he will awake from it and regret the day he let me go.*

"*But when will that be? I can't afford to wait for nature to take its course, and neither can he. If the girl was no longer there, he would come to himself the sooner. And so I've decided to seek your help, dearest Idris and best of friends. Please meet me at a place of your choice as soon as you can.*"

Idris stared at the letter and then read it again. He should have expected that she would not forget in so short a time. Her obsession with the Caliph was too powerful to have faded away so quickly. Alone in her uncle's house, no doubt brooding on the

Caliph's rejection of her and her expulsion from the palace, she had found no outlet for her frustrations. And so, her thoughts had taken a dangerous turn. It placed an onerous responsibility on him not to hurt her more by rejecting her wishes, yet at the same time to do just that. He was uncertain what these wishes were, but he needed to prepare for the worst. His immediate worry, however, was how to meet her undetected. But he was certain he would have to do it to prevent some desperate action she might take.

He thought hard about it and decided there was only one way a meeting with Hind could be arranged. It would have to be through Um Jaafar's stewardess—Maryam. She had been specially assigned to this position as one of the privileges Um Jaafar, the mother of a possible heir to the Caliph, enjoyed. Maryam was close to Um Jaafar, went on special errands for her, and was her liaison with the rest of the palace and the world beyond it.

But how to gain Maryam's help without Um Jaafar finding out, and, through her, the other wives? His only chance was to rely on Maryam's promise to say nothing about the meeting. They had always been friendly, and he had found her sensible and discreet. In any case, he had no intention of telling her the real reason for the meeting with Hind. He would simply say she had asked for financial help to buy gifts for her family when she joined them. She was ashamed of having to do this and had begged that no one should know.

To Maryam, this was not an unfamiliar situation. Wives, even the Caliph's, had no wealth of their own unless it came from him, or separately from their families. None of the wives at the Dar al-Huram had their own means and didn't normally need any. So, Maryam agreed to accompany Idris to see Hind and gave him her word she would say nothing about their meeting.

The best place to meet, they decided, was the Street of Booksellers. This was a special place of bookshops and book lovers, originally granted by the Caliph to encourage his people to read, and they thought unlikely to attract others from the palace at certain times of the day.

When the time came, Maryam extricated herself from her duties to Um Jaafar and made straight for the house of Hind's uncle. When she and Hind emerged, they were identically veiled in black, and only distinguishable by the differences in their shapes. Idris, waiting a short distance from the house, joined them, and they set off on foot.

It wasn't far to their destination, and they soon mingled inconspicuously with the crowds. None of them had ever been to the Street of Booksellers before, and at the sight of the books spread out on the ground outside the bookshops for passers by to browse among, a pang of nostalgia shot though Hind. It brought back vividly the memory of her life with the Caliph, the books he sometimes read to her, and their sweet companionship. For a moment, she was transported back to those ecstatic times and lost herself in their magic.

The sound of Idris's voice speaking to Maryam brought her back to the painful present, standing outside one of the bookshops halfway along the street where they had paused. Idris asked Maryam to go into the shop and pass the time somehow, while he and Hind talked alone. He knew Maryam to be resourceful and was confident she could be relied on.

He drew Hind away to the side of the street and found an uncrowded spot where he thought they were unlikely to be overheard. He looked around but could only see strangers strolling past the book stalls and chatting. No one gave the man or the veiled woman with him a glance.

Hind faced Idris. She could hardly wait to speak. Involuntarily, she grasped his arm and if they had been alone would have thrown herself in his arms, as she had done before. He felt the same way, only more passionately. The glimpse of her pale, sorrowful face behind the veil had stirred him. She opened her mouth to speak, but only sobs came out.

"Shh! Keep your voice down," he urged her. "Now tell me what you meant when you said the lady Murjana would have to go away."

Unnoticed by them, a man was walking slowly along the street in their general direction, pausing here and there to greet the booksellers he knew. One of them took his arm and invited him into his shop.

"Salam, Abu Mansour," said the bookseller. "I've just had a new delivery from the copyist at the Translation Academy. You will find these interesting, I promise you."

Abu Mansour liked the man and had often bought his books.

"All right, I'll come in. But I can't stay long. God knows, I have enough books at home I haven't even read yet," he said smiling.

It was his habit to take a break at the end of his morning work and before his afternoons at the bimaristan. If he didn't spend it sitting quietly reading in his courtyard, he would stroll to the Booksellers' Street and enjoy browsing through the latest books, and this was such a morning.

But as he followed the bookseller to inspect the new books, he glimpsed a couple he had vaguely noticed before, standing outside the bookshop. Though he didn't know the woman, the man left an instant impression—it was Idris beyond a doubt. The doctor was surprised to see him there. Idris seemed absorbed in listening to the woman, unaware of Abu Mansour's scrutiny.

At first, Abu Mansour wondered with a shock if it was Murjana. But this woman was taller and had a fuller figure. He had no idea who she might be and would have liked to satisfy his curiosity. But snooping was not in his nature, and he thought of his assistant. How Younis would have relished the chance to probe this mystery. Idris's presence in such a place, and with an unknown, veiled woman was so unusual, Younis would have been unable to resist the challenge of finding out.

But Abu Mansour assumed there was some good reason for the head eunuch being there, and so he put the coincidence of meeting him in such an unexpected place out of his mind. It was while leafing through a book he had taken to read by the light from the shop window that he found himself close enough to the couple outside to overhear their conversation.

Idris was saying something to the woman, but in such a low voice that Abu Mansour had to strain to hear it.

"No, madam, I can't do it. It's too much."

She was weeping quietly. "If you don't help me, I swear I'll die. I'll kill myself."

They said no more and started walking toward a bookshop lower down. Abu Mansour went out into the street and looked after them as unobtrusively as he could. When they reached the shop, the two of them stopped and another veiled woman came out to join them. She looked familiar; he was sure he had seen that plump, veiled figure before somewhere, walking briskly around.

As she drew near to the other woman and said something to her, he suddenly realized who she was.

PART IV

PART IV

29

The meeting was rowdy and uncontrolled. Hamza could see that Usama was having a hard time trying to restore order. Musa was at the door to stop more young men from coming in.

"Brothers, brothers, please!" entreated Usama. "Let's calm down and show each other some respect. Remember, we're here to fight the Abbasid, not ourselves."

"Yes, and we can see what a success you've made of it, brother!" jeered a man at the front. Others immediately joined in.

They were in the main room of the house where Hamza and Musa had met Ismail a week before. The owner, Abu Hussein, was one of a small number of well-to-do Shiites, and his house had become a meeting place for the dissidents ever since the Caliph's last assault on them in the woods outside Baghdad. Abu Hussein was on pilgrimage to the great shrine of Karbala' in the south, and they had his blessing for their resistance; it was he who had given them the money to buy weapons for the struggle.

The meeting had been called for by the group of young men who were now disrupting it with shouts and angry insults. They were all fighters and had been in the battle, or skirmish, as Abu Ubaydah had called it, in which several of their comrades had fallen. They still smarted from that defeat. Their numbers much reduced and their leaders killed, they had been unable to mount another raid against the Caliph. It made them all the more frustrated and vengeful.

So, they looked to Ismail, the man they had taken on as their new spiritual leader and chief strategist, to direct them toward the next move in their war against the Caliph. Having turned away from the imam for what they considered his surrender to the Caliph, they followed his nephew instead. Ismail was also of the blood of Ali, the first imam, and acceptable in the eyes of Shiites. Some even believed him more legitimate than the present imam.

Usama tried again to calm everyone down.

"Come, brothers, put your anger aside and let's talk. What are your grievances?"

Yusuf, an older fighter who took on himself the role of spokesman for the others, answered.

"Brother Usama, we have waited many months for guidance in our war with the Caliph. We want to know what's the next step. But we've heard nothing from brother Ismail or you. The boys are restless as you can see and won't wait any longer."

Usama was alarmed. Nothing could be worse for their cause than a chaotic, uncontrolled lashing out at any target they thought was connected to the Caliph. It would ruin the months of planning he and the others had put their energies into. He wished Ismail would come soon; he was afraid he couldn't restrain the young men much longer. Hamza picked up on his anxiety, the more so as several of the fighters present had pointedly ignored him. No one was overtly hostile toward him, out of respect for his brother whom they had all admired. But he was nothing like his brother. In the days when the last battle against the Caliph's forces was being planned, Hamza was nowhere to be seen, and not since his brother's death either. He wasn't one of them, and they didn't understand why he was at the meeting.

Ismail arrived in the middle of this atmosphere. He strode to the front where Usama and Hamza were standing and took charge. At his appearance the room grew quiet. He saluted everyone.

"*Al-salam-u-aleikum wa rahmat-u-allah wa barakatu.* Peace and God's mercy and his blessings upon you, brothers. Forgive my lateness. You are as dear to me as my own children, and I won't let you be dissatisfied." He had a remarkable ability to soothe the young men and make them listen to him. "First, tell me why you've come here."

Yusuf spoke up again. "Brother Ismail. We came to ask what's to be done against the enemy, now that his forces have won and think we're completely defeated. We waited to hear how we can avenge our fallen brothers. And I tell you now, our young men won't be fobbed off with speeches and promises."

"So, what do they want? To fight again?" And, facing the room, he asked, "Do you feel ready to take on the Caliph's men once more?"

There was a general muttering, but no one answered.

"We don't know, brother," said Yusuf eventually, "that's why we come to you for guidance." The other men nodded.

"That's good. Well, this is my answer on your behalf. No, we're not ready to fight the Caliph's army again. And maybe we never were."

There was anger in the room at this, with shouts of denial and disagreement.

"So, the blood of our martyrs has been shed in vain?" cried a man at the back. "Shame!" And the rest took up the refrain.

Ismail waited for the noise to subside. Usama was glad to leave him in charge, and Hamza seemed to have shrunk further into his corner.

"You've misunderstood me, brothers. We had to fight and we rightly aimed to win. It wasn't our fault the odds against us were too great. We don't have a large army, or unlimited weapons. But we fought bravely and our martyrs are in heaven."

He paused, as if remembering the martyrs. Everyone was listening intently again. "To admit that we're no match for the Caliph's army isn't treachery or failure. It's to recognize reality so we can deal with the war against the Caliph in a different way. That's all."

An expectant hush fell on the meeting as they waited to hear what that way might be.

"As it happens some of us have worked it out." Ismail chose his words carefully. "A different way, one that might be more successful than anything we've tried so far. Will you trust me to do the job?"

"What is this different way?" A few men shouted out.

"I can't say as yet. If I did, it could wreck the whole plan."

No one was happy at this. He asked again, "Will you trust me?"

When they had all gone, mystified but also hopeful that Ismail really could provide salvation, the four men who had met the previous week stayed behind. Musa made doubly sure no one was in the house beside them and one servant who was far away in the kitchen. Ismail sat down with a tired sigh. He looked at Hamza.

"Well, brother Hamza, you saw what happened here. The men won't wait much longer. I managed to calm them down tonight, but only by assuring them we would deliver on our promise."

Usama too was looking at Hamza.

"Everything's progressing as we would hope, brothers," he said brightly. "I've talked to my sister and she knows what has to be done."

Ismail's eyes were fastened on him searchingly. "You're sure she understands?"

The memory of Murjana's horrified reaction and her running away from him in the courtyard was fresh in his mind. But he nodded confidently at the others.

"So, how will it be done?" persisted Ismail.

Hamza had come prepared for this question. "I will give Murjana the opium when I visit her. I won't let her have it for too long before the deed in case it's discovered. I've told her how much she has to use, but not to take any chances I'll measure out the dose when I give it to her. That way, there'll be nothing left for anyone to find. She will know how to place it in the Caliph's favorite dish. She also knows he must eat it last thing at night before he retires. He will then go to sleep naturally."

Ismail was impressed. He could see Hamza had given the matter careful thought, far more than the usual poisoner who was sloppy and soon discovered.

Usama was still doubtful. "Could the poison be traced back to us?"

Ismail turned toward him. "How will anyone know the Caliph was poisoned?" he pointed out. "If he dies in his sleep, it'll be put down to his age. He's not a young man, and remember how ill he was only a few months ago. In any case, if anyone sees Murjana putting something into her husband's food, I expect they'll think it's some extra delicacy."

Musa, who had been quiet until then, now spoke, "I know something of Hamza's sister, and I very much doubt she can carry it through."

This was a bombshell no one expected. Hamza stared at him, wondering if he somehow knew of the conversation in the courtyard.

"I remember how sweet-natured your sister was and how she behaved when I told you all about Yahya's death. She was shocked and grieved, no doubt about that, and she wanted his death avenged. But I don't feel her capable of doing this."

Ismail frowned. "I thought you knew your sister, Hamza. Is this true?"

Hamza was furious with Musa. He tried to control his anxiety in front of Ismail. "My sister is not bloodthirsty or murderous, if that's what you mean. But she has a sense of duty that overrides her natural delicacy. Of that, I'm sure."

"We've been relying on you, Hamza," Usama joined in. He had never liked the man and regretted that they were forced to depend on him. "If you had doubts about her, you should have said so a long time ago. We wouldn't have built up our hopes then. At the very least we should have known before the meeting with the brothers tonight and the promises we made to them." His voice was full of disapproval. He looked at Hamza steadily, and waited.

Hamza was filled with dismay. He felt himself losing his hard-earned credibility with Ismail, whom he both feared and admired.

"You've got this all wrong, brothers. Just because Musa tells you he felt such and such when he met Murjana—which was only once, mind—it doesn't mean she's incapable of playing her part in our plan."

Ismail and Usama exchanged glances.

"Very well, Hamza," said Ismail with an air of decision. "She's your sister and you're in charge of her. You've promised to carry our plan through to the end, and we will hold you to that."

Then in a kinder tone, he added, "I don't underestimate the difficulties. You're a brave man, brother, and I pray to God for your success." He patted Hamza on the shoulder and stood up, indicating the end of the meeting. Hamza was gratified by Ismail's endorsement of him, but under no illusion about the enormity of the challenge facing him.

Though he had been angry with Musa's blabbing about Murjana, he knew that his friend was right. Hamza had been worried about her ever since her marriage and what seemed to be her growing attachment to the Caliph. He saw her increasing reluctance to go through with the plan agreed between them and how it had come to a head when he explained what had to be done. It had forced him to the reluctant conclusion that it was unlikely he could rely on her. But he would have to, at least in order to gain access to the palace and the Caliph. It was a conundrum, and he mulled it over all the way back to his uncle's house and late into the night. By daybreak he had decided that he had no choice but to speak to Murjana again. This time he would be gentle and persuasive, beg her to remember their beloved brother and his unavenged death. But in his heart of hearts, he suspected it would not work, and he would have to find another way. There was no one else he could trust. With reluctant resignation he realized he had no alternative but himself. He would have to do the deed.

The watcher followed Hamza all the way home. He hung around for a while, but no one left the house after that. As the candles were extinguished in one room after another, he gave up and took himself off.

It had been a disappointing evening. He had started off by watching the house where the meeting took place, frustrated that he could not get in. The door was opened only to those who gave their names and were carefully examined. They had all seemed to know each other personally in any case, and if he had tried to go in he would soon have been discovered. It was annoying because he had sensed the meeting was important from the time he shadowed Hamza going there.

Hidden in the dark, he had heard raised voices and angry shouts from time to time, and after a short while a man he recognized as their leader, Ismail, had come striding along the alley and was admitted into the house. The watcher had waited, concealed around the corner from where he peered out frequently, checking the scene. There was no street lighting here as in the center of

Baghdad. What illumination there was came from torches placed at both ends of some of the bigger roads like this one, but the rest was in darkness. If it had not been for the light coming from inside people's houses, the watcher would have stumbled in the dark, drawing attention to himself, or lost his way getting there.

He had known he was taking a risk being in that area at night. Although the dimly lit streets had a reassuringly cosy atmosphere, it was deceptive. They hid many dangers in their shadows. It was the time when Baghdad's underworld of criminals and thieves came to life. They were most active in the wealthier districts of the city, but nowhere was safe. He could easily have been taken for a burglar as he lurked in the dark, and had prayed no diligent householder was out checking his vicinity. Worse still, a real burglar might take him for a competitor and club him over the head without hesitation. There were no public guards here and crime went largely unpunished. But he had suppressed his feeling of fear and fixed his eyes on the house where the meeting was taking place.

It was well lit and he had seen the comings and goings of people outside. As he watched, a crowd of noisy young men came out from the house talking heatedly. The meeting had evidently come to an end, the signal for him to try and find out what they were saying. He had left his corner and walked slowly in their direction, careful not to look at them as he pretended to search for something in the sack he was carrying on his shoulder. No one had noticed him. The snippets of conversation he had overheard were all variations on the same subject—a promise of some kind and how it might rid them of "the enemy." Some of the comments were skeptical, but on the whole, the men had an air of optimism. When the last of them disappeared from the street, he had gone back to his corner spot and waited.

A short while later, he had seen Ismail and another man leave the house, followed by Hamza and his friend, whom he recognized from having seen them together before. They had stopped a couple of feet away from the corner where he was hiding.

"I'm sorry if you felt I betrayed you talking about your sister, but I had to speak according to my conscience."

"No, my friend, you only spoke the truth as you saw it. How can I blame you for that?"

"What will you do?"

"It'll be all right. Don't worry."

They had moved off and continued walking up the alley. The watcher saw them part halfway along, and saw Hamza resume his way home.

As the watcher left the vicinity, he thought about what he had seen and heard: the noisy but serious meeting, the optimistic young Shia men, and lastly the private conversation he had just listened to. He tried to put the pieces together. Whichever way he looked at it, he felt uneasy. He did not understand all that was going on, nor had anyone asked him to. His assignment had been to carry out certain instructions, which he had done faithfully. Nevertheless, he felt the situation was urgent. And if so, he should deliver the information he had gathered without delay.

30

The Caliph's inquisition on the Quran's createdness did not go down well in Baghdad. No one had ever heard of such a thing, and even when they found out, many were none the wiser and wondered what the point of it was. The inquisition targeted prominent judges and teachers of Hadith, who were all theologians of high standing and widely respected. It upset many of their adherents and provoked the disapproval of wider society. As for the common people, the Caliph believed they needed protection from the religious distortions and false beliefs peddled by so-called pious *ulama'*. Some of these, it was said, thought nothing of fabricating hadiths and passing them off as genuine in order to plant some self-serving idea or other.

The Caliph identified scores of these self-appointed interpreters of the faith who misled the public, and he wanted them brought down. He was still invigorated by his decision to force the conspiracy they were fomenting against his authority out into the open. They would be asked repeatedly if they endorsed the doctrine of the Quran's createdness until the judge was satisfied, and then they had to sign their agreement. Most ended up doing so, but it was not an unqualified success for the Caliph. Some had agreed because it was the simplest course, others declared they were doing so under duress, and the rest bowed their heads in obedience to the Caliph's order. This hardly counted as universal acquiescence, but the Caliph's inquisitors could squeeze no more out of them.

It disappointed the Caliph, but after some dozen prominent men had been tried in this way, something began to happen. A few of the traditionists began to concede that the rationalists had a right to be heard and they were prepared to listen. This had never happened before, and it seemed a promising start. Perhaps they were genuinely converted, but the Caliph thought it more likely they had been sobered by their head-on collision with his authority. Nevertheless, a dialogue of sorts started even among diehard adherents of one side or the other, and, for a while, it galvanized the intellectual atmosphere.

To encourage this trend the Caliph instructed the governor of Baghdad, charged with the administration of the inquisition, to be lenient with those interrogated. And so it went on until it was the turn of Amr ibn Uthal. This was a tense moment in the inquisition and the intellectual elite of Baghdad awaited the outcome keenly. Ibn Uthal's followers gathered outside the court where he was being interrogated with cries of *Allah-u-akbar*. They prayed loudly for his safe deliverance until dispersed by the court guards.

No one was surprised when Ibn Uthal refused to sign the endorsement. He was arrested and held in a dungeon inside the court without food or drink. Different interrogators kept him awake all night and resumed the next day; he had nowhere to sit but the hard floor, and he was kept for hours in the dark. Still he would not sign. Reluctantly, they tortured him for two whole days. But he still did not sign. Those few who had undergone a similar ordeal and remained recalcitrant stayed in prison. But on the third day of his captivity, Ibn Uthal was released on the Caliph's orders. It was a triumph for Ibn Uthal and his followers, who thought it was a sign from God.

"Whatever I do for the people, it's not enough to overcome their willful ignorance," the Caliph complained. "They'd rather blindly follow a man like Ibn Uthal, who offers them nothing but prayer and parrot-like recitation of scripture, than use their brains to think and better their lives."

Abu Mansour had been among the first to hear the outcome of Ibn Uthal's trial. He had followed the debate from the beginning, and, like the Caliph, was wholeheartedly on the rationalist side, whether mu'tazilite or any of the other similar movements. The Caliph had consulted him about his intention to institute an inquisition long before its public announcement, and Abu Mansour had wondered at the time about the advisability of taking such a step.

"Looking back, my lord, do you think it was wise to have gone down this path? You must know how badly the inquisition has gone down with people." No one other than the doctor could have said such a thing to the Caliph. Ever since the inquisition, the Caliph would hear no criticism of it. He was convinced it was the only way to rid the land of a rival authority that threatened the stability of the state. But he knew Abu Mansour would never give him false advice and had only his good at heart.

"What else could I have done? Leave these men to rampage through the realm, telling their lies and leading the people astray?"

"As to that, I honestly can't say. But there could have been another way, not so alien to people as this, and not so harsh on one of their heroes, whatever we may think of him."

The Caliph was thoughtful.

"There's a lot of unrest among the people, my lord, and things which shouldn't be said are being openly talked about."

"What do you mean? The old accusations about the death of my brother? I'm used to that, and the protests always die down in a short time."

Abu Mansour was thinking of something quite different, and it would affect the Caliph to his core. Abu Mansour's mother, Um

Hasan, had unwittingly come out with it as they sat under the large tree in the courtyard of his house. Green almonds were in season, and she was salting them in a bowl for him to eat.

"There's a rumor going round that the Caliph set up the inquisition because he's sympathetic to the Shia," she said.

"What nonsense is that?"

"And they're saying it's his new wife's influence over him. She and her family put him up to it. I don't know about that," she added, "but I do think our Caliph was wrong to put the venerable Sheikh Amr through such an ordeal."

Her news worried Abu Mansour. He knew the traditionists who rejected the mu'tazilites also rejected the Shia as sects outside orthodox Islam. They accused the Caliph of being favorable toward Shiism because he spoke of caliphs and imams interchangeably, and insisted that Shiism should be part of mainstream theology. In response, the Caliph would have said that, irrespective of his enmity toward Shia splinter groups who threatened the security of the state, he respected the right of the Shia to have their own vision of what faith meant; that vision only enriched the diversity of ideas in his realm he held so dear. This was lost on the traditionists, and all they saw was his partiality for a branch of Islam that did not accord with theirs.

At first, Abu Mansour had wondered whether he should tell the Caliph straightaway, or hold back until the situation calmed down. There had been a popular uproar in the wake of Ibn Uthal's imprisonment and release, and his supporters had whipped up people's resentment against the court and the judges who tried him, and, behind that, the Caliph himself. They lost no time in seizing the opportunity to spread their conservative message to the faithful, who now flocked to swell the ranks of their followers. At the same time Younis and also Saad reported that the rumor of the Caliph being under his wife's influence was gaining ground. Suspicions about her Shia origins, which no one had cared about previously, now surfaced as a ready explanation for the Caliph's unpopular inquisition. It was not a Sunni-Shia split as much as it was a battle of what was seen as the pious versus the godless.

As always at such times, people carried the various disaffections with their lives over into something else, usually unrelated. So, they lamented Ibn Uthal's ordeal and focused their wrath on the Caliph's Shia wife and her community. It did not look as if this hostility was waning, and Abu Mansour decided he would have to tell the Caliph.

"It concerns the lady Murjana, my lord."

The Caliph stared at him. "The people are saying that you are under her influence, and as she is a Shiite, your sympathies with the Shia have increased because of her. And that, they think, is the real reason for the inquisition." Abu Mansour laid the facts before him with no attempt to soften the impact. The Caliph said nothing. He was already aware of what Abu Mansour had told him through his chief wazir, who had detailed the rumors and how they had been spread by Ibn Uthal's supporters to the whole of Baghdad. He did not know where it would all end.

To Durayd and Uthman, the chief wazir, Abu Hisham, said privately afterwards, "Everything around the Caliph's wife just goes from bad to worse. First it was her family's scheming against him, and now she sets off trouble between the Sunna and the Shia."

"To be fair to her, she hasn't set off anything," said Uthman. "It's the *ulama'*, who'll use anything to discredit their opponents."

"Nevertheless," muttered Abu Hisham, "it's an ill wind." And then, checking to see they were not overheard, he dropped his voice and said,

"I wish to God our master had never married her!"

If Abu Mansour thought the same, he gave no sign of it. The Caliph sighed heavily.

"What should I do? Set Murjana aside to satisfy this narrow-minded rabble and the men who control them?" He shook his head. "I will not harm a hair of her head, and I will not waste another moment on any of them."

"As you say, my lord."

But Abu Mansour had a sense of foreboding. The storm clouds were gathering, and he wondered how long it would be before the storm broke.

⊞

Murjana had not seen the Caliph so preoccupied since their wedding. She was aware of the inquisition he had imposed on the *ulama'* and knew it had not been well received. But she had her own preoccupations since her last visit to the family and could think of little else. It was a visit she had dreaded beforehand, and it proved fully as disturbing as she feared.

When she came back to the palace on the afternoon of that day, she felt she never wanted to see Hamza again. It made her guilty to think like that, but she could not help herself. As they drew near to the palace, a sudden fear seized her that she would find the Caliph gone. She knew it was quite irrational but could not shake it off. They passed through the gate and, barely waiting for Idris, she walked on fast, nearly breaking into a run as she reached the courtyard. Without turning to thank the eunuch for serving her that day, she rushed toward the door of the private apartments.

In her haste she did not see the Caliph sitting quietly by the flowerbeds reading. As she ran past him, he caught hold of the back of her robe and dragged her toward him. She almost fell over him. Breathless with relief, she knelt and put her arms tightly around him as if they hadn't seen each other for years.

"Oh, my lord, I'm so glad to see you."

"And here I am," he said, kissing her. "Sit down and tell me all about your day without me."

But she would say little beyond making a few bland remarks about the house and the family. He was supposed to assume it had been an unremarkable visit, and when he asked how soon she wanted to see her relatives again, she was vague. He could see she was not herself, and he sensed something had happened that day. She ate little at dinner, and when night came, she had her maids prepare her for bed as quickly as they could and then dismissed them. She lay down and waited for him to join her, and when he did, expecting to talk a little and hold her in his arms as he normally did when they were first in bed, she did not wait and pulled him eagerly toward her. Taking him aback with the urgency of her passion, she pressed the full length of her body to his as if to feel each part of him against her skin. Moaning slightly, she clasped him to her and kissed him deeply, moved against him, and kissed him again. He was bemused, but responded with equal passion.

"What is it, my love?" he whispered when he could draw breath. He half sat up to look at her in the dim light, but she reached up wordlessly and drew him down again where she clung to him as if for dear life. There was a desperation in her he could not fathom. It was not lovemaking she wanted, but something more.

"Tell me, my darling, what's the matter," he said again. "I'm here and I will never leave you. Do you doubt that? Is that it?"

She shook her head and put her face against his chest. Her cheeks were wet. He could feel she was racked by emotions he could not unravel. Somewhere in it was love, he was sure, but much else besides. She seemed to want reassurance, though about what he did not know. He put up his hand to stroke her hair, wanting to soothe her, but she caught it and held it to her cheek, then turned it over and kissed the palm, sobbing. Her mysterious grief was unbearable to watch.

He held her close against him and rocked her gently from side to side. In a while she quietened down, and with a final convulsive sigh, stopped crying. Still she had said nothing, but was now exhausted. Her arm across his chest and her face buried deep into his shoulder, her body slowly relaxed and her breathing grew soft and regular.

From nowhere a strange idea came into the Caliph's mind as he lay sleepless beside her. What he had just experienced was no less than Murjana's farewell to him. A chill hand laid itself across his heart as he thought it. He shook himself free, closed his eyes tightly, and made himself breathe evenly. Murjana should tell him what was tormenting her, and that would put an end to such morbid thoughts.

31

After the meeting with the rebels, when he had embarrassingly been called on to give an account of himself to Ismail and the others, Hamza had not been able to settle down. The decision to speak to Murjana and enlist her help in gaining access to the Caliph was constantly on his mind and he knew he could not delay much longer.

Rumor had it that the Caliph's spies had heard of the rebels' meeting, and it might be only a matter of time before his soldiers acted against them. Ismail sent word asking him about his progress with their project, as he called it, and it made him more nervous.

He thought of the approaches he might use with Murjana, but he was worried he had already ruined his options. Their disastrous encounter was still fresh in his mind: the crude pressure he had tried to put on her and his bullying tactics. No wonder she had run away. To bring her back into the fold, he had to be softer, more affectionate, and earn her trust once more. He had been alarmed when they last spoke, and he saw the extent of her involvement with the Caliph. If he hadn't known better, he might have thought she was in love with him. But he could not believe that, knowing as she did the plan they had used to entrap the Caliph. She couldn't have forgotten and thought herself a normal wife enjoying a normal marriage.

His request for permission to visit her in the palace was granted by the Caliph's chamberlain, and the time and date agreed. Yazan wanted to go with him, but Hamza refused, reminding him he was now an apprentice to a ceramics merchant in the souk and had duties there. He was on the point of leaving when his aunt Zubeida stopped him and held out a covered oval dish.

"Take this to Murjana and tell her it was baked this morning. It's saffron and almond cake, her favorite. Tell her not to mind the slight bitterness, it's the crushed almonds. I put in extra."

"I can't take food into the palace, Aunt. It will look as if they don't feed her enough."

Zubeida dismissed this. "Nonsense. You tell them it's a special delicacy from her aunt. No one will mind. And if they do, you can bring it back and we'll eat it."

When Hamza reached the palace and gave his mount to the grooms at the entrance, he carried the dish self-consciously through to the courtyard where he found Murjana waiting for him. The first thing he noticed was her pallor and the shadows under her eyes.

"Dearest sister," he said warmly and kissed her with unaccustomed affection. "I've brought you a little present from home. Here, your favorite cake from our aunt." He handed her the dish, and Murjana's expression suddenly brightened. She uncovered it and saw what it was.

"How kind. It really is my favorite. Please thank Aunt Zubeida. We will eat a little of it straightaway." With that she ordered the servants to serve sherbet and slices of the saffron cake. They sat in the courtyard, Hamza attentive throughout and on his best behavior. He had lost his closed, gloomy expression, and smiled frequently and held Murjana's hand from time to time. She was puzzled, having expected something totally different, and lost a little of her wariness.

When she had first heard of her brother's request for a visit, she was filled with apprehension. A repeat of their last dreadful encounter was more than she could have borne. But she had no choice except to welcome him. The Caliph, assuming they would want to discuss family matters, had left her to see Hamza alone.

As the cake was served, the smell of freshly baked almonds wafted into the air. Hamza took a bite of the honey and nut mixture and indeed found it a little bitter. Murjana didn't mind.

"That's how it's supposed to taste," she said with her mouth full. "Dear Aunt, so good of her to remember."

Hamza was about to agree when he was struck by a sudden thought. Of course—*the cake*. Why hadn't it occurred to him before? *It was the perfect solution.*

He looked up and smiled at his sister, his spirits suddenly lighter. She in her turn had also regained some of her sisterly affection for him. If only his good mood would last, she thought; it was so much easier that way. A scene of the happiness she might enjoy with the Caliph if that happened flashed before her.

"Is there anywhere we can talk, dearest Murjana?"

The wariness came back. "Why can't we talk here?"

"Please, Murjana, I'd like to talk, but somewhere private. Don't worry, it won't be like before, and I'm truly sorry about that."

Murjana hesitated, unsure what to make of him. "The only really private place I know in the palace is the animal menagerie. There's no one there but the keepers, and once they've fed and cleaned up after the animals, they usually leave, and the place is deserted."

This sounded good to Hamza and he agreed. Murjana led the way from the courtyard and along the walkway toward the menagerie. When they arrived, there was great noise from the elephant and the chimpanzees in their cages, but no one was to be seen. They stood beside the outer fence of the animal enclosure.

"What do you want to tell me, Hamza? I'm sure we won't be overheard here."

"Dearest sister, you know I love you and want only the best for you. I confess I've been harsh recently and I beg you to forget my bad temper and stupid ways. It was only that I was so anxious to do what we agreed on."

He took her hand in both of his and kissed it. She said nothing.

"I've been really unkind and insensitive toward you. I should have understood how difficult it was for you to withstand the Caliph's love and all his flattery and gifts he's showered on you. No girl could resist that. Please, dear sister, forgive me."

Murjana had not quite expected this, but he sounded sincere, and she didn't know how to respond. Undeterred by her silence, Hamza pressed on.

"I can understand that you've grown fond of the Caliph. It's only natural. I'm not blaming you for that and would never condemn you, even though we know what he's done to our family."

Murjana put her head in her hands, which he interpreted to signify remorse at having forgotten her duty to their brother. He quickly put his arm round her.

"Don't be sad. It's not too late. We will make it up to him."

Murjana shook her head from side to side. "No, Hamza, I won't. I can't. I know I promised, but that was before I knew what you really wanted. Don't ask me to do it. It's beyond me to do."

Hamza controlled his anger. His voice was smooth and persuasive when he spoke.

"I know how shocked you were when I told you. And I should have realized you needed time to take it in. But now that you've had a few days to think, can't you see that there's honestly no other way? If you know of one, tell me and I swear to God I'll take it." She shook her head again. "We have to carry this through. For the sake of our brother and all the other brothers and sons and husbands who've paid the ultimate price to free us from tyranny."

She hung her head sorrowfully. "Hamza, you must believe me," she begged in anguish. "I can't do it, and I don't believe it's right to redress one wrong with another."

"Dearest sister, there's no need for this upset. I think you misunderstand. It's only a small thing I'm asking for. There isn't that much for you to do."

She looked confused.

"When the time comes," he explained patiently, as if to a child, "everything will be prepared beforehand. You will receive it ready and discreetly hidden so no one will know. All you have to do is make sure the Caliph takes it."

She felt herself cornered and tried to play for time. "What if I'm discovered?"

"Ah, so that's what you're afraid of. How could you be discovered? No one would suspect a loving, grateful wife like you when the Caliph had so honored her humble family with his favor? A woman who'd reached the top like you would be mad to give it all up." The bitterness had returned to his voice.

She didn't know how to escape him and fell silent.

"Oh, Murjana." His voice was gentle once again. "If you'd seen the dream I had last night, you wouldn't hesitate as you're doing now."

She stared at him, her eyes large in her head. "What dream?"

Hamza struggled to master his emotions. His face had lost color and a haunted look came into his eyes. He said in a hushed monotone, "It was in the early hours before the dawn prayer. Yahya appeared before me as lifelike and real as you are now. He was dressed in dusty, torn clothes, his face smudged with dirt and his hair matted. His eyes were wild and desperate. He put his arms out entreatingly towards me as if to bring me closer to him. And then he said in a voice so sorrowful, so full of pain it broke my heart, 'Avenge me! If you ever loved me, avenge me, or you will have no rest in this life or the one hereafter.'

"'How, Yahya?' I cried, 'tell us how we should avenge you.' But the vision was already receding. An echo of his voice trailed behind him, unmistakable and as clear in my ears as your voice now. 'The Caliph,' it said, 'the Caliph'. And then I woke up, sweating."

He was agitated and breathing fast. Murjana burst into tears, "Oh, Yahya, Yahya."

Hamza put his arms round her again and they wept together. Her tears were not all for the ghost of her poor brother, but for herself too.

32

Abu Ubaydah sat waiting in the anteroom to the Caliph's private chambers, deeply troubled. Though he had previously decided to refrain from setting a watch on the lady Murjana, the plot against the Caliph was too serious to be subject to such protocol. So, he had gone back to his old strategy of watching her and her family.

He appointed Salim, another of his spies and a man of usefully nondescript appearance who easily merged into the background wherever he was. Salim had made Abu Ubaydah aware of the lady Murjana's movements when she went to see her family, her stolen visit while there to the imam's house, and of her brother Hamza's meeting with the Shia rebels. His final report was of Hamza setting out for the palace to see the lady Murjana, at which point he had stopped his surveillance for fear of being discovered by the palace.

For Abu Ubaydah, the picture Salim's reports painted was so alarming that he decided he would have to inform the Caliph of his findings immediately. Although there was no definitive proof as yet, the sequence of events from the killing of the Banu Shaaban son to the conspiratorial behavior of his siblings left no room for complacency. He could only assume that the meeting between Hamza and the lady Murjana that had just taken place was a further stage in the conspiracy against the Caliph.

At his request, Abu Ubaydah saw the Caliph alone. He then gave a detailed account of all that had happened from the time of the battle against the Shia rebels up to Salim's last report. The Caliph listened intently throughout, his face inscrutable.

"I believe the lady Murjana has received her brother here recently, but I have no information about the meeting between them." The Caliph nodded but did not comment. His expression was closed. *He knows*, Abu Ubaydah realized with a shock. *He may even know what transpired at the meeting as well.* If he was right, it could only mean that the Caliph was already suspicious of his wife and her family. But that would not accord with the Caliph's skepticism about the warnings his officials had given him. There was something here Abu Ubaydah did not understand.

"Thank you for filling in the gaps in the story, Abu Ubaydah, it explains a great deal. Perhaps you should have told me about Yahya ibn Shaaban from the start."

And would you have listened? thought Abu Ubaydah. *If I had told you the lady was the devil incarnate, you would not have believed me.* But he only said, "As soon as I realized, I tried to reach you, my lord. But you had already left for Famm al-Silh." *And that was in the past*, he wanted to add. The real issue was what the Caliph would do now with the information he had.

"I'd be grateful if you would now suspend your spying operations, Abu Ubaydah, and leave matters to me." He spoke politely but firmly, and Abu Ubaydah's freedom of action was thereby ended. "I must also ask you to keep what you've discovered to yourself. No one should hear any of it until I say so."

And then he added, "I'm not angry with you. You're a good and faithful servant and I won't forget your vigilance over my safety and the country at large. You've exceeded the call of duty, and I will reward you at the appropriate time."

He rose from his seat and patted Abu Ubaydah on the shoulder. He seemed calm and in control, without disquiet or distress. Abu Ubaydah wondered how his master could preserve such equanimity in the face of what he had just heard. Was it even possible he meant to ignore it completely; that, still so blinded by love for his wife, he could believe her and her family innocent bystanders in the conflict between Sunni and Shia? He found that difficult to believe, but was at a loss to explain it in any other way. Eventually, he gave up trying and reminded himself his duty was to obey the Caliph's commands and nothing more.

⊡

In the days that followed his meeting with Abu Ubaydah, the Caliph came to a decision. He summoned his chief wazir to see him.

"I would like to have a few days' rest away from state business and my normal duties, Abu Hisham. For that reason, I intend to move to the Small Palace which will be my home for a short while. You'll remember that was the place of my convalescence under the care of Abu Mansour. I found it soothing and restful at the time, and hope to find it like that again."

Abu Hisham was surprised. He could see no conceivable reason for the Caliph wanting a rest at that moment. The situation in the country was relatively quiet; no new insurrections had been reported, and the unrest caused by Ibn Uthal's imprisonment was contained for the time being. Even the runaway Abdullah ibn Rida had been rearrested and was back in jail, awaiting the Caliph's pleasure. If there was anything to worry about, it was likely to arise from a renewal of the war with Byzantium. No new hostilities between the two sides had occurred recently, although the frontier between them was perennially unstable and could break down at any time.

No, he thought, the Caliph must have another reason for wanting to move, and it worried him. What if it was the lady

Murjana's idea and not the Caliph's at all, for her to have him alone to herself? And then what would she do with him? Abu Hisham wondered how they could keep the Caliph safe outside the Golden Gate where they had a good network of spies. He had a sense of fear and unease.

⊞

Murjana had been surprised by the Caliph's announcement of their departure for the Small Palace. She too had her memories of that house, her visit to the Caliph's sickbed, and the scene that had ensued. For a hopeful moment she wondered if he intended for their coming stay to be a second honeymoon in sentimental memory of that first passionate encounter.

Her whole world had changed in the few days after her return from visiting her family and the tortured night that followed. For no reason she could understand, the Caliph became a different man. Although he was as polite and correct as ever towards her, his manner was cold but for the strange light that burned deep in his eyes whenever he looked at her. Gone was the warm passion she used to bask in, the love for her she had thought unshakable, and the intimate conversations in the night when he confided his innermost thoughts and ideas to her. It was a change so complete as to make her wonder if she had dreamed it all. She had no one to ask and no one to open her heart to.

When Abu Mansour paid a visit to the palace the day before their journey, she was almost tempted to turn to him. If anyone understood the Caliph, it was he. He would know how to advise her and keep her confidences. But there was no way to reach him. During his visits to the Caliph, they normally sat alone in a separate chamber distant from the private apartments, and she had no one like Maryam, Um Jaafar's stewardess, to send a message with. There was no help for it; she was on her own and would have to face whatever the Caliph had in store for her.

She did not have long to wait to find out. They left the Golden Gate the next day and arrived at the Small Palace before noon. It had been handsomely prepared for their arrival and gleamed with cleanliness and polish in the spring sunlight. To her surprise, she was shown into the room that had been the Caliph's sick room. But it looked different to the lugubrious place she remembered entering so timidly the time before. The windows were wide open and light was streaming in. The hangings on the walls were rich and colorful, and the marble floor was covered with silk rugs. Vases of flowers sat on the bedside tables, and a large bouquet was laid across the bed. The whole room looked to Murjana like a bridal suite.

As soon as the thought struck her, she felt her heart lift. It must mean that all was well, she told herself. If the Caliph had ordered their room to be prepared as if for their wedding night, he could not be angry with her. His odd manner was probably nothing to do with what she feared, that she had offended in some way, but was more about his other responsibilities. Such things had never affected his behavior towards her before, but perhaps he had not had to confront whatever big problem she imagined him to have now. She decided to put all gloom behind her.

The Caliph was nowhere to be seen, and she occupied herself with a walk around the garden. By the time it was evening and he still had not appeared, she started to worry again. But word soon came that the Caliph awaited her for dinner in the hall.

She had the maids prepare her bath and anoint her with oil of ambergris. Then they dressed her in a wine-red velvet tunic with flowing sleeves, and her hair was brushed and oiled. She knew she looked beautiful as she entered the dining room. The Caliph stood up for her. He had instructed all male servants to leave the room, and only the females and eunuchs were to attend on them. He asked Murjana to remove her veil.

"I want to see you as you are."

His tone was quite unlike himself, hard and a little menacing. He indicated she should sit down, and when she had done so, ordered one of the eunuchs to fill their glasses with wine. She looked at him searchingly. There was not a flicker in him of the man she knew.

He spoke and ate little, although the dishes served were of the finest. Murjana too had lost all trace of appetite and ate even less. But he insisted she drink the wine as he was doing. She longed to ask him what had gone wrong, why he had brought her to this place, but was too afraid.

After the meal was over, such as it was, she rose and asked his permission to leave. He nodded absentmindedly, as if it was the same to him whether she stayed or went. He had said virtually nothing all evening, and his expression was impenetrable. Entering the bedroom again, she thought of her earlier optimism and realized he must be playing some cruel trick on her. Perhaps the room was not to be a nuptial chamber at all, and he had meant for her to sleep alone in it.

She did her ablutions and performed the evening prayer. The maids then prepared her for bed and, leaving the candles burning on the side tables, left her. Sleepless, she stared at the ceiling and the shifting shadows the candle flames cast across it. Time passed, and when nothing happened, she sat up to extinguish them and try to sleep.

Before she could do that, however, the Caliph entered the room. He was in his night robes and held a book in his hand which, she presumed, he had been reading. He put it down on the chest of drawers against the wall and came towards her. She could not see his face well in the weak light and stayed sitting up. She watched him take off his robe and then sit silently on the side of the bed next to her. She kept her eyes on him, stiff with apprehension about his next move.

He suddenly got into bed beside her. Instinctively, she turned towards him. But instead of the tenderness she had learned to expect, he seized her roughly by the shoulders and pulled her down into the bed. He threw the bedclothes back, exposing her body to the cold night. She shivered, but did not dare move to cover herself.

There was nothing erotic in his actions; they were cold and deliberate. He put one hand beneath her buttocks and the other under her shoulders and moved her effortlessly into the center of the bed beside him. She lay paralyzed with fear, remembering this was what she had dreaded happening on their wedding night.

He was not brutal or violent in the way she had heard some of her friends describe their husbands, but he might just as well have been. No sooner had their bodies touched than he gripped her, and his lovemaking, if that was what it could be called, was hard and fierce, without passion or regard for her, almost as if she were not there. It made her feel degraded and cheap, like a slave-girl.

He never kissed her once and, apart from his harsh breathing, he made no sound. When it was over, he sat up. His expression was no easier to read than it had been in the dining hall before. Slowly he put his tunic back on and looked at her body, studying it with detached interest.

"You know," he said in a conversational tone, as if they were sitting together quite normally, "I made a big mistake with you from the very start. I thought you were someone else, put you on a pedestal above every woman I ever loved, even above my own self. I saw in you a rare kinship with me, as if we were one spirit and one body. And for a while I felt ennobled by the love I found with you, raised above humankind, a man who walked with the angels, uniquely blessed by God. It filled me with a happiness I had never felt before."

He paused. When he spoke again, his voice was bitter and filled with distaste. "I was wrong about you. You were not that

kind of woman. It was all a hoax and a deception, and I fell for it."
The face he turned on her was dark with anger. "Yes, I was wrong.
You're *this* kind of woman, good for only one thing."

And leaning over, he pulled her to him. She tried to push him
away and draw herself towards the top of the bed. But he was too
strong and pulled her down again. This time he was harsher and
more punishing; she shut her eyes and started to weep helplessly.
He ignored her and at the end sat up against the wall and stared
silently into the dark. After a few moments he rose from the bed,
picked up his robe, and left the room. She lay unmoving amid the
crumpled bedclothes, the tears still streaming down her cheeks.

Despite what she had been through, she knew that if he
should return she could not protest or refuse him. She was
utterly trapped. The man she knew had gone, and in his place was
someone she did not recognize. It was clear no tears or pleading
would move such a man, and she could only pray that her ordeal
would soon stop.

But it did not. He visited her bed again in the following days,
always with the same cold anger, distaste, and a barren lustfulness
that found no satisfaction. Inside him all the while was a terrible
anguish she sensed, despite her misery, but did not know how to
respond to. By the time their stay at the Small Palace ended, she
was reduced to such a state of humiliation she was glad of the
thick veil she could hide beneath.

Her fevered mind went round and round, trying to understand what had happened to change the Caliph into this hateful
stranger. He was angry, but he was also vengeful, and she could
think of only one reason for that. Yet she and Hamza had been
so careful. All their contacts had been discreet; they had always
made sure no one overheard their conversations and had succeeded so well that the other members of the family, the closest
people to them, suspected nothing. Even their last, and riskiest
encounter at the palace if anyone had found them out, had not

been overheard, Murjana was sure. And no one else could have betrayed them. It was a puzzle.

But the fear that, despite all those precautions, the Caliph had still somehow found out nagged at her. And the more she thought about it, the more plausible it seeme. It suddenly dawned on her that if her suspicions were correct, she and her brother were in great danger and might have little time to avert it. The thought filled her with alarm. There was no alternative but to let Hamza know, and at the earliest possible moment.

33

Murjana made arrangements to visit her uncle's house the moment she was back at the Golden Gate. Hamza was surprised to see her when she arrived, and asked why she had sent no message to say she was coming.

As soon as they were alone in what had been her old bedroom, she explained there had been no time to warn him. They did not have long, and she had urgent information she must impart to him. He looked at her with slight alarm.

She dropped her voice to a whisper. "Listen to me, Hamza. We're in danger. I had to let you know as soon as I could."

And then she told him of the change in the Caliph and the ordeal he had put her through at the Small Palace. She had hoped things might improve when they returned to the Golden Gate, but they only got worse. The Caliph started to avoid Murjana's company altogether. He no longer shared her bed, not even for those episodes of tortured lovemaking he had subjected her to, and she slept alone at night. He took his meals without her, and she hardly ever set eyes on him. It suggested to her that the situation was accelerating.

"What situation? What're you talking about?"

She told him about the conclusion she had come to that

would explain the change in the Caliph's behavior towards her. "If I'm right, and I think I am, he knows what we've been planning. And his revenge will be terrible."

Hamza started at her, shocked. She could see he sensed she was right. He told her he had always been afraid of the Caliph's spies, who were everywhere. Even though he had been careful, it was no guarantee of escape from their vigilance. And now it seemed they had caught up with the two of them. He tried to think of what best to do; Murjana waited, conscious that time was passing and she would soon have to return to the palace or risk being discovered.

Hamza was frowning with the effort of concentration. And then he said there was nothing for it, they'd have to make their move as soon as possible. It would have been much better had they more time to prepare, but the Caliph could be upon them very soon. They must start planning at once.

Without waiting for her reply, he started to ask her about the Caliph's dining habits. What were his favorite dishes, how adventurous was he about trying new tastes? Had she introduced him to their aunt's saffron cake, given him a slice of the one Hamza had brought to the palace that day? His eyes darted about the room unseeingly as he rattled off more of his thoughts. He seemed to be unaware of her silence as he talked.

Murjana stopped him. She took his hand and looked earnestly into his face. "I came here to warn you because unless something is done, we, and especially you, are in danger. I didn't mean for you to bring forward your plan of murder, for that's what it is."

Hamza's mouth fell open.

"It's all over, dear brother. I weakened when you came to the palace to see me and told me of your dream. I loved Yahya just as much as you, and I mourn his passing with all my heart, as you do. But I've made up my mind. I can't commit murder to avenge him, and I won't. That is a sin before God no better than the sin that took him from us."

She then told him of her visit to the imam, how she'd been so troubled in her mind that she turned to him for help. She had opened her heart and told him everything. Hamza put his hand to his face, horrified.

She had no right to do that, he said angrily, those secrets were not hers to tell. But she assured him she'd given no names, just told the imam of a plan to take revenge on the Caliph for his crimes against her family. The imam guessed the rest, and what he said had sealed her decision. She did not dare to tell Hamza that the imam had asked to see him at once.

"These are terrible things you've told me, my daughter. It's a mercy your uncle doesn't know. Send your brother to me as soon as you can, he needs guidance and help. The plan he has devised must be stopped immediately. How has he strayed from the path of our faith so much that he could think of something so evil? It must be the influence of Ismail and his band of mad followers. They don't know right from wrong, or good from evil."

He had then put his hand on the top of her head as if in blessing. "Be strong, Murjana. Never have any doubt, the taking of life, no matter how just a punishment it might seem to those who suffer injustice, is a sin. Make that your basic, unchanging creed, and never be tempted to give in to revenge."

Remembering those words, she raised her eyes and looked into her brother's. "Hamza, it's wrong to take one life for another. I can't go through with it, and I ask you to put it aside too. Please go to our imam. He will guide you back to the true path."

Hamza fought to control his anger and disappointment. "So, what have you decided to do?"

"I will confess all and assure the Caliph of my loyalty."

"Have you gone completely mad?"

She shook her head. Since seeing the imam, she had looked back and realized she had not known what she was doing when she agreed to Hamza's plan. It had been a bit of a game to her and she never thought it would ever come to anything. But she had gone along with it to please him.

She leaned forward and touched his arm. "I'm sorry, Hamza. I know I misled you, but I could never have agreed to killing the Caliph had I properly understood."

"You must have understood! How else could we have avenged our brother?" Hamza was furious and also frightened. "I can see how you feel, dear sister, and I won't ask you to do anything against your will. Just help me in this one thing: let me come to the palace and be with you. Nothing more."

She shook her head again. "Don't ask me. I can't put the Caliph in danger."

She wanted to go on and say, "I've grown to love him, Hamza. I didn't know it until these last few days. He was cruel to me, but all I could do was long for his forgiveness. I never knew he was so precious until I lost him. It wasn't like that at the beginning. I loved all the attention, all the finery and the luxury of palace life. I enjoyed his adoration and what I thought was my power over him. I even imagined one day telling him what to do with matters of state because he often confided such things to me. And all the while I had no idea that I was growing to love him for himself, not just for his love of me. Those fine things he said he saw in me I saw in him too, but had not the words to describe them. I know you and I did not intend for any of that to happen, and I beg you to forgive me."

But she could never have said those words to him, knowing what a betrayal of their brother they would seem to Hamza. And not just to him. What of her own disloyalty? How could she reconcile her love for Yahya with her love for the man on whose orders he had been killed? Guilt and remorse shot through her. Did she not dishonor her brother's memory each time she longed for his killer's embrace? Would Yahya's shadow never leave them? Would his ghost never be satisfied until she had sacrificed her own happiness for his death?

To Hamza, she said he must feel she had let him down, and pleaded for forgiveness. Hamza, who seemed to have collected himself in the meantime, smiled and put his arm around her shoulders. He assured her he understood her feelings, now that she had explained. He thanked her for having fulfilled her promise to ensnare the Caliph as requested at the beginning. It was not her fault that she misunderstood her mission or had now changed her mind. She could not believe what she was hearing.

"There is nothing to forgive, dear sister. I release you from any further commitment if it makes you so unhappy. You must know that I wish nothing but happiness for you." He sighed. "When I think about it, it was a wild idea and probably impossible to carry out, even if it had been right. In that, you and our imam are the true voices of conscience and righteousness in our community, and you have saved me from a terrible sin."

At his words Murjana experienced a joy she had not felt for months. Her spirits soared. He had absolved her of all responsibility and released her once more to live like other people.

In her relief she did not pause to wonder at his rapid change of heart, but if she had, she would still have refused to let it spoil her happiness. She hugged her brother and promised she would not betray him to the Caliph. He would know nothing of names or individuals, only that there was no plot against him anymore.

⊞

Abu Ubaydah made his way reluctantly to the chamber in the palace where he had met the others before. He had not seen any of them since that time and never told them about his audience with the Caliph.

When Abu Hisham sent him word to come to the meeting that evening, he nearly made an excuse. The last thing he wanted was another session of hand-wringing and indecision like the one before. He had done his duty and warned the Caliph, and could see no further reason for meeting the Caliph's palace officials. But in the end, he accepted Abu Hisham's invitation, and when he arrived found everyone else already there.

"Greetings, Abu Ubaydah," said the chief wazir. "I'm sorry that we started without you. We've been talking about the change in the Caliph since his short trip to the Small Palace."

Abu Ubaydah, who had not seen the Caliph since the time he made his report about Murjana and her brother, had no idea what Abu Hisham was talking about. Durayd explained about the Caliph's short break away from the Golden Gate, and how he seemed to have changed towards his wife on their return.

"He shuns her company, sleeps separately, and behaves as if she wasn't there."

"And he doesn't visit his other wives either, in case you were wondering," added Idris. Abu Ubaydah shook his head. He was thinking that the Caliph must have taken his report seriously after all.

"We don't know what made our master change, but it's the best news we could have hoped for," continued Abu Hisham, smiling with satisfaction. Durayd looked at him reprovingly. Abu Hisham corrected himself hastily, "It's not that any of us would want to see the Caliph unhappy, but in view of our anxieties and yours, Abu Ubaydah, it's surely good news that he's become more cautions and now avoids the lady."

"Perhaps," said Idris. "But he's miserable. I've rarely seen him so unhappy."

"Better unhappy and out of harm's way than the alternative," said Abu Hisham. He went on, "We were wondering what made our master change so dramatically. Did you by any chance speak to the Caliph, commander? Because none of us did, and we're puzzled."

Uthman, who had been silent until then, looked up. Abu Ubaydah debated with himself whether he should tell them the truth. In the end, he could see no harm in it. He gave them a summary of the report he made to the Caliph, expecting them to disapprove of his spying on the Caliph's wife. But no one objected, and he went on to tell them about the Caliph's calmness and indifference to Abu Ubaydah's findings.

"It was as if he knew already and had decided to ignore the warnings. I really can't explain it otherwise."

The rest were pensive. Then Durayd spoke. "However the Caliph seemed to you when you reported to him, something happened to change his mind. I would say he's now well aware of the danger from the lady and her family. It's clear he's on his guard, and at the very least it'll save us the worry of having to watch over him."

"Yes," said Abu Hisham, "but it's not enough for him to be wary and to avoid his wife. More needs to happen. She and her family must no longer be a part of his life."

Everyone looked at him. "So long as she remains in his vicinity, she will be a danger to him." They nodded in agreement. "So, Abu Ubaydah, you're the military planner among us. What do you say?"

Abu Ubaydah looked from one to the other of them. He did not care for Abu Hisham's manner towards him, as if he were some foot soldier in his employ.

"What do you mean, Abu Hisham?" he asked, having guessed what was in the other man's mind. "Divorce? Banishment?"

"Divorce will leave the lady probably embittered and even more vengeful. And anyone can return from banishment, secretly or otherwise. No, I was thinking of something very different."

34

Murjana did not know which was the greater: her longing to see the Caliph or her fear of him. His anger and silence were formidable. But since she thought she knew the cause, she was desperate to put an end to both their suffering.

Two days had passed since her visit to Hamza, and in that time she had not glimpsed the Caliph once. Her lonely life had resumed with only the servants for company. That would not have happened had she been with the harem, where the women might comfort each other at times of neglect by their husband, even if they were often rivals for his attention. But that avenue was closed to her, and she felt truly alone.

As she wandered restlessly around the courtyard one morning, it was Jaafar who came to her aid. The Caliph's son couldn't help observing the change that had come over the household since his father's return from the Small Palace. Murjana would often sit alone with his father nowhere to be seen, and it was obvious that something had gone wrong between them.

Used to the ways of rich men, and the Caliph's several marriages, it would not have surprised Jaafar if his father had already begun to tire of Murjana. He remembered how, not long before, his father had repudiated his favorite wife, Hind, whom no one believed he would ever divorce. Yet he had not only left her but also expelled her from the palace.

That it was now Murjana's turn seemed to Jaafar entirely plausible and, attracted to her as he was, his heart leapt at the thought. He said nothing about it to his mother, but maintained a watch on events, keeping Murjana in his sights. He made sure of bumping into her as if by chance whenever he could. Once or twice, he saw her tear-stained face behind her veil and felt his heart would burst with emotion. It made him surer than ever that his father had discarded her.

"Won't you sit with me, Jaafar?" said Murjana when she saw the boy hovering in a corner of the courtyard. She sat down on the cushions and patted the place beside her. He nodded shyly and sat down awkwardly next to her. He wanted to hold her hand, but did not know how. She asked him what he'd been doing and if he'd been to the hunt, for which he had a liking.

"My lord father does not approve of me hunting. He thinks I spend too much time at it. But I don't see any harm in it. If only someone could speak to him on my behalf." He looked at her pointedly.

"I would do so without hesitation if your father were to visit me." She did not care how that might sound to the boy, whom she imagined still saw her as his father's favorite wife. But he did not seem surprised, and took her words to heart.

"I will make him come! He will not refuse me."

Bringing his father back together with Murjana was the last thing Jaafar wanted. But he could not overcome the urge to impress her with his gallantry. He was also curious to see if his suspicions about the rift between her and the Caliph were correct. So, he rose and bowed.

"I will go to find my father," he promised.

There was no sign of him for several hours after that. Lunch was served in the courtyard at her request, but she ate little, listening out for footsteps the whole time. Eventually she went into her bedchamber and lay down. She dosed off after a while and awoke with the afternoon prayer.

When the maids came to dress her, they told her the Caliph was waiting for her in the majlis. She finished dressing, put on her veil, and walked the few steps to the room. A part of her didn't believe the Caliph would really be there; their estrangement felt longstanding and irreversible.

Jaafar was at the door as she came in. He ushered her in silently and walked ahead of her to where the Caliph sat, his back against the light. Murjana could not see his expression as she walked forward behind Jaafar. The three of them were alone. Reaching his seat, she fell to her knees before him. He made no attempt to raise her up, and she stayed kneeling.

"I understand you wanted to see me."

"Yes, my lord. But we must be alone."

There was a silence. Jaafar looked dismayed.

"I see no reason for my son not to hear anything you might have to say to me. He will stay."

Murjana shook her head. She knew she was playing for high stakes and would have to brave the Caliph's displeasure or his downright rejection. But it was her one chance to redeem the situation between them, and she could not afford to lose it.

"I have things to say that are for your ears only, my lord. No one else can hear them. I beg you to grant me this one wish, and I'll ask for no more."

The Caliph shifted on his cushions. "Very well. For this one time only. But it will not happen again."

He indicated that Jaafar should leave and stop anyone from coming in until he gave the order. The boy was put out, but not too much. He was now certain that his father had rejected Murjana, and assumed she wanted privacy to try and persuade him to take her back. His offer of help to her had borne fruit, and he need have no regrets about making it.

When the door closed behind him, Murjana, still on her knees, took off her veil. She was pale and her large eyes were serious.

"I beg you to listen to me fairly and with an open mind until the end." She paused to collect herself fully. "You believe that I've betrayed you, my lord, and that my brother and I are plotting to do you harm."

She could feel she had his full attention, although his closed expression did not change. "It will never happen. I swear it by all that I hold dear. My brother will swear it too, if you summon him."

She told him the whole story, from the family's initial grief at the death of Yahya to her brother's desire for revenge in which she had shared. She told him of her love for her eldest brother, whom she had always looked up to, and her anguish at losing him. But it might have ended as anger and grief but no more, she said, had Hamza not come under the influence of Ismail and the other dissidents. She placed the blame wholly on them, and held back nothing: her growing doubts and worries, her meeting with the imam and what he had told her, and then her final confrontation with Hamza when she had rejected his plan for good.

"He rejects it too, regrets he ever got involved, and will never raise a finger against you."

She rose from her knees and timidly sat next to him. The Caliph looked at her desperate face and forgot his anguish for a moment. He didn't know if it was naïveté or guilt that made her confess to such high treason as if it had just been a silly mistake. She touched his hand, afraid he would draw it away. But he didn't and went on looking at her.

"I wouldn't harm a hair of your head, my lord. You must believe me." She did not know how to make love speeches. She had never needed to before; his eloquence and passion had carried them both.

"Your harshness towards me these last days has been too much to bear. Your hatred was like a stone in my heart. I could not go on living if you never forgave me, never came back to me." She paused, searching for the right words. "I didn't always love you. You were too grand, too powerful, and too far above me. It's not easy to love a man like you. But without my knowing how, it still happened. My love for you has made me forget every pledge I made to avenge my brother, and everything that came before you."

The Caliph was touched, despite himself. Was it possible she was telling the truth? Her artless candor in telling him a story so damning of her and her family, apparently without fear of his retribution, made him wonder. Perhaps it was the greatest proof of her innocence, and he found himself hoping it could be so. He was tired of hatred and revenge, and every fiber of his being urged him to believe her.

Yet it was hard. His sense of betrayal by the one person he had trusted with his innermost thoughts, his very soul, the woman he worshipped and who was the love of his life, had been indescribable. He had reeled with shock and disbelief. It awoke in him all the fear and distrust he had felt for everyone around him at the time of the war against his brother. He had seen enemies lurking in every nook and around every corner, and had not known a moment's ease until he had purged them all. He didn't want to return to that time of constant suspicion and unhappiness.

And so, he forced himself to see Murjana, not as the devious traitor who would lure him to his death, but as she really was: a young girl without mother or father, living a sheltered life under her uncle's guardianship, and clinging to her brothers for security. Her loyalty had been to them above all others and made her easy prey for adventurers and ruthless schemers. He had glimpsed her vulnerability many times, and it had aroused his deepest instincts to protect her. But others must have seen it too. And wasn't it more likely that they had put it to good use for their own purposes than that she had connived to do him harm of her own accord?

Her pained and anguished face whenever he tormented her at the Small Palace came into his mind, and he was suddenly ashamed. It had all been a dreadful mistake. Murjana was a victim, not a criminal. He could see that now. She should never have been subjected to the cruel ordeal he had devised to punish her.

Her eyes were on him as these thoughts went through his head. He could see she was still nervous. Gently, he lifted her hand to his lips and kissed it.

"Forgive me, Murjana, forgive me."

▣

They retired early that night. No one was allowed to disturb them. The supper the stewards served was left largely uneaten, and the servants who came to do the routine preparation of the Caliph's bedroom before his bedtime were dismissed.

At last, they were totally alone. It had been unusually warm for spring, and the bedroom windows were open to the soft breeze. The courtyard candles glinted in the twilight, and the torch nearest the window lit up the room inside with an intimate glow. The air was tranquil, and the waters of the fountain cascaded rhythmically into its marble basin. It was a scene to delight the Caliph who felt himself replenished each time he sat in the courtyard.

But this time was special. There was joy in everything around him, the palace, the world, the whole universe. He lay with Murjana in his arms, not speaking or moving. If he could have captured that moment he would have locked it into a magic bottle to savor each time he wanted to remember the happiness of that night.

Murjana was back with him, more a part of him than she ever had been, and they would try every pleasure and taste every delight of all the lovers in the world who had loved as they did.

The night of their reunion was not merely a coming together, but a resurrection of two people condemned to death and then returned to life and vigor. They slept little, and with the coming of the dawn Murjana sat up and looked down at the Caliph, who was also wide awake.

"My sweetest lord, I want to make you a pledge before God, who is my sole witness. I love and honor you, and I will do so till my dying breath. I will never betray you, not even for the sake of my dead brother, not because you are innocent of his blood, but because I can't. Whatever you have done, you are as precious to me as the memory of my mother, as dear to me as I am to myself. I want for you never to die and leave me, and may God forgive me for denying the death He has ordained for us all. I want the two of us to live forever."

It was the longest speech the Caliph had ever heard her make and it moved him unutterably. He sat up and she saw there were tears in his eyes. He whispered, "Oh Murjana, how can I answer you? You are the queen of my world, my heart, and my soul, and all that I am is yours till death."

He took her gently in his arms and closed his eyes. If there is a paradise in this world, he thought, then I have found it.

PART V

Baghdad, April 830

PART V

35

When Durayd left him outside the Caliph's bedchamber, Abu Mansour felt an overwhelming urge to follow him back to the majlis and not go into the room. He had a premonition of the impending horror awaiting him. But he composed himself and moved forward into the room.

The scene that met Abu Mansour's eyes as he stood inside the Caliph's bedchamber was worse than he had feared. The lamps were still lit, even though it was daytime, their light competing feebly with the shafts of bright sunlight that came through the shuttered windows.

He couldn't help but note how much the room had changed since he had last seen it when the Caliph was ill. The marriage had transformed it into an opulent place, magnificently furnished with the finest carpets from Armenia, its windows hung with curtains of satin brocade from Damascus, and huge wall mirrors framed in wood and mother-of-pearl, matching the chests of drawers and bedside tables.

His eyes went to the bed that stood against the farthest wall. It was wide and low, and draped in a rich velvet coverlet. Over it, prostrate and unmoving, was the body of the Caliph covering that of his wife, who lay still under the bedclothes.

Abu Mansour could not tell which one of them had met a terrible fate, or if by awful chance, both of them had. The thought of some macabre death pact came to his mind. His alarm at the sight was so great he felt impelled to break the silence.

"*Al-salam-u-aleikum.*"

There was no immediate movement from the bed. But then the Caliph turned his head toward him. He's alive, thought Abu Mansour with immense relief, and in the same instant realized the lady Murjana had still not moved. The Caliph stared at the doctor, and then rose to his feet.

"Thank God, you're here, Abu Mansour." His voice was hoarse. "I've been keeping vigil over Murjana, waiting for you. She hasn't woken yet, and I can't rouse her."

Abu Mansour drew closer to the bed and looked at the Caliph's wife. Even at such a moment, he could not help being moved by her outstanding beauty: her oval face and sculpted cheekbones, her full lips, and the long dark hair spread out on the pillows. She wore an expression of serenity, and her body was utterly still. He knew the signs, and did not need to examine her to know what had happened.

"My palace doctors have seen her already, but they had no idea of what was wrong with her. I knew that only you could help." The Caliph was trying hard to control his palpable agitation. Abu Mansour asked for permission to open the shutters. The sunlight that streamed into the room only emphasized Murjana's pallor. He had no doubt the palace doctors had reached the same conclusion that he had, but were too afraid to tell the Caliph.

Abu Mansour went through the motions of examining her, but without rushing, so as to give the Caliph time to face the reality. He bent down over Murjana and felt for her pulse. He put his nose to her mouth and tried to smell her breath, and then held his handkerchief against her nostrils. It didn't stir. At that, he straightened up and looked solemnly into the Caliph's face.

"I'm sorry, my prince. Please forgive what I am about to say. But I must follow the dictates of God and my profession. The lady Murjana is dead."

The silence that followed these words was absolute. Not a breath stirred. The Caliph stood as if he had been turned to stone. And then it came, a low howl as from an animal mortally wounded. It filled the room, growing louder and louder. The Caliph clutched at his robes, and bent his head over his breast, utterly desolated.

"No! No! No!" he cried again and again, shaking his head from side to side.

Abu Mansour could only stand by quietly, waiting for the Caliph's anguish to abate. He felt uncomfortable intruding on his grief and thought he ought to leave. But in the end, he stayed out of pity. Eventually, the Caliph's agony gave way to an abandoned, inconsolable sobbing that would have tugged at the coldest heart.

"It was my fault, all my fault. I should have been more careful," he kept muttering agitatedly.

Abu Mansour was not sure what he meant. But it was often the way of bereaved people to blame themselves for the death of a loved one. He did not interrupt, and after a while the Caliph controlled himself. Looking at Abu Mansour through red, swollen eyes, his lips dry and cracked, he spoke in a cold, dead voice, "Murjana did not die by any natural means. She was in the fullest health. Nothing ailed her. Only yesterday we walked together, and then we dined. You were with us for dinner and saw how she ate and drank with appetite, and how she shook me playfully after the meal whenever she thought I was getting sleepy. It's true that later in bed it was she who slept before me and didn't stir at my touch as she normally did. But it was nothing more than the tiredness after a long day in the sun."

He continued in this vein, making ever wilder accusations, and Abu Mansour could only feel compassion for his ravings.

It was a natural enough reaction; a grieving lover bereft of his beloved and venting his anguish on those he imagined had snatched her from him. He said nothing and waited.

After a while the Caliph's agitation subsided and he grew quiet. His face took on a closed, determined expression.

"Hear me, Abu Mansour. I will not rest until her killer is found."

"Indeed, my lord. But we have yet to know the cause of this tragic death."

Had he been addressing his students, he would have said, "We never jump to conclusions without evidence."

"I don't know how the act was committed," the Caliph responded, "but I must know who was responsible."

He paused and looked into the doctor's face.

"And you, Abu Mansour, will tell me."

The doctor was taken completely by surprise. The Caliph's request was the last thing he expected. Why would his master ask something of him so outside his experience and professional skills? He did not know how to refuse the Caliph's command. But he could not take on a responsibility so alien to him.

"Forgive me, my lord, but I'm not a sleuth. That is not my profession. I try to help the living as best I can, but that is the limit of my competence. I beg you to look among your many agents who are far cleverer than me in such matters."

The Caliph did not react angrily, but he was unmoved by Abu Mansour's protestations.

"My agents are competent as you say, and will do what's required of them. But in this matter, I trust no one except you. Only you have my interest at heart, and only you understand what Murjana meant to me. You must do as I ask."

◫

News of Murjana's death spread quickly around the palace, and a messenger was sent hastily to inform her family. It would not be long before the whole of Baghdad heard about it as well, and speculation about how the Caliph's wife had met her end would soon follow. It was not uncommon for young women to die, but it was usually the result of poverty or childbirth. Since neither of these applied to the lady Murjana, inevitably there would be whispers and rumors that her death was suspicious.

Abu Mansour paid little heed to any of this. Mindful of the Caliph's urgent command, he knew he had little time. He hurried to his house in the company of a palace guard who, at his request, was carrying the remnants of the food served at dinner the night before. Not much was left after the kitchen had disposed of the leftovers, but Abu Mansour had in mind one particular dish that only the Caliph and his wife had eaten and whose remains were still there. "Send word to Ahmad that I need him here urgently," he instructed Younis.

The box of food the palace guard had deposited was in the doctor's dispensary, much to Younis' curiosity. The household was not yet aware of what had happened, since there was nothing unusual in Abu Mansour being called to the palace. Only Saad knew from Younis of the urgency with which their master had been summoned to the Caliph's presence, and they were both curious to learn more.

As soon as Abu Mansour had taken off his robe and washed his hands, he turned his attention to the food box. When Ahmad appeared, breathless from his journey to the house, Abu Mansour took him immediately into the dispensary, but did not have the heart to dismiss Younis, whose excitement had reached fever-pitch.

"You must be quiet if you want to stay with us, Younis."

He explained the circumstances to Ahmad, and said they would have to test the food for traces of anything abnormal.

"Are we looking for anything in particular, sir?"

"Yes, Ahmad, we are. You remember how I taught you to test for opium. That is my first suspicion, having examined the color of the deceased's lips and fingers, and smelled the odor around her mouth. If I am wrong, we will test for other substances." The young man nodded.

Abu Mansour opened the box. Inside were the remains of several dishes, including two pieces of saffron cake, one a paler orange than the other. Looking carefully, he saw that the reason for the difference in color was that it had a smaller amount of saffron on top.

"We must test all the dishes one by one. I doubt we'll find anything odd in any of the ones we all shared last night, since I am unharmed. After we test them, we'll concentrate our efforts on the two pieces of cake which only the Caliph and his wife ate, to see if their ingredients are the same."

Younis brought out two beakers and two spatulas for the cakes, with small bowls for the rest. He was dying to say something.

"Didn't I tell you, sir, about what I saw in the souk? I know it's him!"

"Yes, you did, Younis. But we don't know what's in these cakes yet, and even if we find something, it doesn't mean there's a connection with the person you're thinking of, or anyone else we know."

They set to testing and recording what they found. There was nothing remarkable in any of the dishes until they came to the cakes. Here they came upon what Abu Mansour had suspected ever since he saw the lady Murjana that morning. But only one of the pieces of cake—the paler-colored of the two—contained opium.

Abu Mansour straightened.

"Well, I think that tells us all we need to know. Thank you, Ahmad, and you too, Younis. What we've discovered, we must keep to ourselves for now. No one must know about it. I'm relying on your absolute discretion."

When Younis left the dispensary, he found Saad waiting eagerly to hear what was happening. But mindful of his promise to his master, he shook his head firmly.

"Don't ask me any questions. I can't tell you anything."

36

amza hurried over to the house where he usually met the others. He left behind him a scene of indescribable grief as the news of Murjana's death sank in. His aunt was prostrated, and her daughters could not stop crying and beating their breasts. Abdulhamid was inconsolable. Yet another of his brother's children had gone. He was bewildered by the evil luck that dogged his family, as if someone had laid a curse on them all. In the midst of the general distress, Hamza's extreme agitation did not seem unwarranted. He said he couldn't bear it any longer and needed to get some fresh air.

But immediately on leaving the house, Hamza went quickly down the alley toward the usual meeting place, making sure that Yazan did not follow him. Once there, he found Ismail and Usama waiting for him inside. Musa was not with them. The two men dispensed with the usual greetings, and quickly got to the point.

"Well, brother Hamza," said Ismail. "What happened?"

"I swear before God, I don't know."

"You assured us nothing could go wrong."

"Look, she was my sister. I didn't want this to happen."

Afraid of the two men, Hamza was intensely agitated. "It was meant for the Caliph. I made sure he had the right cake. I don't understand how they got mixed up."

"Perhaps whoever you entrusted with the task guessed what you were doing and wanted to protect the Caliph."

"No, that's not possible. I sent our old servant, who is faithful and devoted. He's been with us all his life, and I'd trust him with mine. He took my aunt's cakes as a gift to the Caliph and Murjana. She told us the Caliph wasn't fond of saffron, and our servant asked the stewards to make sure they served him the cake with less saffron. He swore he did, and I believe him."

The men started at him, unconvinced.

"You never told us you were going to handle it this way. You said you had a foolproof method. We trusted you. And this was it? It was bound to go wrong."

"How else could I have done it? You knew that my sister refused to help me, and without her we couldn't have been able to do anything. But I found a way to change her mind. She believed me and got the Caliph to trust me and think I was a changed man. And it was because she trusted me that I could get her to offer the Caliph my aunt's specialty and slip the cakes past her."

Ismail thought about Hamza's explanation.

"But it still went wrong. Someone else must have known about the cakes. Can you think who it might be? Someone in your family? Someone who spied on you without you knowing it?" Having a low opinion of Hamza's competence, he thought the latter was the most likely.

Hamza shook his head.

"No one in my family has any love for the Caliph. But I'm sure no one had any idea what we were doing."

"Well, it's too late now. We have to work out what's best for us to do. The Caliph will want to find out how your sister died. He won't realize he was the one intended, and may think his enemies meant to attack him through his wife" He looked worried. "Whatever he decides, it'll come to the same thing for us. He'll send his men after everyone he suspects, and we'll be top of the list."

Ismail paused abruptly, suddenly aware of his surroundings, and listened to the sounds from the street. He got up and checked that the windows and front door were closed. Reassured that there was nothing to worry about, he continued.

"Brothers, we need to leave as soon as possible. We can't take the risk of staying here a moment longer."

"How can I leave?" Hamza objected, nearly in tears. "My sister's not even buried yet, and I must be there for the funeral and the condolences. Running off now would be tantamount to admitting guilt, even if the Caliph doesn't know how I'm involved. You do what you think best, but you'll have to leave me behind."

"And have the Caliph's men arrest and torture you? You'll tell them everything and none of us will be safe. No, brother Hamza, you will leave with us, and do so tonight."

⊞

Idris was a troubled man. He had had a sense of impending doom ever since he heard of Murjana's death. He remembered his last, frustrating encounter with the lady Hind, how none of his appeals against the actions she wanted taken to displace her rival had changed her mind. When they parted at her uncle's front door, she had looked at him through her veil with an expression of such deep sorrow it touched his heart. Her hand resting on his arm, she had said, "Dearest Idris, my best and only friend, if you will not help me, then I am alone and must find my own way."

"What do you mean?"

"You know more than anyone what I want most in all the world. It's the only way to bring me the happiness I once knew. If you don't relent, I'll have to make my own plans."

Idris felt himself to be in an impossible position. She affected him every time he saw her. He longed to make her happy again, but he could not bring himself to do what she asked. She had given him unmistakeable hints of a closer relationship between them if he helped her, and, although a part of him sensed it was a bribe that could be withdrawn once he had done her bidding, there was an allure in it that tempted him.

"There's nothing that would make me happier than to serve you. But in all conscience, I can't agree to this. And I fear for you if you try. How will you do it? And what if you're discovered? It's no small thing that you're contemplating."

"You mustn't worry about discovery."

She paused, wondering how much she should tell him. She knew he cared for her and was sure he would never betray her. Besides, it was just a conversation between them, nothing more. She spoke in a whisper. "It will be a simple matter of indigestion, eating something that disagrees with the stomach, that's all. All you need do is tamper with the food, and it's all over. No one will suspect you, or me for that matter."

With that, Idris's hesitation came to an end. He made up his mind.

"No, my lady. Neither of us should do anything like that. I grieve for your unhappiness, but this is not the way. Never speak of such things ever again."

⊞

Maryam sat with Um Jaafar and reported on the day she had spent with Idris and the lady Hind. She spoke of Hind's obvious sadness and the way she had clung to Idris, although not actually touching him. On the Street of Booksellers, they had stood together at one point deep in conversation which looked to be of a private nature. Maryam was too far away to hear them, but the lady looked upset and cried.

"And you couldn't make out what they were talking about? Could it have been about her sadaq?"

"I don't think so. That was a simple transaction and wouldn't have been a cause for upset. It was more like a request she made of him, and I could see him shaking his head, which was when she started to cry."

Um Jaafar had a good idea what the conversation would have been about. Hind was obsessed with the Caliph and had never accepted her divorce from him. Um Jaafar guessed that Hind's banishment to her uncle's house had given her time to brood over what had happened, which would only have made matters worse. Although Um Jaafar herself had not been divorced, she had a sense of what that felt like. She had been still young and, she thought, pleasing to the Caliph when he married Sulafa. No amount of reassurance from him that it was merely a marriage of convenience, and that he still held her, Um Jaafar, in high esteem, repaired the hurt she had felt. Nor did it make up for the loss of the passionate nights she had known with him, her first and only lover. She still thought about that and could not help imagining how that passion was now in the possession of a new wife. If she allowed herself, she too would be as jealous as Hind and wish the Caliph had never set eyes on the girl.

But she never gave free rein to such thoughts, and unlike Hind, she had been gifted with a son. Jaafar was the apple of her eye and destined to be his father's heir. She clung to the importance it gave her as *Um Walad*[*] and the consolation it brought.

"Did you believe the story about Hind's sadaq?" she suddenly asked.

Maryam thought for a minute. "I did at first. But I never saw any money change hands, and I couldn't see how something like that would be so upsetting."

---

[*] Literally, "mother of a son," a special status enjoyed by wives and concubines who had given birth to a potential heir to the caliphate.

Um Jaafar mulled this over. Clearly there was more to the meeting than met the eye.

"You've done well, Maryam. Please keep all this to yourself."

When Maryam had gone, she sat and thought about what she had heard. She could only conclude that Hind was planning to do something to the Caliph's new wife, but dared not think what it might be. One could speculate endlessly, she thought, since no one knew the cause of Murjana's death, and the mystery surrounding it was enough to cause a cloud of suspicion to hang over everyone.

At the other end of the palace from Um Jaafar's apartment, the Caliph's chief wazir was also pondering the mystery of Murjana's death. Abu Hisham had no idea how she died, but it was certain that someone knew, and that person was a potential suspect. Increasingly, he started to feel that he himself might be considered such a suspect.

Ever since Murjana's death, he had imagined there was a change in the behavior of people around him. He thought the men with whom he had conferred secretly about the problems created by the Caliph's marriage were avoiding him. Durayd was always busy, Idris spent most of his time at the Dar al-Huram, and Uthman had vanished altogether. Even Suleiman hardly greeted him when they came across each other.

He tried to think back over the meetings they had held. Had he been careless? He searched his memory with ever increasing alarm and then recalled that, in the course of an outburst, he had once made an unwise remark about the Caliph being better off if he were rid of the lady Murjana, who had brought nothing but trouble into his life. Surely everyone must have known he wasn't serious, and had no intention of putting his words into effect.

But, thinking about it now, he couldn't be sure that his words hadn't been misconstrued. Panic gripped him. And then he wondered if it was someone else of their circle who was the suspect. What if, in his zeal and loyalty to the Caliph, one of them, possibly Uthman, or even Idris, had taken it on himself to do away with the lady and put the Caliph out of danger for good? It would have been the ultimate expression of devotion to their master, and he could see that both men had that sort of loyalty. And yet, was it possible they would go that far?

The more Abu Hisham thought, the more bewildered he became. Finally, in a daze of fear and anxiety, he went back to the safety of his house and family and tried to forget.

37

The Caliph's order to find the lady Murjana's murderer left Abu Mansour with deep misgivings. He knew he must obey, but he disliked having to fulfill an assignment he felt he had not the skills for. After a while, however, he managed to set aside his dismay and accept that he would have to carry out the task to the best of his ability.

As a physician, he had always approached the diagnosis and treatment of disease by methodically applying logic and experience to each step before arriving at his conclusion. It gave people under his care the feeling that he understood their ailments and gave them the best therapy to fit their diagnosis and was a reason for his great popularity. He saw each disease as a mystery to be elucidated, and the mystery of Murjana's death was no different.

So he used the identical method and estimated that it would take him roughly two weeks to complete the task. He canceled his clinic work and took leave from the bimaristan, the better to devote himself to his assignment.

Unlike the process of diagnosing a disease, however, he found he didn't know where to start. Having established the cause of the lady Murjana's death, his next step was to find out who had placed the poison in the cake that she ate, and why only one of the two virtually identical pieces was affected.

After a period of consideration, he decided to begin by drawing up a list of those around the Caliph who had any reason, however far-fetched, to wish him or the lady Murjana ill, since targeting her would hurt him almost as much as killing him. His next move would be to find out who had access to the palace kitchens and hence to tampering with the food she ate that night. Matching these two discoveries should establish the identity of the perpetrator. To that end, he had a question for the Caliph's chamberlain.

"This is all most tragic, Master Durayd, and I am sorry to have to burden you with what might seem a strange question. But it's important and I think you're likely to know the answer. I assume you have access to the palace kitchens if you needed it. Can you tell me who else has it, beside the kitchen staff?"

Durayd was not put out by Abu Mansour's question. He was reminded of the doctor's equally strange questions at the time of the Caliph's illness, which had turned out to be so crucial to his recovery. He thought about his answer.

"Usually anyone inside the palace can enter the kitchens, although in the normal course of things, most people would have no business there. From outside, delivery men and perhaps a few special individuals known to the kitchen staff can do the same. But no one else."

Abu Mansour thanked him and crossed him and his colleagues off the list.

After them came Ibn Uthal and his followers, who had been angry at his detention and inquisition on the Caliph's orders. They had contended that the Caliph was under his Shiite wife's influence, a matter that had worried Abu Mansour at the time. It was possible to conceive of someone from among their ranks conspiring to harm the lady Murjana, or the Caliph.

He spent some time making inquiries of the chief wazir,

who received regular reports about unrest among the people. Abu Hisham had ordered his network of palace spies to gather information on Ibn Uthal's followers in the wake of his detention, and they had attended the Friday mosque sermons in the part of Baghdad where his disciples congregated, as well as the traditionist public meetings. But they found no evidence that the resentment people felt at the time of Ibn Uthal's interrogation had amounted to anything more than a temporary protest, and after a while it had died down. So another possibility was removed from Abu Mansour's list.

He then turned to those he considered the more likely suspects in terms of motive and opportunity. At the head of this group were the Caliph's wives, two of whom had strong reasons for wishing the lady Murjana's departure from his life, by whatever means. His conversation with Idris had made him first suspect the lady Hind, who had not forgotten her repudiation at the Caliph's hands, and had brooded on her revenge ever since, according to the eunuch's account. It was the woman who had taken her place that she had in her sights, not the Caliph who had rejected her.

"I wish I could say that the lady had grown calmer with time."

Idris looked sad as he said this. His sympathy for her, and perhaps something more, became evident to Abu Mansour. In his experience, it was not unusual to come across eunuchs who retained manly emotions, often because they had not been completely castrated in boyhood or, as probably in Idris's case, castrated when puberty had already started.

"Would you go so far as to say that the lady might have made her own plan to harm the Caliph's wife without you knowing?" Abu Mansour asked.

Idris shook his head vehemently, showing he had considered the possibility.

"She longed for that and wanted my help. But I turned her down."

"Do you know if she had access to any poison she could have used?"

Poison was traditionally said to be a woman's favorite weapon. But, living outside the palace, and with no way of reaching the lady Murjana except through Idris, who had refused to be a party to her schemes, she would have needed an accomplice. Hind was the perfect suspect—passionate, vengeful, and unscrupulous in her desire to rid the Caliph of Murjana.

Abu Mansour decided he would need to see her. And the Caliph, who had his own suspicions of her, gave him permission.

They met in a small room far away from the Dar al-Huram. Idris was with them, but no one else. Hind was veiled from head to foot. With her full figure and proud bearing, he immediately knew her to be the woman he had seen with Idris in the Street of Booksellers. He supposed it was there that she had begged for Idris's help, and he realized that his curiosity about them had not been misplaced.

"I hope you will forgive a few questions I wish to ask. I understand that you're living in the house of your uncle. Do you often go out?"

She shook her head, and he could see her eyes watching him through the face veil.

"I would like to ask if you ever make visits to the palace, the Dar al-Huram in particular." She turned toward Idris as if appealing for his help. Standing behind Abu Mansour, he remained silent.

"I don't ever come here since my lord sent me away," she answered.

"But you could come if you wished to?"

"The lady Hind would have to ask the Caliph's permission first," said Idris.

"But you might like to visit a friend among the other ladies. Would our master deny you that?"

"He might. But there is no one I wish to visit."

She sounded upset.

"I can understand there will be sensitivities with the Caliph's wives, but not all of them, surely? Do you have no friend among them?"

Idris could not understand where his questions were leading.

"We all liked Um Jaafar, so I suppose I could say I would like to see her again, if I could."

"And is that where you were on the night before the lady Murjana died?"

"No, no. I wasn't."

"Where were you then?"

"At my uncle's house," she said, flustered.

"I realize how upsetting it must have been for you to be forsaken for a younger woman. Did you ever wish her dead?"

She made an effort to calm herself.

"No, I did not."

She looked at Idris.

"I spoke of his leaving her, but only as a longing. I wouldn't have harmed her, although I was angry and upset."

"And also rejected?...Would you have welcomed her removal so the Caliph could return to you?"

She said nothing.

Abu Mansour was impressed by her strength of character and self-control. She was a fighter and, whatever her denials, would not have given up the battle for the Caliph easily.

He visited the other wives in the Dar al-Huram, and made up his mind about each of them. If Hind had been the perpetrator of the crime, her accomplice could only have been Um Jaafar. She was the most loyal and faithful of the Caliph's wives, apparently selfless in her devotion to him and his son. So much was obvious when he conversed with her.

Of all the Caliph's harem, she did not cover her face, which had not been the custom in her country. Abu Mansour took an instant liking to her. She had a graceful, dignified demeanor, although she could not be regarded as beautiful.

"Forgive me, but I need to ask you some personal questions."

"Of course. You're trying to find the person responsible for this dreadful crime. Ask as you please."

"How did you feel when your husband decided to take this last wife?"

She thought about it quietly. "I accepted it. I had seen the Caliph's marriages to three women after me, and it seemed natural for him to take another."

"Were you worried he would divorce you?"

She shook her head calmly.

"Is that because you felt secure as Um Walad?"

"Partly."

"You see, I'm wondering if you felt secure at all. The lady Murjana was young and you could see she might give him another son. With this difference—that such a boy would be the fruit of a passionate love between the Caliph and a new wife whom he adored."

He saw he had hit a raw nerve. Um Jaafar's equanimity was badly ruffled, and she tried to regain her placid expression.

"I doubt any of that would happen as you say, Abu Mansour. My husband has loved Jaafar since his birth. I cannot see him replacing the son he prizes so much with another. But even if that were to happen, I wouldn't begrudge my lord his happiness."

Abu Mansour did not believe her. In spite of the serenity she struggled to display, she clearly resented the Caliph's new marriage deeply. She had probably never stopped loving him, or ceased regretting his having put her aside for other wives. But she had hidden it under the guise of the wise and understanding elder wife, managing to fool many people, not least the Caliph himself.

Um Jaafar was not blind to the lady Murjana's beauty and how captivated he was by it. If she did indeed bear him a son, the consequences for Um Jaafar were potentially devastating. Jaafar might be displaced as the heir by the new son, and the valued status of Um Walad that she had enjoyed for all these years, and that had been her compensation for the loss of the Caliph's love, could vanish.

The temptation to prevent such an eventuality might have been enough to persuade Um Jaafar to assist Hind in her designs on Murjana. But a big obstacle stood in the way of the plan, one that the women must have soon faced: it would not be easy to gain the access to the Caliph's private apartments they needed. And neither woman would be allowed to enter in person. If Abu Mansour was right about the plan, they must have thought of a solution.

"This is pure speculation, Um Jaafar. I hope I have not offended you. I know our master holds you in the highest regard, but who knows what might have happened if he were to be blessed with a new son."

At that moment, Maryam, Um Jaafar's stewardess, came in with a tray of sherbet. Looking at her again reinforced his recognition of her that day in the Street of Booksellers with Idris and the lady Hind. But, more importantly, it struck him that she was allowed entry to all parts of the palace—including the Caliph's apartments.

Abu Mansour went home and sat in his courtyard, reflecting on the progress of his investigation and what he had learned about the case. His list of suspects had yielded only one serious possibility: the Caliph's wives who could have conspired against Mujana and brought about her end. He went over the details of his inquiry and found the inferences he had drawn to be logical. Both women had strong motives, could easily have acquired opium, which was sold by many apothecaries in the souk, and had access to the palace kitchens.

But there was still a flaw. For the plot to work, Um Jaafar's stewardess would have had to be taken into their confidence, or told some story plausible enough to dupe her into putting poison into the cake. Neither was at all likely, and Abu Mansour discarded the whole idea. Motive, however persuasive, he knew was not enough on its own. He would have to think again.

From the start, he had based his investigation on the assumption that the murderer's intended victim was the lady Murjana. He had thus excluded her family from his inquiries, for they would obviously not wish to harm their own daughter. At the same time, this was a family that, from all accounts, had a deep grudge against the Caliph and wished him ill. There was no more effective way to take revenge on him than to kill his cherished wife. Yet, who of them would do such a thing?

He went to see Abu Ubaydah again.

"I am at an important point in my investigation and would benefit from your help once more, Abu Ubaydah. At our last meeting, you spoke of the palace officials' anxieties over the Banu Shaaban family, but said little about your own concerns. I sensed at the time that you knew a great deal about the family, and would appreciate your sharing that knowledge with me now."

There were no objections, and the commander told him what his spies had uncovered of the family's closeness to the imam, and Hamza's friendship with the Shia dissidents who were sworn enemies of the Caliph. But the spies had not been able to penetrate the rebel fraternity or attend their meetings. It was not clear if they had any significance or what role Hamza played for them, if he had one at all.

Abu Mansour was suddenly reminded of the incident Younis witnessed at the apothecary shop in the souk when Hamza, after buying opium, was seen talking to another man.

Abu Ubaydah then told him about the execution of the eldest Shaaban brother, Yahya.

"This is important. Does the Caliph know?"

"He does, but he took no action as far as I know."

This didn't make any sense, and the commander could shed no further light on it. Abu Mansour would have to investigate the family, and Hamza in particular. He had not forgotten the man's strange visit to his clinic and possibly to his lecture at the bimaristan afterward. Younis, whose suspicions the doctor had dismissed, may have been on the right track all along.

Put together, these incidents left no doubt about Hamza's quest for a poison—for opium, in particular—which it seemed he had finally obtained. But to what end? If revenge on the Caliph was the aim, he would hardly have targeted his own sister, even to avenge their dead brother. It was a paradox Abu Mansour could not explain.

At the launch of his inquiry, Abu Mansour had decided to search for whoever had tampered with the cakes that were served at the Caliph's dinner, and identify whoever was most likely amongst those hostile to the Caliph or his wife. He had assumed all along that the poison came from inside the palace. It was a natural enough assumption, given the difficulty of entry for visitors from outside, and so he had looked for a perpetrator who could have entered the kitchens and planted the poisoned cake, unobserved. But the more he thought about it, the more he had to acknowledge the possibility that the cake was not made on the premises and had been brought in ready-made.

In the immediate aftermath of the lady Murjana's death, the chamberlain's first act had been to summon the head cook and the kitchen staff to explain how the Caliph's food had been prepared and by whom. Terrified and dreading their instant dismissal or worse, they denied they had seen any strangers in the kitchen, or had any friends visiting on the day of the Caliph's dinner. But thinking it over again, Abu Mansour decided it was now essential to repeat the interrogation, and he would start there. After that, he would complete his inquiry with a visit to the Banu Shaaban, the last of his suspects.

He reasoned that, if he had not managed to fulfill the Caliph's order and find his wife's killer by then, he never would.

38

The Caliph found the wait for Abu Mansour to complete his inquiries and report back intolerable. He thought of nothing else, remained shut away behind the doors of his private apartments, and spoke to no one. It was reminiscent of the days of his sickness. At his request, his attendants served him silently, wondering when it would all end.

The palace was in official mourning. Activity on all fronts was muted, and all nonessential meetings were canceled. The intellectual gatherings the Caliph cherished were halted. The weekly diwan was suspended, and all foreign and other visits ceased. Public displays and celebrations were prohibited throughout Baghdad in mourning.

If ever the Caliph had needed the comfort of religious faith, it was then. The Quran teaches that death is preordained by God on the appointed date, and at the appointed hour. Striving to know the cause and manner of his wife's death, as the Caliph was doing to see if he could have prevented it, was futile. It would have made no difference in the end. No matter how much he raged or what he did, death would have found Murjana, if not in that place, then in another, and at the same predestined hour.

Had he been able to believe in such a creed, like many others, he might have found some respite from his anguish. He would have surrendered his fate to God and shed his sense of responsibility for Murjana's death. But he had no such faith, and so he remained in a state of grief and despair, set on a path of revenge against whoever had killed his wife.

⊞

When finally the next morning it was announced that Abu Mansour had arrived at the palace and was heading for the private apartments, the Caliph came out into the courtyard to meet him. It was the first time since Murjana's death that he had done so. It was also the first time he allowed the servants to put her clothes and jewelry away. Up until then, they had been forbidden from touching anything that belonged to her, and were to keep the room just as it had been at the moment of her death. It was where he spent his days and nights, still smelling her perfume, holding her clothes to him as if to recapture her essence, and sleeping on his accustomed side of the bed opposite to where she used to lie.

"Salam, Abu Mansour!"

The doctor bowed. "Peace be upon you, my lord." As he straightened, he searched the Caliph's face for signs of illness. But, though it was pale and haggard, the sleepless eyes haunted and lackluster, he did not look ill.

When, long afterward, he looked back on that fateful day, Abu Mansour would always remember the scent of spring flowers in the air and the pale early sunlight that bathed the courtyard. The beauty and tranquillity of that scene, bearing no hint of the turbulent times to come, would stay with him, a lasting reminder of how it was when life was normal.

"We have prepared the small audience chamber, my lord," said Durayd, who accompanied them to its door. There the Caliph thanked him and gave orders not to be disturbed.

"I am so pleased to see you, my lord," said Abu Mansour. They were now alone. "I know how patiently you've been waiting, and I regret the long delay."

The Caliph nodded. In his eagerness to hear what Abu Mansour had to tell him, he barely noticed how tired the doctor was looking, as if he too were laboring under some great strain.

"It has not been easy, my lord. As you know, this is unaccustomed work for me. And it was all the harder because, the whole time, I was burdened by a sense of my own responsibility in this tragedy."

"What do you mean?"

"I cannot mourn the lady Murjana as you do. But I grieve all the same at her untimely death. And I cannot forget that it was I who brought you together, and it was I who urged you to marry."

"You did, and I am grateful for it."

"Perhaps you shouldn't be. Because in doing these things, I also brought you unimaginable sorrow that was not meant to be."

The Caliph was moved by Abu Mansour's words.

"Never say that, Abu Mansour. When you brought Murjana into my life, you gave me the greatest joy I ever knew. It wasn't you who took her from me, but others. And that's why I wait impatiently to know who it was."

There was a knock at the door, and the servants came in with sherbet and cakes. The Caliph waved them away impatiently, and when they had gone, Abu Mansour sat quietly for a while, sipping his sherbet thoughtfully. Then he set down his cup slowly.

"When I began the assignment you had given me, my lord, I confess I didn't know where to start. You asked me to find out how the lady Murjana died and who was behind it. You were convinced that her death was unnatural. I am able to confirm that you were correct. She was the victim of poisoning." He had the Caliph's full attention.

"But who was the poisoner? That was what took up the rest of my investigation."

Abu Mansour knew that the Caliph was impatient for him to disclose his final conclusion. But he was determined to give as thorough a report as he could, in order to dispel any lingering questions or doubts in the Caliph's mind.

He ran through the list of suspects and what his investigations had revealed in each case, including his inquiries about the Caliph's wives, which he related as delicately as he could. The Caliph listened without interrupting, although some of the revelations the doctor offered were evidently a surprise to him. But he did not comment, waiting for the end.

After what must have seemed like an age to the Caliph, Abu Mansour came to the final part of his account.

"Lastly, I turned to the likeliest suspect of all, whom I had excluded at the beginning because the facts were irreconcilable. It was only when I started to wonder if it was you, and not your wife, who was the intended victim that I hit upon the person with both motive and access." The Caliph stared at Abu Mansour.

"It was the lady Murjana's brother, Hamza. Once I'd put the facts together, it became quite obvious. He had harbored feelings of anger and revenge against you ever since Abu Ubaydah's troops killed his eldest brother, Yahya. I learned that he and his fellow conspirators blamed you for that and many other acts against their community, and concocted a plan of murder. The lady Murjana, who also grieved for her dead brother and wanted to avenge him, was to be an essential part of their plot. So, Hamza was well placed to put his plan into effect."

The Caliph's face was ashen. He held up his hand to silence Abu Mansour.

"Enough, Abu Mansour. You needn't go on with your speculations. Your quest for the murderer of my dear wife can now come to an end."

The doctor stopped in mid-flow. He had been about to detail the case he had carefully prepared against Hamza, and did not understand the Caliph's interruption.

Letting out a deep sigh of resignation, the Caliph said, "Don't look any further for the perpetrator of this terrible deed. You're looking at him."

Abu Mansour was stunned.

"Yes, I am my wife's murderer. If you're confused, Abu Mansour, don't be."

He paused for a moment.

"I didn't send you on a fool's errand when I asked you to investigate the lady Murjana's death. I meant it in good faith, desperately hoping you would find another perpetrator. If you did, it would absolve me of the awful crime I have committed. You've done well, my dear friend, and told me much I didn't know. But let me now save you further trouble and explain.

"Long before my marriage, I was aware of these vengeful plots against me that you describe. And so, I put my agents onto the Banu Shaaban family. At first, I discounted the gravity of the situation and thought it was more rumor and gossip than anything else. When my agents reported on the activities of Hamza, my wife's elder brother, I wasn't unduly worried. He appeared to be keeping company with a group of loud-mouthed bullies with inflated opinions of themselves, Shia dissidents already known to us and of little account. Nevertheless, I instructed my spies to keep them under surveillance."

The Caliph stopped for a moment. Abu Mansour could see he was finding it hard to continue his account of the steps that led him to carry out the unspeakable crime he had confessed to. But then he went on, "I knew of the whispered meetings between my wife and her brother. I wasn't sure what they were about, and it was only when Abu Ubaydah told me how their eldest brother, Yahya, had been executed on my orders that I understood the whole story and could make sense of the plan they were putting together."

"So, why didn't you arrest Hamza and his accomplices there and then? Surely, such treason was intolerable."

"The facts were not sufficient, Abu Mansour. I had nothing but inference and conjecture to go on. I could not risk accusing the man who was my wife's brother of a wrong if there was any doubt at all about his guilt. So, I pretended to be unaware of what was happening, and waited for proof."

If the situation hadn't been so grave, Abu Mansour might have been tempted to commend the Caliph, as he would his students, on his admirable approach to the importance of evidence. The Caliph's expression took on a look of pain.

"Although I knew that proof had to be found, I dreaded finding it. And when I did, it was as shattering as anything I could have imagined. When Hamza came to see his sister at the palace that last time, I set Uthman, my secretary, to mount a watch on their meeting. That I should spy on my own wife was abhorrent to me, but I had no choice."

He paused.

Abu Mansour remained silent, reluctant to interrupt the Caliph's train of thought.

"On Hamza's arrival, the two of them went to the animal menagerie, perhaps thinking not to be overheard in such a place. But the man Uthman had concealed behind the enclosure fence overheard everything they said and reported back to me."

The Caliph recounted the conversation between brother and sister in precise detail, as if he had gone over it in his mind many times.

"What I heard banished every lingering doubt I had, not about Hamza, whom I had long ago recognized for the scoundrel he was, but about my wife. And oh, how it grieved me."

He tried to control himself.

"I don't need to tell you, of all people, what that meant to me. I struggled with myself, tried to shake off my fear that she had indeed betrayed me. I made a thousand excuses for why she spoke and behaved as she did, anything to tell myself she was innocent and I was wrong. But that last talk with her brother haunted me. When I put all the facts together, it was impossible to find any explanation that absolved her of guilt."

There was total silence in the room. Abu Mansour sat unmoving, his attention focused on the Caliph.

"I couldn't convince myself of her innocence, hard as I tried. The facts were too damning, and I knew there was no escape from what I must do." His expression was grim as he looked at Abu Mansour. "It was then I put in train the process that would end with her execution."

Abu Mansour was appalled at what he was hearing. But he forced himself to respond, speaking in as reasonable a voice as possible.

"Surely, my lord, it was Hamza and the villains he consorted with who were responsible."

"You're right. Don't imagine they'll be spared. They've fled for now, but they will soon be caught and face the punishment that awaits them." His face clouded over. "But all the time I knew that eliminating them would not be enough while the heart of their conspiracy, my wife, lived on. I looked back on the affection she had shown me, and I saw it as no more than a snare designed to gain my trust."

He seemed to sink down into his seat, his shoulders hunched and his body stooped like an old man's. After a few moments he continued.

"Her personal betrayal of me was painful enough. But it was her treason against the realm that I could not overlook. If I didn't act, the flame of sedition her family's treachery had ignited would spread like wildfire, and it had to be put out.

"It was no easy decision. While it would no doubt please Ibn Uthal and his followers, it would anger the Shia in equal measure. I had to make a choice, and the stability of the state was above everything."

Abu Mansour knew how dearly the Caliph held that security, and saw it as his duty and mission to protect the country from all threats, whatever the cost. But he couldn't restrain himself any longer.

"I knew the lady Murjana. Not as you did, my lord, but enough to see through to her good heart and lack of guile. I could never think ill of her, although I confess I didn't know about that last meeting with her brother. I can see how it must have caused you to doubt your wife."

There was no answer from the Caliph. Abu Mansour pressed on.

"But even with all that, I can't help thinking there's another way to see what happened at that meeting with her brother, contrary to how it must have seemed."

Abu Mansour was on dangerous ground. His words could be understood to contradict the Caliph's conclusion, and he would need to tread carefully.

"I find it hard to believe the lady capable of such a deed, or even of contemplating it. Is it at all possible she might have appeared compliant with her brother's plan just to appease him, but have rejected it afterward?"

The Caliph turned his eyes toward Abu Mansour, his expression full of sorrow.

"Do you imagine I didn't want to think so, too? Didn't long for you, Abu Mansour, to dispel my fears as you used to in the past? How many times do I remember confiding my suspicions about the lady Murjana, even before my wedding to her. I used to tell you I doubted her, not because I thought her evil in herself, but because of her family's influence over her. And each time, you reminded me of her innocence and the love she bore me, and helped me to dismiss my doubts.

"But my fears turned out to be correct. In the end her family's influence was too strong for her. She could not overcome her guilt about her dead brother and her duty to avenge him. And I know it tormented her, so much so it made her succumb to Hamza's demands. Not only at that last conversation between them, but before, and perhaps from the beginning of our acquaintance."

Abu Mansour could do nothing but listen as the story's dreadful logic unfolded.

"So you see, I had no choice. I made my decision and gave my instructions to Uthman, the only one amongst my officials whose discretion and loyalty I trusted. I asked of him only one thing. That when he arranged for the deed to be carried out, he would ensure that it was merciful and she would not suffer."

They lapsed into silence, each wrapped up in his own thoughts. The atmosphere was charged with tension and unspoken emotions. Neither noticed the time passing, and when the call to prayer suddenly rang out from the Grand Mosque, they were both startled.

Soon after, there was a sound of shuffling outside the door as the servants prepared for the Caliph's emergence to go to prayer. It was followed by a discreet knock. Durayd spoke through the gap in the door, "Forgive the interruption, my lord, but it's time for the noon prayer."

Neither the Caliph nor Abu Mansour could have torn themselves away at that moment from a story they knew must be pursued to its tragic end.

The doctor rose and went to speak to Durayd. When the chamberlain had gone and the sounds of the palace died down, the Caliph resumed.

"I made my decision. But I was still tortured by disappointment and rage at my wife's betrayal. I visited the worst humiliation and vented my anger on her without mercy. Her bewilderment and misery at what I was doing should have invoked my pity and made me question her guilt. But I had hardened my heart against her. How I hated myself for doing it, and what remorse I felt afterwards."

"But you were surely redeemed, my lord," said Abu Mansour gently. "I never saw you happier than at that last dinner we had together."

"Only because she gave me absolution. She confessed everything, what she knew about the plotting of her brother and his friends, how he attempted to recruit her to their cause, and her doubts and then her decision to reject it all. She begged me to believe her. She swore her brother was a reformed man and had taken an oath never to harm me. I could see she believed it."

"And you believed her."

"Her innocence made me wonder about my decision, the artless way she revealed a plot so vile against me as if it were a bit of mischief that she and her brother could make up for by repentance. No schemer who genuinely planned my downfall could have thought I would be taken in by anything so absurd, or feigned such lack of guile."

He paused, remembering.

"I was finally convinced. It wasn't so hard, because the truth is, I wanted to believe her with all my heart. So I let my guard down and let her dispel my doubts. I could have turned out to be wrong and have placed myself in danger. But my love of her was too great, and I abandoned my plan."

He looked at Abu Mansour.

"The rest of the story you saw at dinner that last night."

"I did, my lord, and I was very happy to see it."

The Caliph shook his head. "She did not live. She did not live." His voice was wooden and expressionless.

"Let me guess, my lord. You withdrew the order to go through with the plan to kill her, but you were too late? Is that what you think happened?"

The look the Caliph gave Abu Mansour was full of desolation.

"I was not in time. I killed her, Abu Mansour, as surely as if I had fed her the poison with my own hand. There is no forgiveness for what I have done. I will pay for it all the rest of my life."

The spark of passion that had animated him before suddenly died. He looked spent and forlorn.

Abu Mansour let out a weary sigh. It had all gone far enough, and he could no longer put off the moment when he must take the story onto its final, dreadful conclusion.

"It is true, my lord, that at one time you wished the lady Murjana dead and that you planned to do the awful deed. But that was as far as it went. Though you thought the order to execute your wife was carried out as you had instructed, I doubt that Uthman would have complied. He knew what she meant to you and that you were in a rage. My guess is he would have waited until he had consulted with your close ministers before he thought to take such a grave step."

The Caliph stared at him. "What can you mean?"

"I mean, it wasn't you who committed that last, heinous crime against your wife...You are not her murderer."

39

Had any but Abu Mansour uttered those words, the Caliph would have dismissed him for a sycophant and a fool trying to ingratiate himself with false words of comfort. But he knew that Abu Mansour did not speak except from some special knowledge. He frowned.

"What makes you say such a thing, Abu Mansour? You heard my admission, didn't you?"

"I did, and I say again that you were not the murderer. Because I know who the murderer was."

It took a moment for the Caliph to take this in. And then he erupted with pent-up rage and despair.

"Who is it? Where is he?"

Abu Mansour held up his hand.

"You cannot do anything, my lord. The murderer is beyond your reach."

"No one and nothing, except God himself, is beyond my reach!"

"Oh, but this murderer is. You see, death has already claimed her."

There was a stunned silence, as if all life in the room had suddenly been sucked out of it. As the fearful implication of what Abu Mansour had said sank in, the Caliph froze.

"I'll have to start at the beginning."

⊞

"You will remember, my lord, that I had reached the point in my account when I was telling you that of all the suspects in this case, the most likely was the lady Murjana's brother, Hamza. He had the means and the access he needed. Earlier on that day of our last supper together, I discovered that Abdulhamid's old servant had visited the palace kitchen. He had been known to the staff since your marriage to the lady Murjana, and often came with dishes her aunt made for her. So, he was a familiar figure, and no one thought to mention him to your chamberlain."

The Caliph sat, hardly moving.

"On that day, the old man had come with a present of two saffron cakes, one of them made with less saffron than the other in view of your dislike of the spice. These were delicacies made with special care by the lady Murjana's aunt as a token of esteem for you, which your wife had asked for in celebration of your reunion. I was able to examine the remnants of those cakes afterward and found that one of them, the one with less saffron, had been poisoned with opium."

He paused while this information sank in. No sound came from the Caliph.

"There's no doubt in my mind that it was Hamza who was responsible for tampering with the cake, intending for you to ingest it. He and the lady Murjana and their aunt were aware of your dislike for saffron, but only he could have made use of that fact for his own ends.

"Unfortunately, I didn't know any of that at the time we had supper. Toward the end of the meal, when the sweetmeats were brought in, the cakes were placed on the table. The full saffron cake was put before the lady Murjana, as I had declined to eat any, and the lesser saffron one was placed in front of you. I don't think you were aware of the difference between the cakes, or that the lesser saffron one had been made especially for you."

The Caliph shook his head.

"Your steward entered the room at that point and you turned to speak to him, taking your eyes off the table. In those brief seconds, I saw your wife quickly swap the cakes, so that the one with less saffron ended up with her and the other was in front of you.

"I had bent down at that moment to pull my robe away from my shoe, and she thought no one had seen her. But I was just in time to glimpse what she did, although I didn't know what to make of it. And I certainly had no suspicion of what the cake she had taken for herself contained.

"If I'd known, it would never have happened. But I didn't, and I watched her eat a slice and encourage you to do the same with yours."

"Which I did," muttered the Caliph, his voice barely audible. "I ate it for her sake because I knew she had made her aunt prepare it to please me."

For a moment or two nothing more was said. Then sighing, Abu Mansour resumed his account.

"So it's clear that Hamza was the would-be murderer and you, my lord, the intended victim. But as things turned out, it was his sister, your wife, who took the poison, instead of you."

The Caliph said nothing.

"When you set me the task of finding the lady Murjana's killer, I already suspected that the answer lay in the swapped saffron cakes I'd noticed. But I didn't know how. And I resisted anything that implicated the lady Murjana herself in her own death. I desperately hoped to find another way to explain how the deed was done. And so I looked at all the possibilities, no matter how far-fetched."

He paused. His tone was filled with sadness.

"I can only think that, in the end, she didn't trust her brother, no matter what assurances she may have given you. And, although she didn't know for certain if there was anything wrong with the cakes, she could not take the risk of endangering your life. And if she turned out to be right, it was a fate she somehow felt she deserved…

"Opium has a bitter taste, and the almonds and syrup the cake contained might not have disguised it completely. Perhaps she noticed it as she got to the affected section and was suspicious. Still, she ate it.

"Somewhere inside her, I feel, there still lingered a guilt about her brother, Yahya, and what she believed was her betrayal of him."

He paused.

"By instilling her with such ideas, Hamza had penetrated her soft heart and natural sense of honor far more than he knew. And yet, I can't help thinking there must have been a wild moment of hope before the effects of the drug overwhelmed her that she wondered if she had been wrong and the cakes were harmless after all. Despite the sacrifice she was willing to make, her sheer youth and lust for life would have surged up in her and made her long to live."

In all of his worst moments, the Caliph had never imagined a possibility like this. At Abu Mansour's words, he put his head in his hands.

"Oh, my God, my God," he kept repeating in an agony of pain and regret, oblivious to everything around him.

Abu Mansour watched his anguish. But he had an anguish of his own. Like the Caliph, he had at first accepted the inquiry into the lady Murjana's death because he was anxious to find a perpetrator other than the one his inner eye had led him toward, once he realized the Caliph was the intended victim. But as his investigation proceeded, the possibility that some third party had committed the crime began to fade. After the Caliph's misplaced confession of guilt, the truth could no longer be evaded.

If only it had not been left to him to be the bearer of such dark news.

Mute with grief, the two men sat unmoving in the quiet of the chamber, and in their minds was the picture of a vibrant, beautiful girl whose light had been cruelly and prematurely extinguished forever.

For the Caliph, there was no resignation or acceptance of his fate. Only rage at the finality of death, and utter desolation at the impossibility of Murjana's return.

EPILOGUE

The imam stood before the Caliph. It was an unaccustomed encounter, and they eyed each other warily. The Caliph was flanked by his commander, Abu Ubaydah, and his physician, Abu Mansour, men the imam did not know. It had been many years since he had met the Caliph, not since his arrival in Baghdad and his subsequent incarceration in his house. Despite that, the imam's reputation for wisdom and erudition had spread, and it made the Caliph sometimes wonder if he should arrange for a meeting between them. But it never happened, and even when Murjana tried to intercede on the imam's behalf, the Caliph had procrastinated. Now, he wished he had not.

The imam inclined his head to the Caliph courteously, but did not bow. It was said that he acknowledged the authority of no man, only God.

"To Allah we belong and to Him we shall return. I knew and cherished the lady Murjana more than I can describe. She was as dear to me as a daughter. I can scarcely express the sorrow I feel at her passing, though I know it is God's will."

The Caliph thanked him and introduced the others.

"Please don't be disturbed by the presence of these old and

trusted friends. They are here to bear witness to what passes between us."

He invited him to sit down, and they all settled themselves in a circle on the cushions.

"Your grief at my wife's death is but an echo of my own, Imam. I cannot describe what she has meant to me, or how my life will change forever by her absence. But I did not invite you here today to tell you about my loss and sorrow."

He stopped, weighing up his words.

"It was to say I have decided this must be the last tragedy that occurs between us. The enmity, hatred, and suspicion that have ruled our relations for so long are no tribute to the memory of so precious a being as Murjana. There must be no more victims. The war of Muslim on Muslim has run its course and must end."

The imam received these words with a look halfway between doubt and relief.

"I can't but welcome these sentiments, sir," he replied. "For years now, I've thought the same. But I never imagined I might find an ally in you." The imam's face was suddenly suffused with light. He seemed overcome.

"God bless you."

"As of today, Imam," the Caliph continued, "your confinement is ended. Abu Ubaydah here will see to it that your guard, and the watch we have ordered over you, are immediately removed."

The imam sat still, taking it all in.

"In a further pledge of my good will, I am declaring an amnesty for those of your followers who are detained unjustly for peaceful dissent against me. From now on, no one will face punishment just for holding opposing views."

He turned to Abu Ubaydah. "See to it there are no more round-ups, assaults, or executions of Shia dissidents."

The commander bowed. The Caliph turned back to the imam.

"I've been blind, Imam. It should not have taken the death of one as beautiful in mind and spirit as Mujana to open my eyes..."

He paused. Then he rested a hand on Abu Mansour's shoulder.

"Before God, and in the hearing of this dear friend, I swear that from now on, there will be no supremacy of Sunni over Shia, nor Shia over Sunni. We are one people under Islam. It does not matter if we choose to worship in different ways. Our God is one, and our Prophet is one. And that should be our legacy. That generations to come will live together as one, undivided, harmonious community."

His expression darkened.

"Without it, the curses of in-fighting, division, and fragmentation will sap our strength and make us easy prey for the unbelievers, the invaders, and the enemies of Islam."

He slowly searched the faces of everyone present.

"And that must never be allowed to happen."

Historical Note
Baghdad in the ninth century

The Baghdad of the ninth century, the setting of Murjana, bears little resemblance to the unstable, dilapidated city of sectarian conflict and foreign intervention it became at the dawn of the twenty-first century. Seeing the unsafe streets and run down nighborhoods of this Baghdad, with its intermittent energy supply and general impoverishment, one can hardly imagine that at one time it was a city at the forefront of civilization.

In 830 AD, the time of the novel's main events, Baghdad was under the rule of the Abbasids, the second Arab dynasty of the newly established Islamic State. They succeeded the Umayyads, the first rulers of the Near East following its conquest by Islamic forces in 640 AD. The Abbasids built Baghdad in 762 AD, which they named Madinat al-Salam, the City of Peace, and made it their capital and the center of an Islamic Empire that stretched from Spain to Samarkand, from Iran to modern Afghanistan, and from India to the edge of China.

None of this had been dreamed of when the Islamic conquests first began following the death of the Prophet Muhammad in 632 AD. The Arab armies, bringing with them little more than their new religion, Islam, and their language, Arabic, surged out of Arabia to conquer the Levant. In a short space of time, they had spread their hegemony over the surrounding lands, and from there to places much further afield. Within a hundred years of the Prophet's death, the Arabs had become the masters of a vast empire larger than that of the Romans at its height.

In its heyday, from the eighth to the tenth century, the so-called Golden Age of Islam, Baghdad was deemed to be one of the world's most glorious cities, rivaled only by Constantinople. It was home to the flowering of a new civilization imbued with enormous creativity, no doubt the result of the mixture of peoples and cultures the Arabs came to rule. The city was renowned for its architecture and its advanced urban planning and engineering. Its status as an emporium of trade and commerce and a foremost shipping center made it accessible to the whole world.

It soon became the hub of an intellectual and scientific explosion that spanned mathematics, astronomy, medicine, and philosophy. Today, we still have some of the medical, scientific, and philosophical textbooks and treatises that were its legacy. The medical literature of the period has been the main source for the depiction of medical practice set out in this book. Accounts of conditions such as "the disease of *'ishq*," or love, and its treatment as described in the story are all taken from this literature.

Medieval Arabic medicine was based on the ancient Greek medical theory of humors. This theory held that the body contained four fluids, or humors: blood, phlegm, yellow bile, and black bile, which had to be in balance, or equilibrium, with each other to ensure normal health. It was their imbalance in quantity, or a change in their properties that caused disease. Although the Arabs had access to Indian and ancient Egyptian medicine, the humoral theory of the Greeks was the major medical system they employed. It was transmitted to the West through Arabic medical writings and dominated European medical thinking until the nineteenth century. It still survives today in such terms as, "equilibrim," "ill-humored," "phlegmatic," "melancholic," "sanguine," and the kind.

The disease of *'ishq* that is a central theme of the novel was believed to be a distinct medical condition akin to madness. Its features are illustrated by a colorful anecdote linked to Ibn Sina (Avicenna), the foremost tenth-century Persian/Arabic physician, which is given here in abbreviated form. It tells the story of a young Persian prince who fell ill with a mysterious malady no one could diagnose. His health steadily declined until he took to his bed, and there was great fear for his life. Ibn Sina was called in to save him. After examining him, the famous physician applied the pulse test. Placing his finger on the young man's pulse, he noted how its rate increased at mention of a certain family. At which point, he asked if they had daughters, and finding that they did, stood up and declared the problem to be solved: the disease was love and the cure was marriage.

I have incorporated elements of this famous story into the account of the Caliph's malady, which has many of the features described in it, including a similar cure. The other features are derived from several medical sources and epitomise the essence of the contemporaneous humoral theory.

◻

The ninth-century Sunni-Shia friction the book describes was not the vicious sectarian strife it became in modern times, but it was already beginning then. Its roots went back to the death of the Prophet Muhammad when a dispute arose about who should succeed him as head of the Muslim community. One side held it should only be of the Prophet's bloodline, that is Ali, his cousin, and Ali's wife, Fatima, the Prophet's daughter. The other side believed the successor should be the one considered most able as decided by consensus. The first group became known as the Shia of Ali, that is, the party of Ali, and were called Shiites, while the other group were called the people of the Sunna, or Sunnis, those who followed the actions and sayings of the Prophet. The Shia did not accept the legitimacy of the first Islamic dynasties, and, in the case of the Abbasids, they had a special grievance.

In their war to oust the Umayyads from the leadership of the Islamic state, the early Abbasids relied on Shia support, promising that the Shia imam would be the head of religious authority in the state if the Abbasids won. But once in power the Abbasid caliphs reneged on their promise to the Shia and went on to persecute them. This was not on religious grounds but for reasons of power politics. The Shia of the ninth century were in the main a pious community who lived simply and believed in social justice. They shunned the opulence of the Abbasid upper class and preached the kind of Islam the Prophet himself had preached. As their message started to attract greater numbers of followers, the caliphs increasingly saw them as a potential threat to their authority. Dissidence on that scale could not be tolerated, and resulted in the persecution and alleged murder of many Shia imams. That, in turn, led to the appearance of small violent rebellions amongst what had been a peaceable Shia community.

The Abbasid caliph, who also bore the title Commander of the Faithful, was supremely powerful: at the head of government, the army and the final point of reference for all matters related to the state. Although that power declined with the later disintegration of the Abbasid dynasty, at the time of the book it was at its height, and the caliph was a figure both feared and admired. The title "caliph" is the abbreviated English rendering of the Arabic "khalifa," or successor to the Prophet Muhammad. As such, he was the head of both religious and temporal power.

Many of the events and characters described in what follows are fictitious, but not all. The Caliph and the physician are both based on real historical figures of the era. The former is modeled on the fifth Abbasid caliph, Abdullah al-Ma'mun, (reg.813–833), an outstanding intellectual, free-thinker, and scholar, who could almost be the Platonic "philosopher-king" of Arab history.

This caliph is associated with the famous translation academy in Baghdad known as Bayt al-Hikma, the House of Wisdom, mentioned in the book. His involvement with the mu'tazilite movement, an unorthodox religious sect, was likewise historical. The tussle with the traditionists, the "*ulama*'," this movement caused over what we would now see as the obscure doctrine of the creativeness of the Quran did take place; the traditionists' leader, Ahmad ibn Hanbal, head of one of the four main schools of Islamic jurisprudence which bears his name, and known in the novel as Amr ibn Uthal, led to the institution of the Caliph's *mihna*, or inquisition.

In middle life al-Ma'mun fell for a young woman named Buran, on whom the book's character, Murjana, is loosely based. His costly and extravagant wedding to her, of which we have detailed accounts, was the basis for descriptions of the Caliph's wedding to Murjana recounted in the story.

The physician, Abu Mansour al-Tabrizi, is a representation of the famous tenth-century clinician of Persian origin, Abu Bakr Muhammad ibn Zakariyya al-Razi, (c.865–925), a physician and polymath whose clinical observations and the teaching textbooks he wrote guided generations of medieval doctors. Some of these discoveries included the condition he named, "The catarrhal disease when the rosebuds first open," which corresponds to our modern day allergic rhinitis or hay fever, and is the earliest known description of this disorder.

The court poet, Abu Firas, is based loosely on the famous Arab poet, Abu Nuwas, (756–814). This man was a controversial figure, a drunkard and a promiscuous homosexual, known for his profane utterances and irreverent attitude towards authority. However, his poetry was greatly admired and he was tolerated because of it. I have chosen a few verses and put them together in a different arrangement. Rendering the beauty and subtlety of his language into English is virtually impossible.

Creating a picture of a now vanished Baghdad and its everyday life is an enormous challenge and has required considerable research. No social histories of Baghdad exist as such, although much information can be gleaned from near contemporary accounts that enable one to build a picture of life in the city. Indirect sources have also been useful, for example, medical textbooks, cookery books, poetry, and, of course, the Arabian Nights, many of whose stories supposedly took place in the Baghdad of Harun al-Rashid, al-Ma'mun's father.

Glossary

Glossary of Names

Abbasids: second Arab dynasty; capital, Baghdad; ruled 750-1258 AD

Abdullah ibn Rida: governor of Khorasan

Abdulhamid: devout Shiite and Murjana's uncle

Abu Aziz: head of the Banu Aziz family and Abu Mansour's patient

Abu Firas: court poet and notorious reprobate

Abu Hisham: chief wazir, or prime minister

Abu Mansour: physician to the Caliph

Abu Ubaydah: Caliph's senior military commander

Ahmad: Abu Mansour's student apprentice

Ali: (as in personal name) Abu Mansour's grandfather

Amr ibn Uthal: prominent religious leader with many followers

Anas: member of Mu'tazilite minority religious sect

Ayesha: Murjana's cousin, daughter of her aunt Zubeida

Banu Aziz: wealthy Baghdad family

Banu Shaaban: prominent Shia family in Baghdad, known for their piety

Dar al-Huram: women's quarters inside the palace

Dar al-Tiraz: dressmakers' palace quarters

Durayd: Caliph's chamberlain

Falluja: Iraqi town, about 43 miles west of Baghdad

Famm al-Silh: small hamlet on the banks of the Tigris south of Baghdad

Hamza: Murjana's elder brother and dissident conspirator

Harthama ibn Fadl: wealthy landowner and previous governor of Khorasan

Hasna: Caliph's half-sister

Hind: Caliph's fourth wife

Idris: head eunuch

Imam: spiritual head of the Shia community

Ismail: chief Shia dissident

Jaafar: Caliph's eldest son and heir from his first wife, Um Jaafar

Karkh: major marketplace or souk in west Baghdad

Khadija: Caliph's stepmother; mother of his half-brother, Muhammad

Khalid: friend of Yazan ibn Shaaban at the palace

Khorasan: largest province in Persia; included what is Afghanistan today

Al-Mansour: second Abbasid caliph, who built Baghdad; ruled 754-775 AD

Mansour: the father of Abu Mansour

Maryam: Caliph's first wife's personal assistant

Merv: capital city of Khorasan

Musa: friend of Hamza and co-conspirator

Saad: head of Abu Mansour's household servants and freed slave

Salim: spy working for Abu Ubaydah

Sulafa: Caliph's second wife

Suleiman: head doctor at the palace

Talha: retired soldier and Abu Ubaydah's spy

Um Hasan: Abu Mansour's mother

Um Jaafar: Caliph's first and most senior wife

Umayyads: first Arab dynasty after the Prophet Muhammad's death; capital, Damascus; ruled 705-750 AD

Usama: Shia dissident

Uthman: Caliph's personal secretary

Yahya ibn Shaaban: Murjana's oldest brother and Shia dissident

Yazan ibn Shaaban: Murjana's youngest brother

Younis: Abu Mansour's clinic assistant

Yusuf: Shia dissident

Zeinab: Caliph's third wife and his first cousin
Zubeida: sister to Abdulhamid and Murjana's aunt

Glossary of Terms

'Attar: spice-seller in the souk; also sold perfumes and drugs

'iddah: three-month period following divorce to cover the possibility of pregnancy, the resulting child being the divorced father's responsibility

'ishq: hectic or passionate love; more akin to powerful infatuation

Abna': descendants of the Khorasani soldiers who fought with the Abbasid armies against the Umayyads; they settled in Iraq and had a favored status

Ahl al-Kitab: literally, the People of the Book; this referred to Christians and Jews, who both had written scriptures, and were accepted in Islam as valid fellow religionists

Ali: (as in followers of) another designation for the Shia

Ambergris: waxy substance produced in the digestive system of sperm whales; used in perfumes, and extremely expensive

Barid: the postal system, efficient and highly developed at the time to cover Iraq and many surrounding areas

Bimaristan: hospital

Dar al-Islam: the Islamic community

Dirham/dinar: units of currency used in Iraq throughout medieval times

Diwan: regular meetings with the Caliph for the public held at the palace

Hakim: the ideal Arab physician, a wise and learned man

Hammam: public bath

Hiera: bitter medicines of Greek origin, widely used for abdominal ailments

Ijaza: stamp of approval inscribed inside books that students had read to the satisfaction of their teachers

Jihad: to fight for justice

Kufr: unbelief; a serious allegation for Muslims to make against anyone they believe is a *kafir*

Majlis: refers to a meeting place, where seats are arranged along the walls facing each other, and also means any formal gathering of people

Maqam: musical form involving songs and traditional instruments invented in Iraq

Mihna: inquisition instituted by the Caliph to try anyone denying the Quran's createdness

Mu'tazilites: a religious/philosophical movement that flourished under the Abbasid caliph, al-Ma'mun; it drew the animosity of the traditional Islamic community

Qalansuwa: tall, peaked hat, usually black, worn in Abbasid times

Qiyan: especially and expensively trained slave-girls whom only the rich could afford to own

Rabi' al-Thani: Arabic name for the month of January

Sadaq: woman's dowry promised by her husband to be paid on divorce

Sherbet: fruit juice diluted in water

Shia/Shiite/Shii: alternative Islamic sect for those who believe that the Prophet's successors should be descended through his blood relatives; that was his cousin, Ali, and Fatima, the Prophet's daughter and wife of Ali. Today, Iran is the center of Shiism

Sirwal: wide-legged trousers usually worn under tunics

Sunna/Sunni: mainstream Islam; refers to the *sunna,* or the way of the Prophet, whose successors or "caliphs" are chosen by consensus. The vast majority of today's Islamic world is Sunni

Tannour: traditional round oven for baking bread

Ulama': traditionist religious scholars

Um walad: status of being the mother of the caliph's heir; it had many privileges attached

Zirbaj: specially prepared chicken dish

Acknowledgments

Murjana was a lonely book to write. By the time I came around to writing it, the colleagues in medieval Arabic medicine and history, whom I had worked with on those topics in the 1970s and who would have been natural partners in such a project, had gone on their different ways. I myself had also moved into new fields, principally, Palestine and the conflict with Israel.

For years, my absorption with this intractable issue edged out all others, until a long-time friend and medical colleague, Dr. Keith Baker, recalled me to my previous life as a physician and medical historian. By giving me the initial idea of a historical thriller where the "detective" would be a medieval Arab doctor, he set me on a path that took me back to my, at one time, extensive research in medieval Arabic/Islamic medicine. Without him, *Murjana* would have never been written.

I also recall my enormous debt to my father, Hasan Karmi, whose expertise in classical Arabic and the legacy of Islamic civilization came back to inspire me. He would have been fascinated to read *Murjana*.

I cherish and value the help of many friends who gave me much encouragement in the writing of the book. Among these, I record my gratitude to Christopher Penfold, coincidentally Keith's brother-in-law, who went out of his way to give me editorial help with *Murjana*. I greatly appreciated his sensitivity to some aspects of the story, and his shrewd advice on plot and style.

My dear friend, Adel Kamal, who had edited all my

..s, took to this latest one with enormous ..tment. I owe him a huge debt of gratitude ..e plot line and writing of the early drafts. His ..pathy and understanding of the historical period ..llously illuminating. I so much regret that he never .. the end, due to his death in 2023, a year before the book's ..ication.

Special thanks are due to Tom Suarez, who read the book carefully and gave me invaluable advice on several aspects. His shrewd eye for inconsistencies and errors was enormously helpful, and his friendship a constant support.

I am also grateful to friends who read and advised on parts of the book, among them, Gill Emberson, Tim Llewellyn, and Ahmad Majdoubeh.

Last but not least, my thanks are reserved for Michel Moushabeck, whose interest in the book and commitment to seeing it in print were heart warming. Thanks are also due to all at Interlink Publishing for their editorial help in seeing the book through to publication. I am grateful for their hard work and dedication.